TWO THYRDES

TWO THYRDES

by
BERTIE DENHAM

St. Martin's Press
New York

The author's copyright extends to the song *Called to Arms*, the words of which have been written by the author.

TWO THYRDES. Copyright © 1983 by Lord Denham. All rights reserved. Printed in the United States of America. No part of this book may be used or reproduced in any manner whatsoever without written permission except in the case of brief quotations embodied in critical articles or reviews. For information, address St. Martin's Press, 175 Fifth Avenue, New York, N.Y. 10010.

Library of Congress Cataloging in Publication Data

Denham, Bertie, Baron, 1927-
   Two thyrdes.

   I. Title.
PR6054.E47T8   1986   823'.914   85-25149
ISBN 0-312-82752-0

First published in Great Britain by Ross Anderson Publications.
First U.S. Edition
10 9 8 7 6 5 4 3 2 1

To: J.J.B.
R.G.G.B.
H.M.M.B.
And G.P.P.B.

Table Plan in Dining-room 'D', House of Commons

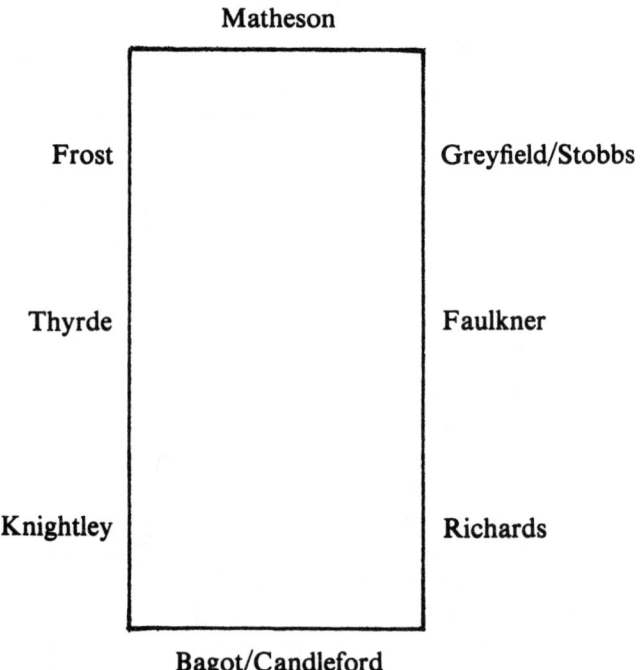

PRINCIPAL CHARACTERS

'1944 Club' Members

Derek (Derry), 2nd Viscount Thyrde
Derek, 3rd Viscount Thyrde, *his son*
Sir John Bagot, Bart., M.P.
Billy Bagot, 2nd Baron Candleford, *his son*
Colonel James Matheson, D.S.O., M.C., M.P.
Henry Matheson, M.P., *his son*
Peter, Earl of Greyfield
Peter Stobbs, M.P., *his son*
Leonard Frost, M.P.
later to become Lord Frost of Highgate
Lieutenant Alan (Dick) Richards, U.S. Army Air Corps,
later to become 4-Star General, U.S.A.F.
Roger Faulkner,
later to become Director of The Farmwell Foundation
Lieutenant Stephen Knightley, Royal Navy

Others

Third Officer Molly Stanton, W.R.N.S.
The Hon. Mrs. Matheson (Tisha), *Lord Frost's daughter*
The Hon. Charles Mallicent, *Derry's younger brother*
Commander E. F. Jackson, D.S.C., Royal Navy, *of Norfolk House*
Brigadier G. Broadbent, D.S.O., O.B.E., *of The War Office*
Tom Barraclough, *of the village garage at Thyrde*
Sir Makepeace Brotherton, Q.C.
Detective-Chief-Inspector Harding } *both of New*
Detective-Sergeant Pollock } *Scotland Yard*
Lord Stanstead, *Chairman of British Light & Power*
Mr. Justice Pierceworthy, *a High Court Judge*

All the characters in this book are fictitious. No character is based on any real person, living or dead, and any similarity between the name or other attributes of any of the characters and those of any real person is coincidental.

TWO THYRDES

Prologue 18th December, 1944

"Hey, steady on, Derry! There is such a thing as a black-out, you know."

Derek, *2nd* Viscount Thyrde, pulled the thick velvet curtains together again. He had been trying to catch a last glimpse of the trees across the lawn, cedars mostly, but more particularly of the tall beech that stood over by itself, to the right of them and a little further back. All that he had been able to see was his own reflection against the blackness of the night outside and that wasn't very clear either. His tie looked good, though, a perfectly shaped black figure of eight with the ends squared off, nestling into the stick-ups of his collar and above the white gleam of his shirt front. He had taken trouble over that.

He turned to face his younger brother, who was still sitting at the table in the little room off the main dining-room of Thyrde House. Ridiculously young he was looking, with the single-winged O of an observer standing out bright and new on his R.A.F. uniform and his attempt, not very successful as yet, at growing a moustache.

"Don't worry, Charles. They tell me there hasn't been a German bomber over for weeks."

"Not them I was thinking about, old boy. But, if old Adams sees so much as a chink of light, he'll be up here on his bicycle, all note-book and truncheon, before you can say 'knife'."

Derry walked over to the table and sat down. He put some more brandy in Charles's glass and then topped up his own.

The two brothers sat in silence.

"It was a blessing really," Derry said at last. "You haven't seen much of her over these past two years. She was never really herself again after Father died."

Charles nodded. Then he raised his glass. "Well, here's to Mama. God bless her, poor old girl. One thing, though," he nodded across to the third place at the table, empty now but

Prologue

showing signs of recent occupation, "bit of luck your being able to get back from Holland, even if it was for the funeral." Suddenly he looked anxious. "By the way, how is my sister-in-law? She's all right, isn't she? She was looking bang-on tonight, but it's not like her to want to hit the hay so early."

"Yes, she's O.K. But it *is* the sixth month, you know. She says she always gets a bit tired towards the evenings and she's determined to keep on the billetees. Look, Charles, there's something I want you to do for me."

His brother looked at his watch. "Well, I don't know about that, old boy. I've got to be back on the Station by eleven at the latest."

"No, this may not be for years, yet. Long after the war's over, probably, but I must tell you about it now. As you know, I'm leaving at squeak of dawn tomorrow and I had to wait until we were alone."

"Ah, that's all right, then. Well, let's see, the roads are pretty empty at night and if I push the old bus along a bit I can do it in twenty minutes. That gives you exactly half an hour."

Derry got up again, glass in hand, and walked over to the fire where, half buried among the fluffy white wood ash, there still remained a nugget or two of dullish red glow. He turned and stood with his back to it and looked across to the table, where his brother had pulled his chair out and now sat with one leg crossed over the other.

"I feel that this is a bit of an occasion," he said. "No, apart from Mummy, I mean."

"Hence the glad rags, eh?"

Derry smiled. "In a way. But I think that this may be the last night that I will ever be dining at Thyrde. You see I've got the strongest of premonitions that when I go over this time I shan't be coming back."

"Don't talk rot, Derry . . ." but Charles broke off as his brother held up his hand.

"I posted off a packet to the solicitors, this morning, a covering letter with it – I spent a long time writing that, but I'm still not sure whether I got it right. Then I tried to ring up old Frimble and explain it verbally, but the line was so bad and he's so deaf that I don't think he understood. I want you to see that my instructions

Prologue

are carried out."

"Has it occurred to you that I'm just as likely to buy it as you are?"

"If that should be the case, my dear Charles, you will be absolved from any further responsibility."

"What are the instructions, then?"

"They're a bit complicated, I'm afraid. It's a sealed package and I've told the solicitors that it is to be kept intact. If I survive the war, I'll be able to make any further arrangements myself. If I *am* killed and my child turns out to be a girl, the packet is to be destroyed unopened. If it's a boy, however, the packet is to be given to him, still unopened, when he's grown up – but only if he's ever in such severe trouble that there seems to be literally no way out."

"What sort of trouble?"

For a moment Derry looked helplessly at his brother.

Then, "I don't know," he said. "Disgrace rather than physical danger, I think, but . . . no, I just don't know."

"And I am to be the sole arbiter as to what sort of trouble might be regarded as severe enough and whether the packet should be handed over or not?"

"If you would Charles."

Charles got up from his chair and walked over and put a hand on Derry's shoulder.

"Of course I will, old boy. But it's all a lot of nonsense. I bet you anything you like you'll live to a ripe old age."

As things turned out, Derry Thyrde's premonition was proved to be right. His brother, Charles Mallicent, would have lost his bet.

1. Now. Narrative of Derek, 3rd Viscount Thyrde

The struggle for domination was over. That had been the first phase. It was teamwork from now on, teamwork all the way. And from now on, as the tempo quickened and whilst quickening became ever more perfectly co-ordinated and synchronised, it was pace for pace, effort for effort, in a mutual eagerness to reach the end while, paradoxically, seeking to postpone that inevitable end for as long as possible until, with an expertise that can only be achieved after much practice and a total familiarity, patiently acquired, each with the technique of the other, we reached our respective goals at the identical moment and flung ourselves panting on the metaphorical grass.

With the possible exception of football pools, it is the one pastime in the whole world in which to win is only marginally better than to lose. It is the draw – the score draw, of course – that is all important.

'A—ah,' said Julia, 'that was good. The best ever. And I particularly wanted it to be tonight.'

'M-mmm,' I said.

Always before it had been she who was drowsy afterwards and I who became instantly, maddeningly, awake. But this time, for some extraordinary reason, the roles had been reversed.

'Do you know what day it is today?' She had raised herself up, one elbow on the pillow, chin supported in hand.

'No,' I said, 'but whatever it is it's tomorrow. Go to sleep, darling. Good night. *Thank you* and good night.'

'It's exactly a year today since we've been together – well, properly full time together, that is.'

'Happy anniversary,' I murmured. My pillow had an enticing softness to it and I could feel myself floating blissfully away.

'Wake up, Derek. This is serious. All this time together and we still don't know, either of us, whether we want it to be permanent.'

'I love you madly, passionately. Will that do?'

Now

'But you still don't know yet whether you want to marry me, do you? Well, be honest. Do you?'

'Not at this time of night.'

'Well, I'm not sure either.' She was sitting up in bed now. 'I've been doing a lot of thinking lately. We can't let it drift on like this forever. I'm going away tomorrow – today, I mean – for at least six months or a year. To stay with my aunt and uncle in Canada. At the end of that time, if neither of us has met anyone else, we should be sure.'

'Hey ...!' For a moment she had me worried.

And then, suddenly it came to me.

What was it she had said? Asking me if I knew what day it was. It must be April the first. All Fool's day! But I was damned if I was going to let her see how nearly I had fallen for it.

'We'll talk about it in the morning,' I said and I turned over and went to sleep.

But in the morning she had gone. And so had her suitcases. It was still only the twenty-ninth of March.

I had a miserable breakfast. Coffee of the instant variety, black and bitter, burnt toast – and a letter from the bank.

The manager was very nice about it. After the long association that his Branch had enjoyed with my family and myself, he would have liked to help me, but my farm overdraft was too high already, my personal one more so and, much though he regretted it, the answer was "no".

Farming some five hundred acres round a big house in the country, with a flat in London and a none-too-cheap foreign car, doesn't sound the usual sort of background to bankruptcy, but I had had a lot of expenses lately and this was the time of year when cash flow problems were at their worst. What I desperately needed now was a bridging loan of some twenty-five thousand pounds. The land, the house and most of the furniture were entailed, an entail that couldn't be broken until my eldest son, when I had one, reached the age of twenty-one – an event that now seemed remote in the extreme – so such a loan would have to be unsecured. And this was the way out, the door to which my bank manager had firmly but regretfully just slammed in my face.

The only thing for it was for me to give up the one job that I really enjoyed, that of being an unpaid Opposition Whip in the

Now

House of Lords. I was panicking unnecessarily, of course. I always do. Things would have sorted themselves out somehow and it almost certainly wouldn't have come to that. But the maddening thing was that I hadn't told Julia about any of all this yet. I hadn't wanted to worry her unnecessarily — after all, the worst might not actually occur. If I had done, she wouldn't have chosen this of all moments to walk out on me. And all that I could think of at that moment was that the worst *had* occurred and that it was now too late.

I picked up the Daily Telegraph, looking for diversion rather than for comfort. There was hardly likely to be very much good news there. But, for once, I was wrong. The Labour government had been defeated by one vote on a vote of confidence in the House of Commons the night before. A General Election within the next few weeks was now certain. The Tories were favourites to win.

Not that it would make a lot of difference to me now, I thought. Even the salary paid to a junior Government Whip in the Lords would hardly be enough to get me out of trouble. But still, I had better get along to the House and find out what was happening. There was certainly no point in hanging about dismally here.

I went outside into a grey, wet, rain-sodden morning that matched my grey, wet, rain-sodden thoughts. Not even the friendly frog-like face of my green Citroen CX GT1, barely three months old and waiting patiently for me at the kerb, did a lot to cheer me up. I got in and slammed the door, cursing it out loud when the engine refused to start first time. It was almost as if I had hurt the poor thing's feelings. Its windscreen wipers keened pathetically as I drove off in the general direction of Westminster.

Two streets on, I was forced to stop. An approaching taxi had drawn up, all but blocking the Citroen's path between it and the cars parked at meters on my left. The driver was leaning over in his seat, conducting through the far window what seemed to be an endless financial transaction with his late fare. I decided to chance it. As I was inching forwards, I became aware that the taxi-driver had temporarily broken off negotiations and, head now through the window on my side, was watching my progress with indulgent interest.

'I could get a' aeroplane through there,' he informed me kindly.

Now

The obvious reply, that if I were driving an aeroplane I would go over and not through, occurred to me just too late. He had gone back to counting out small change. I proceeded with what dignity I could.

The head reappeared.

'... sideways!' it said.

On this, of all mornings, there was a new policeman on duty at the Peers' Entrance of the House of Lords. I had the added frustration of having to sort through the various credit and membership cards in my wallet with the growing conviction that I had mislaid the one that I needed, my Palace of Westminster pass. At last I found it, a little rectangle of plastic-covered card consisting of a surprisingly flattering colour photograph of D. Thyrde on the left and, on the right, obscured by three broad red diagonal stripes just in case anyone might otherwise be able to decipher it, a facsimile of my signature. I held it out.

The policeman smiled. 'Can't be too careful, these days.' he said. 'Thank you very much, Lord *Thryde*.'

'Pronounced "Third", as in "first, second and...".' 'I said.

There is something about the interior of the Palace of Westminster, and more particularly that part of it whose red carpets and red leather upholstery, as distinct from the Commons' green, mark it out as the territory of the House of Lords, that has a sense of permanence and even timelessness about it. The hushed atmosphere; the dim light, relieved only by the gilding of embellishment and coat-of-arms, some mellow with the patina of age, some bright and newly done; the spotlessness, lovingly achieved by an army of early-morning daily ladies; the attendant doorkeepers, custodians and policemen, who glide rather than walk and when stationary seem, like the linenfold panelling, to have been carved to the design of Pugin himself; all these combine to put personal worries, however serious, into perspective and make them seem so ephemeral that it would be almost an impertinence for them to intrude. And it was under this increasingly soothing influence that I walked up the stairs and along the corridor to the room of Thomas, Earl of Lavenham, the Conservative Chief Whip.

I found him sitting down, his lank form drooped over his desk, engaged in a rhythmic transfer of papers from his in-tray to his out, with only the formality of adding a ritual and hieroglyphic

Now

initial L to each, as it passed in between.
He looked up and smiled. 'Ah, Derek ...' he said. But something of the morning's calamities must have remained on my face because the smile faded.
'What's up with you? Girl-friend been giving you hell? Young Julia Elton – she still your current bird?'
'She's suddenly stopped being current,' I said.
He nodded slowly. Then he tactfully changed the subject.
'Look, Derek, I can't promise anything, of course. That's for Charles Fortescue to decide, when and if he becomes Prime Minister. But if we do win this election, I take it you'd be prepared to stay on as one of my Whips?'
'I'd like to, Tom,' I said, 'but...' and I gave him a brief résumé of my dreary financial problems. Again, he nodded sympathetically.
'No need to worry now. I'll ask you again after the election. Time enough to make your mind up then.'
I left Tom Lavenham to his papers and went off in the direction of my own room, rather cheered by this respite until, turning into the cross corridor, I saw the figure approaching from the far end. That tall, bulging shape could only be one man and, at that particular moment I thought, Billy Bagot was just about the last person I wanted to see.
Billy Bagot! I hadn't been able to adjust myself to thinking of him as Billy Candleford yet, even though it was some months since he had succeeded to the title. It was partly resentment, I suppose, because his father, Johnnie, had been such a nice old boy. Johnnie Candleford had sought me out when I had first started coming to the House of Lords – our two families, he told me, had always been very close although that seemed to have lapsed with my own father's death – and since then he had gone out of his way to be friendly whenever we had met. I had been as much surprised as delighted to learn that he had left me five thousand pounds in his will.
But son, Billy, was a different sort of man altogether. I had met him once or twice with his father and quite a lot since. A great craggy man, he always reminded me of one of those potato faces that one used to make as a child, using a real potato on which one pegged a choice of eyes, ears, noses and mouths from a purpose-made plastic set. There was a half-moon mouth, I remember,

Now

which one could use either way, pointing up for happiness, down for dismal sorrow. Billy had made no secret of the fact that he had resented his father's legacy to me, stinking rich though he was, and insignificant the sum in relation to everything that he himself had been left. Whenever we had met since, his bulging eyes had been reproachful and the ends of his half-moon mouth had pointed firmly down.

Still, there was no avoiding him now.

But, when he got closer, I saw that his hand was held out to me and his face was set in a very definite grin.

'Derek!' he said. 'Just the very person I wanted to see. You *are* coming to the "1944 Club" Dinner this evening?'

'Good Lord,' I said, 'it's not tonight is it?'

Normally it was an occasion that I did attend whenever I possibly could. Some weeks before, I had filled in and sent off the form, saying that I would be there. But all the rigmarole of dressing up for a formal dinner seemed to have lost its attraction now.

'I'm afraid I'll probably have to give it a miss.'

'Oh, I say,' he looked genuinely disappointed, '*do* come. I'm told it's the first time for years that all the members will be present and it'd be a shame to spoil that. Even Dick Richards has flown specially over from the States for it.'

I felt myself weakening. The United States Air Force general was the one member of the club whom I had not yet met.

'He's chairman, this year, isn't he?'

'Yes and, as you know, it's my first dinner. I really would be most grateful if you'd change your mind.'

But I still wasn't very enthusiastic about it and, if only I'd had the strength of mind to keep on saying "no", this whole story might well have ended there.

'Oh, all right,' I said.

And it was with even less enthusiasm that I walked along the Law Lords' corridor of the House of Lords that evening, down the narrow red-carpeted stairs, past the big Harcourt Room on the right and into the passage off which lay the four private dining-rooms of the House of Commons. What was I doing now, I thought, paying the best part of twenty pounds which I couldn't afford, to eat a meal that I hadn't chosen myself, with a lot of

Now

people who weren't particular friends of mine anyway?

I was greeted just inside the door by a rigid hulk of a man in his late fifties, iron-grey hair swept back at either side. Everything about him was aggressively English, but belonging to an England of a good forty years back. Single-breasted dinner-jacket that could only have been conceived in Savile Row, high waistcoat and, unbelievably, at the neck of his cream silk shirt a stick-up collar, round which, perfectly tied and the one modern thing about his appearance, was a wide-bowed, matt black, wild silk tie. This could only be the American Air Force General. He was known for his passion for all things English, to a degree that amounted almost to a caricature.

'Lord Thyrde?' He had a quiet, deep voice in which it was impossible to detect any trace of accent at all. 'Richards is my name. I've been looking forward to meeting you. Call me "Dick".'

'Derek,' I said, as I shook his hand.

'I knew your father. You'd hardly remember him, I suppose?'

'I never even saw him', I said. 'He was killed six weeks before my twin sister and I were born.'

He nodded. Then he looked me up and down. 'You're not unlike him. He had a moustache, of course,' even here he put the accent on the second syllable of the word, 'and he was in his early twenties then. How old are you now?'

'Thirty-four.'

He smiled. 'Well, get yourself a drink. You know every one else, I think.'

I helped myself to a gin and tonic and looked around. Room D is the smallest of the four dining-rooms which are available for members of the House of Commons who want to give private parties for their constituents and friends. Across the middle was a white-clothed table, laid for eight. It was a friendly, cheerful little room and, of the four, it was the one that I knew best. For it was in this room that the members of the "1944 Club" invariably met.

I saw that I had been the last to arrive. Billy Candleford caught my eye and waved. He was talking to Stephen Knightley, a farmer from somewhere down in deepest Hampshire. Against the curtains of the single window, stood Leonard, Lord Frost of Highgate – with the death of Billy's father, he was the oldest member left. With him was Dr. Roger Faulkner, a recent Nobel Prize winner who was the director of a research establishment not

Now

very far from where I lived in Northamptonshire.

Over to the right, the remaining pair, Peter Stobbs and Henry Matheson, were both M.P.'s and, as has become the custom with similar functions based on the Palace of Westminster, they were the only members present who were still wearing ordinary daytime suits.

'Gentlemen!' Dick Richards spoke quietly but with an authority that brought each separate conversation to an instant mid-sentence halt. 'I think perhaps we ought to sit down. Billy,' he put his hand on the chair at the head of the table, 'you're here in your father's old place. I'm on your right.'

With the ease that comes from long familiarity, the rest of us sorted ourselves out into our respective places, and dinner began.

The "1944 Club" was a dining club whose members met once a year. It had had its origins in a party, given in 1944 to celebrate his own birthday, by Johnnie Bagot — Billy Candleford's father, to a random selection of his friends. My own father had happened to be one of the guests. Over the comparatively short period of its existence, it had accumulated to itself a number of eccentric and rather endearing traditions of the sort that one usually associates with an institution of far longer standing. Each member, for instance, occupied the same place at the table, year after year. The chairmanship changed annually, passing from member to member in rotation. The chairman of the day did not, as one might have expected, move to the head of the table, but presided over the dinner from his own accustomed place.

The places of members who were unable to be present at a particular dinner were nonetheless fully laid, the appropriate knives, forks, spoons and glasses being removed as course succeeded course. This custom had been inaugurated in honour of my father, the only one of the original party who had been missing from the first anniversary dinner, having been killed shortly before it was held. During the first of my two chairmanships to date, only two other members had been present, Leonard Frost who was the nearest that the club possessed to a secretary and old Johnnie himself. But the tradition had still been maintained, even though it meant removing more clean implements than used ones each time. In view of the full complement of members, it would not of course be necessary tonight.

Now

When any member died, his eldest son was automatically elected. This stemmed from the third dinner. Old Colonel James Matheson had died not very long after the war and, after a decent interval, Henry had been invited to take his father's place, both metaphorically as a member of the club and literally round the table. Shortly after my twenty-first birthday, I too had been asked to join. The arrival of the letter sticks in my mind because, oddly enough, it was the occasion of the last major row that I remember having with my mother. She begged me not to have anything to do with it. Looking back on it, I think that it must have been pure resentment at the implied suggestion that I was capable of being a substitute for my father in any way at all. In the end I did join – she hadn't seemed to be able to produce any valid reason why I should not – but without telling her and I had always taken care never to mention the "1944 Club" or its functions in her presence since.

Somewhat naturally, in view of the Parliamentary preponderance of the membership, here too much of the conversation was about the Government defeat on the vote of Confidence the night before and everybody seemed to be taking it for granted that the Conservatives would now get in.

'Well, young Derek,' said Leonard Frost on my left, 'I suppose you've already got your seat booked on the government Front Bench?'

Tall and thin but stooping now, his hair tumbling down to his collar and gleaming in the artificial light white enough to justify his name, Lord Frost of Highgate had long been an intermittent drinking mate of mine in the various bars of the House of Lords. He was a member of that part of the right wing of the Labour Party that considerably overlaps the Tory left.

I shook my head. 'You're jumping the gun a bit. Too many imponderables, still.'

'Such as?'

'Well, there's the little formality of our winning the election for a start. Then, whether or not they offer me a job – that's by no means certain. And lastly, if they do, whether or not I can afford to accept it which, the way things are going at the moment, looks highly unlikely.'

'Oh, your lot will win, all right. *And* they'll offer you a job, no question about that. But I've always looked on you as the

Now

supreme example of gilded youth.'
'You tell my bank manager that! If I can't raise quite a lot of money in a very short time, I'll be in dead trouble.'
Leonard had a mannerism of which he was probably totally unaware. Every now and then, he would smoothe back his white tresses, quite unnecessarily, into place with quick alternate stroking movements of either hand – and he did this now.
'You'll manage it, if you really want to. You'd be a Lord-in-Waiting, I suppose. Or have you got your sights set higher than that?'
'No. Lord-in-Waiting'd suit me.'
'Lord-in-Waiting?' said General Dick Richards. As so often happens, the other conversations round the table seemed to have come to an end simultaneously and every one else was now listening to Leonard and myself. 'Is that to The Queen? Does it mean you'll have to leave politics?'
'No.' I explained the system by which government Whips in the House of Lords were appointed, whereby the Chief Whip and his deputy were automatically made Captains of the two Royal Bodyguards, the Gentlemen-at-Arms and the Yeomen of the Guard respectively, and the five junior ones became Lords-in-Waiting. The official Court duties attaching to these posts were minimal and combined rather well with the more mundane but full-time preoccupations involved with the day-to-day running of the House of Lords.
'It's like this, Dick,' Leonard explained, 'when you become President of the United States, Derek here will meet you at London Airport on The Queen's behalf, every time you come here on a State Visit.'
I shook my head. 'I'm afraid not,' I said. 'When that happens you'll rate some one infinitely more important than me.'
All this time, Peter Stobbs had been glaring at me through his heavy horn-rimmed spectacles. He was a little man and they and the floppy bow tie, white spots on red which he invariably wore, had become his trade-mark – a gift to the cartoonists. A large circle for the face, two smaller interconnected ones for the horn-rims, a white-spotted bow of exaggerated size and floppiness and some of them didn't even bother to fill in the features in between. He was noted for his schoolboy humour and the high-pitched whinny of a laugh with which he accompanied each manifestation

Now

of it.

'What have you ever done to deserve office?' he said.

I raised my eyebrows. 'How about the hereditary principle? Isn't that good enough for you?'

'You know damn well it isn't.'

His father had been Peter, Earl of Greyfield, a bumbling man whom I remembered as a Tory of sorts in the early years of my membership of the "1944 Club". Young Peter, on the extreme left wing of the Labour Party, had renounced the earldom on his father's death, some years' back, so that he could keep his seat in the House of Commons, but he liked it to be known that he would have done so on principle in any case.

'Then just exactly what,' I said, 'do you think you're doing here tonight?'

Peter glanced at Henry Matheson on his right, from him to Billy Candleford and then back to me. We four owed our presence here solely to the fact of our having been our fathers' sons. There was a sudden gust of laughter round the table, in which Peter's falsetto giggle almost immediately joined.

With the advent of the next course, I turned to Stephen Knightley the farmer, a stocky red faced man with hair cut brutally short at back and sides, who was sitting on my right.

'I hope *your* lot at least will be able to do something about devaluing the "green pound",' he said.

For one who professes to be a politician as well as a farmer, I had always been ashamed of the fact that the *Common Agricultural Policy* was a complete mystery to me. But should I try to bluff it out or should I confess my ignorance and ask him to explain it?

'Er ...' I said.

I needn't have worried. The gleam of an all-too-often-thwarted pontificator came into his eye and, without waiting for such a request he launched straight into a long and complicated exposition. He lost me after the first few sentences, but I punctuated the remainder of the discourse by interspersing "yes-es" and "noes" at what I hoped were appropriate places.

'The Germans, for instance,' said Stephen. 'They're not frightened of food prices – theirs are the highest in Europe – because they know how important to them their farmers are. You can rely on *them* to get their priorities right.'

Now

It did occur to me to mention that Germany had not always been noted for "getting their priorities right", but I let it go. His admiration for that country, not unmixed with a tinge of envy, was plain to see.

'I say, Dick . . .' I had noticed that Henry Matheson, at the foot of the table, had been talking across Peter Stobbs to Dr. Roger Faulkner who was opposite to me. Henry, tall, dark-blue pin-striped suited, blue-black hair plastered slickly back on his head, dark blue tie, was firmly to the Tory right. He was married to Leonard Frost's daughter. Immensely serious, it was always said of him that he was incapable of smiling. He had a scar on the left-hand side of his face which gave his mouth a permanently twisted look and perhaps that was the reason. He was leaning forward now, the mouth poised open for a moment, '. . . I told Roger that I'd always wanted to see Farmwell and he's suggested that the seven of us should go down there together and he'd show us round.'

'It would have to be fairly soon for me,' said Dick Richards. 'I'm flying home, today week. But that may be too short notice.'

Roger Faulkner had a habit of tilting his head back and surveying any one that he was talking to, through the thick-lensed rimless spectacles perched on his formidably prominent nose, as though they were a particularly complicated piece of circuitry – his field was electronics. He also had the slightest of stammers, except when he was talking on his own or a closely related subject, when it miraculously disappeared.

'N..othing easier,' he said.

We all got out our diaries and, finding that the following Tuesday suited all of us, we settled for that. I had always heard that a visit to the famous Farmwell Foundation, particularly if lunch was included, was a thing that it would be foolish in the extreme to miss.

I sat back and looked round the table at the odd assortment of people and wondered, as I often had in the past, why it was that this particular gathering should always go so superbly well. A more diverse collection it would be difficult to imagine. Leonard Frost and myself, for instance; and the two M.P.'s, Henry Matheson and Peter Stobbs, now chattering away together as though they were each other's best friends whereas I doubted whether, apart from this occasion, they ever addressed a single

Now

word to each other outside the Chamber. Then there was Roger Faulkner, the dedicated laboratory-bound scientist, as against General Dick Richards who had spent so much of his life in action – and in the American services at that. Billy Candleford, even he seemed to be fitting in well, and Stephen Knightley, this was probably the only day in the whole year that he didn't spend in gumboots, thickly coated with Hampshire mud. There was quite a difference in generations too. Leonard must be getting on for seventy now. I, at the other end of the scale, was the youngest by far, Peter next, some ten or twelve years older than me and the other five were very much of an age.

The food and wine were invariably good, and that may have had something to do with it, particularly the wine. Not in the same class as the wines that old Johnnie had provided at the original dinner, of course, those had been something to dream about. Most of the founder members probably still did. Almost every year, one or other of them had to be forcibly prevented from reminiscing about their dim distant glory. Even so, we did ourselves well enough even now. The port had just completed its first circuit. I glanced at the menu in front of me. Croft '55.

There was a rap on the table.

'My Lords and Gentlemen . . .' Dick Richards was standing up now. 'The Queen!'

We all drank.

Before the conversation had time to restart, he rose to his feet again.

'As you know, one of the strictest of our rules is that there should be no speeches and I don't propose to break that tradition tonight. But this is a sad occasion because it is the first time that Johnnie Candleford, so beloved by us all, has not been present among us. Now the very last thing that Johnnie would have wanted is any sort of mourning so, for this one occasion only, I shall ask you to stand and keep a moment or two of silence.'

We stood, while perhaps thirty seconds ticked away.

'And now I shall have to improvise because the formula of words to which we have grown so used is, alas, no longer appropriate.'

He raised his glass.

'My Lords and Gentlemen, to the memory of Johnnie Bagot on this, his birthday.'

Now

But it was only a slight variation on the words of the toast that had been proposed in that room and on that date, or when it had happened to fall at a weekend on the nearest convenient weekday to it, every year since 1944.

i. Then. Narrative of Derek (Derry), 2nd Viscount Thyrde.

It all started with that confounded birthday party! Wednesday, the twenty-ninth of March, 1944. Not that I did not enjoy it at the time. In fact it was a jolly good evening from start to finish, but I did not then know what an impact it was destined to have on my own life, let alone the difference that it might have made to the whole outcome of the war.

I had managed to wangle a few days' leave and had left Yorkshire earlier in the day, from where the Second Battalion, Grenadier Guards, were waiting impatiently for the invasion which we all knew to be imminent but which we had almost given up hope of ever coming to pass. For a wonder my battered old M.G. two-seater had refrained from breaking down on the way and, shortly after 6.30 p.m., I had parked it under the bronze statue of *Richard Coeur de Lion* in Old Palace Yard. Mounted and armed, his sword bent by bomb blast was held high in symbolic defiance of England's enemies. The sky was a monotonously uniform mid-grey and there was a thin drizzle as I walked across the cobbles towards the Peers' Entrance of the House of Lords. To my right the massive shape of Victoria Tower loomed menacingly over me, the scaffolding that extended up to nearly half its height giving the illusion that it had suffered from the ministrations of some monstrous spider. The lugubrious rise and fall of a distant siren was piercing its way through the damp atmosphere as I pushed open the double swing doors and went inside.

The door-keeper on duty looked at me doubtfully, as I slung gas-mask and ash-plant on the peg allotted to me and put my blue forage cap over them.

"Are you a peer, Sir?"

"Yes," I said, "I'm Lord Thyrde. Hold on a minute, I've got my pass somewhere."

I took my wallet out of the top right-hand pocket of my service-

Then

dress jacket, extracted a small oblong of blue card with rounded corners and handed it to him. The signature of Lord Ancaster, the Lord Great Chamberlain, which it bore was a printed one – not even in facsimile. Any spy worth his oats would have had no difficulty in providing himself with a passable imitation of one of those, but it seemed to satisfy the door-keeper.

"Beg pardon, m'Lord, but one can't be too careful these days," he said.

I went on up the stairs and along the corridor. The Palace of Westminster, after four and a half years of war, presents an atmosphere of gilded shabbiness. It always reminds me of those gallant dowagers that one sees at parties nowadays whose faded, sometimes darned even, ball gowns seem to invest their wearers with a special kind of dignity that something straight from the dress-makers, with its suggestion of scrimping and saving of coupons if not actual scrounging on the black market, could never hope to attain.

The first ante-room that I came to was previously known as '*Prince's Chamber*', but it has been re-named '*Peers' Lobby'* in the rearrangement since the Commons, their own Chamber having been destroyed by bombing in 1941, have been occupying ours behind the two pairs of locked doors on the left. There was a single peer, whose face seemed vaguely familiar, sitting writing letters at the further of the two octagonal tables. He got up and came towards me.

"Thyrde, isn't it?"

A shortish man, a good ten years older than me – that would put him in his mid to late thirties – his neck bulged slightly over a stiff white collar that had become at least a size and a half too small for him. He was wearing the dark blue with twin diagonal stripes of an Old Harrovian tie.

"We're to be fellow guests. Of Johnnie Bagot. Dinner to-night, I understand." He spoke in jerks with a sort of breathless urgency. "Met here before, remember. Greyfield," he said and he held out his hand.

And then I did manage to place him. Peter Stobbs, Earl of Greyfield, was one of the people to whom I had been introduced some eight months before when I had come to take my seat. His father, the first Earl, had figured in one of Lloyd George's more suspect honours lists at the end of the last war, thereafter

Then

multiplying his already not inconsiderable fortune by speculating in Germany. Peter Greyfield had been the only son and nothing had been too good for him. In the late 'twenties and throughout the 'thirties, he had owned a number of successful race-horses, but recently there had been rumours that even his bank balance was beginning to show signs of strain.

"Yes," I said, "Uncle Johnnie's my god-father."

Greyfield nodded. "Jolly good chap, Sir John. Work on Committees together. Walk down together, shall we?" he said.

* * *

"Ah, so you two know each other," said Sir John Bagot.

Although he was in fact no relation, Uncle Johnnie had always been part of my life. He and my father had been at school together and, left a widower with one small son after only a year of marriage, he had come down to stay at Thyrde at least three times a year for as long as I could remember. But kind and attentive though he always was to me, I had somehow never managed to get very close to him. It was almost as though his character was surface-deep only and lacked a third dimension. I had been told that he had never been the same again since his much-loved German wife had died in child-birth. He was a plump man in short black coat and striped trousers, with a protruding tummy and a bristly but close-trimmed moustache. He was fifty years old exactly. Today was his birthday, which was the reason for the party tonight.

"I think you know everybody, Peter. You can look after yourself. Now then, Derry my boy, who don't you know?"

There were four other people in the room, two in uniform, two not. Without waiting for an answer, Uncle Johnnie turned to the nearest who had been hovering just behind him, a tall man with a lean brown face, a few years older than himself, wearing the uniform of a Lieutenant-Colonel in the Scots Guards.

"Do you know my god-son, Lord Thyrde? Derry, this is Colonel Matheson."

I shook hands with him. "How do you do Sir," I said.

"Knew your father well. He and Johnnie and I all got into the House at the same time, don'cha know. We missed him sadly when he went up to the Lords."

Then

"Don't let the fancy dress fool you," said Uncle Johnnie. "Old James here only plays at soldiers – attached to the Brownies or some such nonsense. He's really only a humble Member of Parliament like myself."

"That'll be enough from you, young Johnnie. When you start being humble, I'll know it's time for us all to apply for the Chiltern Hundreds." The Colonel winked at me. "Don'cha know?" he said.

"You two can talk later," said Uncle Johnnie. "Now then, Derry, that fellow over by the window is young Roger Faulkner." He pointed to a chap of my own age, thin and not very strong looking with heavy spectacles and a large nose, whom I had already recognised and who was now talking to Lord Greyfield. "He's some form of back-room boffin. Quite brilliant, they say."

"Yes, I know him," I said. "He was in m'tutor's at Eton."

"Well, those other two. The bearded chap in the Wavy Navy's called Stephen Knightley. He's in the same ship as my boy, Billy. Billy couldn't get away, so I asked Stephen instead. And the fellow he's talking to, who looks like a golliwog, is another M.P. friend of mine, Leonard Frost. Bit of a red, he is, silly young fool, but not a bad chap at heart. Reason I asked him is he's corporal i.c. my section in the Palace of Westminster Home Guard. You're sitting between them at dinner. Come on, I'll take you over to meet them."

But at that moment, he was called back to the door to welcome a new arrival, a man in the olive-grey belted jacket and pinky-grey trousers of the American Forces. The table I had noticed was laid for eight, so the party must now be complete. I walked across the room to talk to Roger Faulkner, who was now by himself.

I had not met him since we had both left school shortly before the war. What I remember chiefly about him was his passionate championship of the new Germany and its economic miracle. I wondered how he felt about it now.

"Hello, Beaky."

He winced slightly and I made a mental note to desist from using a nick-name that he had obviously long outgrown.

"Hello, D. .erry," he said. He peered through his spectacles at the 1939–1943 medal-ribbon, dark blue—red—light blue, which was perched lonesomely above my top left-hand pocket.* "Lucky

* Later to become the 1939–1945 Star.

22

devil! In the thick of it, I suppose."

"There's not a lot of *it* to be in the thick of at the moment," I said. "How about you? What are you doing now?"

"Oh, I'm in a research job. I was all set to try and bluff my way through the medical when they found out that I had a Higher Certificate in Physics and Maths coupled with a scholarship to Magdalene. Now I'm tied up in some d..ismal hole in Northamptonshire. That's where you live, isn't it? All I really want to do is to have a crack at the so-and-so's."

"I should think you're doing that pretty effectively where you are now," I said.

At that moment we were joined by Uncle Johnnie, bringing the American over with him, who I now saw had Air Force wings over a respectable row of medal ribbons which put my poor *one* to shame. He was a tall man with dark hair cut very short, and could not have been much older than me.

"This is my god-son, Derry Thyrde, and another young friend, Roger Faulkner – Lieutenant Alan Richards. It is Alan, isn't it?" The airman looked startled for a moment. Then he grinned.

"That's right," he said. "Sounds kind of funny to hear it, though. I'm never known as anything but 'Dick'."

"We'd better sit down," said Uncle Johnnie. "Don't want to make the staff late, getting home in the black-out. You're here on my right, Dick." He called the others over and directed the rest of us to our places, Roger next to the American, then Greyfield and Colonel Matheson at the far end. I introduced myself to Mr. Frost on my left and Lieutenant Knightley on my right and sat down in my own place with my back to the single window with its black-out curtains already drawn.

A very elderly waiter hobbled round with the wine and I glanced at the left-hand side of the menu.

Le Montrachet, 1934. Shipped by Louis Latour.
La Mission Haut Brion, 1926.
Graham's, 1908.

"My word, Johnnie, you're doing us proud this evening."

I looked up. Colonel Matheson was gazing almost in rapture at the glass-ful of pale straw-coloured liquid that he was holding up to the light.

Stephen Knightley, on my right, I liked immediately. With his

Then

dark brown hair and trimmed beard, he looked like a rather younger and, of course, commissioned version of the man in the middle of a packet of Player's Navy Cut cigarettes. He was two years older than me. As soon as he had left school, he told me, he had started to grow a moustache of which he became inordinately fond.

"I only grew mine when I passed out of O.C.T.U.," I said.

"Well, when I joined the Navy it was a choice between shaving it off or growing a beard as well. When I look at myself in the glass now, I'm still not sure whether I made the right decision."

Like myself, he was on leave, but his had started a couple of days before and he was spending it in London where I gathered he was rather keen on some girl. It was only Uncle Johnnie's insistence that had persuaded him to tear himself away from her on this particular evening. I told him that I thought I might be coming up to London again myself on the following Tuesday and we arranged to meet at his club, 'The Senior', for lunch.

Mr. Frost, to whom I talked as soon as the next course arrived, was a pale-faced man in his early thirties with a wild tangle of black hair and I found him rather heavy going to start with.

"What's going on in the House of Commons," I asked him.

Immediately his listlessness disappeared.

"Committee Stage of the Education Bill. And it's been an education to all of us, I can tell you."

"Why, what's happened?"

"Haven't you heard? We beat the Government by one vote last night. Equal pay for women teachers. And you'll never credit what the Tories have done now. You're a Tory, I suppose?"

"I don't know. I've never really thought about it. My father was," I said.

"They're going to remove the whole clause, as amended, from the Bill tomorrow – Mr. Churchill announced it in the House today – and then replace it in its original form at Report Stage, in a week or two's time. And they're going to achieve that, if you please, by making it an issue of confidence. They know that nobody will dare to risk bringing the Government down."

"Sound tactics!" Colonel Matheson, on his other side, was nodding approvingly. It was the first time that I had realised that he had been listening.

"Sound tactics?" Mr. Frost scrubbed at his mop of hair several times, with his right hand followed by his left. The effect was negligible. "I never thought that even the Tories could sink as low as that."

"Hey, break it up," said Johnnie Bagot. "No politics tonight."

There was an uneasy silence. "Well, Derry," said Uncle Johnnie, "when's the invasion going to come?"

"I don't know," I said, "but it can't be too soon for me."

"Nor me!" I was surprised by the vehemence with which Stephen Knightley spoke. "The sooner we beat those swine the better. They're rotten to the core, the whole darn race of them and I hope we kill as many of them as possible. There's no good German but..."

He stopped short and looked round at me. To his credit he did not ask me why I had kicked him under the table, but I had done so too late. The words left unsaid had been all too obvious. Colonel Matheson was looking at Johnnie Bagot with his mouth open. Lord Greyfield folded and unfolded his napkin. Roger Faulkner stared down at the table-cloth in front of him. Even Leonard Frost was shifting about uneasily in his seat. It was plain that, like myself, they were all thinking about Uncle Johnnie's adored German wife.

The silence was broken by Lieutenant Dick Richards.

"Well, I guess I'd better come clean", he said.

We all stared at him.

"My mother and father were German. They emigrated to the States before the last war. They were naturalised of course, but even so I guess that makes me one too." He smiled. "I don't know about good, but I'm far from being dead yet."

There was laughter all round and from that moment the awkwardness was forgotten. If anything, Richards's quick-wittedness in overcoming it made the party go better than before. The atmosphere in that dingy, once cream-painted little room with its nondescript Palace of Westminster prints started to come alive and almost achieved an entity of its own. The claret may have had something to do with it of course.

Colonel Matheson held up his glass to the light. "Superb, Johnnie," he said. "Great depth and perfectly balanced. I wouldn't have believed it but it's got even more character than the neighbouring Chateau Haut Brion itself."

It was indeed delicious, with a slightly almondy flavour to it,

Then

and it seemed to be in plentiful supply. The port that came after it was pretty good too.

When the decanter was almost empty, Colonel Matheson stood up and rapped on the table.

"I'm under strict orders. No speeches! But we can't let this occasion go by – without saying thank-you, don'cha know – so I'll ask you to raise your glasses. Gentlemen, to Johnnie Bagot. Happy birthday."

"Happy birthday," we all said.

Johnnie Bagot stood up too and emptied his own glass.

"Well, that's all, boys," he said. "I'm afraid you must go home now."

"I say," Lord Greyfield looked conspiratorially round the room. "Night's young, yet. Let's go on somewhere. Why don't we all go to *The Bag*?"

There were murmurs of assent.

"I'm game if you are," said Uncle Johnnie. "You'll come, James? Right, I can take one other in my car. Two, with a squash."

"I've got a jeep outside," said Dick Richards.

In the general movement that followed, I managed to take Stephen Knightley on one side and explain to him about Johnnie Bagot's wife. The small area of his face that was not covered in beard turned a brilliant red.

"Good Lord, I never knew," he said. "I must go and apologise to the old boy at once."

"No, don't do that. It's all passed over now. Come on, I'll give you a lift to *The Bag*."

Stephen looked doubtful.

"I say, isn't that the place where . . .? I think I'd rather not."

"It's not obligatory, you know," I said unkindly, "and the girls aren't at all what you'd imagine. If you go off now, you'll start breaking the party up. After that brick you dropped, I think you owe it to all of us not to do that."

* * *

The Bag o' Nails is a night-club that is situated in a dark alley off Regent Street. Its membership list, were such a revealing document ever to be published, would read like an omnibus

Then

volume of Burke's *Peerage* and *Landed Gentry*. I rang the bell and, as the door opened and we went in, I saw on Stephen's face much the same sort of apprehension that Lot's guests must have shown on their first arrival in Sodom.

"Good evening, m'Lord," said the attendant. "We haven't had the pleasure of seeing you here for some time."

I signed us both in and took him down the stairs and into the room below, saying 'hello' to Millie, the guiding spirit of the establishment, and introducing a reluctant Stephen to her, on the way.

"You're sure we're only coming in for a drink?" he said.

The others of our party were already installed at a large table on the left. On the far right, a four-piece band was playing softly to an empty dance-floor. There was one other party, smaller than ours and all in uniform, drinking and laughing. At two other tables were grouped six or seven moderately pretty girls, all in long dresses. They were talking sporadically among themselves and, as I looked around them, one of them caught my eye and smiled invitingly at me. There were two other men, each at a smaller table. One had a partner already and their heads were bent close together, talking with an earnestness that might have been taken for laying the foundations of a life-long relationship. In fact I knew that they were negotiating a more fleeting and financially based transaction. The other man was still alone. He was holding an empty glass and eyeing the field speculatively. We walked over to our table and took the two empty chairs, I next to the American with Stephen on my left.

It was the first time that I had had a chance to talk to Dick Richards. He told me that he was stationed at Chelveston in Northamptonshire which is only about fifteen or twenty miles away from Thyrde.

"Quick thinking on your part at dinner," I murmured to him. Across the table, Uncle Johnnie was deep in conversation with Colonel Matheson and Frost. "Saved what looked like being an embarrassing moment." I told him about the late Lady Bagot being a German. He nodded slowly.

"I guessed something like that was up. Incidentally, it was true what I said — about my own parents, I mean."

"Doesn't it make you feel a bit awkward being at war with Germany, then?"

Then

"Not unduly. I dislike the Krauts as much as any one, more possibly, but I don't go much on the Communists either. All this talk about dear old Uncle Joe and our brave Russian allies makes me want to vomit. I sometimes wonder if we've got our priorities right and whether we oughtn't to be fighting them instead."

A second bottle of whisky soon appeared.

"Well, Johnnie," said Colonel Matheson, "I'll say it again, it really has been a splendid evening. I haven't enjoyed myself so much for weeks."

"Nor I," said Mr. Frost. "Let's have another dinner next year. Same date, same party — all of us who came tonight."

Colonel Matheson leaned forward. "That's not a bad idea. I don't see why we shouldn't be able to repeat the same atmosphere we had tonight and with any luck the war'll be over by that time, so we'll have something else to celebrate as well."

Uncle Johnnie made a slight gesture of acceptance with his hands. "If you like," he said.

"Not a bit of it, Johnnie. You'll be our guest next time."

"And we can't ask Sir John to organise it again either," said Frost. "One of us should do that."

"You suggested it," I said to him. "That counts as volunteering where I come from."

He looked at me for a moment with what I gave him the credit for being simulated annoyance. Then, "All right," he said.

The room was beginning to fill up. The other party like ours had acquired a full complement of partners. There were a few couples already on the floor, gyrating slowly wrapped in varying degrees of clinch.

"Well, if nobody minds," said Lord Greyfield suddenly. "Feel like a spot of exercise. Just the odd dance or two."

Dick Richards and I turned in our chairs and watched him as he walked over to one of the tables where the diminishing supply of spare girls were still sitting, paused for a moment to survey the occupants, and then leaned over to speak to one of them and led her out to dance.

"Say," said Dick in my ear, "can a non-member do that?"

"Certainly," I said. "But you'll have to make your own financial arrangements — even to dance."

"Sure." He stood up, put his chair back to the table, and hitched the waist-band of his trousers more securely over his hips.

Then

Then, without hesitation, he walked straight over to a girl in blue.

I was debating with myself whether or not to follow his example, when a brief glance at Stephen's face decided me against it. I really would have lost my name with him completely. Mr. Frost, however, suffered from no such inhibition. He beckoned over the head waiter who, after a brief murmured consultation, went to fetch one of the remaining girls for him. As he ushered her back in our direction, Frost got up and walked to meet her. Clearly not for Leonard Frost, M.P., were the hit and miss methods employed by the other two.

When the music stopped, Colonel Matheson jumped smartly to his feet. "Come on, let's all move over a bit," he said. "Make room for the girls, don'cha know."

He reached for a chair from a nearby unoccupied table, placed it firmly next to his own and held out his hand to invite Frost's partner who was the first to arrive to sit in it. Stephen, I noticed, kept manoeuvring his chair so that it remained equi-distant between mine and Roger's on his other side in order to pre-empt the possibility of a similar fate occurring to him. A waiter arrived with three opened bottles of champagne, which he put on the table one in front of each girl. The Colonel leaned over solicitously to pour out some for his next-door neighbour. When the band started playing again, we all stood up as he escorted her off to the floor. I saw Uncle Johnnie watching them with an indulgent smile on his face as they cavorted round. I caught his eye and he winked. When they returned he took his wallet out of his pocket.

"Well, I must be off now. Do you think that we can get hold of the bill?"

"Certainly not," I said. "You've done enough already." I looked round the table. "Perhaps who-ever leaves last can settle the bill and contact the others about their share?"

A gleam of triumph came into Mr. Frost's eye.

"You've just volunteered," he said.

"That's very good of you all," said Uncle Johnnie. He stood up. "Coming James?"

"Eh?" said Colonel Matheson. He looked reluctantly at the girl beside him. "Oh, all right. You'll let me know what I owe you, Thyrde? Good night, my dear." He leaned forward and kissed her cheek. "Good night, all of you," and he followed Uncle Johnnie across the room and out of the door.

Then

I asked Dick and Roger to give me their telephone numbers. Stephen and I had exchanged ours earlier in case our luncheon should fall through and the others I could contact at their respective Houses of Parliament. Stephen Knightley, Roger Faulkner and I were left at the table when the others went off to dance again. None of us had very much to say. I re-filled my glass, infuriated by having allowed myself to be inhibited by Stephen's moral scruples – there seemed to be no spare girls left now, any way – and at the same time having let myself in for staying until the end, when Lord Greyfield came back.

"Must be off now. Wife'll be worrying. This is Lord Thyrde," he said to the girl. "He'll look after you." And he left.

I glanced round at Stephen but he was studying the table-cloth as though it contained secret orders that he had been told to memorise and then immediately destroy. I looked back at the girl. She was a brunette and not at all bad looking, short and plumpish wearing a pink dress with narrow shoulder straps.

"What's your Christian name?" she asked.

"My friends call me 'Derry'."

"Come on, Derry, then. Let's dance."

* * *

From that moment on, the evening began to look up considerably. Her name was Irene, she told me, and she pronounced the final 'e'. She snuggled up to me closely on the dance floor and responded to every movement that I made even before I had made it. Not that we moved very much. Sometimes we sat at the table and talked, occasionally coinciding with Dick or Mr. Frost and their partners – Stephen and Roger had by now gone – and eventually they too left. She was marvellous company. I remembered what I said to Stephen earlier that evening about the girls at The Bag. She might have been somebody's sister, if you know what I mean. Her hair smelt vaguely of flowers.

Suddenly, as we were dancing, she disengaged herself slightly, put a hand on each of my shoulders and looked up at me.

"Would you like to come home with me? Nothing to pay or anything like that."

"I'd like to," I said, "I really would. But I can't tonight. I've got a full day to-morrow and I must drive back to

Then

Northamptonshire."

I looked at my watch. It was already 3 a.m. "Good Lord, is that the time?"

I sent for the bill and paid it and while she was collecting her coat I went upstairs and ordered a taxi for her. Both she and it seemed to take an unconscionable time to arrive.

"Excuse me, m'Lord." It was the head waiter. He handed me a folded sheet of paper. "This was found under your table. It must belong to you or one of the other gentlemen who were with you."

I unfolded it. It was cartridge paper, about foolscap size or perhaps a little bit bigger, folded in three, with the little holes and round impressions made by drawing-pins in each of the four corners. Held lengthways, a thin irregular line ran across the top of the sheet, with a more squiggly dotted line about an inch or an inch and a half below it. Double straight lines ran down from the continuous one, some apparently random and three others together in the approximate shape of a fan. The rest of the sheet was covered with little blob-like shapes and dots with figures against them, all this in Indian ink, but arrows had been pencilled in here and there, and in the top right-hand corner was a brown ring that looked as if it might have been a stain left by a carelessly placed tea-cup, if someone had not written in thick blue crayon in the middle of it '$2\frac{1}{2}$ C.A.'

"Not mine," I said. "It must belong to one of the others. I'll be in touch with them next week anyway and I'll ask them all then."

I had re-folded it and put it away in my wallet, when Irene arrived.

"Look," I said, "I'll be staying up in London next Tuesday. I'll see you here then, shall I?"

She reached up and kissed me gently on the lips. "Promise?"

"Promise," I said.

And I really meant it. If things had turned out differently, I would have kept that appointment.

The fact that I had to let her down still gives me a twinge of conscience when I think about it, even now.

* * *

I had turned off Watling Street and I was half-way up the steep hill between Hockliffe and Woburn when the engine spluttered and died. The M.G. had no doubt decided that it was time that it made up for its impeccable behaviour of the day before. I got out to have a look, but I already knew from bitter experience what was wrong. A cam-shaft coupling had sheared through. Luckily, I always carried a spare with me now. But what in the day-time would have been a comparatively simple operation, tinkering about with cars has always been something of a hobby of mine, took a long time by the light of a torch. It was twenty-five minutes to eight when, oily and exhausted, I drew up outside the front door of Thyrde House. A journey that I should have done easily in a couple of hours had taken over four and a half.

Breakfast, I thought, and then bed. I went into the dining-room and found that there was an occupant at the table already. One of my mother's billetees, who was head boffin at a nearby hush-hush establishment, was engaged in putting a thin smear of butter, from a dish that held his individual ration, onto a slice of toast. His boiled egg had already had its top removed.

"Morning, Professor Tomkins," I said. "You're up early."

He got up and held out his hand. "Hello, Lord Thyrde, welcome home."

I poured myself out a cup of coffee at the side-board and we sat down. He had a busy day in front of him, he told me, and wanted to be in his laboratory early so as to get everything ready before his colleagues arrived.

"Oh, by the way . . ." I suddenly remembered the paper that I had been given at the Bag o' Nails. I took it out and passed it over to him. "I've got to trace the owner of this. Can you give me any idea what it might be?"

He unfolded it, glanced at it, then bent forward and peered more closely. He looked up at me over his spectacles and spoke in a very low voice.

"Where," he asked, "did you get this?"

I told him about the party the night before and the last-minute discovery of the paper under the table.

"Who else was at the party?" He took a note-book out of his pocket.

I gave him the names and he wrote them down. "Why do you ask?"

For a moment he did not reply but folded up the paper and put it inside the note-book which he returned to his pocket.

Then, "I think I'd better take care of this, if you don't mind."

"Hey, I don't know about that..."

"This paper," he said, "is of quite inestimable importance. It also happens to be stolen and it belongs to me. I last saw it — quite by chance, I was looking for something else — in my safe at Farmwell, early yesterday afternoon."

2. Now

Farmwell — *The Farmwell Foundation for Technological Research*, to give it its full style and title. We were sitting at lunch in the Director's official dining-room. Dr. Roger Faulkner was at one rounded end of the long table, General Dick Richards as Chairman for the year of the "1944 Club" on his right and I on his left. Roger had invited in six of his departmental heads to have lunch with us, so that members of the home team could alternate round the table with the seven guests.

I had driven up from London alone that morning and we had gathered for coffee in the director's office at eleven o'clock. Then we had been taken round various departments to see projects in progress.

Over a glass of sherry before lunch, I had been buttonholed by Leonard Frost. He had been brought by his son-in-law, Henry Matheson. Henry, it seemed, had a board meeting in Birmingham early the next morning and would be driving straight on so Leonard would be short of a lift back to his house on Highgate Hill.

'Grand, come with me. Glad of the company,' I said.

At the beginning of lunch, the Secretary of Farmwell who was on my left, Henry who was on his other side and I had discussed for a time all that we had seen and heard that morning. But Henry had wanted to go into everything in detail and from a standpoint of such apparent technical knowledge that I had soon dropped out of it and, as Roger was still preoccupied with the American, I was left for the moment to my own devices.

On the wall behind Roger's chair, there was an oil-painting of Farmwell as it had been in an earlier incarnation, back in the days of the war. The work, no doubt, of a local artist and painted from a point that must have been just across the road from what are now the main gates, it showed a higgledy-piggledy collection of single-storey huts, the entrance blocked by a metal pole with a

Now

guardroom to one side. A red-capped Military Policeman, his face a magenta blob, stood at ease outside its open door, bayonet fixed on his Lee Enfield rifle which was a slightly crooked streak of brown. In the foreground, a passing and totally irrelevant farm labourer, cur-dog at heel and pitchfork over shoulder, his sole purpose in life being to balance the composition of the picture, was slouching stolidly and perpetually by.

'That's how it l..ooked when I first came here.' I glanced sideways and saw that I now had Roger's attention. He had turned in his chair and was following through the thick lenses of his spectacles the direction of my gaze. 'We've come quite a long way since then.'

It was indeed a marked contrast to the massive complex of Stockbroker-Queen-Anne red brick blocks, reception offices, high railings and the tortured writhing of wrought-iron gates, that was Farmwell now.

'Well, Derek, what are your impressions so far?'

'Fascinating,' I said. 'But quite a lot of it's way over my head, I'm afraid.'

He laughed. 'That's inevitable with the highly sophisticated state that technology's reaching now. And there's quite a lot we haven't been able to show you, of course. Ministry of Defence projects – we still do quite a lot for them. But there is one thing that I think will interest you, an every-day practical example of the sort of thing that the micro-chip will be able to achieve in the home. A completely new device that is going to revolutionise domestic central heating. You'll see that this afternoon.'

We came back to the director's office just before four and there we found waiting for us a man in a brown cotton overall coat, covering T-shirt and jeans. He was in his early twenties and I judged from the line of his cheek-bones that his face would have had the ascetic gauntness of total dedication had it not been masked and softened by a bushy red beard.

'This is Mr. Foster, Gentlemen,' said Dr. Roger Faulkner. 'What you're going to see now is the brain-child that he's been working on for the last six months.'

The red beard split in a wide beam, which its owner swept round the room until he had focused it on each of our party in turn.

'Afternoon all,' he said.

Now

It was the final item of our tour. Roger went over to the safe and unlocked it, taking out a white cardboard box the size and shape of a shoebox, which I subsequently discovered was exactly what it was, and after a moment's hesitation gave it to the red-bearded man.

'I'll leave you to explain it to them, Reg.'

Reg Foster took it and held it to his chest for a moment, directing down towards it the look of wonder and total love that one usually associates with a first-time mother who has received, from the hands of the midwife, her new-born child. Then he put it down on the leather-topped desk, removed the lid and extracted and unwrapped from its enswathing tissue paper a black metal box, some eight inches by four, by four again. We all crowded round.

He took a Phillips screwdriver from the top pocket of his linen coat and ruthlessly started the operation, undoing the single screw. Then he took off the top of the box revealing its intestines, an obscene jumble of metal and coloured-coded plastic that looked as though some one had carelessly stepped on the working parts of an old fashioned wireless set and trodden them flat.

'This, Gentlemen, is the *Controller*,' he said. 'And that . . .' he pointed with the business end of the screwdriver to a remarkably undistinguished-looking piece of electronic offal, 'is the EAROM'.

I was beginning to feel faintly queasy. I never did care much for insides.

'And here . . .' Reg paused to grope in the cardboard box again, like a child taking a lucky dip in a bran-tub at some village fete, and triumphantly withdrew and unwrapped a smaller metal box — square this time, painted white, it was equipped with four push-buttons spaced like the dots on the "four" side of a die. 'Here is one of the *Thermocouple* units. The controller is programmed to act on instructions that it receives from the thermocouples — signals which its microcomputer has converted from *analogue* into *digital* — but it modifies these in accordance with the usage experience that the microcomputer has also built up and stored in the EAROM.'

He looked round at us anxiously. 'All clear, so far?'

Henry Matheson nodded wisely . . . but his single "yes" was drowned in the otherwise unanimous chorus of "no".

Now

'You've lost me,' said Billy Candleford. His potato face had an expression of mock perplexity that the manufacturer of the little plastic accessories would have been hard put to it to supply.

'Me too,' I said. 'How about the ci-devant Earl?' I had noticed the floppy bow tie bobbing about next to me, out of the corner of my eye. Peter Stobbs shook his head and whinnied.

'I haven't got your massive intellect, Derek,' he said.

'You must remember that my friends are laymen, Reg,' said Roger Faulkner. 'They don't speak quite the same language as you and I. Perhaps you'd better let me tell them.'

The red-bearded man seemed to be quite content with this. He just stepped back a couple of paces and stood there eyeing his creation with the same air of maternal pride while his director took over.

'As you know,' Roger said, 'the normal central heating system is turned on in the morning and off at night, by means of a timeclock that can be set by the owner of the house. Its objective is to keep each room in the house, irrespective of whether or not it is being used at the time, at an even temperature that has been previously determined, again by the houseowner by setting a dial on one central thermostat which is usually sited in the hall. An enormous amount of energy is wasted in this way, to a degree that is quite unacceptable, both nationally to the Government and individually, with the rocketing prices of gas and oil, to the consumer himself.'

One answer, he told us, would of course be to have a thermostat in every room but that would be expensive and in any case it wouldn't answer all the problems. The system that Reg Foster had been developing at Farmwell was better in almost every way.

Each room would be furnished with a thermocouple — Roger picked up the square white box with its four die-spaced buttons. This would be situated in a part of the room representative of the temperature as a whole and preferably near to the door. It differed from a thermostat in that, while it was capable of determining the temperature, it couldn't take any action about it itself. It merely relayed the information back to the controller — he pointed to the larger black-painted gadget — which would then decide what to do about it, issuing separate instructions to every radiator in the house. The controller was in fact a computer. It

37

Now

possessed a memory bank and this was how it worked.

'The thermocouple will be made of plastic in its finished form and the two buttons on the left will be marked "on" and "off". The occupants of the house will have to school themselves to press the "on" button every time they come into a room if they are the first to do so and the "off" one if they are the last to leave, in just the same way as they would with the electric light switch. Hence the reason for its siting just inside the door. To begin with, the controller will react immediately to the press of the button, but this in itself is wasteful. Ideally, the heat should be turned on about half an hour before the room is to be used and off a similar period before the last person is likely to leave. After a bit, the controller's memory will have built up experience of the behaviour patterns governing the use of rooms by that household and will be able to make the necessary adjustments accordingly. It's surprising how regular the habits of the average family are.'

But that wasn't all. We would notice that there was no dial on the thermocouple with which to set the required temperature. The two buttons on the right would be marked "H" for hotter and "C" for colder respectively. If a particular room was noticeably too cold, pressing the "H" button would cause the controller to raise its temperature by approximately $2\frac{1}{2}$ degrees. Similarly, the "C" button could be pressed if the room became too hot. And if these minor adjustments were not enough, the appropriate button could always be pressed again. Here too, the controller's memory would gradually acquire experience as to the temperature bracket in which the family liked a particular room to be kept at any particular time.

'Well, that's it, Gentlemen,' said Roger Faulkner. 'There *are* other more sophisticated refinements that I haven't had time to go into, but I've given you the broad general idea. The whole system will undoubtedly ensure a dramatic reduction in each family's consumption of fuel. Any questions?'

Three of us spoke at once.

'What about bath-water?' said Stephen Knightley. 'Will it control that as well?'

'How much will it cost?' asked Henry Matheson.

But I was thinking of the ever increasing difficulty of maintaining Thyrde House at a temperature even marginally above absolute zero.

Now

'How soon can I get one?' I said.

Roger smiled and held up his hand. But he answered all three questions together. 'Yes, with some slight adaptations, of course. Hard to say, depends on production. The initial outlay would be heavy, but you'd soon get that back in savings on fuel. Fitted to an existing system, about five hundred pounds for the average house, I should think. Our work is complete on it, but *British Light & Power*, the company we've developed it for, want to carry out the final tests on it themselves. Lord Stanstead, chairman of B.L.P., is coming over with some of his top men to collect it tomorrow. If all goes well, it could be on the market in a matter of eighteen months. Any more?'

No one else spoke, so he beckoned forward the red-bearded man who re-wrapped the two gadgets and stowed them away in the box, which he gave to Roger. Then he beamed all round again and hurried off, anxious no doubt to start off his next assignment with the right amount of early pre-natal care.

Roger locked the box back in his safe and removed the key.

'I must ask you,' he said, 'not to mention what you've just seen and heard outside this room. I shouldn't really have shown it to you, but we're all friends here. I've already had an approach, verbal of course, from a smaller firm but one which in this limited field are trade rivals of B.L.P. They'd somehow got wind of this development and offered me a substantial sum of money to let *them* have the results instead. Then they had the cheek,' he picked up a single sheet of paper from his in-tray and I caught a glimpse of an impressive-looking embossed letter heading at the top, 'to follow up with this – it came this morning – doubling their initial offer.' He looked down at it with distaste. 'I'm not quite sure what to do about it.'

'Snap it up,' said Leonard Frost.

'No, tell 'em it isn't enough,' said Dick Richards.

'I didn't mean . . .' then Roger intercepted the wink that was passing between them and smiled. 'I suppose they'll have taken care not to put anything down on paper that actually constitutes a breach of the law. Still, it just shows how careful you've got to be.'

He tossed the letter back into his in-tray, slammed the key of the safe down on top of it and then pressed the button of a bell. Almost immediately, a secretary came in from the next door office, carrying a tray of tea. While we were drinking it, General

Now

Dick Richards made a short speech of thanks on behalf of all of us. Then, Leonard walking with me, we dispersed to our respective cars.

The girl who had been reading *Harpers* in an armchair by the fireplace got up as soon as we came into the drawing-room, which was on the first floor.

'Ah, you two haven't met, have you?' Leonard said. 'Derek Thyrde, my dear. Derek, my daughter, Tisha — Henry's wife,' and he went out to fetch some ice.

My immediate impression was of a slim girl in a white cashmere polo-necked sweater and a soft blue tweed skirt just not too long to allow a glimpse of an exciting pair of legs. She held her small breasts high, and thrust forward, in a way that was somehow disturbing and served to accentuate the flatness of her tummy. Her face was lean, but softened by a small rounded chin and a slightly pouting and eminently kissable mouth, and her dark curls were cut close to her head.

'My father's told me a lot about you,' she said.

By far her most compelling feature were great big eyes of a luminous greeny-brown. She must have been every bit of twenty-five, but there was a look of almost childish wonder about them. I was receiving the full benefit of it now.

'What's "Tisha" short for?' I asked. *Letitia* seemed too ghastly even to contemplate. 'Patricia?'

But Tisha shook her head.

'Would you believe "Beatrice Ann"?'

I looked her up and down.

'Frankly, no,' I said.

She laughed. 'It was the nearest I could manage to the two names when I was tiny. And when I grew up, I couldn't stand either of them, let alone the combination. So "Tisha" sort of stuck.'

'Suits you, too,' said Leonard, who had come back and was now busy over the tray. 'Don't you think so, Derek? What'll you have?'

Henry, it seemed, had dropped her when he had picked up Leonard that morning and, over my second gin and tonic, I sat and looked at Tisha Matheson, while she scolded her father over the various shortcomings that she had discovered during the day.

Now

Just my luck, I thought, now that I myself was on the loose again. A super bird like that and married – for all I knew happily, too. Even in these permissive days there are still certain taboos. After all, both her father and her husband *were* my friends.

I stood up and made my goodbyes.

'I must go home, too, father,' said Tisha. 'I only really waited until you came back.'

'Can I give you a lift?' I said.

'Wouldn't hear of it,' said Leonard. He made one of those quick smoothing of the hair movements of his. 'There's a mini-cab place just round the corner.'

'Absolutely no trouble.' I turned to Tisha. 'Where do you live? Westminster? I'll virtually be driving past your door.'

No trouble? Up to that moment, I hadn't even begun to appreciate what trouble really meant.

'Why do you keep a cosh in your car?' Tisha asked suddenly. 'Is it to give your birds a sporting chance of self-defence?'

We had been driving in companionable silence for the first part of the way. I had become aware that the white-sweatered figure in the seat beside me was rummaging about in the front pocket of the Citroen, with a curiosity that I found rather endearing.

'Cosh?' I glanced sideways at her. Her short curly hair was of that rich, dark colour that is to all intents and purposes black, but which in a horse one would refer to as brown. The little instrument that she was now holding was about six inches long with a black handle and a weighted silver head.

'Oh, that,' I said. 'No, that's a *priest*. What you use for bonging a salmon over the head, when you've finally got it onto the bank. Do you fish?'

'No, I never have. Not for salmon, that is. I've always wanted to.'

'I go up for a fortnight on the *Chanisgil* every year.'

'On the how much?'

'C, H, A, N, I, S, G, I, L, pronounced "Hanny-skill". It's a river in Sutherland.'

'That's gaelic, is it?'

'Yes,' I said. '*Cain* – genitive of *cu*, or dog: *eisg* – fish: *gile* – white. A "white fish" is what they used to call salmon or sea-trout, locally, so a "white fish dog" is an otter.'

Now

'River Otter!' said Tisha, putting the priest back into the pocket. 'That's nice.'

'Not if it eats all the white fish before I can get to them,' I said.

She grinned round at me. I caught a tantalising glimpse of little white teeth, moist between half-open lips. The alternatives before me, of either cooking something for myself in a lonely flat or else going out to one of my clubs, all at once lost their attraction.

'Have dinner with me tonight? Before I drop you off at your flat?'

'Why not?' Tisha said.

She took a long time choosing. I hadn't taken her to one of my usual places – they were too reminiscent of Julia. I had recently heard well of a new place off the King's Road and I took her to that. It was small, candle-lit and crowded and the occupants of the other tables – we had only just managed to get the last one – all seemed to be eating with total confidence. The menu read like a gastronomic encyclopedia. Over it I could just see the top of her head.

I took out my cigarette-case, a habitual pipe-smoker I carry one for those occasions when pipes are more than usually antisocial, and held it open in her general direction. 'Do you smoke?'

Tisha lowered the heavy cover of the menu and looked at me, with eyebrows raised.

'What! Me, with my husband an M.P.?'

'Tobacco not hash, you fool.'

She smiled and shook her head. Then she reeled off her choice of food from the vast double sheet in front of her and I was able to begin my researches into the companion volume that dealt with the wine.

With her sitting opposite to me in the flickering half-light of the candles, her big eyes shrouded by long natural lashes looking seriously into mine, it was hard to remember that we had only just met. Without any conscious intention of doing so, I suddenly found that I was telling her all about myself. My work; my farming; my wife, Diana, killed out hunting barely eighteen months before. And Julia, that still hurt, but somehow it seemed to have fallen more into perspective now.

It was an evening of pure fun, but I thought it wiser not to

Now

prolong it. As soon as we had finished our coffee, I asked for the bill and paid it. Then, following her directions, I drove her back to her flat, part of a complex in one of those streets just off the embankment. I parked the Citroen under a street lamp near to the main entrance of her block and went round to open the passenger door.

She got out. 'Coming up for a drink?'

'Just a quick one, then.' I reached in, extracted the priest and held it out, the handle towards her.

'Perhaps you'd better take this, just to be on the safe side.'

Tisha didn't smile. She looked at me for a moment in silence, almost as though she were giving the suggestion serious consideration.

Then, 'I think I'll take a chance on it,' she said.

I laughed and threw the priest back onto the seat of the car, before I slammed the door.

The brandy was good. Far too good to hurry. But she was looking so damned desirable lying there, contemplating the ceiling with her head back, in a way that emphasised the line of her slim white neck, long legs stretched out and crossed at the ankle just below the hem of her skirt, cne hand dangling over the arm of her chair, that I didn't trust myself. The white wool of her sweater swelled gently up and down. I swallowed back the contents of my glass.

'I'd better go.' I started to get up.

Tisha didn't move. But she let her eyes travel slowly downwards until they were focused on me from between half closed lids.

'One more?'

Resolution faltered. 'Well, maybe just a spot,' I said.

I walked over to the bottle and poured myself out just enough to cover the bottom of the glass. Then I screwed the top back on again.

'Hey . . .' I hadn't heard her move on the soft carpet but, a fraction of a second before, I had sensed that she had followed me across the room. I turned. 'What about me?' Her glass held out appealingly, that little girl expression in her eyes.

I didn't mean to. I swear it. But I couldn't help myself, her face was looking up at me an inch or two away from mine. I took her glass gently from her and put her empty and my full one down.

Now

Her waist seemed so small that the fingers of my hands might have met round her had it not been for the thickness of the wool. Her two eyes seemed to move infinitesimally closer together, until with the distortion of proximity they became one. Her arms slid round my neck as I felt the warm dampness of her mouth on mine.

Minutes later, she disengaged herself and took me by the hand. Without a word, she led me to the door and out across the hall. One of the pair of lamps on her dressing-table was lit and I remember thinking vaguely that she must have left it on all day. But after that there was no time to think. All the loneliness, all the sense of inadequacy and rejection of the past few days must have been building up inside me until they were needing, demanding, seizing the opportunity for, an outlet now. And Tisha, from the urgency of her responses, must have been suffering from her frustrations too.

Only when it was over, her curls nestling jet black now against the whiteness of the pillow, did she speak.

'Do you often do this, with girls you've only just met?'

I leant over and traced one of the tiny frown lines that ran across her forehead with my finger.

'All the time,' I said.

'Close encounters of the Thyrde kind?'

I was woken by a noise that I couldn't quite place. The single lamp of the dressing-table was still on – neither of us had had the energy to get up and turn it off the night before. In contrast to it, the sky showed black against the glass of the window, although outside it must have been starting to get light.

And then the noise came again. A tiny muffled choking sound that could have been a sob, not quite suppressed. I levered myself round. Tisha was lying, facing me, her eyes wide open but unfocused, her cheeks glistening wet. As I watched another tear grew at the corner of her lower lid and, when it was fully formed, coursed slowly down her cheek until it spent itself, merged in the general wetness that was there. I noticed that a small patch of pillow was already quite damp.

I put out a hand and reached to touch the tiny round of bare shoulder that was peeping out from underneath the sheet. She moved it gently but emphatically away.

'What's the matter?'

Now

'I'm sorry,' Tisha said. She was looking at me now. 'It's just . . . it's just that it's the first time I've ever been unfaithful to Henry. And I *do* feel so bad about it now.'

Suddenly a full realisation of the enormity of what I had done came over me. What could I say? Nothing. Absolutely nothing! But I said it, all the same.

'I really am most awfully sorry.'

Tisha shook her head. 'It's my fault. I knew what I was doing and there's no excuse. I led you on.'

Then she sat up.

'You must go now, Derek. Quickly, please! And promise me you won't try to see me again — ever!'

I looked at her. Sitting up there naked in bed, even with her tears — or perhaps because of them — she really was lovely.

'If that's what you want.'

'And you won't tell any one? Promise?'

'Of course not!'

'People do, you know.'

'Not me. I'm old-fashioned.'

Tisha managed a grin through her tears. They were flowing freely now.

'I didn't notice you being very old-fashioned last night,' she said.

I got up and sorted out my clothes from the heap by the bedside, just as we had shed them, hers alternating with mine, the night before. When I was fully dressed, I went out into the hall, Tisha padding after me with bare feet on the polished wood-block floor.

Even then, I wondered whether I should stop and argue.

'You won't let anyone see you go?' There was a plea in her small tremulous voice. The little inverted delta of dark hair where her legs met looked strangely decent somehow, as though she had paused for long enough to put on the bottom half of a miniscule bikini.

I leant and kissed her cheek.

She stood there, looking pitifully young and vulnerable, as I said "goodbye".

ii. Then

"Hello!" I said.

Her hair, so fair that it was almost white, was piled up under a tricorn hat. Her eyes were the palest of pale blue. She had no make-up on which was just as well. Nothing could have been an improvement on what was there already. The navy blue jacket fitted superbly her almost but not quite boyish figure, each of the sleeves encircled by a single ring. The bell had rung just as I had been crossing the hall from the dining-room to the library beyond, so I had opened the door myself. But what was a Wren – and such a Wren – doing at nine o'clock on a Monday morning, at the top of the steps that led up to Thyrde House? And why did the Navy always seem to succeed in snaffling the prettiest girls?

"Lord Thyrde?"

She looked me up and down and a slow smile came over her face, disclosing two very white top teeth with the slightest of gaps in between. I had to admit that my appearance warranted it. I was wearing a cream cotton shirt, open-necked and flapping at the cuffs, and a shocking old pair of grey flannel trousers and in my hand I had a copy of the *Daily Mirror*, folded open at the strip cartoons on page seven. I had just discovered to my disappointment that *Jane* had all her clothes on that morning. It could hardly have been otherwise, I suppose. She was meeting her boy-friend, *Georgie*, off a train.

"Yes, that's me," I said.

She gave me a very smart naval salute and handed me a buff envelope.

"Third Officer Stanton. I was to deliver this to you personally."

"Does it need an answer?"

Again, that devastating smile. "I rather think you'll find it does," she said.

I took her into the library and sat her down before tearing open the flap. It was on naval-headed paper and in official service form.

Then

From: Commander Jackson, D.S.C., Royal Navy
To: Captain, The Viscount Thyrde, Grenadier Guards
You will accompany bearer to my office forthwith, please.

Just at that moment, the telephone rang. I picked it up and took off the receiver. It was a trunk call.

"Is that you, Derry?" I recognised the voice of the adjutant of my battalion.

"Hello, Charlie," I said.

"Look, old boy, you'll be getting some orders to-day by special messenger."

"I think I've just got 'em. The messenger *is* pretty special too!"

I glanced across at the Wren who tried, not very convincingly, to look displeased.

"Signed by a Commander Jackson? Well, I've been told to ring you up and confirm that they're genuine. You're to do what they say."

"What's it all about?" I said.

"Search me. Probably wants you to swab down the deck of his battleship for him. Well, enjoy yourself."

I put the receiver back on the hook and stood up.

"Your commander chap will hardly want to see me looking like this. Give me five minutes and I'll be with you," I said.

* * *

We reached the grey importance of London not much later than eleven o'clock. Miss Stanton had driven the Royal Navy Hillman fast and well. Her name was Molly, she told me. Both her parents were dead and she had been brought up by an aunt in Suffolk since the age of fifteen. She made straight for St. James's Square.

She parked the car opposite a vast modern barrack-like building in the south-east corner of the square, all windows and red brick, with the even more topical touch of sandbagging at street-level, which I subsequently found to be called Norfolk House. Two military policemen, one British, one American, saluted us as we went in and I followed Molly Stanton down to the basement, where she knocked on a door.

"Come in."

The naval officer, who had been writing behind a paper-littered

Then

desk in the artificial light which was all that was available, got up and came round to meet us.

"Lord Thyrde? Good of you to come at such short notice."

He made it sound as though I had really had a choice. He was a thick-set man with the reddish sort of face that one usually associates with a life-time spent on the sea. His grey hair had been cut short and bristled up from his head, with the exception of a single forelock brushed ruthlessly back from his forehead. His jacket, shiny and threadbare with three rows of faded medal ribbons, was unbuttoned disclosing a cardigan of thick navy-blue wool, the sleeves of which came down a good three inches below his cuffs. He had the most penetrating eyes that I had ever seen.

He indicated two chairs on the near side of his desk and went back to his own. Then he picked up an envelope and passed it across to me.

"What do you make of that?"

I opened it and extracted and unfolded the contents. It was the paper that Professor Tomkins had taken from me the previous Thursday morning, but I saw that it had become a good deal more tatty in the intervening time. It had acquired several more fold marks; there was a tear now, that extended from one of the drawing-pin holes to the edge of the paper; a small ink-blot, recent in origin and emanating I suspected from a leaky fountain-pen of the professor's, had appeared near to the brown circle which looked as though it might have been a stain left by a tea-cup.

I concentrated, but in vain, on the latter's cryptic designation, '$2\frac{1}{2}$ C.A.'

"I'd like you to look particularly at the irregular line that runs along the top of the paper and the dotted one beneath it."

I did so, but I was no further forward.

"I don't know, Sir," I said. "Is it a map perhaps, or a plan of some sort?"

He nodded. "More or less. Now will you please describe to me exactly how that paper came into your possession?"

As fully as I could remember them, I told him about the events on the night of the birthday party.

"Yes," he said, "that's very much how I've heard it already. I can't tell you how fortunate it was that you recovered that paper. It contains information that would have been quite disastrous if it had fallen into enemy hands." He spoke very slowly. "It's no

Then

exaggeration to say that it might well have made the difference between our winning and losing the war."

The paper had been stolen from Farmwell, he told me, at some time during Wednesday afternoon or evening, probably the afternoon. The exact time was unimportant – the paper could have changed hands, possibly more than once, between then and the time when it was discovered under the table at the *Bag o' Nails*.

"What *is* important is that it was almost certainly dropped there by one of the members of your party. Whoever had possession of it must be working for the enemy."

"But ... for someone to get his hands on something as explosive as that and then just to drop it about somewhere. Isn't that ... well, so careless as to be almost unbelievable?"

"Yes, but people are sometimes. Only last month, one of my immediate superiors left a brief-case containing the entire outline plans for ... for something every bit as important, if not more so ... in a taxi on his way back from lunch. We had the devil's own job getting it back, I can tell you. Now *you* know all seven. Can you think of anything – anything at all – that might give us a clue as to which that person might be?"

"Not off hand," I said. It was an appalling thought that one of my fellow diners at that congenial party must have been a traitor and a spy. "Well, let me go through them. Sir John Bagot, for a start, had a German wife. He was absolutely devoted to her. I was very young when it happened, but I've always heard that he changed completely after her death."

"Good. Go on."

"Then there's the United States airman, Lieutenant Richards. His father and mother were German – he's only a first generation American. Oh yes, and he did say that as far as he was concerned, he'd just as soon we were fighting the Russians instead."

Commander Jackson was busily making notes as I spoke.

"Lord Greyfield. He's always been stinking rich, but a lot of it was tied up in Germany and there have been rumours lately that he's liable to go bust at any moment."

"Yes, there could be a purely financial motive, I suppose."

"Then there's Leonard Frost, the M.P., but he's a left-wing socialist."

"Ah, but there's something we've found out about him. He used to be a member of the British Union of Fascists. He only became

Then

disillusioned when he went out to Germany to see the system working for himself."

"Next Roger Faulkner, he's a scientific prodigy of some sort. I was at school with him. He used to be a great admirer of Germany but he tells me that he's disillusioned now."

Commander Jackson looked up at me.

"Did you know that he works at Farmwell?"

"Good Lord! No, I didn't," I said. "How many's that?"

"Five. Two to go."

"Stephen Knightley, then. He's in the Navy. But he seems to have got an almost pathological hatred of the Germans. Who have I left out?"

"Colonel Matheson."

"Ah, yes. Well, I don't know very much about him. I'd never met him before and I hardly spoke to him at the party."

"Colonel Matheson," said the Commander, "lived and worked in Germany for several years. He only came back to England a year or two before the war."

He took a tobacco-pouch out of his pocket and started to fill a very old and blackened cherry-wood pipe.

"Won't whoever it is have left his finger-prints all over that thing?" I asked.

"No, you can't get finger-prints off paper. They reckon they'll find a way of doing it some day, but not yet. How much leave have you got left?"

"Two days, Sir. I'm due back in Yorkshire on Wednesday."

"It's cancelled, I'm afraid. You'll be working for me from now on."

I looked at him bleakly. Suddenly life at Helmsley, with all its repetition and uncertainty, seemed unaccountably attractive.

Commander Jackson nodded sympathetically. "Worried you might be missing the balloon going up? I'll try and get you back with them before your lot go over," he said. "I can't promise but I'll see."

* * *

So far as Commander Jackson and his men had been able to discover, nobody had yet been back to the *Bag o' Nails*, or even telephoned, to ask about the missing paper. But they had had to

Then

be careful, so they could not be certain of that. There was just a chance that the spy had not yet realized the vital nature of the information that he had had, however shortly, in his hands and nothing that we now did must give him the slightest suspicion as to what dynamite it really was. Only the discreetest of enquiries could be made at Farmwell itself. There might still be an accomplice there, because it was more likely than not to have been an insider who had first stolen the paper. Professor Tomkins was that day being switched to another billet and I was not in any circumstances to get in touch with him again. As to the seven who had been present at the birthday party, the Commander had of course people at his disposal who were highly skilled at intelligence. But any enquiries made however skilfully by a stranger might just put the guilty man on his guard – and that was where I came in. I already had a built-in excuse, in collecting the money for the Bag o' Nails bill, and what could be more natural than that, chancing to find myself in the neighbourhood of each one of them during what they would still think was the remainder of my leave, I should seek them out in person with that in mind. Pretty mercenary it would make me look, but I thought that in the circumstances I could live with that.

And I was not to be alone.

"Third Officer Stanton, here, will be working with you. Two heads are better than one and she *has* had a certain amount of training in intelligence, which you frankly have not. She'll be in plain clothes, of course, because you'd better introduce her as your girl-friend. I don't suppose that will be any great hardship?"

It was the one bright spot in the whole proceedings so far. I glanced round at the Wren, Molly, where she was sitting beside me. Her eyes were fixed firmly on the ground.

"I think I can bear it," I said.

"And you'll need a car. You've got one, I suppose?"

"Only an old M.G.," I said. "It's far from reliable and I've just about used up the last of my petrol ration."

"Petrol's no problem. Haven't you got anything else at home?"

There was indeed another car at Thyrde. It was a Rolls-Royce 20–25 two-seater, drop-head coupé, which had been barely five years old when it had been laid up soon after the beginning of the war. It had been Rolls-maintained throughout its early life and I knew that it would be in first class running order now. There was a

Then

young lad living on the estate who had begged to be allowed to come and look after it from time to time. Tom Barraclough had been knife-and-boot boy in the house before the war and he worked for the local village garage now. Four days before, I had looked at it longingly when I had put the M.G. away beside it and everything about its appearance had testified to young Tom's loving care.

There was only one snag – it simply drank petrol. It was not with a very great deal of hope that I mentioned its existence now.

Much to my surprise Commander Jackson accepted the suggestion without hesitation.

"Well, I think that's all," he said. He looked down at the notes he had made. "As you see, it's a pretty open list. It might be any one of them – with the possible exception of young Knightley. And we can't discount even him at this early stage. Any questions?"

"Just one thing, sir." It had been worrying me on and off for the last few minutes. "How do you suggest we raise the subject with these people when we do talk to them? After I've dunned them for their share of the bill, I mean?"

"Only one thing you can do," he said. He picked up the stolen paper from where I had put it down on his desk. "You take this round with you and show it to each of them in turn. Don't let it out of your hands, of course, but tell them exactly how you got it on Wednesday night and ask them if it belongs to them."

"What?" I gaped at him. "But . . . isn't that a quite enormous risk? If that paper's anything like as important as you say it is?"

He did not answer for a moment. He just looked down at the paper in his hand. Then he nodded slowly.

"It is," he said. "But it's a risk that we must take."

* * *

"I see you're still not happy about it," said Commander Jackson.

I had marginally modified my original conviction that he had gone stark raving mad, but it was still a considerable understatement.

"But why can't I just tell 'em about the paper? Describe it to 'em from memory as best I can?" That had been my first

Then

suggestion.

That, the Commander had told me, would be quite fatal. Nothing that we did must run the slightest risk of arousing the suspicions of the guilty man and the only natural thing for me to do in the circumstances would be to take the actual paper that I found, and about the real importance of which I must be seen to have no idea whatsoever, round with me until I had established its rightful ownership. And Molly Stanton and I were not to be alone. At least for as long as we had the paper with us, we would be followed everywhere we went by Commander Jackson's men. We would not see them – and we were not to try – but they would be there all the same. For that reason we were not to allow ourselves to be separated. To do so would entail using two sets of followers and the Commander simply could not spare the men.

"But how can we be sure that your men won't lose us?" I asked.

"Look," he said, "I've laid on an exercise for you this afternoon. You will start from a pre-arranged point, on foot and alone. From then on, go anywhere in London, do anything, use any form of transport. My men will be shadowing you, your object will be to shake them off and you'll have exactly two hours to do it in. If you fail to do so, will that satisfy you?"

"I . . . suppose so."

"Good. Now, on this one occasion only, I want you to see if you can identify any of your followers. If you suspect anybody, challenge him. Go up to him and say 'Donald . . .'. If your suspicions are correct, he will reply '. . . Duck', and that particular man will be out of the game. Where are you going to have lunch?"

"I thought of going round to White's," I said.

"All right, you can start from there. Leave White's Club at 2.0 p.m. precisely and the exercise will finish promptly at four. Come back here at, say, 5.30 and you can pick up Miss Stanton. I'll have everything else ready for you then. Good-bye and good luck."

Molly and I stood up and saluted.

When I was half way to the door, I turned.

"You will promise to tell me, Sir . . . if I have managed to shake them off?"

Commander Jackson was writing again and he did not look up, nor did his pen pause for a moment.

"You won't," he said.

Then

* * *

It was exactly one minute to two, when I walked out of the door of White's and stood at the top of the steps. I had worked out my itinerary and a plan of sorts over lunch. I waited until the second hand of my watch had gone round a complete circuit before I started down the steps.

I walked down St. James's, unhurriedly as though I was just out to enjoy the fineness of the day, and turned left into Jermyn Street, returning the salutes of a couple of passing guardsmen as I went. In Duke Street I paused outside the window of Dunhill's, the tobacconists, and glanced around me for a taxi, feeling in my pocket instinctively for my tobacco pouch as I did so. And then I put it reluctantly away again. I would have to move quickly and a pipe would only be in the way.

Two taxis were approaching me up the hill, both with their flags up. Dim memories of Sherlock Holmes came back to me – not the first, nor the second – so I let them go by. There was a third rounding the corner from King Street at the bottom. That too was empty and by the time that it was level with me there was not another in sight, so I hailed it and got in.

"Leicester Square Underground," I said. "I'm in a bit of a hurry, so as quick as you can, please." The driver nodded and let out his clutch. As he turned right into Piccadilly, I looked out of the little window at the back. As far as I could see there was nothing following, but I knew that they would be there somewhere. Not even I was optimistic enough to think that I could shake them off as easily as that.

Past the gutted church on the right; round Piccadilly Circus, with the monument boarded up where the statue of Eros used to stand, and into Coventry Street; past the gaping hole that had once been the Café de Paris; past the Prince of Wales Theatre on the other side, with its posters proclaiming Sid Field in *Strike a New Note* – 'Final two weeks' – and along the top of Leicester Square. I took out a couple of half-crowns and passed them through the partition to the cabby. As he drew up at the Underground, I opened the door and darted down the steps. I only needed a tuppenny ticket, but I bought a shilling one to confuse any one who might be watching and ran down the moving staircase to the Piccadilly Line.

54

Then

I was going West and I could hear a train approaching that platform, but there was one already standing, doors open, on the east-bound side. It was an unexpected bonus and I made for that instead and stood just inside. As the doors were on the point of closing, I slipped through them and over to the train now standing on the other side. I made it just in time. As the train moved off, I sat down in the seat nearest to the doors and looked about me.

There were four other men in the compartment, all reading news-papers, two in bowler hats, one wearing a trilby and the fourth who was nearest to me, a cloth cap. There was a poster opposite to me, a Fougasse cartoon of an underground train similar to the one in which I was sitting. 'Careless talk costs lives.' Hitler's face was peering out from underneath a seat. I looked again at each of the four men. Perhaps I ought to challenge them, but it was difficult to decide now which seemed most suspicious – perhaps the cloth-capped one just had the edge.

I leaned towards him. "Donald . . .?" I said experimentally.

"Eh?" he shouted. The other three looked up.

"Donald . . ." I repeated, louder.

"You've got it wrong mate. Don't know nothing about no Donald. My name's Bert."

I sat back. He had effectively put paid to the other similar approaches that I had planned.

At Hyde Park Corner, I slipped out – again just as the doors shut, and I could swear that I was the last to leave. Up the moving staircase, towards the Hyde Park exit, up the steps and into the sunshine outside.

I walked along the pavement, past the Decimus Burton Screen, dodging the traffic that was going into the park at the first gate, and then that which was coming out at the third, and left into Park Lane. There was a suitable gap in the traffic just before I came opposite to the Dorchester and I crossed over and walked along the pavement on the other side. I was looking about me in earnest now – it was time that I had another go at trying to thin out the opposition – locating anybody who looked suspicious enough to challenge. But there were so many people milling about in both directions that it was difficult to decide.

Wait a minute! That girl half hidden in a door-way. I could have sworn that she was watching me, but when I looked more closely her eyes were fixed firmly in the opposite direction.

Then

Commander Jackson had referred each time to the people who would be shadowing me as 'men', but even after my brief acquaintance with him, I had a feeling that it was just the sort of trick that he might play. Anyway, I had nothing to lose. I walked straight up to her.

"Donald..." I said.

I had realised my mistake a fraction of a second too late to stop myself. The sticky red spludge of a mouth split into a smile that found no echo in her apathetic lash-encrusted eyes.

"Hello Donald darling," she said. "Would you like a good time?"

I walked on until I came to Grosvenor House, in through the main entrance, and across the hall to a locked door, where I stopped and rang the bell. It was soon opened by a boy in livery and I went through into the premises beyond.

Owned and managed by Grosvenor House, the name of the *International Sportsmen's Club* is frankly misleading. Most of its members are insular to a degree and many of them would not be able to tell a pelham-bit from a polo-stick, but its principal advantage to me now was that it possesses a separate entrance of its own, round the corner in Upper Grosvenor Street, and it was this that I made for now.

"Look," I said to the hall-porter, who was an old friend, "there's some one I want to avoid. Can you call a cab and have it waiting outside for me, facing away from Park Lane? When it's there, tell the driver that he's to move off as soon as I get in. Then watch for a moment when there's no one in sight in the street and give me a call."

I put a ten-bob note into his hand and stood and waited.

After a minute or two, he came back grinning. "All clear now, m'Lord."

I hurried through the revolving door, ran to the taxi and jumped in.

"Victoria please," I said through the partition, as soon as we were moving. "Near to the underground station and try and see that we're not followed."

I had decided that I would try a change of tactics and this time when the underground train drew into Westminster Station I was standing by the doors. I was first out, ran up the stairs, thrust my ticket into the collector's hand, across the ticket-selling area and down two steps to where, set in the wall on the left, was a heavy mahogany-coloured door. I had my key-ring in my hand, the appropriate key already selected, and I let myself through and slammed the door behind me. I was now in St. Stephen's, another of my clubs – this time a political one – and every member is entitled to a latch-key for the basement door.

The door has a history. In late Victorian times, an important vote was on and the Liberal Whips, lulled into a sense of false security by the sparse attendance on the benches opposite, had allowed those of their members who had more pressing engagements to go home. But a large number of Tories had been secreted across the road in St. Stephen's Club, which possessed a division bell. When the bell rang, they all trouped down to the basement, out by this door, through the tunnel under Bridge Street and into the Palace of Westminster in time to win the division and bring down the Government. The story may or may not be true, but it was this same door that represented another of the means by which I had planned to tilt the odds in my favour now.

I ran on up the stairs, past the hall-porter who must have thought that I had gone mad and out onto the embankment beyond. There was a tram already waiting some forty yards down the road to my left and I ran towards it. A number 31, I saw as I got nearer, and it moved off while I was still ten yards away, but I quickened my pace and jumped onto the platform just in time.

I had been lucky enough to pick a tram that went through the tunnel opposite Waterloo Bridge which was just what I wanted. The Commander's men, if any of them were still with me, would be doing well to follow me through that.

I got off at Holborn Subway, ran through the underground station and up to the street above. I narrowly missed being run over by an army motor bike, its rider giving one horrified look at my uniform, as I dashed across the street and onto a number 289 'bus that was waiting on the other side.

At Gamage's I got off, straightened my service-dress jacket and went in. I stopped just inside the door, where I could see out into the street without myself being seen, until a single taxi drew up. I waited until the recent occupant had paid then I ran out and jumped inside.

"Drive on," I puffed. "I'll give you the directions as soon as I've

Then

got my breath back." He looked a little oddly at me, I thought, but he let out his clutch immediately. At last I could relax.

"I've got a bet on," I said through the partition. "A friend of mine reckons he knows London pretty well, and he's bet me a fiver that I can't lose him. With any luck I've shaken him off already. I don't know what sort of a car he'll be driving, but dodge about a bit, if you will, just to be on the safe side. I don't mind where you go."

I could see him nodding his head. "Right ho, Guv'. Leave it to me." Plainly the idea appealed to his sporting side.

During the next twenty minutes, I had no way of knowing how effective he was being at losing any one who might still be following, but after the first three he had certainly lost me. We weaved in and out of side streets, down back alleys that I never knew existed, narrowly missing dustbins on either side. I could swear that we never stopped at a single set of traffic-lights. At some point, I do know, we crossed the river, though by which bridge I really cannot say. Later, below us to the right, I caught a glimpse of the two as yet completed red chimneys of Battersea Power Station.

"How much more, Guvner?" I looked at my watch. It was exactly three fifty-five.

"Can you find a street near here that's likely to be empty? It's a condition of the bet that I've got to be standing in the open at exactly four o'clock."

He nodded, drove on for another hundred yards or so, turned left, then almost immediately sharp right and on and over a fairly major road. He pulled into the side and I got out.

We were in a narrow street of terraced Victorian cottages, in soot-bespattered brick. Further down on the left, there was a single van parked against a bomb-site, but it seemed to be unattended. Across the road, a small child of indeterminate sex dressed in a dingy frock turned and looked at me, but without interest, then it went back to its occupation of bouncing what had once been a tennis ball against a low brick wall. A black and white cat which had been sunning itself on a concrete path got up and stretched lazily. It padded over and rubbed itself affectionately against my trouser leg. I saw that it had no tail. A Manx? There was no one else about.

I took the pouch out of my pocket and filled and lit my pipe.

Then

The smoke curled luxuriously upwards. It was exactly four o'clock.

"You've done marvels," I said to the cabby. "I really think I've won my bet."

I could hardly wait until half-past-five to see Commander Jackson's face.

In fact, it was barely five-and-twenty past when I was standing in the basement of Norfolk House, and knocking at the Commander's door.

"Come in."

He motioned me into a chair and his face was grim, as he went on writing. I went on sitting. Dashed unsporting of the old boy, I thought, to take it out on me just because I had won.

"Here!" I looked up. He tossed a large envelope across the desk to me. "Perhaps you'd like to have a look at these, while you're waiting?" It was unsealed, and there was a batch of photographs, enlargements some ten inches by eight, still limp and barely dry, inside.

I looked at the top one. It was of me, standing on the top step of White's. The second showed me outside Dunhill's, gazing anxiously down the street. The next was a bit blurred, taken as I dived from the taxi into the underground at Leicester Square. But the fourth, of me in Park Lane, was in perfect focus. It was a remarkable photograph by any standards — you could see every powdered wrinkle of her face. I hope to God he keeps *that* one to himself, I thought. It was even possible to pick out the figure one on the pound-note that I was pressing into her hand.

With a growing sense of disillusion I riffled through the rest. There, was the rear of my taxi as it drew away from the portico in Upper Grosvenor Street; there was I, dashing from the taxi into Victoria Station; I, running for the tram along the embankment pavement, outside St. Stephen's Club; I, coming out of Gamage's, with a sickeningly smug expression on my face; and, last of all, there was I, lighting my pipe in that grimy street in south London, with that infernal black and white cat arching its tail-less bottom in the air at my feet.

I glanced across the desk to where Commander Jackson was writing. But he was not writing any more. His pen was poised in mid-air and he was looking straight at me.

"Yes," he said. "That's how good we are."

Then

* * *

"Devious old so-and-so," said Molly Stanton. She was laughing up at me from the corner seat opposite. I had waited to tell her the full story until we were sitting in the train. "Just like old Jackie to do a thing like that. I really am sorry, Lord Thyrde, I ought to have warned you."

"Look, if you're going to be my girl-friend, you'll have to get used to calling me 'Derry'."

"All right, ... Derry," she said.

She had changed into a light blue tweed coat and skirt, and she had let her hair down. It hung in a sweeping curve almost hiding one eye.

"He was right about one thing," she said, "it really does show just how good his chaps are. Happy now?"

I instinctively touched my top pocket, where the recovered paper was now sizzling away gently to itself in my wallet.

"Happi*er*," I said.

The taxi, for which I had telephoned to the local garage earlier in the day, was waiting for us outside Bedford station and young Tom Barraclough was driving it.

"How's the Rolls?" I asked him after we had started. "Is she in good heart?"

He beamed. "Tip-top condition, Mr. Derry, Sir."

"Good. Miss Stanton and I are going to be using her from now on."

The freckled face beneath Tom's ginger hair radiated pleasure all the rest of the way.

Every room in the house itself being full of billetees, I had arranged for Molly to be put up by my agent and his wife. Commander Jackson had agreed to this and Tom drove us straight there – they only lived across the stable-yard. I carried her suitcase in for her and introduced her to Mr. and Mrs. Ford. Then, as I said 'good-night' to her, I leaned forward to kiss her cheek but instinctively she shied away.

"Girl-friend!" I whispered.

Cautiously, she advanced her cheek again. I left them and walked across the yard and in at the back door.

There is a picture that hangs above the fireplace in the library, which I think I like better than any other in the whole world. A

Then

medley of grey-blues, greens and purple-browns, it is a water-colour of the Horse-shoe Pool on the River Chanisgil. Later, when I had poured myself out a whisky and soda from the tray which old Andrews, the butler, had left ready, I went and stood in front of it, soaking in the memories that it conjured up. The smoky bustle and excitement of Euston Station. The coarse white linen sheets of the sleeper train. The sound of milk churns clanging together, when we stopped at Crewe. Breakfast in the Station Hotel at Inverness. The winding puffer-train that carried us yet further north. The apprehension as we approached the final bend, the old ruined castle perched precariously on the cliff-top, would it still be there or would just one more winter of storms and erosion at last have sent it crashing to the sea below? But there it always was. The first meeting with Donald Mackintosh, the ghillie, dour but infinitely wise and patient, he would be away to the war now too. Gut casts soaking overnight, filling tooth-mug and basin in every bed-room in the lodge. Salmon fish-cakes in the morning.

And then the Horse-shoe Pool itself. The sharp bend in the river, swing foot-bridge beyond, from which it took its name. How many fish had I caught there? Five? Six? That little swirl in the water, close against the gravel on the far bank – just about a yard and a half below that, that is where he used to come.

It all seemed a very long time ago.

3. Now

It must have been about nine o'clock that night when I reached the Horseshoe Pool, give or take a quarter of an hour. It was the end of my fourth day on the Chanisgil. The light was beginning to go.

There is something about salmon fishing, the peace of the surroundings, the conviction that it is always the next cast which will be the successful one whereas in fact only one in several hundred ever is, the challenge of single combat – a matching of wits and skill, self against fish – that makes all one's worries, and God knows I had had enough of them lately, seem totally irrelevant and causes them to retreat to a distant point some half way up the surrounding hills. All worries – except for those connected with the actual fishing, that is. Is the river too low? The water too cold? The wind strong enough? The sun too bright? Is my fly the right colour and size? Have I got a knot in my cast? *Is somebody else catching more fish?*

Luck in fishing, as in cards, runs in streaks – the good and the bad. This time I was very definitely onto a losing streak. I had started out on the Monday morning with my brand new Bruce and Walker carbon fibre rod – a Christmas present from Julia – and the optimism which the first day on the river always brings. I have a record in my fishing book of every fish that I have ever caught, the name of the pool, the type of fly used – on the Chanisgil it is sacrilege even to mention any form of bait – its weight to the nearest half pound, the name of the ghillie or friend who has netted or gaffed it for me and, in the final column, the running total to date, after adding that particular fish. The six fish that I had caught last year brought the grand total up to one hundred and ninety-nine. On Monday, I had been looking for my two-hundredth fish.

I had risen two fish on that first day, each in a separate pool and with quite an interval in between. The first had just touched the fly

Now

and the other hadn't seemed to be very enthusiastic about it. Neither of them would come again.

On Tuesday, my confidence had only marginally been diminished and had come flooding back in the mid-morning when I got the first feel of a fish truly hooked, only to depart again just as quickly and in even greater volume when the nylon broke two and a half minutes later, caught round the snag of a submerged rock. I had had another one *on and off* at lunch-time. That same afternoon I had caught a kelt – last year's fish, all skin and bone, on its way back to the sea.

My only Wednesday fish had got off after nearly ten minutes, lost at the gaff taking my fly with him, solely because a well-meaning but irrationally parsimonious friend, who had happened to be passing, had insisted on giving me a cast made up from his reel of nylon saved from the previous year, when I had had to replace mine the day before.

Thursday so far had been blank, not a breath of wind and bright sun all day.

None of this, I am ashamed to confess, would have been quite so bad if others had been suffering a similar fate. But all this time the people on the other beats, and even the man who had the second rod which was to have been Julia's on my own beat, had been catching their one's and two's a day. Fishing is above all a competitive sport, success in it being measured not so much in numbers of fish caught as in *numbers of fish caught in relation to those caught by other people.* I can never quite make up my mind which is harder, to be a good winner or a good loser – trying to moderate one's pleasure at one's own success in deference to the feelings of others, or trying to simulate a pleasure at the success of others that one can never really feel. Fishing brings out the best and the worst in people – with me it is invariably the worst. Competitiveness turns into jealousy and jealousy into black despair, which in turn evaporates and seems petty and childish in retrospect the moment that a spell of bad luck has come to an end. I always wish that I could behave when I am losing fish at least well enough not to feel so ashamed of myself as soon as I start catching them again. It is the thing that I enjoy doing best in the whole world, but like all great pleasures it has its ingredient of pain.

It was in near desperation therefore that I had had an early

Now

dinner that evening, so as to be out on the river by eight o'clock and I had fished two other pools first, both with no result. I had never caught a fish on the Horseshoe Pool before, although it was considered to be one of the best on the river, certainly on this particular beat. I stood on the gravel high up in the pool, too high probably, but I wanted to be sure that my flies would cover the whole of the swirl on the far side. The *Walker* rod sent out the line smoothly, effortlessly, as I eased it from the reel a little bit at a time, until the tail-fly landed with a hardly noticeable plop four or five inches from the stones of the opposite bank. I kept the point of the rod up, so that the dropper – the higher of the two flies – bobbed half-submerged in the ripple of the streamy bit. I watched it come slowly round until it reached the stiller, deeper water in the middle, when I inched the line in by hand to keep the flies working until they had almost completed a quarter-circle close against my own side. Then I took one step to my left, downstream, and repeated the process.

Watch round, pull in, step down, cast again.

This was the time of day that I had always liked fishing best. The river, which throughout the morning and afternoon had been an unbelievable picture-book blue, had now dulled into a satisfactorily uniform dirty-grey. The twin distractions, of passing road-traffic on the one side of it and of the little diesel train that chuntered periodically round bends and up slopes on the other, had gone, leaving undisturbed the sounds of approaching darkness. The querulous fretting of a lost lamb in the distance, the distinctive whistles of plover and oyster-catcher, the crunch of nailed wader on gravel and the regular lapping of wind against water, punctuated every now and then by the louder and more ragged *pil-loop* of a jumping fish.

Watch round, pull in, step down, cast again.

It was two or three feet below the swirl that it happened. Suddenly there was a break in the rhythm, a petulant, worrying, nagging sensation at the end of my line. Automatically, irritated almost, I jerked back. The line tightened, the rod bent and then . . . with a feeling of almost intoxicating excitement, I knew that he was on. Quickly I switched the rod over to my left hand. Now was the time for judgment – too little pressure and he might wriggle the hook out of his mouth, too much and I might pull it out or even snap the nylon – I walked downstream the few paces until I was

Now

opposite to him, keeping that pressure constant as I went. He moved slowly down to the bottom of the pool, turned and moved equally slowly back up to the top where he turned again. He was still deep down, I hadn't seen him yet. He was hardly the most dramatic of fish but drama was one thing that just at that moment I felt that I could do without. I mustn't lose him now. Not this one. He moved steadily back again, I keeping level with him all the way. And then he stopped. No movement at all. The cast was completely under water, only line showing above, and the rod had the same bend on it . . . but he was still, terrifyingly still. Had I lost him? That had happened to me more than once in the past, the fish off and away and the fly somehow having managed to get itself embedded in a rock on the bottom. On one occasion I had stood there 'playing' such a rock for a full five minutes, sure that it was still a fish. Cautiously, experimentally, I turned the handle of the reel a couple of clicks. There was a very slight movement in response. Yes, he was still there. He moved away. Then there was a throbbing, vibrating, almost a twanging sensation transmitted up the line, as though he were trying to rub the hook out of his mouth against the sandy bottom. I always hate it when they do that and what little confidence I still had began to seep away. Then there was a series of short sharp tugs. Steady now! Let him go, if he wants to . . . I took my hand off the reel and lowered the tip of the rod fractionally to ease up on the pressure . . . then a sharper tug . . . followed by a sudden surge . . . let him go . . . *he went*!

There is nothing, absolutely nothing, so frustrating – so devastatingly deflating, as that moment when the flies, freed suddenly, dance impudently in the air above the surface of the water and the rod becomes an inert and useless thing in one's hands. That elusive two-hundredth had foiled me once again.

I carried my rod up to the top again and, step by step, fished the whole pool down. Nothing! I hadn't really thought that there would be. The light had all but gone. Now I couldn't even see the swing-bridge, barely a hundred yards beyond the opposite bank where the river curved sharply back behind it. Surely there couldn't be any point in going on. Disconsolate, I turned away from the water – the end of yet another fishless day.

And then the bat came.

Where it had come from Heaven alone knew, the nearest

Now

building must have been well over a mile away. Yet there it suddenly was, flitting, floating, wheeling, weaving, ducking down to within an inch of the river surface and up again, like something out of a vintage horror movie, a black shadow against the not quite black yet that was now the sky. Immediately, something that an old ghillie had once said to me – not from the Chanisgil, from some other river – flashed into my mind. 'As soon as the first bat flies, take off whatever you're using and put on the biggest fly that you can find. That's when you'll catch fish.' There was only one fly of any size in my box, a *Dunkeld* some two inches long. That should be big enough at any rate, 2– or 3–0 – even in this light I could see the gold on its body glint. I untied the flimsy cast that I had been using, made up another for a single fly from a new roll of fifteen-pound breaking-strain nylon and started from the top, yet one more time.

There was no doubt about it when he came this time, he meant to have it. He took at almost the identical cast – there must have been two fish there, the first would never have come again – and he took deep, a vicious plucking that nearly bent the rod double, and then he was away up the river and into the pool above at a speed that caused the line to cut my finger and set the reel spinning with a high-pitched whine. At the far end he jumped, a twirling flash of luminescent silver, and with an instinctive reaction that was far quicker than ever conscious thought could have achieved I lowered the point of the rod just in time. Even so I was convinced that I had lost him. The rod was straight, the line flapping, but there was just a chance that he had turned and was coming towards me. I walked quickly backwards, down the river and away from it, reeling in furiously all the time, and suddenly there he still was, the bend was back in the rod and fish, line, rod, my own hands, once more seemed to combine and develop a live entity of their own. He went on past me and down to the bottom of the pool, where he jumped again. Then he started back, slower this time but still very much in command, towards me, away diagonally, downstream, up, across to the other side, taking me on a conducted tour of the limits of the pool. Then he went down to the bottom end again. But he didn't stop this time, he carried straight on down the river, pulling line out after him all the way. I followed him down the bank as far as I could but some twenty yards below the pool my way was barred. There was a birch tree

Now

overhanging the river — I could hardly see it now, but I knew from long familiarity with the pool that it was there, and there I had to stand. And still he took line out until it was down to the *backing*, the thin cord that attaches line to reel. Now, if ever, was the time when I had to exert my authority. Once he was round the bend the line would foul the shingle on the other side of the river and I would have lost him. I jabbed my finger onto the line to stop it, the rod curved almost to danger point, there was a moment of suspense ... and then, it eased slightly and I knew that from now on he would increasingly respond to my pressure rather than I to his.

Slowly at first, then more quickly, I wound him in, he reacting now like a recently disobedient gun-dog puppy, slinking reluctantly but apologetically back to heel. On and on he came. When he was almost within reach, I took the rod in my right hand and felt for the gaff, clipped onto my coat pocket, with my left. Using the fingers of my rod-hand to ease out its hook, I extended it fully and switched rod and gaff again. Then I reached forward — but I was being too precipitate — he shied away in a sudden flurry of movement and was off downstream again. He wasn't done yet.

Every extra second that he was on now would increase the danger of his getting away. I must turn him and keep his head upstream if I possibly could. I held my finger on the line again ... allowed the rod to bow still further ... and, as he expended his remaining energy in a final roll, I coaxed him round and then he was floating towards me, his lower jaw skimming the top of the water as I steered him in. By the time that he was close enough for me to use the gaff, I realised that he was half-beached already and that it wasn't necessary. I dropped it on the gravel at my feet, leaned even further forward, grasped him firmly round the narrow of his tail and carried both fish and rod well back from the water's edge. (Many a fish has been lost, regaining its freedom at the last moment, by slithering back into the river off the bank.) Without thinking, I groped in my coat pocket for my priest before I remembered that maddeningly I hadn't been able to find it when I had been packing before leaving London, but I found a suitably shaped stone and used that to knock him on the head with instead.

Back at the road, I turned on the headlamps of the Citroen and carried my *white fish* round to examine him in their light. Well in excess of ten pounds I reckoned, his flank, dusty now, was flecked

Now

with what looked like little two-inch threads of white cotton. Long-tailed sea-lice! Sure proof that it was less than twenty-four hours since he had come in from the sea.

As I drove back down the strath, I was aware of a sudden transformation that had taken place. The night, the road, the river, the hill rising steeply on either side, though marginally darker of course, these to all outward appearances were much the same as they had been twenty minutes before. But the thin film of gloom, that in my eyes had been obscuring everything and turning the entire landscape into a dull flat monotone, had lifted. I had caught a fish at last. Life had become three-dimensional again.

There used to be a ruined castle that stood on the top of a cliff to the south of the little town of Chanisgil, but both cliff and castle had been swept away some years back to make way for a smart new bypass road. On a similar clifftop to the north lay another landmark of far more recent origin, the Strathchanisgil Hotel, kept mainly for fishing people by Donald Mackintosh, a ghillie long retired from the river. This one had been spared by the planners and it was for this that I was making now.

Once off the river, reality returns. Julia had gone leaving in me a . . . a what? An aching void or merely a disconcerting break in what had become an agreeable routine? The trouble was that I simply hadn't yet been able to make up my mind. But anyway a gap of some sort, and Tisha — what fun it would have been initiating her into the joys of fishing — Tisha, who might have done something to fill that gap, had never quite arrived.

As for my financial problems, they seemed miraculously to have been relieved, but it had happened in such a way that it would almost certainly turn out to be a mistake and if that were so the relief would only be illusory after all.

But even reality, however grim, has a soothing veneer to it which makes one feel that things can't really be as bad as all that — when one has caught a fish. And I was proving this to myself for the umpteenth time — the two-hundredth, to be precise — as I drove through the gates and down the short drive that led to the lighted yard of the Strathchanisgil Hotel.

I met old Donald Mackintosh, the proprietor, as I walked into the hall.

'Ah, so you've got one.' He examined the fish which I was

Now

carrying, as though it were some rare species of which hitherto he had only heard tell. 'Where was that?'

He nodded when I told him.

'Aye, many's the one I've seen your father take just there.' He held out his hand. 'Give it me. I'll weigh it and put it in the fish larder. Your lordship will be wanting a drink, no doubt.'

I handed it over gratefully and made for the bar.

I stood in the doorway for a moment, acclimatising myself to the atmosphere of smoky, noisy, cheerful fug, the glint of light on half full glasses, the window at the far end, black now but through which in the daytime it was sometimes possible to make out the distant shape of a North Sea oilrig, fishing prints on warm buff walls. Peter, the young merchant banker who had taken over the other rod on my beat at short notice, was sitting at a large round table surrounded by chairs. He was new to the river, but the men who were with him were all old friends. Evander, *his* ghillie; Willie, who had been with me earlier that day and on the three preceding ones; Dougal, Murdo, Kennie and John – they were employed elsewhere on the river, I had caught fish with each one of them, over the years. To my left young Donald – he was every bit of fifty, but he was always known as 'young' Donald to distinguish him from his father – was behind the bar.

The conversation faltered to a stop as they realised that I was standing there and every face looked up towards me enquiringly. I held up one finger. There was an instant outbreak of congratulations. There is only one exception to fishing jealousy, in which ghillies share in possibly even greater measure than their principals, *everybody* is genuinely delighted to see a spell of bad luck end.

'Fill 'em up, all round,' I said to young Donald, 'large ones, please.' And I went over and sat down at the one empty chair. He was soon back with a tray-full of glasses, which he distributed round the table.

'I've got in a bottle of that *Talisker* you were asking for earlier in the week,' he said, as he handed the last of them, containing two fifths of a gill of peat-brown liquid, to me. 'Oh, I almost forgot, Lord Thyrde, two gentlemen from London were asking for you. I've put them in the private sittingroom.'

'Hell!' I said. 'I suppose I'd better go and see what they want.'

I got to my feet and put the glass, to which I had just added an equal quantity of water, down on the table, as yet untouched. Then I changed my mind and picked it up again. The best single malt whisky in all Scotland, it was far too good to leave behind.

The private sittingroom, three doors down the passage to the left, was a prim, cheerless room. The few pieces of furniture, scattered around it with apparently no general purpose in mind, contrived to avoid both comfort and aesthetic merit. Its monotone prints, whose artist seemed to have had little to say and hadn't been very enthusiastic about saying it anyway, had thin, natural oak, frames. There was a coldness that exuded from the pale-green paint of its walls.

The short man in brown tweeds scrambled up, hand outstretched, from one of the two antimacassared armchairs as I came in.

'Lord Thyrde?'

He gave an impression of total roundness. He had a small round body, round face and a round beaming smile.

'Let me introduce myself, my Lord. I'm Detective-Chief-Inspector Harding. And this is Detective-Sergeant Pollock.'

The tall, spare man in a dark blue suit, who was leaning by the fireplace, inclined his skull-like head fractionally, you could scarcely have called it a nod. His hair was sleek and black, his elbow was on the mantelpiece and a bony wrist extended well above the cuff of his coat-sleeve. I found myself thinking how well he went with the room. The little Chief-Inspector would have looked far more at home in the bar.

I glanced awkwardly down at the full glass that I was still holding.

'Can I get you both a drink?'

The little man shook his head gravely.

'Thank you, no. We're on duty.' And then, as though to counter any impression of churlishness that he might have given, he smiled again. 'Later, perhaps.'

Reluctantly I put my own glass down on a small round table that stood in the middle of the room in useless isolation, remote from any chair, then, I taking the other armchair, the Chief-Inspector and I both sat down. Sergeant Pollock, whether from protocol or personal preference, remained where he was, draped around the far side of the fire.

'Well now to business, my Lord. We won't have to keep you

Now

long, I'm sure. Some weeks ago I believe that, together with a party of your friends, you visited an establishment called ...' he took a small notebook out of a briefcase that was leaning against his chair and opened it at the first page, '... the Farmwell Foundation for Technological Research?'

'Yes,' I said, 'I did.'

'There, among other items, you were shown ...' again he referred to the notebook, '... an electronic device, designed to regulate domestic central heating.'

'That's right.' I was getting more and more mystified as to what this was all about.

Chief-Inspector Harding looked up at me. 'Were you aware that shortly afterwards the establishment at Farmwell was broken into, a security guard attacked and injured and that device stolen from the safe in which it was kept?'

'Good Lord, No! Is he all right? The guard, I mean.'

'Yes, he was only suffering from shock, a mild concussion and a flesh-wound in the head, from all of which he seems to be completely recovered. In fact,' he smiled, 'I rather think that it has given him a topic of conversation which he will make the fullest possible use of for the rest of his life. But the reason behind this visit is that it is virtually certain that it was one of the members of your party who was responsible. At the moment we are still very much in the dark as to which.'

I stared at him. 'You *can't* be serious!' I ran quickly through the members of the "1944 Club" in my mind. Billy Candleford? I couldn't imagine him having the energy. The two M.P.'s, Henry Matheson and Peter Stobbs? Surely neither of them would do a thing like that. Stephen Knightley, the farmer? Far too staid! Leonard Frost? He was the one whom I knew best. That only left the American, General Dick Richards. The remaining member of the "1944 Club" was Roger Faulkner, the Director of Farmwell himself. It didn't seem to make sense.

'Can I do anything to help?'

'Well, yes, my Lord. Since you're kind enough to ask, there is one thing. We've been making enquiries, purely a formality of course, but you'll appreciate that in a case of this kind we have to investigate every possibility. It seems that some weeks ago you applied to your bank manager for a bridging loan of twenty-five thousand pounds which you urgently needed, a request which he felt reluctantly obliged to turn down. And that, between the dates of . . .' he riffled through the pages of his notebook until he had found the place that he wanted, '. . . Monday the 9th and Thursday, 12th April, inclusive, a number of payments were made into your bank account, at various branches of various banks and in cash, and that these payments together made up that exact sum of twenty-five thousand pounds. Now it would be a very great help to us if you would be good enough to enlighten us as to the origin of these payments?

The whole tenor of the conversation had suddenly altered. It had now come round to a point where it was far too close for comfort to me personally. Only that morning, I had had a letter from my bank manager, forwarded on via the friends with whom I had stayed on my way up to Scotland, telling me that in view of the fact that the overdraft on my Private Account had just undergone such a satisfactory reduction he was now prepared to agree to my request for a bridging loan on the Farm Account, if I still wanted it. *If I still wanted it!* I had had no idea whatsoever how or why this could have happened. The "how" was now apparent but, as to the "why", I was still just as much in the dark as the Chief Inspector and I explained this to him.

Was it my imagination, or could I now detect a predatory gleam in the eye of the watching Sergeant Pollock? But Chief-Inspector Harding couldn't have been nicer about it. He nodded sympathetically when I had finished.

'I shouldn't worry too much about it, my Lord. I have no doubt that a satisfactory explanation will emerge in due course. Now there is something else.' He reached down into his briefcase and extracted an object which he handed to me. 'This was found in the bushes outside the building where the guard was attacked. The medical evidence is fairly conclusive that this is the weapon with which the wound was inflicted.'

It was the missing priest!

There must have been any number of similar ones made but, the first few times after I had started using it some three years ago, until I grew tired of doing so, I had filed a little notch on its silvery head for each fish that I had killed with it. And there, identifying it beyond any doubt at all, those same notches were. My immediate panic resolve was to deny all knowledge of it. But, when I looked up, I knew at once that he had been able to tell from my

Now

expression that I had recognised it.
I held it out to him resignedly.
'It's mine,' I said.
He took it without a word, returned it to the briefcase and extracted something else, small and gold this time, which he handed to me in its place.

'The security guard found himself grasping this when he came to,' he said. 'His mind's still a total blank about the whole episode – otherwise things would be very much easier for us.'

Here at last was something that I didn't recognize. I had never even possessed, let alone worn, a signet ring. For a moment it was a tremendous relief, an anticlimax almost ... until I turned it round in my hand and looked at the engraving. An owl, three flowers on a single stalk protruding from its mouth, a jagged collar round its neck, flapping its wings and perched precariously on a rather snazzy-looking cap – the whole surmounted by a viscount's coronet.

The entire interview now seemed progressively to be taking on the quality of a nightmare of the type where you're being chased by a lion and first you can't get the door of your car open and then, when at last you do, you fall out through the bottom. I had known that owl from my childhood at Thyrde, where it still adorns every fork, spoon and plate, together with innumerable other objects that are scattered throughout the house. I could even recite its full heraldic description off by heart.

On a Chapeau Sable turned up Ermine an Owl Argent gorged dancetty Sable wings displayed Argent holding in the beak a Spray of three Roses Gules barbed, seeded, stalked and leaved proper.

The crest of the Mallicents – and mine was the only viscountcy in the family.

I looked up helplessly at Detective-Chief-Inspector Harding.

'I'm the only person in the whole world who is entitled to wear that ring,' I said, 'but I swear that I've never seen it before in my life.'

He nodded his head solemnly several times before replying.

'I'm afraid that I shall have to ask you to accompany us back South to Northamptonshire to assist us with our enquiries.'

The words carried with them an all too ominous connotation.

Now

'Does that mean that you're arresting me?'

'Arresting you, my Lord? Oh dear me, no.' He was beaming again now. 'If I were going to arrest you, I should have to caution you first. Is that not right, Sergeant Pollock?'

The sergeant's lips parted slightly in what I could only suppose was an attempt at a smile. He hadn't spoken yet.

'No, purely a matter of routine, I do assure you. For instance, it may be that you can account satisfactorily for your movements on the night of Tuesday, April the Third, between the hours of, say, 11.0 p.m. and 2.0 a.m., the following morning. That would clear up the matter once and for all.'

I took out my diary and leafed through the pages frantically.

Then, almost in slow motion, I shut it up again and returned it to the inside breast pocket of my coat. Tuesday, 3rd April, had been the actual night of the visit of the "1944 Club" to Farmwell. The night which I had spent with Tisha. The night about which I had promised her faithfully never to tell a living soul.

'I'm afraid I can't,' I said.

The glass of Talisker remained on the small round table, still untasted.

And I never *did* find out how much that fish weighed.

The next thirty-six hours passed extraordinarily quickly. They let me drive my own car down and I drove through the night, the two detectives taking it in turns, one to sit beside me while the other slept in the back. We reached Farmwell soon after nine o'clock in the morning. A room had been made available for us in the village police station – a cell I suppose it was, because in addition to a table and chairs it contained a bed and on this I was allowed all too brief a rest, sleep I did not find possible, before the questioning in earnest began.

The detective work of the Chief-Inspector and his Sergeant had been painstaking, even if it had led them ultimately to the wrong conclusion. It had been just after 3.0 am that the security guard had recovered consciousness enough to raise the alarm but, although the assault had taken place in a passage not very far away from the Director's office, the actual theft had not been discovered until the following morning. When Lord Stanstead, the Chairman of *British Light & Power,* had arrived to claim the gadget that had been developed for his Company, the key of the

Now

safe had been found to be missing and it had taken some time for a duplicate to be located. It was only when the door had been opened, revealing the absence of the device, that the local police had been able to piece together from the rather disjointed statements of Dr. Roger Faulkner the sequence of events that had led up to the theft. He had remembered locking the device away in the safe, in the presence of the seven of us. He had remembered showing us the letter from the trade rival of B.L.P.'s, which had annoyed him so much, and giving us a résumé of its contents. And he had remembered putting the key and the letter down on his desk, again in our presence. Thus far, I myself was able to confirm. When our party had left, his secretary, as to whose reliability and loyalty he in any case had no doubt whatsoever, had gone home too. Dr. Faulkner himself had stayed on in his office working late, this apparently was something that he often did and on this particular occasion he had had a lot of work to catch up on, after a day spent in supervising our visit. By the time he had realised how late it was getting, it was eleven o'clock – he distinctly remembered looking at his watch. He had tidied up the papers on which he had been working and gone back to his own house which was in another part of the establishment, but before leaving he had looked on the desk for both letter and key. Finding neither there, he had concluded that, at some stage during the evening, he must have reopened the safe, put the letter into it and subsequently mislaid the key. The latter point had seemed relatively unimportant to him at the time – he was quite satisfied that the general security arrangements for Farmwell were adequate – and indeed it had quite slipped his mind until it was brought back by the questioning in the morning.

When he had remembered it, Dr. Faulkner had come to the conclusion, with the utmost reluctance because we were all of us friends of his to a greater or lesser extent, that one of the members of the "1944 Club" must have pocketed both the key of the safe which contained the device and the letter which disclosed the name of a ready and unscrupulous buyer and subsequently returned to steal the device itself.

The local police had been dubious to say the least. The Director was noted for his absent-mindedness, but in view of the eminence of the suspects, who included two MP's, three peers, a distinguished American General and a farmer of hitherto

Now

irreproachable character, they had decided to call in Scotland Yard.

To begin with, Detective-Chief-Inspector Harding and Detective-Sergeant Pollock had shared their doubts. And they had still been sceptical when, on Monday, 23rd April, an anonymous telephone call had been received suggesting that it was I who might have profited by the theft – in spite of its engraving, they had failed to connect the signet-ring with me until I had enlightened them. But they had approached my bank manager who had had no alternative but to give them the information that they asked for. And on three points Dr. Faulkner still proved to be unshakable. Both key and letter had been on his desk *before* the members of the "1944 Club" had left at 5.15 pm. Neither had been there when he himself had left soon after 11.0. And he had been there alone – no one else had come in – throughout the intervening time.

The questioning went on all day, but the questions were always the same – as were the answers. Yes, I had received payments amounting to a substantial sum of money. No, I hadn't got the slightest idea as to whom they had come from or why. Yes, the offending priest was mine. No, I hadn't seen it since about ten o'clock – it could have been ten-thirty – on the evening of the visit to Farmwell. No, the signet ring did *not* belong to me. But yes, it was my family crest and the viscount's coronet on it could only refer to me. And no, no, no! I could *not* account for my movements on that particular night.

On the Friday night I did sleep, but by then I had been both cautioned and charged.

On the Saturday morning, a special session of the local Magistrates' Court was arranged for my exclusive benefit. In the circumstances, it was remarkably painless. The charge was "Robbery", I was remanded for Committal Proceedings which were to be held at the same court on Tuesday, 5th June, and bail was fixed in the sum of five thousand pounds. At first this presented a difficulty. It could no longer be done, it seemed, "in my own recognisances" and I had to find someone to stand surety for me. But here luck was with me. I was allowed to ring up from the court and my Uncle Charles, bless him, was willing and even anxious to act in this capacity, there was a police station next door to his flat in London where the desk-sergeant knew him well, he was able to

Now

sign the necessary papers and the whole thing was fixed up on the telephone.
 The proceedings had started at ten am. and by eleven I was on the road to London.

Back at my flat, I made the first of two telephone calls. The Tories had indeed won the General Election. Polling Day had been Thursday, my last day on the river, but Chief-Inspector Harding had given me the news during the questioning on Friday. My first job must be to tell Tom Lavenham, my Chief Whip, that I was definitely a non-starter now.
 But it was the second that I had been dreading. I found the number in the little blue book, *Dod's Parliamentary Companion*.
 'Hello.' It sounded like her, but I couldn't be quite certain.
 'Is that Mrs. Matheson?'
 'Yes.' The voice sounded flat, uninterested.
 'Look Tisha, Derek Thyrde here. I know I promised never to get in touch with you again, but something awful's happened. I must see you. May I?'
 There was a long pause.
 'Tisha . . .?'
 Then, 'It doesn't matter . . . now. Henry's left me.'
 'I'll be right round,' I said.

'Was it because of me? Henry leaving you, I mean?'
 'No. He doesn't know about that. Things were going badly wrong, long before you came on the scene.'
 Tisha had met me at the door and I had told her the whole story. Yes, she would go on seeing me – that was the first question that I'd asked. And yes, of course she would help me to clear my name. But there was a "but" in both cases.
 'I know you'll think it's silly of me, *but* can we forget that night and start all over again? As though we'd only just met? I'm really not an easy lay and I'd rather not go to bed with you again until I'm sure this time. It may take a little longer than it would in normal circumstances, but it'll be worth waiting for. Please?'
 And,
 'Of course I'll come to the police with you, Derek, and tell them everything. Now – straight away, if that's what you really want. *But* . . . it'd be like taking all my clothes off in public. I really don't

Now

know what it would do to us ... to you and me. Let's try it the other way first. Try and find out who really did steal that thing, I'll help you, and then we won't have to tell anyone what happened that night. But if we can't, if we've tried everything else and there really isn't any other way, then I'll give you your alibi, swear that you never left me that night – in court, if necessary. I'll have got over the shock of Henry leaving me and ... oh, I'll know you so much better by then, and it won't be half so bad. Do you understand?'

I wasn't any too keen on either of the conditions, but somehow I didn't argue much. Suddenly I felt ridiculously happy – everything was going to be all right now.

'Come on,' I said, 'it's a lovely day, I'll take you out for a drive.'

I took her up the M1 to Thyrde. The sky was liquid blue and even if the puffy white clouds that inched across it did have a greyish tinge at the base of them nothing was going to spoil the day for me now. We had called in at Justin de Blank's in Elizabeth Street to buy ourselves a picnic lunch first and Tisha kept me supplied with bite-sized pieces on the way. Far behind us, it seemed, we had shaken off such trivialities as Farmwell, central-heating devices, policemen and Magistrates' Courts and now there was only Tisha – dark curls prancing, white shirt swelling, Tisha grave, Tisha laughing, Tisha inquisitive – on the seat beside me. And then we were on the minor roads, fields on either side painted a brilliant poster-colour yellow with oil-seed rape in full flower, little weed-like patches of it having spilled over onto the grass verges, making the native dandelions seem dowdy in comparison. And finally, the gates of Thyrde and the long straight drive. The avenue which had been the glory of my childhood had succumbed to Dutch elm disease some years back, but now the double rows of young lime trees with which I had replaced it were at last achieving undisputable ownership, their branches sprinkled with half-opening leaves.

I took Tisha everywhere, showed her everything and, being Tisha, into everything; the house; the garden, that my mama still visited at least once a week to see that nothing was being neglected (secretly, I always suspected, hoping to find that something was); the water-garden, which had been the nearest that she had been able to achieve to the lake that she had always craved; the stables, empty for the moment; the agent's house beyond, in which old James Ford had lived until he had retired to

Now

his native Gloucestershire. I had moved into it myself for a couple of years – before my marriage to Diana. But now that too was empty.

'What's that?' said Tisha suddenly.

She was pointing at a brick building, the only one on the whole estate; ivy was covering the wall on one side and had spread in a cluster over the orange-red roof-tiles; the mortar between the bricks looked as though someone had daubed it with apple-green paint, but I knew from previous close inspection that it was lichen. Stable one side and, carriage-house once presumably, but garage in more recent years, the other, it went with the agent's house; in front of it were the grass-grown remains of what had been a cobbled yard.

'A shed,' I said unhelpfully.

Rather meanly, I was hoping to avoid having to go to the trouble of opening up that too for her, but Tisha had walked over to it and was peering through the window. The glass was smeared white with neglect, but there was one pane missing.

'There's something in there.'

'Oh, that's nothing. It's only an old Rolls.'

She looked round at me, appealing. 'Do let me see.'

There was nothing for it but to take the ring of keys out of my fob pocket. One of them fitted the padlock and the hinges yelped in protest as I pulled open the pair of ill-hanging doors.

Swathed in plastic sheeting stippled with swallow droppings, there was a vast shape inside. I hauled back the plastic, rear to front, in much the same way that one shows off a horse on a Sunday morning visit to the stables. And then I stood back.

Most of the bonnet was still covered and, in any case, there was only a black plastic cap on the top of the radiator where the mascot should have been – worth over a hundred quid, that was safely locked away in a cupboard in my dressingroom. The lines were still there of course and it was possible to visualise something of their former elegance. But the canvas hood, bleached by the years, was frayed and threadbare. Corrosion in the form of a powdery white dust was showing through on swept mudguard and curved bootlid, their once-fawn paintwork faded to a dirty drab. Between the rear bumpers one could barely make out, through the grime on the glass that covered it, the registration number – JB 5555.

Now

Tisha was at my side.

'Oh, Derek! He's t'riff.' She was looking up at me with an expression in her eyes that nearly had me foundering but, alas, it wasn't me with whom she had fallen in instant and total love.

'My mama gave it to me on condition that I never sold it,' I said. 'She and my father did most of their courting in it. I used to drive about in it quite a bit at one time.'

'Can we get him back on the road again? Please, Derek. Do let's try!'

I looked doubtfully at the shabby hulk of lifeless metal.

It seemed unlikely that it would ever go again.

iii. Then

The Rolls started at the first push of the button. I cast a final guilty glance towards my faithful M.G., where it was standing neglected and reproachful, and then I drove out of the garage and round to the back door to pick up Molly Stanton who had walked over from the Fords' house earlier to join me for breakfast.

"I say, this *is* doing it in style," she said.

A trickle of ash-blonde seeping out from beneath her head-scarf, she looked ravishing, swathed in Burberry though she was. It was a clear morning, but chilly, and I was glad of my British Warm over-coat. My wrist-watch told me that it was eight-thirty, but I knew that it was lying. It was still only half-past six by the sun — double summer-time had started two days before.

I drove off down the elm-lined drive which ran dead straight for fully two hundred yards, the random etching of branches and twigs overhead glowing red with late flower against the cream and blue of the sky. It would be hard to imagine seeing Thyrde without its elm avenue, but I doubt if I will ever have to. Approaching their prime now, those trees I have been assured are good for another sixty or seventy years.

"Who do we see first?" said Molly, when we had stopped for petrol. "Fill her up," I had said, much to the surprise of the boy who was working the pumps. I had had to flourish a fist-full of coupons in his face before he would believe me.

"The American, Dick Richards," I said. "And after him Roger Faulkner, the boffin."

I had rung them both up, as soon as I had got in the night before, and also Stephen Knightley to tell him that I was bringing Molly with me. I had suggested that in the circumstances we should lunch at the House of Lords — and on me — instead.

I counted out coupons and money and we were on our way again.

A long expanse of gleaming fawn bonnet-top away to the front

Then

of me, the wings of the mascot seemed to be soaring now until the tyres skimmed the surface of the tarmac. I settled back in my seat, the tang of leather upholstery pleasant in my nostrils, the steering-wheel solid and reassuring – a symbol of power and security – in my hands, an awareness of the lovely girl beside me ever present in the forefront of my consciousness, while the engine crooned along the road like a motorised Bing Crosby.

We reached the American Air Base at Chelveston some five minutes early, so I stopped just short of the main entrance. The sentry who was leaning against the barrier had obviously not heard the Rolls approaching, but he looked up when I got out and slammed the door. Then he went back to his occupation of cleaning his finger-nails with the tip of his bayonet. Dick Richards had not yet arrived.

"Can we have the hood down?" said Molly. "It's such a lovely day."

"Will you be warm enough? And what about your hair?"

"Oh, don't worry about that. It's a mess anyway."

She got out to help me, took off her head-scarf and shook her hair so that the silky fairness of it fell back into position half obscuring her right eye. It looked far from a mess to me.

If the Rolls had been impressive with its hood up, it had now been transformed into an open two-seater to dream about. The three near-side wheels, front, rear and the spare which was positioned against the side of the bonnet, together made up an off-centre triangular pattern achieving a perfect balance against the sweeping fawn body-lines that ran long and straight above, from *The Spirit of Ecstasy* on the radiator-top, through the base of the gently tilted wind-screen and the chocolate canvas of the hood-cover to the boot-lid, and long and curved below.

"Say, isn't that just something?" Dick Richards had joined us. He was wearing a dark leather flying-jacket, his name printed above the top left-hand pocket. "You wouldn't care to part with her, I suppose?"

I laughed and shook my head and then I introduced him to Molly. Immediately the Rolls lost his attention. But after a minute or two of conversation he turned reluctantly back to me again and took a thick wad of bank-notes, which was held together by a gold clip, out of his pocket.

"Well, Derry, what's the damage for last Wednesday night?"

Then

I produced the bill on which I had already done the necessary arithmetic.

"It came to £17. 3s. 6d. in all, I'm afraid. I made it up to the round nineteen quid with the tip. Split between the seven of us, that's two pounds fourteen and three each."

He passed over three pound notes and I gave him two half-crowns, a six-pence and a threepenny-bit in exchange.

"Look," I said, "I hope you don't think I'd have routed you out at this ungodly hour just for that. There is something else, but I didn't want to talk about it over the telephone."

I took the wretched '$2\frac{1}{2}$ C.A.' paper out of my wallet and held it out to him.

"This was found under the table after you'd all left that night. It looks as though it might be pretty important to some one, so I thought I ought to find out who it belongs to."

He glanced at it briefly and handed it straight back.

"Not guilty! Means nothing in my young life."

He walked slowly round the car examining every part of it. Then he came and stood in front of Molly, and looked her up and down too, an attention that she at least seemed to find by no means unpleasant. He grinned and waved a hand in the direction of the Rolls – but he was still looking at Molly.

"Some body-work!" he said.

* * *

To get to Farmwell, which lay an almost exactly equal distance in the opposite direction, we would have to go right past the end of the drive at Thyrde again, but to make it more interesting for Molly I took her back a different way.

I drove along a series of hedge-lined roads, through little villages in which hens, scratching and pecking lazily in the dust at the roadside, were suddenly activated by our passing into squawking, hurtling bundles of feathers, near-suicidal at the bonnet-front. In one, a very old farm-labourer hobbled along, his back bent under a wooden yoke, hands steadying the chains which held a brimming milk-pail on either side. In another a shepherd, walking dogs at heel along the grass verge, looked up and waved as we went by.

This, I thought, was England at its best. The England of

Then

summer, cricket on the village green and pewter tankards on a trestle-table at the boundary, where the old men used to sit comparing the antics of the distant white-clad figures with their counterparts remembered from matches long past. The England of autumn and the first evocative note of the hunting-horn in the mists of early morning, with the corn-stooks standing golden on the stubble and the leaves just beginning to turn. The England of winter, shooting-sticks spaced along the ridings of white-rimed woodland, the shouted jokes of approaching beaters, one to another across thirty-yard intervals, suddenly stilled by the whirr of a cock-pheasant from the undergrowth, and giving place to *Mark Over* in a delighted cry. The England of this spring morning, an open two-seater down a country lane with a laughing blue-eyed lovely, hands loosely laid on lap, silken whisps of cream-coloured hair wafting in the slip-stream, on the seat beside me.

And this was the England that one out of seven men, all known to me, had conspired with The King's enemies in seeking to destroy.

* * *

"All right," said Roger Faulkner, "L . . et's have a look at it."

I passed it over to him, the '$2\frac{1}{2}$ C.A.' paper in all its obscurity. We were sitting on precarious wooden folding chairs round the oil-cloth-covered top of a folding wooden table in the canteen at Farmwell. An old lady in the village shop, who had been engaged in the act of snipping off *personal points* coupons for a small boy intent on buying a Mars Bar, had paused for long enough to direct us. Roger had bought us tea from the woman behind the urn on the counter and he had slopped it in the saucers while bringing it over. I had already dunned him for his two pounds fourteen and three.

He peered at it closely.

"N . . o, it's not mine," he said at last. He put the paper down on the table narrowly missing a small puddle of canteen tea, took off his spectacles, polished their lenses meticulously with his handkerchief, replaced them on his beaky nose and leaned forward to stare at the plan again. "Leave it with me. I can almost certainly find out something about it."

Then

"I'm afraid I can't do that," I said. "I'm seeing the others today and I must show it to them too."

"Look, Derry, I think this may be something very important . . ." but I picked up the paper quickly and buttoned it away firmly in my top pocket to stop further argument.

Molly and I finished up what remained of our uninspiring pale brown liquid and then we went back to the car, Roger flapping around us like one of the hens that we had recently encountered.

As I let out the clutch and the Rolls started to move forward, "I still think," he called out, "that you should leave that p. .aper with me."

* * *

We joined Watling Street at Stony Stratford.

Molly's father had been in the Navy, she told me, and she had hardly been able to wait to leave school so that she could join the Wrens. But it had not been until August, 1942, that she had been summoned to the training centre at Mill Hill. While she had been waiting she had worked full-time in her aunt's garden in Suffolk.

"Only vegetables, of course," she said. "Dig for Victory and all that, but I've always had a passion for gardening. The one thing I long for is a garden of my own. Something that I can really plan for and work out years ahead, with nobody to please but myself."

"The garden at Thyrde's pretty good," I said inconsequentially. "You haven't seen it yet."

On her first day at Mill Hill, she had been issued, not with the uniform that she had hoped for and expected, but with overalls, even though they had been navy-blue – and it had not been long before she found out why. For the first two weeks her life had consisted solely of mops and long-handled brooms and endlessly scrubbing and cleaning the concrete floors of rooms and corridors. That fortnight had seemed like a life-time. But when it was over, oh the bliss of it, they had been sent to *slops* to collect their uniforms.

"Slops?"

Molly grinned. "Sorry, I forgot I was talking to a "pongo".* It's where you collect and sign for your *issue*. But I felt like a different

---

* The derogatory term applied by naval personnel to a member of the Army.

person the moment that I got out of those disgusting overalls. First the new white shirt and the struggle to put on a semi-stiff collar with back and front studs. Then the black tie and those awful issue stockings, the skirt and coat and, final touch, the round hat with 'H.M.S.' on it. It all became a bit of a bore after we got used to it, but that first time I felt like Cinderella being dressed for the Ball. It was only the local Toc H canteen we were going to, but it seemed better than a ball to us then."

At the beginning of the fortnight, they had been sorted into groups according to the category of the work that they would later be doing. Cook, steward, boat's crew, *writer* – "secretary, to you" – admin. and the various technical jobs. She, with one or two others, had been taken into a separate room and asked whether they would be prepared to do a special job.

"You were the Mata Hari brigade?"

"No, that came later."

She could not tell me what the job had really been – they had had to take an oath of secrecy that bound them, not only until the end of the war, but for life.

"Thirteen shillings a week, we were paid. I remember the thrill of lining up for the pay parade on Fridays. You held your upturned hat out in front of you with both hands and they dropped the money into it. Then two steps backwards and ..." she broke off. "Oo, look at that."

We were driving through Redbourn, the last village before St. Albans. There was a stuffed bear standing upright outside the door of a public house on the right.

"Yes, he's nice isn't he. We always used to wave to him when we were driving up to London this way as children. I'll give you three guesses what that pub's called."

"The Bear?"

I shook my head.

"Oh, I know. The Warwick Arms?"

"No."

"What, then?"

"The Chequers," I said brutally.

"But ... why does it have a bear in front of it, then?"

"Perhaps the land-lord likes stuffed bears?"

There was an awful pause before Molly decided to ignore it. In the middle of the previous year, she had been sent to O.C.T.U.

Then

She had not found it unenjoyable, but she had missed the excitement and the sense of fulfilment of the work that she had been doing and being marched through the village, led by a petty officer and singing ghastly songs, had been a poor substitute. Then, half-way through the course, Molly had been sent for. She had approached the door of the office certain that she was going to be chucked out. Instead of her Commanding Officer, whom she had been expecting to see, she had found an elderly Commander sitting at the desk — and not a very smart one at that!

"Commander Jackson?" I asked.

Molly nodded. He had asked her a lot of questions, all of which had seemed totally irrelevant — her home life, her schooling, her likes and dislikes. Then, as soon as she had been passed out, she had been posted to Norfolk House.

"And that was that." She grinned at me. "Now it's your turn," she said.

* * *

Stephen Knightley was paying off his cab outside the Peers' Entrance, as we drew into Old Palace Yard. He turned to look at the Rolls and when he recognised me he walked over to meet us, beard and uniform bristling with the aggressive efficiency of a naval officer.

"Is that yours?"

"Yes," I said, rather smugly. It was a car of which any one would have been proud to acknowledge ownership.

"How did you get the petrol?"

"Oh, I just happened to have some left," I said hurriedly. "Let me introduce, Lieutenant Knightley — Miss Stanton."

Stephen saluted her and they shook hands. Then he looked at the car again and seemed to be on the point of saying something. But apparently he changed his mind, because he suddenly turned without a word and followed Molly inside.

His own girl-friend, whom I had suggested on the telephone the night before that he should bring, had apparently been unable to come being far too busily tied up at her munitions factory.

"What sort of war-work do you do, Miss Stanton?" he said as we sat down at the table.

"I ... er," Molly looked at me helplessly. "Well, nothing very much, I'm afraid."

Stephen changed the subject. But his tacit disapproval was only too plain to see.

We were half-way through luncheon when I felt a hand on my shoulder.

"I say, Thyrde."

I turned and got up at the same time. Lord Greyfield's chubby face was looking anxiously at me.

"The other night. Hope you didn't mind. My landing you with Irene. How did you get on?"

"Not too badly, thank you," I said.

He nodded with an air of proprietorial satisfaction. "Good girl that. Knew you'd appreciate her. One of the best at the..." and then he noticed Molly who was listening fascinated and his expression changed to one of contrite horror.

"Well... really only stopped... The bill, that night. Find out what I owe you," he said.

I told him and he took out his cheque book and balanced it awkwardly against the wall with his left hand as he wrote.

"Thanks. Oh, by the way," I said, as I put the cheque away in my wallet and took out the paper in its place, "this isn't yours, is it?" I unfolded it for him and explained the circumstances in which it had been found.

He shook his head. "Nothing to do with me. Never seen it before. No, not mine," and, with another appalled glance in the direction of Molly, he left.

"Let's have a look at that," said Stephen, who during the previous exchange had been staring out of the window with a concentration that the view of a dingy grey stone wall with blocked up windows across the court-yard hardly merited. I passed it over and he studied it carefully.

"What do you make of it?" I said.

"Well, it's a stretch of coast-line, that's obvious, probably taken from an admiralty chart. You see that line along the top and the dotted one below it, those must be the high and low water levels. And those other dots with figures against them will be the various depths in fathoms. But, other than that, where it is and what it's all about, I can't tell you."

After that we got on to the inevitable subject of the war.

When Stephen started telling us about his experiences in

Then

Atlantic convoys, his hatred of the Germans became even more apparent.

"By the same token," he said, "I'd decided not to mention it, but you really shouldn't go swanning about in that great Rolls of yours. If you realised the lives it costs bringing petrol over to this country, you'd be more careful."

It was turning out to be a more than usually sticky luncheon. I was not quite sure which of us was in more disgrace, Molly for doing nothing to increase the nation's resources or me for wasting them. When I paid the bill, I took Stephen on one side and asked him for his contribution for the previous Wednesday. He felt in his pocket.

"But I'm not going to pay for the champagne for those ... those *women*."

I must say, I thought it was a bit much when he was brimming over with my food and drink, but I did not argue.

I let him off with the odd fourteen-and-three.

* * *

"I'm lost," said Molly. "Where are we?"

"It's quite simple," I said. "This is *The Commons' Lobby* which used to be *The Peers' Lobby*. Through those doors there is what used to be the Chamber of *The House of Lords* but the Commons have been sitting there since 1941 so now it's *The House of Commons*. Beyond that is what used to be ..."

"I know. *The Commons' Lobby*?"

"No, *The Prince's Chamber* but now it's *The Peers' Lobby*. That leads on into what used to be *The Royal Gallery*, and still is, and beyond that again is what used to be *The King's Robing-Room* and is now *The House of Lords*. *The Commons Lobby* was down that way, past what used to be *The Central Lobby* only it isn't 'central' any more and just short of what used to be *The House of Commons* and is now nothingness."

"I used to be *Third Officer Molly Stanton*, but I'm not sure whether I am now," Molly said.

In one corner, a group of men whom I assumed to be M.P.'s were talking excitedly. One of them detached himself, as Molly and I were waiting to attract the attention of the Principal Doorkeeper who was offering snuff to a passing Member, and came

Then

over towards us. I recognised immediately the unruly black hair of Mr. Leonard Frost.

"Ah yes," he said, when I had introduced him to Molly, "the bill the other night. How much do I owe you?"

I had the greatest of pleasure in taking the money off *him*.

Then I showed him the paper and told him where and how it had been found. He glanced at it and shook his head.

"Certainly not mine. I'll take it in and show it to Bagot and Matheson, if you like. They're bound to be in the House."

"Well, I've already sent a message in," I lied. "I think I'd better hang on to it, if you don't mind."

"Please yourself. Good-bye, Miss Stanton," and he departed inside the Chamber, scrubbing at his hair, right hand, left hand, right, left, as he went.

Uncle Johnny, when I did finally manage to extract him, arrived followed closely at heel by Colonel Matheson. I was beginning to get the impression that those two habitually hunted in couples. They shook hands with Molly, the Colonel's eyes immediately springing to life and animating his brown face.

"Well, Derry my boy, what can we do for you?" said Sir John Bagot." Surely you and Miss Stanton don't want to listen to The Education Bill and it's a bit early yet for tea."

I shook my head. "No, we've got to rush off, I'm afraid." I took the paper out of my pocket again. The Colonel dragged his attention away from Molly and peered forward to see it.

"I say, Johnnie, you been dropping state secrets about the place? They shoot yer for that, don'cha know."

Uncle Johnnie waved the paper in his face, snatched it away and then gave it ostentatiously back to me.

"I'll tell you exactly what that is," he said. "It's a plan of the dispositions of the Home Guard around Camberley in the event of enemy attack, but don't for God's sake give it back to James, here. He'll only lose it again and if *those* were to get into enemy hands, we really would be in the soup."

Colonel James Matheson nodded happily and went back to talking to Molly.

It was with considerable relief that I re-folded the paper and buttoned it safely into my top pocket again.

* * *

Then

"Well, that's the lot," I said to Molly. We were sitting outside in the Rolls again. "Any ideas yet?"

She shook her head. "I really don't know . . ." There was a pause. "But I *do* hope it doesn't turn out to be that gorgeous American."

"No?"

The sudden surge of jealousy must have been apparent from my tone, because she looked round laughing at me.

"Tell you what," I said, "let's go to a flick tonight – after we've reported back to Commander Jackson." I reached behind my seat for that morning's copy of *The Times* and passed it to her folded to the back page. "Have a look what's on."

"Let's see. There's *For Whom The Bell Tolls*, that's at The Carlton."

"Too gloomy," I said. "All about war."

"I've seen it, anyway. *Madame Curie* at The Empire?"

"Too clinical."

"Wait a minute, what about *The Desert Song* at The Warner?"

"That'll do grand. It's in Leicester Square, so we can have an early dinner before it and then walk over to *The Four Hundred* afterwards."

"Oh . . ." She looked down at her tweed coat and skirt and felt the hem. "Derry, I can't. I haven't got anything to wear. I took my only decent dress down to Thyrde and, anyway, I couldn't go *there* with my hair looking like this."

"It was just a thought," I said.

"Hold on. I can borrow something from Pat, the girl I share a room with. She's on night duty at the moment and she takes the same size as me. And I might be able to get my hair done at Harrods while you go and see old Jacky."

"Hoy," I said. "Remember our instructions. We've got to stick together all the time."

She grinned. "There are places, Lord Thyrde, where even you can't follow me," she said.

And so to Harrods we went.

There had been a hole dug in the road in Hans Crescent, fenced off by poles with a red flag on them, and I turned the Rolls round, reversed it and parked close up against that. I took Molly's arm as we walked across the road, inside and along to the lifts. The Hairdressing Department was on the fourth floor.

91

Then

We stood for a moment in the entrance to that peculiarly feminine preserve with its looming domes of hair-dryers, the atmosphere heavy with the scent of soaps and lotions, the chatter of scissors and the sound of running taps. Five customers in varying stages of completion were already installed, their ages seeming to range from the old to the very old, the nearest of them a thin little woman whose mottled hands were thickly encrusted with diamonds at finger and wrist. Tied by its lead in one corner, a poodle bitch whose mid-brown coat had been evenly trimmed to tight little curls stood yearning towards this last, her mistress beyond doubt, with never wavering eyes. At a sixth basin, an old man in a white coat and pince-nez spectacles with thin gold rims was sitting in the chair reading an evening paper. He folded it, stowed it away carefully behind the bottles on the ledge in front of him, got up and hobbled towards us.

"Off you go," Molly said, "or you'll miss old Jacky. He sometimes leaves the office early."

"You won't move a yard away from here until I come back and collect you? Promise?"

"I promise."

And I had to be content with that.

When I did get down to the street again, I found that some idiot had parked a black Morris Ten saloon, or one that had once been black, slap in front of the Rolls, locked of course and with barely a foot to spare. There was a mascot hanging by a cord from the inside top centre of the narrow rear window. A Mickey Mouse which grinned cheerfully at me through the glass, but it had little cause to do so – it was missing one white-gloved hand. The Morris itself had not fared much better. The right-hand rear mud-guard was crumpled and there was rust showing through where the paint had flaked away, the whole of that half of the bumper had been knocked out of shape too and the number plate was obscured with grease and dirt. I got into my own driving seat, and eventually, with the help of a friendly passer-by, I managed to manoeuvre myself out without giving him the matching dent, that he so richly deserved, on the other side.

* * *

"None of them claimed it then?" said Commander Jackson.

Then

"Didn't expect them to. But did anything strike you as being suspicious about any of their attitudes when you showed it to them?"

"Not really. Roger Faulkner did his best to persuade me to hand it over to him. Said he thought it might be important and got pretty annoyed when I refused. By the way, isn't it a bit risky letting him go on working at Farmwell?"

"No. The thing he's concerned with there is something in which we know the Germans are well ahead of us. Any one else?"

"Well, Stephen Knightley. He was convinced that it was a map of a bit of coast and that those two lines represent high and low water."

The Commander grunted. "That's as may be," he said.

"And Leonard Frost. He was the M.P. that we saw first. I got the impression that he was a bit put out when I wouldn't let him take it into the Chamber to show it to the other two. None of the others seemed to show the slightest interest."

I held the paper out across the desk to Commander Jackson. "Thank God I can get rid of this thing at last," I said.

But he shook his head. "No, you'll have to hang on to that for a bit longer, I'm afraid. Who-ever it is may make another approach to you and he's bound to suspect something if you can't produce it. By the way, where's Miss Stanton?"

I gulped slightly. "Oh, she's all right. I left her having her hair done at Harrods. We're going out tonight."

"What! Didn't I make it clear to you that the one thing above all others was that you have to stick together?"

"Yes, but ..."

"Don't stand there gawping. Get after her, man!"

I turned without waiting to salute and ran out of the office, taking the stairs up to the ground floor of Norfolk House two at a time. I swear that I did that journey from St. James's Square back to Hans Crescent in four minutes flat. The battered Morris Ten had gone and I left the Rolls in the same place but with its rear end half out in the road, without wasting time in parking it properly.

The Hair-dressing Department looked much as I had left it. There, sat the same five customers, she of the diamond hands amongst them. There, stood the poodle, yearning yet. There, was the old man with the white coat and the gold-rimmed pince-nez, now busily intent on sweeping up loose hair-trimmings with a soft

Then

broom.

But of the fair head of Third Officer Molly Stanton, there was no sign at all.

* * *

"Where..." with a supreme effort I managed to keep my voice to a tone that was as near as possible to normal, "where is Miss Stanton?"

The old man studied me with infuriating deliberation. "Ah," he said at last, "you was the young gentleman she came in with. I didn't recognise you at first. She's gone, I'm afraid, Sir. Had a most urgent telephone message – *from Lord Thyrde!*" He was so obviously expecting to impress me that in other circumstances I might have felt gratified.

"I *am* Lord Thyrde – and I sent no such message."

"Oh, I do beg your pardon, my Lord, there must be some mistake, then. And the young lady who took the call wrote it out for me most careful."

He walked over to the corner that was not occupied by the poodle, rummaged in a bin, extracted a ball of rolled-up paper and returned with it, smoothing it out as he came. I took it from him. It was written in school-girl copperplate.

Change of plans. Meet me urgently outside Covent Garden Underground. Will explain later. (sgd) Lord Thyrde.

"How long ago did she leave?"

"Not five minutes gone, my Lord. You'll catch her if you hurry."

I shouted a hurried 'thank you' over my shoulder and rushed off, down four flights of stairs, out into Hans Crescent, past the abandoned Rolls and in at the Underground entrance at the top. Down three little flights and the 'Ticket-and-Change' machines were just ahead of me but there was no time to waste and I made for the head of the moving-staircase, scattering would-be travellers to either side. I pushed past the inspector at the top, causing that official to bellow after me, but there was little he could do so I ran on down past the line of passengers standing on the right. There was a train waiting at the East-bound line. "Mind the Doors" came a contralto yodel from further down the platform and as I jumped in through the nearest set they shut

Then

behind me and the train lurched forward. The compartment was packed, men in dark suits and bowler hats mainly, and jammed back against the door as I was, its angle wedging my forage cap forward, I could only see the people standing nearest to me. At Hyde Park Corner some of the passengers got out and I was able to look around me. Molly was not among those that were left. Surely there would not have been time for her to have caught an earlier train!

At Green Park I hoped to get out and run along the platform to the next compartment, but there were so many people waiting to get in that I did not dare to risk it. The same at Piccadilly Circus and Leicester Square.

When the train moved off from the latter station into the blackness of the tunnel, it was in that hesitant sort of way that always makes one think that it is not quite certain whether it has been right to do so. Sure enough, it jerked to a sudden vicious halt, throwing us all together. At the same moment the lights went out. "Oh God," I thought, "where is Molly and what is happening to her and – *please* don't let it be for long." As if in answer, just as suddenly the lights came on again, the train started moving, more confidently it seemed this time, and within another minute and a half we were drawing into Covent Garden Station. I was the first out.

I ran along the platform, weaving my way amongst the people walking between the train and the two-tier metal bunks for use in air raids which lined the wall, until I reached the exit sign and on through to the lifts. The first was full and the gate clanged shut as I reached it but the second was waiting and empty. "From Knightsbridge, please," I said to the ticket-collector who also worked the lift and I paid him the tuppence that he asked for. I stood there, checking the other passengers as they came in but none of them was Molly, and then came the long journey upward. The gate opened direct into the day-light of a narrow street outside.

I stationed myself by the green-grocer's shop on the corner with Long Acre, looking frantically both ways – there was still no sign of Molly and in all conscience her fair hair ought to have been easy to pick out in any crowd – when I felt a touch on my elbow. A little old woman, whom I had vaguely noticed paying for a cabbage and then waiting for it to be wrapped up in a sheet of old

Then

newspaper, was looking up at me kindly.

"I hope you don't mind my mentioning it, dear, but your pocket button's undone. You'd best do it up or you'll be losing your money."

I smiled at her, said "thank you", and instinctively felt for the top left-hand pocket of my service-dress jacket in which I kept my wallet, as my eyes continued to search. The flap was indeed undone. It was only then that the awful thought struck me. I pulled out the contents and fumbled through them. Then I felt in the now empty pocket again and, in quick succession, all my others both in jacket and trousers. There was no doubt about it. My wallet was there all right, as were my pipe, tobacco, matches and what little money I had been carrying with me. But the '$2\frac{1}{2}$ C.A.' paper, the responsibility for having to carry which had been haunting me every moment of that day until the sudden disappearance of Molly herself had driven it clean out of my mind, *was just not there*.

Half way across Long Acre, stood one of those metal water tanks with the letters 'E.W.S.' stencilled on its side. Mesmerised I watched as, almost in slow motion it seemed, the car that had been hidden beyond it moved steadily out and into view. There was something familiar about that squat, black rear end, dirty and dust-covered ... mud-guard and bumper dented ... number-plate obscured. Suddenly I rushed out into the road and after it, shouting and gesticulating wildly, but too late. As the Morris Ten gathered speed away from me I could see that there was a little object dancing about within the glass of the narrow rear window. It was too far off now to see it distinctly, but I knew with a cold, clear certainty what it was. It was a Mickey Mouse, one hand-less arm lifted in a gesture of fare-well.

Just then, I heard the sound of a motor-horn behind me, but still some way off. A taxi? I pivoted round. It was no taxi, but ... better, infinitely better. First the shape of the silver radiator; then those unmistakable body lines, fawn topped with chocolate; finally the registration number, J.B. 5555.

The blue eyes of Molly Stanton smiled up at me through the open window.

"Thank God you're safe," I said. "No, don't move."

I ran round to the passenger side and flung myself in beside her.

"I know it sounds melodramatic, but ..." I pointed to where

Then the Morris was now disappearing to the left some two hundred yards ahead, "... follow that car!"

* * *

We covered the distance to the turning in about half the time that the Morris had taken. We were round it just soon enough to be able to catch a glimpse of it as, still well ahead, it was disappearing to the left again. Molly was handling the car superbly. It had started raining quite heavily now, making the wood-block surface of the streets slippery and the Morris was nippier as it jigged left and right than the more cumbersome Rolls, but even so, she always contrived to keep it in sight. While we went, I told her my story. And when I had finished – we had crossed Oxford Street by this time and seemed to be heading vaguely north-west – she told me hers.

"I knew there was something fishy about that telephone message the moment I got it, so I went over to where the public telephones are, across the hall, to ring up Norfolk House and check. I tried to tell the old boy who did my hair where I was going, but somehow I couldn't seem to make him understand. When I got through to old Jacky, pretty terse about it he was too – told me he'd sent you back to Harrods with a flea in your ear. By the time I reached the Hair-dressing Department again, you'd come and gone. I rushed down to the street and saw the Rolls still standing there, all lonesome and neglected-like. You hadn't locked the ignition so I brought her along and here we are."

She paused while she was negotiating a horse-drawn van that was making its somewhat erratic way down Marylebone Road.

"Oh, Derry, I *am* sorry. I should have listened to you, but I did so want to go to *The Four Hundred* tonight."

"We will yet," I said.

Molly grinned.

"What are you going to do when we do catch up with him? Ask him very nicely to give it back?"

"Yes ..." I said and I reached behind my seat for the bulky leather holster containing my father's old service revolver, which I had had the fore-thought to bring with me when I had started out that morning, "... with this."

Past Swiss Cottage, up Finchley road turning left after the

Then

Tower Garage at the top, the driver in front was making for out of London, that was obvious now and, whether or not he knew that he was being followed, he was having the luck of the very devil. The traffic-lights had been with him all the way. Only once, when we were approaching the North Circular, did we see their little masked-off crosses glowing red ahead of him, but even then they switched to red-and-amber the moment that his front tyres had touched the rubber pressure-pad that was let into the tarmac. He carried straight on, swerving so as to miss only narrowly some unfortunate citizen who had been crossing quite legitimately on the amber from the right. By the time that we reached them they had changed to green.

It was going up the hill at Hendon that we first started to gain on him and by the time that we were approaching the Mill Hill observatory with its green domes and white walls and could see the thin red-brick church tower, almost oriental looking, on the wooded sky-line to the front of us – was it an angel or saint on top of it, I had always wondered – he could not have been more than forty yards ahead.

"Keep your eyes open at Apex Corner," I said. "He may turn right up the Great North Road."

But the Morris carried resolutely straight on, along the Watford By-Pass.

"We'll get him now," said Molly and she put her foot hard down on the accelerator pedal.

She had spoken just too soon. The driver of the Morris chose that moment to increase his own speed too and was maintaining and even increasing the distance between us. For a moment, it was only for a moment, it passed out of our view round a left-handed bend. Then, as we too rounded it, we were confronted with the sight of what seemed like an endless convoy of slow-moving army three-tonners stretching out along the road in front of us and there was the battered Morris Ten jauntily overtaking the hindmost to the accompaniment of waving arms and ironic cheers from the soldiery within.

"Oh no!" I said.

"Never mind. When we do catch him we'll have the best part of a battalion to help us."

The attention of the soldiers, this time expressed in whistles and cat-calls, had immediately been diverted to her.

Then

"I wish to goodness there was time for me to stop and tell 'em what I think of 'em," I muttered when we too had managed to get by.

"Oh, I don't know, I rather like it," Molly said.

We caught frequent glimpses of the Morris as it overtook, sometimes two in front of us, sometimes three. But when, at last, the nineteenth or twentieth three-tonner load had expressed their aesthetic appreciation of my driver in the identical fashion and we had overtaken both it and the open jeep that preceded it, the road stretched out, long and straight and quite quite EMPTY ahead.

"Quick," I said to Molly, I had had a sudden hunch that amounted almost to a conviction, "turn in that gate-way over there and go back the way we came."

She swung across the road, in to where I had been pointing, reversed out and, in a moment, was retracing our steps and increasing speed again as the leaders of the convoy trundled by.

"Left there, by that garage," I said and I started to explain.

It was an alternative route which we sometimes used when we were driving home from London. There was just a chance – more than a chance I saw when I got out the road atlas, for where else could he have disappeared to – that the driver of the Morris had turned off that way too.

As we hurtled along the by-roads, I noted but did not really take in the various land-marks on either side that I knew so well; the Ovaltine Dairy Farm, roofs thatched with the neat symmetry of an illustrated Victorian children's book; the village of Pimlico which presented such an absurd contrast to its London namesake; the little town of Hemel Hempstead, with its curious fishbone pattern spire rising needle-sharp from square stone tower; I had my gaze riveted on the unfolding road ahead. Past Water end, with its little stone bridge and in its meadows the canal from which, no doubt, it took its name; past the almost matching set of farmsteads spaced one, two, three along the hill-side, each with its cart-track leading up to it, each with its crowning piece of woodland above.

And then, at last, we almost ran *slap into* the Morris Ten.

"Slow down a bit," I said to Molly, "We'll let him go through that village and then we'll get him."

There was a cross-roads in the middle of the village and from the left, as the car in front approached it, a cow wandered aimlessly out. It was joined by a second, then two together and two more. They were dairy short-horns. The leaders stopped and stood there flicking their tails, as they waited almost politely for the Morris to go by, and then they ambled after it, the whole herd surging out in their wake. A flanker swivelled its head round to stare at us as Molly brought the Rolls to a halt, inches from its tail. One of the horns curving horizontally before its eyes was slightly crooked, giving it somehow an expression of comical incredulity — but it was only momentarily. Every movement of its angular red hind-quarters was expressive of outraged dignity as, udder swinging, it rejoined the flow. The Morris, now safely insulated from us, was disappearing out of sight ahead.

"We're not done yet," I said. "Turn right and we may be able to cut him off."

The Rolls was moving almost before I had finished speaking, accelerating even as it turned into and along the winding, hedge-lined road. It was little more than a lane but, as far as Molly was concerned, it might have been Brooklands race-track. I sat there beside her, gripping the seat while I willed myself not to allow my anxiety that we would still be too late to transmit itself to her.

"That's the Whipsnade Lion up there beyond the lime trees," I said, as casually as I could. "It's cut out in the chalk like the White Horse, to advertise the zoo."

"Really? Let's stop and look at it, shall we?"

But she never slackened the pace.

"Turn left at the top. That's the main road ahead."

She accelerated into the turn. In a lighter car we would have taken it on two wheels.

"Now, give her everything she's got." Moments later, "A hundred and fifty yards ahead to the left, that's where the other road joins. See if you can wedge yourself across it and block him in."

I had never experienced a blow-out before. There was a sound like a paper-bag bursting, only magnified many times, from the direction of the near-fore tyre. Then came a smell of burning rubber, a rasping grinding sound, the whole chassis began to shudder, Molly was straining at the wheel in a desperate effort to keep the Rolls steady, until it mounted the grass verge and ploughed to a final and irrevocable halt, with the cross-roads a bare ten yards ahead.

Then

Stupefied, we watched as at that moment the Morris nosed out from the opening on the left, coasted across the road with insolent unhurriedness and was lost to sight towards who knew what destination on the other side.

It was only then, at this culminating blow in what had been an afternoon and evening made up of a series of near-catastrophes, that Molly's composure broke and, for the first time, allowed her true feelings to show through.

She put both her hands close together gripping the top of the steering-wheel and lowered her forehead until it rested forlornly upon them.

"Blast and DAMN!" she said.

4. Now.

'Fucking hell!' said Tisha.

It had been her turn to drive. We had been cruising along a luckily deserted country road, doing every bit of thirty-five miles an hour, when one of the rear tyres had politely but firmly subsided, the car had given a long, slow dignified swerve and had finished up with its near-fore half in and half out of a roadside grip.

'It's your fault,' I said. 'I offer you all the mod. cons. of a brand-new – well, not far short of brand-new – Citroen and you would insist on bringing along this old crock.'

Tisha glared at me. I could swear that there were little sapphire sparks shooting out at me from the depths of those greeny-brown eyes.

'How dare you call Old Rollie an old crock?' she said.

She picked up the latest *Cosmopolitan*, which had arrived crisp and new that morning, from the seat between us and propped it up against the steering wheel.

Then she grinned. 'Well, get on with it then.'

She started to turn the pages. I got out and inspected the damage. It was the near-hind tyre.

I lifted up the side of the bonnet and extracted the hub-spanner, the copper mallet and the various component parts that made up the jack. It had been a long time since I had used them, but I thought that I would probably remember how. By dint of grovelling in the road, I managed to locate the jack under what seemed to be an appropriate metal stay of some kind. I inserted the rod in the jack, the handle on the rod and began to wind.

Several weeks had gone by since that Saturday afternoon when I had first driven Tisha down to show her Thyrde. And quite a lot had happened in the intervening time.

Now

I had spent the following morning in my flat, reading the Sunday papers. There was a mention of my case in all, brief mostly but between them they covered the whole range from the purely factual to downright innuendo. One of the nastier, I remember, read like this.

> *FRIENDS in the House of Lords of popular young Tory Whip Viscount Derek Thyrde, have been wondering why his name has not yet figured in any of the lists of appointments to the new Government. They need wonder no more!*
>
> *Yesterday morning he appeared at Brampester Magistrates' Court charged with a robbery which had been committed during the run-up to the General Election.*
>
> *'Robbery', for the benefit of our less erudite readers, is theft accompanied by violence. Lord Thyrde, family motto 'Strike Thrice', is understood to be contesting the charge.*

None of the reporters had been able to get hold of me on the Saturday but their daily colleagues were having better luck. The telephone bell began to ring incessantly and such calls alternated with ones from friends who were ringing up to commiserate. Among these latter was one from my Uncle Charles.

'Derek, I want to talk to you. Look, tomorrow's a Bank Holiday, so can you lunch with me on Tuesday?'

'It'll have to be short. I'm seeing my solicitor at 3.0.'

'That's all right. Shall we say White's at 12.45, then?'

'Not White's,' I said.

'Eh? Oh, I see your point.' He suggested the name of a little restaurant in Jermyn Street and we settled for that.

I had found him waiting for me when I arrived. Whenever I hear mention of the word 'avuncular', the image that springs

Now

instantly to my mind is that of my Uncle Charles. Greying hair, grey moustache; trim figure, dressed in a way that always makes me feel that my own clothes have come straight off the counter at a jumble sale, he came to the point straight away.

'Look, Derek. First of all, did you do it?'

'No,' I said.

'That's good enough for me.'

I gave him a brief résumé of the events that had led up to the robbery and of the evidence that pointed to me.

'But you have got an alibi?'

'Yes, cast-iron.'

'That's all right then.'

'But there are very good reasons why I can't use it yet.'

'I see,' he said.

And I knew at once that he did.

My solicitor, when I had arrived punctually at his office, had seemed far less prepared to take me on trust. But that I suppose was his job.

Up to about five years before, I had stayed loyal to the family firm of solicitors but, passed from partner to partner as each retired, and finding that although the signature was different the legal fustiness not to mention the tempo of fifty years ago remained the same, I had finally rebelled and gone to a different firm, where worked a congenial friend of mine from Cambridge days. Now, sitting across his office desk from him, I wondered why I had bothered. The face, the voice, the language even, were those of young Sam Thornton, evocative of lunch at the Pitt Club and beagling teas after a long hard day on the fens, but the manner was indistinguishable from that of Frimble, Frimble and Sykes.

He wrote as I spoke, covering sheet after sheet with notes while I outlined the story, his face becoming graver all the time. And when I told him that I had been unable to give the police any account of my movements on the night of the theft, he put down his pen.

'Ahem,' he said. The metamorphosis was complete. The most recent in the sequence of Frimbles had tended to say "ahem" in just the same dry way.

'What happens next, Sam?' I asked.

'Well, the committal proceedings for a start. I think we'll have

Now

to opt for Section One.'

"Section One", he explained was a comparatively recent innovation designed to speed up commital proceedings on occasions when the Defence is not yet ready to submit "No case to answer". Instead of the Prosecution having to go through all the rigmarole of putting their case in full, calling all their witnesses and taking longhand depositions, they merely serve on the Defence and on the Court the written statements – which cover all the evidence that they would have called at this stage. Sam told me that he would arrange for a local solicitor to represent me at the committall hearing. Since I had already been granted bail, it was almost certain that it would be renewed and there was nothing to be gained in getting in any one more high-powered for a mere formality.

'And then?'

'I'll arrange for a consultation with the silk who's to represent you at the Crown Court. I'll see if I can get Sir Makepeace Brotherton. He's the best man there is for ... er, in a case like this.'

'And when will that be?'

'As soon as possible after the committal proceedings. He'll need to have read the statements, and a proof of your own evidence, of course – it's my job to submit that. Then he'll want to hear your and my comments on the evidence of each prosecution witness.' For the first time Sam relaxed and smiled. 'Makepeace Brotherton,' he said, 'has been known to get people off in even more unlikely circumstances than yours!'

'And, after that, the Crown Court?'

'Yes, but that won't be for months yet. Plenty of time for you to drum up some sort of a case for yourself. God knows you need it.'

'How do you suggest I set about it?'

'Oh, I don't know.' He sat and thought for a moment. 'Any sort of information you can get. Anything you can find out about the other possible suspects; which of them particularly needed money; what each of them was doing at the time of the theft. And you'd better get hold of those paying-in slips, the police have probably got the originals but your bank are bound to have kept photostats; they might just give you some sort of a lead. But, above all, see if you can find at least some one who might be able to vouch for your own whereabouts that night.'

Now

I came to the conclusion that the time had come for me to be more open with Sam.

'I already can. In fact, I've got an unshakeable alibi,' I said.

'Good God, man! What are you wasting my time for?' Sam was on his feet. The relaxed stage was over. Frimble was back in full force – and the most archaic one at that. 'Why didn't you tell the police?'

I explained to him that another person was involved – 'Not unusual with an alibi!' he put in, scathingly – about the promise that I had made to that person, sex unspecified, that I would only make use of it as a very last resort and that, given the months intervening between now and the Crown Court, I had every hope that I wouldn't have to use it at all.

'But it isn't as easy as that. You'll be given an "alibi warning" at the committal proceedings.'

I didn't like the sound of that.

'Alibi warning?'

'In effect, it means that we have to give the Prosecution notice, *within seven days of the end of the committal proceedings*, of the name and address of any witness that we might be wanting to call in order to establish an alibi. The whole point of it is to prevent them being taken unawares and to give them a chance to interview the witness for themselves.'

Tisha! Interview the witness for themselves. I could imagine the sort of lines on which such an interview might take place. Just the very sort of "undressing in public" that Tisha had been so anxious to avoid – for our sake, hers and mine.

'What happens if we don't give notice? Does that mean that we'll be totally precluded from using such a witness at the Crown Court?'

'That would be up to the judge to decide.'

'I'm sorry then. I'll just have to take a chance on it,' I said.

I had driven Tisha down to Thyrde again that same night, this time to stay. She had grinned when she had seen the spare room that I had arranged for her, at the other end of the house from mine, and I had made sure that she noticed that my housekeeper's room was in between.

'There's my good boy,' she said.

'Finished yet?' Tisha, *Cosmopolitan* in hand, was leaning out of

Now

the window, watching me.

'I've hardly even started. I can't get the sodding hub-nut undone. Every time I hit the hub-spanner with this hammer thing, the whole wheel turns.'

'Do you mind if I make a suggestion?'

'Please do. Cars aren't my strong point. Every time they go wrong, I scream for the A.A.'

'I think you ought to have loosened the nut before you jacked up the car.'

I began to wind the jack down again. 'Now you tell me,' I said.

Immediately after breakfast the next morning, we had gone to the library to get down to the task of detection in earnest.

'What first?' I said.

'The Rolls. Ring up the garage about it. Please, Derek, you promised!'

'Oh, all right.'

There was a telephone in the room. Mr. Barraclough undertook to send his boys round with the breakdown van to collect it that morning. He was to prepare an estimate for putting it into really first class order but, in the meantime, he was to go ahead with doing whatever was necessary to enable it to pass its M.O.T. Secretly I was sure that even *that* would come to far more than I could really afford, but the smile that Tisha gave me when I joined her on the sofa was worth it.

'The first thing to do is to make a list,' she said. While I had been at the telephone, Tisha had provided herself with a pad and felt-tipped pen. 'There's my father and Henry, of course. Who are the others?'

I gave her the names and she wrote them down.

1. Lord Frost of Highgate.
2. Henry Matheson, M.P.
3. General Dick Richards, U.S.A.F.
4. Billy Bagot, Lord Candleford.
5. Peter Stobbs, M.P.
6. Stephen Knightley.

'There is one other possibility,' I said. 'Dr. Faulkner himself. He did have that letter offering him a hell of a lot of money for that central-heating thing. He could have faked the break-in to put

Now

people off the scent and taken it himself all the time.'
'All right, we'll shove him down as well.'
She wrote,

7. *Dr. Roger Faulkner.*

I looked over her shoulder at the list. Seven names. It was a formidable one, written down like that.
'Hey, what are you doing?'
She had added,

8. *Derek, Viscount Thyrde.*

Tisha grinned at me. 'How do I know that you didn't get up in the night and sneak out and back again without my noticing?'
'Was I in any state?'
She looked at me for a moment and then emphatically she crossed my name out again.
'Seriously, though, that does bring us to opportunity. Whoever it was must have followed us to my flat and stolen that cosh gadget out of your car once we were safely upstairs.'
'I hope to God it wasn't Henry, then ... or even your father,' I said.
Tisha smiled. Then the smile faded.
'You do realise,' she said, 'that all this might come rather close to home, as far as I'm concerned. Statistically, there's a very good chance that either my father or my husband might be involved. I want you to promise me something, Derek. If it should turn out that it's likely to be either of them, Henry or Daddy, that you won't hold back for my sake.'
I leaned over and kissed her cheek.
'I promise,' I said.
'Right then, we'll give each of them a separate page and put down everything we find out as we go along.'
After some discussion, we decided that we couldn't improve on the three lines of enquiry suggested by Sam Thornton. The financial circumstances of each of the seven, their alibis or possible lack of them and the paying-in slips from the bank.
'I'll ring up the bank first,' I said.
I spoke to the manager himself. He was almost tearful in his apologies. He had received an order issued under the *Bankers' Books Evidence Act*, compelling him to reveal the state of my

Now

finances, which included of course my application for a loan and the payments subsequently received, and he had been powerless to disobey. Nor had he felt able to ignore the accompanying request that I should not be informed that such enquiries were being made. The paying-in slips were still at the bank because the police had only taken Xerox copies. No, he could not let me have the originals – he understood that these might be needed later – but he himself would personally see to it that similar copies were put in the post to me without delay.

The telephone rang before I could make the second call. I picked up the receiver.

'Hello.'

The voice was American, female, husky and attractive. 'I have a person to person call from General Alan Richards in Charlottesville, Virginia, for Viscount Thyrde, Northampton *Shire*, England,' it said.

'Thyrde here.'

It took a minute or two before I heard Dick's voice on the line.

'Derek? I've been reading about you in the papers over here but none of them have any details. Tell me what it's all about.'

I explained the almost damning case against me. But I didn't mention Tisha or my alibi.

'Look, Derek, this all seems to be tied up with the "1944 Club" and as Chairman this year I feel that I've got a personal responsibility. I'm sure that the others'll be as anxious as I am to do anything they can.'

'That's very kind of you, but ... one of you won't,' I said.

There was a slight pause.

'I see. We're all of us suspect, I as much as the rest. No, I quite understand – in your place I'd feel the same. But if there's anything I *can* do just give me a ring. I'll fly over at any time.'

'There is one thing that would be an enormous help. And you could probably do it on the telephone from where you are.'

I explained to him my need to find out about the whereabouts of each of the seven at the time in question.

'It may take a day or two, but I'll ring you back,' he said.

Then I dialled my stockbroker's number.

'Simon? Derek here. Is it possible to check up whether a particular person is, or recently has been, in need of money?'

'Just give me the name of one person who isn't these days.'

'No, I'm serious. If I were to give you a list of seven names, would you be able to find out if any of them have been in financial difficulties?'

'Sure, but . . . is it in connection with this trouble of yours?'

'Yes.'

'All right. Give me the names and I'll see what I can do.'

I dictated the list over to him.

The letter from the bank had arrived on the following day.

Tisha and I spent the whole morning in going through the Xerox copies of the paying-in slips and most of the afternoon discussing the results. Exactly thirty payments had been made. Each had been made out to *The Viscount Thyrde* and the address of my bank and even my account number were correct in every case. The handwriting, which was scribbled but still legible, appeared to be the same. Care had only been taken with the name of the payer-in, which had been written in block capitals – P. JANSSEN. Each payment had been made up of twenty, ten, five and one pound notes and totalled odd amounts, all different, the lowest just over seven hundred pounds and the highest just under nine. They had been paid in each at a different branch, not all of my own bank, in Greater London and over a period of four consecutive days. But leading up to Good Friday, they had been a particularly busy four days for banks and, as the manager had pointed out in his covering letter, ones on which the appearance of an individual depositor was least likely to have been noticed – let alone remembered.

'It's hopeless,' I said to Tisha at last. 'We'll never be able to check up on all those. A handwriting expert might be able to do something with the slips, but I doubt it. We'll just have to wait for the other information to come in.'

The telephone had rung that evening.

'It's for you,' said Tisha. 'I couldn't catch his name.'

Simon or Dick, with any luck. I ran and took it from her. But it was only Mr. Barraclough from the garage. The Rolls had passed its M.O.T. and the estimate for further work was now ready for me to discuss with him. I arranged that we should meet him at his house on the following morning.

Tisha had been right. Once the flat tyre was down on the road again and the wheel held steady, a few taps with the mallet and I

Now

was able to loosen the hub-nut by a couple of turns. I checked to see if it would undo by hand and then I began the laborious process of winding up the jack again.

'Sorry Tom's not here to meet you, m'Lord.' Mrs. Barraclough had met us at the door. 'He be gone down to the garage to fetch your car. You come on in, me duck,' she said to Tisha, who looked slightly startled. It was only later that I was able to explain to her that it was a highly localised expression of endearment and that its use signified the highest form of compliment that it was possible to bestow. I had the Rolls's mascot in my hand.

We were shown into the front room, where Mrs. Barraclough apologised and left us. The kitchen floor was awash, it seemed – the electric washing-machine had been playing up again.

I had dim memories of that room as being one of glorious clutter, to the meanest item of which no present day antique shop would dream of denying a place. Mr. Barraclough, as yet unmarried, had lived there with his mother and it had been the kitchen then.

All that was gone now. The cast-iron range, blacked daily and in which coke embers had glowed summer and winter alike, had given place to a gas fire in a stepped marble surround; a trio of improbably bright plaster cock-pheasants, a change from the usual mallard, ascended diagonally the textured paper of one wall; on the top of the upright piano stood a single gilt-framed photograph of my mother and father on their wedding day.

Tisha and I sat perched on the unyielding sofa element of a three-piece suite until Mr. Barraclough, a scrawny, bald-headed man, came bustling in.

'Sorry to keep you waiting, Derek,' he said. He called me "Derek" and "m'Lord" in approximately equal proportions. 'I've worked out that estimate you was asking for.'

Almost a father-figure from my childhood, conveyor to countless children's parties, gymkhanas and school-trains, and confidant on all sorts of unlikely issues, I've never yet been able to bring myself to call him "Tom", but this was clearly to be one of his less formal days.

He handed me a sheaf of papers and I leafed through them. The first three sheets formed a medical diagnosis of the poor old car's bodily condition and that of its internal organs. The surgeon's fee

Now

was itemised on the final page.

Tisha looked over my shoulders as I skimmed down the list with growing horror until I finally came to the grand total – £10,460 – at the bottom of the page.

'I'll have to think about it,' I said.

Mr. Barraclough nodded kindly. 'There may be a bit more to do that we come across once we get started, but that lot'll give you a rough guide. If you leave her another winter, I doubt she'll be worth the saving. Ah, you've got the "Emily" there, I see.'

' "Emily"? Oh this.' I held up the silver flying lady. At some stage in its career, it must have been given a fairly hefty knock. The head was tilted to one side, which gave her a distinctly dissolute look that I had always found rather endearing.

'That's what we used to call them at Rolls-Royce, when I worked there for a spell after the war. They've got another name, more high-falutin, but I never could remember it.'

'Spirit of Ecstasy?'

'That's it.' He held out his hand. 'You give that me, Derek. I'll have it straightened out for you in a jiffy.'

'Actually, I rather like it like this.'

'Please yourself. Glad you're going to use the old car, though. Always did have a soft spot for her. I could tell you a story or two about that there Rolls-Royce ... if I'd a mind to,' he said.

The Rolls was standing in the road outside. Washed, polished to a certain extent – the paintwork was matt but at least the chrome was gleaming – it still looked like a certain candidate for the knacker's yard. I took the black plastic off the top of the radiator and screwed on the "Spirit of Ecstasy" in its place. Then I stepped backwards and lined up the lady's wings with the hinge-line at the apex of the bonnet. Immediately, I became aware of just how much it was that Messrs. Rolls–Royce had owed to the sculptor, Sykes. Age had become dignity. It was an undeniable Rolls again.

'Come on,' I said to Tisha, 'I'll take you for a drive.'

After the power-assisted Citroen, the steering felt like that of an articulated lorry. The engine sounded like one too. I had to keep on reminding myself that the gear-lever and handbrake were on my right-hand side. The sun was shining and we had both side-windows open. Rattled about, exhilarated and wind-swept – my hair was blown all over my face, but Tisha's short curls remained

Now

maddeningly unaffected – we ground along the country lanes. She looked up at me, her face glowing.

'May I have a go. Please?'

She drove us home.

Back outside the house, Tisha looked across at me. 'Sad to think that he won't last long. That estimate was beyond all reason, of course. You couldn't possibly afford all that.'

It was a statement of fact rather than a question. Even so, I thought that I could detect the merest suspicion of hope in her voice.

I had to shake my head.

In the days that followed, the information for which we had been waiting had started to come in.

First from Simon, my stockbroker friend.

Billy Candleford, as I had suspected, was the richest of the lot. Simon hadn't been able to find out exactly how much he was worth but, on the "to him who hath" principle adopted by banks, they would have been prepared to lend him any amount more. *Henry Matheson* was thought not to have a lot of capital but he was a director of innumerable companies and, in addition to his parliamentary salary, Simon reckoned that he must have had an income of a good twenty thousand a year. *Peter Stobbs* had no visible source of income outside *his* parliamentary salary, but it was known that he was sponsored as an M.P. by one of the bigger Trades Unions and there would have been something coming to him on that score. *Dr. Faulkner* again had nothing more than the not over-generous salary that he received as Director of the Farmwell Foundation, but he must have been living well within it, because he had never in his life been known to have so much as an overdraft nor to have left a bill of any size long unpaid. *Leonard Frost* too was a director of several reputable companies and he seemed to have accumulated quite a respectable amount of capital besides. *General Dick Richards*, surprisingly enough, was not by any means as well off as I would have thought. But Dunn and Bradstreet had given him a credit rating modest but reliable. *Stephen Knightley*, like all farmers, suffered from a perennial cash flow problem, but he farmed six-hundred-and-fifty acres all of which he owned and over which, unlike me, he had unfettered control. At two thousand pounds per acre this put him, on paper at least, well into the millionaire class.

Now

Next, from General Dick Richards. He had done a lot of telephoning, poor chap, all transatlantic calls. He gave me the results of his research. God knows what his telephone bill for that month must have turned out to be.

Billy, on leaving Farmwell, had driven on across country to his house in Suffolk where, since his divorce some eighteen months before, he lived alone. He had spent the evening watching television until the programmes ended. A daily woman had come in from the village the next morning and brought him his breakfast in bed. *Henry* had driven up to Birmingham. The booking in the hotel where he usually stayed had somehow gone astray, all the other main ones had been full and he had ended up in a motel. He couldn't remember its name or even its precise location but he reckoned he could find it again if he went up there. The police hadn't seemed all that interested, however, and he was damned if he was going to go to all that trouble merely to satisfy my curiosity. *Peter* had driven North-West to his constituency where he had a pied-a-terre. He had left his wife behind in London, so he too had spent the night alone. *Roger* I already knew about. He had taken care not to waken his wife when he had finally got home to bed. *Stephen* had broken his journey back to Hampshire by staying the night at the Farmers' Club in London. He had eaten out and gone to a cinema afterwards. *Leonard* had been at his house in Highgate. He had warmed up the meal that Tisha had cooked for him during the day, eaten it in front of the television set and gone early to bed. And there Dick's information came to an end.

'I'm terribly sorry to ask, after all the trouble you've taken, but ... where were you that night?' I said.

There was a long pause and then he laughed. 'I was afraid you'd ask me that. Look, Derek, I know you'll keep this to yourself.'

Dick had been staying at the Westbury, but on that particular evening he had rung up a call-girl – the number had been given to him by the commissionaire at another hotel where he had dined – and he had spent the night at her flat. He couldn't remember the address, it was in a street not far from Paddington Station, but he had her telephone number written down in his diary and this he could give me, if I would hold on for a minute.

'No, please don't bother. I really *am* grateful,' I said.

Now

Tisha was looking out of the window again. 'How are you getting on?'
  'Not too badly,' I said. 'I've got the old wheel off, at any rate.' I put the hub-nut carefully down on top of it, where it now lay on the roadside grass.'
  'Let's see. Take new wheel from beside bonnet – I think the one on the left looks the better of the two. Put it on. Do up hub-nut to hand-tightness. Lower jack and then, when tyre meets road, tighten up properly with hub-spanner. Right?'
  'Right,' said Tisha. She went back to her Cosmopolitan. I began the sequence.

On the second day after our arrival at Thyrde, I had driven over to see my mother who lived only two villages away. I had asked her whether there had ever been a signet ring in the family. Yes, my father had had one once – she thought it had belonged to my grandfather – but that had been stolen years ago, before they were even engaged in fact. Talking about it had seemed to upset her and when, over lunch, I had tried to impress on her the seriousness of the predicament that I was in she hadn't shown a lot of interest. 'Of course it'll be all right darling, you'll see. It won't take them long to find out they've just made a silly mistake.' And then she had gone straight on to describe the latest disgusting symptom evinced by her collie, Bridget's, urinary tract. I still regretted the better part of a perfectly cooked fillet steak, red and oozing, which I had had to push queasily away.

Since then, I had been feeling progressively guiltier that I still hadn't taken Tisha to meet her and it had now become an omission that had to be remedied without further delay. I had parked the Rolls outside the railings that topped her low garden wall.

'Good morning. How's the Dowager,' I had called.

The garden itself might have been transported there direct from the Chelsea Flower Show. A blended mass of reds and blues and yellows in a two-yard-strip surrounded a rectangle of lawn shaven to billiard-cloth perfection. A tweed-skirted bottom had obtruded from the section of bed at the far right-hand end. A smooth-coated tricolour collie bitch, attention riveted on all that was visible of her mistress, had been sitting upright and rock-still on the grass between.

Now

The collie turned her head to look at us and gave four or five welcoming thumps on the grass with her white-tagged tail before reverting her gaze to the figure which, having straightened up and turned, was now starting to come towards us.

In her mid-fifties, hair sweeping down almost pure white now over a slightly weather-beaten face, my mother still had the body of a girl of eighteen.

'Sit, Bridget,' she said as she passed. It was quite unnecessary. The collie's head was pivoting slowly but the rest of her hadn't moved an inch.

'This is my Mama — Tisha Matheson,' I said.

They shook hands.

'My father's an old friend of Derek's, Lady Thyrde. They're both members of the . . .' too late, I realised that I had forgotten to warn Tisha not to mention the, for some reason, controversial "1944 Club" in my mother's presence, but she stopped short the moment she felt my elbow in her ribs — '. . . er, what a lovely garden,' she said.

She couldn't have done better, but the conducted tour that ensued as an immediate result took all of half an hour.

'When does your case come up, Derek?' said my mother at last. 'My stupid son's gone and got himself mixed up in a spot of bother, Tisha. I may call you "Tisha"?'

'Next Tuesday,' I said.

'You're still quite sure you don't want me to come . . .'

'Quite sure.'

'. . . because it really wouldn't be *at all* convenient. I've got Sally Armitage coming to lunch and . . .' She broke off. She had caught a glimpse of the Rolls through the railings and the sight of it had immediately driven even such a vital issue as a loquacious hen luncheon party with Mrs. Armitage, to say nothing of a triviality like a court case, clean out of her mind. 'Derek, darling! You've got her going again. I'm so glad.'

'Yes, but not for long, I'm afraid.'

I told her what Mr. Barraclough had said about the terminal state of Old Rollie if left in its present condition and the astronomical proportions of his estimate for putting it right.

'Don't worry about that. You go ahead. I'll pay.'

'You mustn't . . .'

I knew my mother's strictly limited income to a penny — or I

Now

thought I did. Her needs seemed to be pretty small, of course...

'Nonsense, darling. One of my shareholdings trebled in value quite unexpectedly last month and I'm disgustingly rich. This is one thing I'd really like to do. No more arguments, I've made up my mind,' she said.

Blissfully, we had driven back to see Mr. Barraclough and to ask him to put the work in hand.

'But not for a day or two, so that we can use him for a bit first,' Tisha had decided on the way.

On the following Tuesday, Tisha had driven me over to Brampester Magistrates' Court − in the Citroen. Much to her disgust, on this occasion I had refused to rely on the Rolls. My case had been second on the list.

As I stood in the dock this time, a feeling of doom-laden claustrophobia came over me. I was as good as a convicted criminal already. On the raised Bench under the Royal Coat of Arms at the far end sat the magistrates, three of them − on my previous appearance they had only been able to rustle up two. The Chairman was an elderly woman who looked at me through a pair of spectacles with light-coloured rims, as though I were a small boy whom she had just caught stealing the jam. I couldn't help feeling that she would have been happier with a lorgnette. On either side of her sat respectively a middle-aged man with a quizzical rather owlish expression who might have been a local farmer and a younger very pretty woman who was obviously somebody's wife. None of them I knew. Immediately below them sat the Clerk of the Court, surrounded by legal volumes. Nearer to me again was the solicitor who was to represent me, a thin nervous little man who didn't seem too happy about his task and his opposite number − a barrister this one, I had been told − who looked all too confident. The seats allotted to the general public on the left were almost empty but to the right those for the Press were full.

The Clerk read out the charges. Once again the principal one was *Robbery* under Section 8 of the Theft Act, 1968, but this time the Prosecution had furnished themselves with a choice of two alternatives, *Burglariously entering with intent to steal* under Section 9 of the same act and *Occasioning actual bodily harm to the person of Arthur Wills* (the security guard) under Section 47 of the Offences Against the Person Act, 1861.

Now

My acting temporary but not, I fear, unpaid solicitor rose to his feet.

'Er ... I appear for the Defence and we are agreed that there should be a Section One Committal to the Crown Court.'

Then it was the turn of the barrister appearing for the Director of Public Prosecutions.

'In view of possible local feeling, we are both asking that the case should go to the Central Criminal Court.'

The Chairman peered forward.

'Are the Statements in order?'

The barrister picked up a formidable bundle of papers tied round with pink tape and gave it to the Usher who took it up to the Bench.

'Very well. Committed to the Central Criminal Court at a date to be announced later. Bail has been fixed at ... let me see, five thousand pounds. Yes, I think that's in order.'

My man had one more line to deliver.

'I am asking for all the witnesses to be fully bound over to attend the trial.'

'So be it,' said the Chairman.

It was as easy as that.

Late in the afternoon, Sam Thornton had rung up to ask how it had gone.

'Oh, by the way, I've managed to get Sir Makepeace Brotherton for you.'

He told me the date that had been fixed for he and I to go round to his chambers. It was some ten days ahead.

In the evening, Tisha and I had gone over and over everything that we *had* managed to find out about the other seven, and pretty hopeless it was. All of them had perfectly believable stories as to where they had been at the time of the theft. None of them seemed to be in need of money to an extent that would have justified the risk.

'There is one thing,' Tisha said at last. 'That central-heating device. It must be worth quite a lot, hundreds of thousands even, for the thief to be able to lash out twenty-five thousand pounds, merely as groundbait so to speak.'

I stared at her. 'Clever girl!' I said. 'I'd never thought of that. If it's anything like that sort of money, any one of them might be interested in it, even Billy ... especially Billy!'

Now

'How'll you find out? Ring up Dr. Faulkner?'
'No, he's one of them, remember. I'll do better than that.'
All this had been yesterday.

At nine o'clock this morning, I had rung up *British Light & Power*. Lord Stanstead's secretary had consulted his diary. Could I be at his office at 4.30 sharp?

This time we *had* taken Old Rollie. Tisha had been so insistent that I hadn't had the heart to say no. She was to drop me at the railway station and then drive him back to Mr. Barraclough's garage where he was booked in to start his series of major operations. But I had insisted on allowing a good hour longer for the journey than I would have done otherwise — which was just as well!

It was to keep that appointment that I was on my way now.

I gave the hub-spanner a final tap with the copper mallet and straightened up. I picked up the old wheel and stowed it away in the boot, followed by the jack and the mallet and hub-spanner themselves. Then I rubbed as much dirt and oil off my hands as I could with a piece of old rag, threw that in after them, slammed the boot-lid shut and went round to climb in beside Tisha.

She was still immersed. I removed the Cosmopolitan forcibly.

'Bedford Station please, James, and you'd better kick on a bit. I've barely time for one more puncture as it is, if I'm to catch my train!'

'It really is very good of you to see me, Sir,' I said.

Lord Stanstead sat and glared at me. He had been a Cabinet Minister long before my time as a Whip and he was now in the very top league of chairmen of boards. Once or twice it had been my task to ring him up from the House of Lords and ask him to take part in industrial and economic debates. That and saying "good morning" to him whenever we had happened to meet in the corridor had been the limit of our acquaintance so far.

'Well, don't waste my time. I'd have thought that you've caused me enough trouble already.'

In any other circumstances, his tone would have had me quivering like a schoolboy. But I had been through too much just lately.

'You don't subscribe, then, to the convention that a man is

Now

innocent until he's proved guilty?' I said.

The effect was instantaneous and dramatic. He jumped up from his chair and came forward round the desk to meet me.

'My dear chap,' he said. 'Do forgive me, I've got a lot on my mind at the moment. Now then, sit down and tell me how I can help you.'

I told him everything. The full extent of the case against me, even he hadn't realised just how damning it was, and of my need to know how much the thief would be likely to get for the device.

'Well, let's see.' He took out a piece of headed paper and scribbled some figures it. 'We've known for a month or two that the people who wrote that letter to Faulkner — I'd better not tell you their name — have been working along much the same lines as us. It's a very rough guess, but if I were in their position, and assuming that I was prepared to play that sort of game, I'd say that somewhere between twenty and thirty thousand pounds would be a fair price — if you can use such a word as "fair" in this context.'

'Good God! Is that all?'

'Yes, it isn't much of a breakthrough, you know. Once you've decided what you want to achieve, it's just a question of setting up the appropriate circuitry. What they'd be buying is time, their gain of it and our loss of it, that and the advantage of getting their product on the market first. They might go as far as thirty-five thousand, but I doubt it. All they offered Faulkner was eighteen.'

My initial reaction was one of amazement that any one should go to so much trouble, not to mention risk, for such a small return. But suddenly the full significance of what he had been saying did hit me. All this time I had been assuming that the real thief had stolen the device for the money that it would fetch and that I had just happened to be a convenient scapegoat. But I had got it the wrong way round. After paying out my twenty-five thousand, there would have been little or nothing left over. There was ... could be, only one explanation.

I stood up and stared at Lord Stanstead across the desk.

Why, heaven alone knew, but the theft at Farmwell that night had been carried out for one reason and one reason only.

That of discrediting me.

iv. Then

Across the desk from him, Molly and I stood rigidly to attention. I was feeling, as I had not felt since my first year as a lower boy at Eton, when I had had to present yet another *rip* signifying excruciating work to my tutor for his signature, that it was all a dream and at any moment I would wake up; that it was not really me; that I was not really there; but now as then knowing all along, at the back of my mind but with utter certainty, that I really was there. That it really was me. That it had happened — all of it. That it was no dream and there would be no waking up. I could *feel* those eyes of Commander Jackson's boring into me.

"I swear to God," he said, "I'll never use amateurs again."

"I really am most awfully sorry, Sir," I said. "What shall we do now?"

"Do?" the red of his face was turning visibly brighter. "What can you do? Haven't you done enough already? Go back to your battalion, of course — God help them."

"That's not fair, Sir," — it was Molly who spoke this time. "I persuaded him to leave me at Harrods, against his better judgment. And you insisted on Lord Thyrde carrying that paper about with him, in spite of the fact that he protested about how risky it was. It's you and I who are to blame — not him."

"No, I won't have that," I said. "Whatever Molly . . . er, Miss Stanton says, she did have the sense to check up on whether that telephone message was genuine. It was my fault and mine alone."

But Commander Jackson had turned his attention to Molly. She was facing him, her little chin was thrust forward and her pale blue eyes were blazing with an intensity that I hoped that she would never focus on me.

"Not fair, is it?" he said. "You split up which was the one thing that I warned you not to do. Neither of you even bothered to take down the number of the car. And all that I've told him to do is to go back to his battalion." He looked towards me, appealingly

Then

almost. "That's what you want, isn't it?"

It had been. But that had been yesterday. All that I desperately wanted now was to be given another chance to try and do something... anything... to clear up the mess that I had made of it.

"No, Sir," I said.

There was no sarcasm in his voice, only weariness, when he spoke next.

"And what do you think you can do better than – even a tenth as well as – my trained men?"

"Look Sir," I said, "I know I've made the most awful ass of myself but I do still know all of the seven people involved. I can get close to them in a way that your people can't. Will you let us have one more shot at it?"

He sat there for what seemed like a long time, tapping the desk with his pen and looking at me as though he were trying to reassess my character and capability. Then he gave a slight nod.

"You neither of you tried to push off the blame onto the back-up that I promised you. I like that. I'll be having a word or two to say to *them*, later. All right, sit down both of you. I don't suppose there's a lot more damage you can do and – you might just blunder into something useful at that."

* * *

The damage, he told us, was not absolutely irreparable – *yet*. The one really vital piece of information that the paper contained was incidental to its main subject matter and it was not discernible by just looking at it, however brilliant or knowledgeable its present possessor might be. To find out precisely what it signified would require facilities which the Commander was confident that the spy himself would neither have at his disposal nor find it easy to obtain. Nor would he be able to describe the paper over the radio in anything like enough detail to enable the enemy to do so. He would need to get the actual paper physically out of the country and into their hands and that was what we must now at all costs prevent.

At all costs. One solution was obvious – at first sight. We knew that the spy was one of seven men each of whom could be located and pulled in within a matter of hours. It would mean arresting six

Then

innocent men in order to stop one guilty one, subjecting them to every kind of indignity and holding them until the spy could be identified or, if that should not prove to be possible, until the immediate danger that he represented was past. And Commander Jackson would have done it — he had the power to do so, even though they included three Members of Parliament, a Peer of the Realm, an officer in our own armed forces and another in those of our closest ally — if it would have achieved the desired result. But it now seemed certain that the spy had at least one accomplice.

"Your pocket being picked in the underground train, for example. You're sure that none of the seven was in that compartment?"

"Virtually certain."

"And he must have had some one at Farmwell. Unless it was your school chum, of course, in which case, he could have stolen the paper himself in the first place. But that still leaves the train."

And the accomplice might be holding the paper now and not the spy. If that were the case, arresting and holding the spy in common with six others would not only *not* prevent the paper leaving the country but it would also alert the enemy to the lengths to which we were prepared to go to regain it, thereby confirming to them the vital importance that we placed on it, the very thing that we were so anxious to avoid.

Luckily getting the stolen paper out of the country would not be easy for them. At this stage in the war we had virtual control of the Channel; we were now able, with Radio Direction Finding equipment and A.S.D.I.C., to locate any enemy ship that might approach, even under water, long before it came into visual range; and the actual pick-up presented so many hazards that it would entail a great deal of careful planning if it were to stand any chance of success at all, so in all probability we still had a certain amount of time.

Commander Jackson had arranged for the movements of each of the seven to be monitored as far as was practicable by his own men but, since for *them* to make any close enquiries would only risk arousing the suspicions of the spy, there was little chance of their being able to identify him in the meantime.

This then, was the task that was once again to be allotted to Molly and me.

"Your leave was due to be up tomorrow and no doubt some of

Then

them will know that. I'll arrange for you to be posted to the *Department for Inter-Service Co-ordination of Administration and Supply* at the War Office. Report to Brigadier Broadbent there at 0900 tomorrow, both of you."

"Thank you very much indeed, Sir."

The air of calm efficiency that he had been managing to show for the last ten minutes suddenly deserted him again and there was something of a plea in his voice.

"Just get it back, that's all," he said.

* * *

"Welcome," said Brigadier Broadbent, "to the Department for Inter-Service Co-ordination of Administration and Supply."

Grey hair that had once been sandy, moustache trained to either side, still sandy but soon to be grey, he was a bright breezy cheerful man of nearly sixty. You could have shaved yourself in the depth of polish on the Sam Browne belt that bisected his red-tabbed, bemedalled service-dress jacket and used the creases of his trousers to do it with. A gold fox's mask stick-pin held his khaki tie in place and there was an eye-glass, cordless and rimless but so secure that it might have been glued into position, in his left eye.

"Now then," he said to me, "how much do you know about this department?"

"Hardly anything, I'm afraid, Sir."

"Good. Good. Just as it should be. And you, my dear. I understand that you haven't contributed anything very much to the war effort yet and now you feel that you'd like to do something practical. Splendid, Splendid."

Molly gaped at him.

"No, Sir, you don't understand . . ." I said, but the Brigadier held up his hand.

"I know. I know. But we're all play-actors here and it's as well to get into the part from the beginning. Well, I think I've got just the job for you, civilian driver to Lord Thyrde, here. He's going to have a lot to do."

Molly and I looked at each other appalled. God knows it was going to be hard enough chasing after seven different people with the seemingly hopeless task of trying to repair the damage that I

Then

had done, but if at the same time we were going to have to drive round on all sorts of errands for this obscure War Office department, I might as well not even try.

"What exactly will my duties be, Sir?" I said.

"Duties? Duties? Why that's up to you, my dear chap." Suddenly he smiled. "May be," he said, "I had better explain."

The department for Inter-Service Co-ordination of Administration and Supply did not, in a manner of speaking, exist. By this stage in the war, innumerable intelligence organisations had come into being. Some big, some small, they had different functions and worked in different ways, but they all had one thing in common – their personnel needed considerable back-up facilities. Above all they needed cover stories which would enable them to make any journeys, visit any establishments and ask any questions, without arousing suspicion in the people whom they were seeking to investigate.

To meet this need and at the same time to avoid duplication in the use of skilled personnel who were in all too short supply, a special department had been set up. It was headed by four men, a senior officer from each of the three main fighting services and a civil servant, a recently retired permanent under-secretary. And, for reasons of security, the department had no name – or more accurately it had a multiplicity of names, one for every separate operation in which it was engaged. For us, and for us alone, it was to be the Department for Inter-Service Coordination of Administration and Supply.

"And it's not a bad name, either," said Brigadier Broadbent. "Nothing is more instantly believable than red tape – particularly dull-sounding red tape. Here's how it works."

From now on we were to have no further contact with Norfolk House or Commander Jackson unless or until we heard from him. We were to deal instead with this mythical department, which would act as a two-way clearing-house for information. All letters and telephone calls so addressed would be channelled through to him – he was of course the Army member of the quadrumvirate – or his staff and the use of this exclusive name would have the added advantage of alerting them immediately to the fact that the communication referred to our particular operation. Anything that we wanted to know, no matter how stupid it might sound, they would find out for us. Whenever we needed to go anywhere

Then

or meet anybody, we would be issued with orders that would enable us to do so. Furthermore these orders would be so geared as to make it seem natural for us to ask the very sort of questions that we might want to ask. Everything that Molly and I, in our turn, found out was to be passed on through them.

We were to keep as close as possible to all the suspects. I was to start off with an official visit on behalf of the Department to each of the seven and these could be followed up as many times as might prove necessary. In addition he advised me to establish some form of social contact with each of them, if possible connected with a recreation in which they had a particular interest – "Catch a man at his pet hobby, that's when he'll let his hair down" – and on these occasions Molly could take part too. Oh yes, and we were to go on using the Rolls.

"Isn't it a bit conspicuous?" I asked.

"Yes, but they all know you've got it – the spy does at any rate. And in a way it will serve as protective colouring. Nobody in his senses who was doing any sort of secret work would dream of using a car as easily identifiable as that."

Just then, the telephone rang, the red one from among the three of his desk. Brigadier Broadbent picked up the receiver.

"Hello ... Yes, he's here now ... and Miss Stanton ... Right-ho, Sir, I'll tell him."

He turned back to us. "That was your Commander Jackson. I *have* got one piece of information for you but it's only negative, I'm afraid. So far as he's been able to find out, none of your seven friends owns a Morris Ten."

* * *

"Did you notice anything odd about the telephone call?" I said to Molly. We were just leaving the outskirts of Greater London on our way back to Thyrde.

"No, should I have done?"

"Our new boss called Commander Jackson 'Sir'."

"I thought that was just suitable respect shown by a pongo to the Royal Navy," said Molly innocently. "Why? Is a Brigadier-General senior to a Commander?"

"Brigadier," I said. "Brigadier-Generals went out with the horses. We pongos have our verbal niceties too, you know."

Then

"Well, is he?"

"Yes, by a couple of notches."

Molly gave a low whistle. "I always thought there was more to old Jackie than met the eye."

We drove on in silence.

"I still think it's a mistake making us use the Rolls," Molly said at last. "It really is far too conspicuous. Haven't you got anything a bit more ordinary?"

"Only my old M.G. and that's pretty unreliable."

"Even so, it could be better than this."

"Tell you what," I said. "Young Tom Barraclough, the chap who met us at the station, it's him who's been keeping the Rolls in this perfect condition. I might get him to give the M.G. a thorough overhaul, just in case. We'll call in and fix it up the moment we get back."

* * *

"We've really come to see Tom," I said.

The wheels of the Rolls had splashed through water in the potholes to where the cottage stood by itself some half a mile up the lane that led to the woods. Old Barraclough, the game-keeper, had lived on there after his retirement, as had his wife and son since his recent death.

"There's something I want to ask him to do – it's not only for me, it could make a real contribution to the War."

"He'll like that," said Mrs. Barraclough, "been fretting, our Tom have, ever since the Army turned him down on account of his feet, joined the Home Guard straight after, an' I tell him he'm doing his bit, same be every-one else, but I know he feels it's not the same really, an' he worships you too, m'Lord, started growing a moustache, he done, soon as he seen yours t'other day, he's upstairs now, tidying his-self up after working in that nasty dirty garage all day, comes home all grease and such-like, he do, don't get me wrong," the momentary look of disapproval that had crossed her face vanished as quickly as it had come, "he'm a good lad, be our Tom, wouldn't be his father's son else, I'll just go an' hurry him along."

During the merciful lull that followed – Mrs. Barraclough's conversation invariably consisted of one continuous never-ending

Then

sentence – Molly looked in fascination round the room.

The floor, red quarry-tiles polished until they might have been marble; the kitchen-range itself; the monochrome Landseer stags, some belligerent, some at ease, in bird's-eye maple frames; the sampler, '*Unless the Lord bless the House*', colours red for brickwork and green for the stylised fir-trees on either side so faded that they were only just discernible against the general drab of the back-ground; the two oil-lamps, one hanging by gleaming brass chains from the wood-slat ceiling, the other on a table beside the basket-chair, where only Barraclough himself had sat but always left empty now; the hollow cow-horn, one blast from which he had always used to activate the line of beaters at the beginning of every drive; the stuffed jay and magpie, each in its glass dome frozen at the point of alighting; and how much more besides. Above all the atmosphere of frowstiness, the old man had never allowed the window of that room to be opened and the tradition still lingered, the all-pervading smell, not unpleasant but distinctive, part paraffin part boiled cabbage in approximately equal proportions, but I fancy that there was more than a touch of damp in there somewhere too.

The door opened and the grinning freckled face of young Tom, newly scrubbed and bearing the incipient shadow of the moustache, peered round it. He came in hesitantly, followed by his mother.

"How do, Miss. Hello, Mr. Derry ... er, sir ... m'Lord."

" 'Mr. Derry' will do," I said.

Tom looked at me expectantly. I told him what I wanted. There was a pause during which the grin faded to be replaced by a look of disappointment.

"Is that all, Sir? I'll be glad to, of course, but I were hoping..." Suddenly he seemed overcome with embarrassment. Molly came to his rescue.

"I don't suppose Tom would be available if we needed his active help at any time, driving or something like that, would he?" She looked at me appealingly, as did Tom.

I glanced from one to the other. It might not be a bad idea at that.

"Would you do that," I said, "if we were to get in touch with you?"

Tom's delight was instantly apparent but he seemed for a

Then

moment to be groping for words adequate to express it. He found them.

"I don't mind," he said.

5. Now

'I'll just run through the salient points again, if you don't mind,' said Sir Makepeace Brotherton.

I had known the name well enough and heard some of the many stories about him. Who hasn't? But in the taxi on the way to the consultation – Queen's Counsel it seems hold consultations rather than conferences – Sam Thornton had filled in some of the gaps in my knowledge.

His father had been a miner in County Durham, a highly respected man who had first gone to the pitface at the age of fourteen, and who had largely educated himself by reading, when he got home in the evenings, the Bible and the more verbose Victorian novelists in approximately equal proportions. It was after his favourite from among the latter that he had named his three sons. The advantage thus conferred may have been a dubious one, but he had gone to considerable personal sacrifice to try to secure for each of them a better start in life than he himself had had. And he had not been unsuccessful. All three had managed to get into the nearest Grammar School. All three had been commissioned during or soon after the last war, but when they had left the services their subsequent careers had diverged.

William, the eldest, had established himself as a local shopkeeper in a modest but comfortable way. The youngest, who had drawn the even shorter straw, in the way of a Christian name, of "Thackeray", had proved to be the biggest disappointment because he had stubbornly insisted on emulating his father by going back into the mines. Even he had had a certain amount of success. He had become an official in the National Union of Mineworkers, not a very high-up one it is true, but there was something compelling about the strength of his radical views and the blunt-spoken way in which he expressed them and he was often to be seen in front of the television cameras. If at any time the respective leaders of the Scottish or Yorkshire miners seemed

Now

in his eyes to be veering too dangerously towards the Primrose League, there at some point in the background would *Thack* Brotherton be, correcting their course from behind.

But, of the three, Makepeace alone would have justified the old man's efforts. His rise at the Bar had been exceptional. In common with many other great advocates, he combined immense application with a near photographic memory but to these, with Makepeace, was added a third element and one that is sometimes lacking in his profession, a marked degree of sheer common sense. As often as not he had won his cases, not by summoning to his aid some obscure but relevant point of law, but by being able to suggest some everyday explanation for the otherwise suspect behaviour of his client that was instantly believable to the lay mind. Added to this, his own behaviour could be unconventional in the extreme if not verging on the unethical, in that he had been known in the run-up to a trial himself to precipitate events that he could use later during it.

'There's a trick of his,' Sam had said, 'for which he's well known at the Bar. More of a mannerism, really, because I doubt if he even realises that he does it. Whenever he's on his feet speaking, he grips the two sides of his gown and eases them up a fraction of an inch at a time so that the neck hangs lower and lower down his back. But the moment he's sure he's winning, and he's never been known to be wrong about that yet, he jerks his hands down again in one sharp movement and immediately his gown is hanging properly again. You watch out for it, when the times comes. If you see him do that, you'll know you're home and dry.'

I can't remember now quite what I had been expecting, what sort of identikit picture I had been building up subconsciously of Sir Makepeace Brotherton, Q.C., but whatever it was I'm sure that it hadn't remotely approached the reality. A very little man had stood up behind the desk in his King's Bench Walk chambers to greet us, dark hair brushed smoothly back, black coat and striped trousers, he couldn't have been more than five foot two or three. If his desk and chair hadn't been there for comparison, I doubt if his height would have been noticeable, every part of him being scaled down perfectly in proportion, everything but his eyebrows, that is. Those would have been prominent on a man of six foot six and nineteen stone, tangling out nearly an inch in front

Now

of his face.

'I've read the statements, Lord Thyrde, and the proof of your own evidence.' He had spoken very softly but every word was measured and distinct. There was only the faintest trace of North Country in his voice. 'I think that Mr. Thornton has sent me all the relevant facts, but I'd like to hear it from you, in your own words.'

I had gone through it all, including what little Tisha and I had been able to find out since, his Junior making notes and sitting silently by. When I had finished, there had been a long pause during which he had seemed to study my face from beneath those disconcerting eyebrows.

Then, 'I'll just run through the salient points again,' he said.

He got up from his chair and came round and stood a few feet in front of me, gripping a lapel of his black coat in either hand.

'Well now, let me see if I've got it right. Towards the end of March, you were in urgent need of money. Twenty-five thousand pounds, was it not?' He still spoke quietly.

'Or thereabouts,' I said.

'A sum which, reasonably enough in view of the then state of your finances, your bank manager declines to advance to you. Then, on the 3rd April, you visit the Farmwell Foundation where you are shown a device designed to economise in the fuel for domestic central heating, a device which by some curious coincidence subsequently turns out to be worth that same sum of twenty-five thousand pounds?'

'Yes.'

'The Director, not very cleverly perhaps but then he had every reason to believe that he was among friends, leaves in full view on his desk the key of the safe in which he has just locked the device away together with a letter from which, as he had just explained to you all, can be obtained not only the name of a company which it would be reasonable to assume might be unscrupulous enough to buy the device should it be stolen, but also no doubt an indication of the price that they would be willing to pay?'

'Lord Stanstead told me that they were only offering eighteen thousand at that point.'

'Never mind. It would have been obvious that they would be prepared to go higher in the event. You saw that key and that letter lying there on the desk?'

Now

'In company with six others.'

'That same night, between the hours of 11.0 p.m. and, say, 2.0 a.m. the following morning, there follows the inevitable theft, which was accompanied by a vicious attack on a security guard. A fishing priest – which you admit belongs to you – and a signet ring – which incorporates your family crest and a viscount's coronet to which you alone are entitled but of which you nonetheless deny all knowledge – are later discovered, the one outside the building and the other at the scene of the attack. You're quite sure that the ring is not yours?'

'Quite.'

The softness with which he had first spoken had gradually been disappearing. There was a distinct edge to his voice now and the questions followed quickly one after the other.

'And you last remember seeing the priest in your car. What time was that?'

'I don't know exactly. Ten, ten-thirty, possibly. No later.'

'Was the car locked or unlocked?'

'Unlocked.'

'Do you usually leave your car unlocked?'

'No.'

'But you did on this occasion?'

'Yes.'

'Why?'

'I don't know. I must have forgotten, I suppose.'

'How long would it have taken you to drive from where you were then to Farmwell?'

'At that time of night? About an hour and a half.'

'So it would have been quite possible, had you so wished, for you to have reached Farmwell by midnight?'

'I suppose so.'

'Some days afterwards, money amounting to exactly twenty-five thousand pounds – there's that sum again – is paid into your bank account by some person unknown. Now here's an extraordinary thing. This thief who has first gone to an immense amount of trouble, not to say ingenuity, to incriminate you, then, having heard of your need no doubt, immediately becomes considerate enough to make over the entire proceeds of his crime to you.'

I smiled. 'Yes, put like that it doesn't sound very good.' But

133

there was no answering smile on Sir Makepeace Brotherton's face. My eyes left his for a moment and I saw for the first time that his coat had been inching imperceptibly upwards until the collar was now almost halfway down his back.

'Yet, in spite of the weight of evidence against you, and understandably disconcerting as you must have found it, you are not unduly worried because you have an alibi which you know, as a last resort, will account for every moment of your time?'

'That's right.'

'You omitted to tell the police about even the existence of this alibi. You have refused to tell Mr. Thornton exactly what it is. Now I must ask you, in the privacy of these chambers, and alone if necessary – I'm sure that these two gentlemen would leave the room – will you tell me?'

I thought of the pressure which he would surely put on me to use the alibi without further ado. I thought of the persuasiveness of which he was undoubtedly capable and of its probable effect on me. I thought of Tisha. I didn't have to think long.

I shook my head.

'No, I'm afraid I won't.'

He drew himself up to his full height. His tininess, the position that his coat had now reached, no longer seemed incongruous – or even noticeable. At that moment he might have been immaculately dressed and fully six feet tall.

'Won't or can't?' he said. 'I put it to you, Lord Thyrde, that no such alibi exists!'

'No, that's not true.'

'I put it to you that, whatever your intentions may have been when you first went to Farmwell, as soon as you saw that key and that letter lying there on the desk, you immediately saw in them a heaven-sent opportunity for overcoming your financial problems, that you abstracted them when no one was looking ...'

'No ...'

'... that you yourself drove back to Farmwell that night, wearing that ring and taking that priest with you for moral support, that when you were surprised and challenged by a security guard, either before or after using that key to open the safe and remove the device, the ring came off your finger during the subsequent struggle and that, in the sudden panic of making your escape from the building, you flung the priest aside ...'

Now

'No ...'

'... that you subsequently sold the device and that, using an assumed name and a disguised hand, you paid the money into your own account – or, more likely perhaps, arranged for them to do it for you ...'

'No ...'

'... and that everything which you have since told the police, your solicitor and myself is nothing but a tissue of lies. I'll act for you. Of course I will, if you still want me to. I may even get you off, too. But I beg of you not to insult my intelligence or try my credibility too far.'

I got up out of my chair. 'Come on,' I said to Sam, 'we'll find someone else who might at least do me the courtesy of pretending to believe me. I'm sorry to have wasted your time, Sir.'

'Sit down.'

This time the words had a compelling gentleness about them. Much to my surprise I found that, without having taken a conscious decision to do so, I had obeyed. Sir Makepeace Brotherton pulled his coat slowly down to its proper position and walked back to sit at his desk again.

'You stood up to that very well, young man. And of course I believe you. Nobody could be fool enough to make up a story such as you've just told me and expect to get away with it.'

Two points, he told us, had particularly impressed him. First, the anonymous telephone call that had been made to the police on Monday, 23rd April – I was hardly likely to have made that call myself. And secondly, the very fact that I hadn't taken the trouble to provide myself with some sort of explanation, even unvouched for, as to where I had been that night. Unfortunately it wasn't only him who had to be convinced.

'Nonetheless, I meant what I said. I think there's a strong possibility that I might obtain a "not guilty" verdict. But that's not what you want, is it?'

'No,' I said.

'*What*?' Sam Thornton was looking from one to the other of us as though we had both gone suddenly mad. Sir Makepeace smiled at me.

'Will you tell him, or shall I?'

'You, please.'

'Our young friend here is a politician and, if he is to resume his career as such, he must be, like Caesar's wife, above suspicion. That is why being able to prove to the satisfaction of the Court that he was somewhere else at the time becomes for all practical purposes virtually irrelevant, particularly if, as I suspect, the circumstances are such that they would not redound entirely to his credit. Am I not right, Lord Thyrde?'

'All too right,' I said.

'Very well.'

The only way in which I could establish my innocence beyond any doubt whatsoever was to identify the real thief. Unlikely though it might seem, one of seven men – Sir Makepeace agreed that we could by no means exclude Dr. Faulkner himself – must have a grievance against me, real or imaginary, that was strong enough for him to be prepared to face the considerable risks involved in setting up the robbery and planting the false evidence against me. And the fact that he had been able to provide himself with the signet ring, whether or not it was the one that had been stolen from my father so many years ago, argued a certain amount of premeditation.

'Can you think of any one of the seven who has cause, or who might imagine that he has cause, to hold such a grudge against you?'

I barely saw any of them apart from the annual dinner. There was Henry Matheson, of course, but I didn't say so. I hadn't even met Tisha before that night – there could have been no premeditation there. And Billy Candleford's ridiculous pettiness over his father's will. Not very likely as a motive – but I did tell him about that.

'Otherwise, nothing that I've been able to think of,' I said.

'Is there any one else? Any one at all, in the recent past?'

I told him about the attempt early the previous year to blackmail Sir John Elton, Julia's father and the Shadow Home Secretary of the time, into supporting *The Legalisation of Cannabis Bill* of which he had up to then been the leading opponent and about how, more by good luck than anything else, I had been partly instrumental in bringing it to an end.*

'Yes, I remember it well. Could any of these seven have been involved?'

---

* See *The Man Who Lost His Shadow*, Macmillan 1979.

Now

'I don't think so. No, I'm sure not.'

Sir Makepeace thought for a moment. 'Then I think we can largely discount it. We'll bear it in mind, of course, but in view of the risks attaching to this present operation there'd have to be a personal motive – and a strong one at that.'

He made a note on one of the papers in front of him before he went on.

Not one of the seven had a real alibi. All that they had been able to produce had been explanations as to their whereabouts. It would be possible to check up on those, he supposed, but they had all been unvouched for and unvouchable – with the possible exception of Dick Richards – so what was there to check?

Nor, it seemed, was there anything to be gained from the company which had been after the formula, even if we could persude Lord Stanstead to give us their name. They were known to have been working on the same lines as B.L.P., it was impossible to establish how far they themselves might reasonably have progressed, their initial approach to Dr. Faulkner had been oral and there was nothing intrinsically incriminating about their follow-up letter, which had been kept deliberately vague – they had seen to that.

And then there were the paying-in slips. A handwriting expert would be able to certify that these had not been filled in by me, but in all probability he would do the same for each one of the seven. The actual paying-in might well have been done by the receiver of the stolen device.

No, the best course of action now would be for me to establish as close as possible a relationship with all the suspects.

'Go and see them. Talk to them, individually of course. Let each one think that, as far as you're concerned, he is the only one that you feel you can really trust. Ask him for his advice and even help, should the need arise – six of them should be glad enough to give it and even the seventh might let something slip. Oh yes, and don't tell them what we *have* found out – that the device is worth no more than the amount that was paid into your account and that there's nothing in it for him. That's one thing that I doubt if he knows that we know. It's little enough but we might as well keep that one small jump ahead.'

If we were able to establish the identity of the thief, the charges against me would be automatically dropped and we must hope that this would happen before my own case came up for trial. But it might be that it could only finally be established by questioning the other suspects in open court and this was how, with my permission, Sir Makepeace intended to conduct the case. It was not, he warned me, without its risks. He wouldn't be able to call me to the witness box, for example. If he did that, I was sure to be asked in cross-examination to explain where I myself had been that night and refusal to do so might even mean adding contempt of court to the other charges against me. It would mean his insisting that each of the seven should be available throughout the duration of the trial and this he proposed to do. They wouldn't like it, of course – that was just too bad. By constant questioning and re-questioning, he might be able to force one of them to admit something, but if he were unsuccessful I would almost certainly have lost the sympathy of the court.

'Er . . .' Sam Thornton had been shifting uncomfortably about in his chair. Sir Makepeace raised one formidable eyebrow in his direction. 'Is that quite . . . proper, Sir? I mean . . . calling them into the witness-box with the sole purpose of trying to get them to admit their own guilt?'

His expression indicated that Sir Makepeace had been suggesting something akin to shooting a sitting pheasant or heading a fox.

'*Proper*, Mr. Thornton? This isn't a game, you know. My first duty is to my client, is it not?'

'Yes, of course.'

'The main case against Lord Thyrde, here, is that he is the only one against whom there are any suspicions?'

Sam nodded.

'How can it be improper then for me to seek to demonstrate that one of the others – all seven, if necessary – is as suspect as he?'

Sam Thornton subsided into his chair with all the resigned submissiveness of a punctured tyre.

Even so, it was a question of weighing in the balance the pros and cons of two diametrically opposed methods of approach, that of merely trying to establish doubt as to my own guilt or that of seeking to incriminate someone else – the probability of obtaining a bare acquittal as against the possibility of total exoneration but carrying with it the alternative of a long prison sentence instead.

Now

'Are you prepared to take that risk?'

'I've got little choice,' I said.

'In the circumstances I think you're right. And, if the worst comes to the worst, we can always fall back on that alibi of yours.'

'But haven't I rather burnt my boats over that — by not giving notice within seven days of the committal proceedings, I mean?'

'Not entirely. The court of trial still has the power to give leave to the defence to call such a witness, even if no notice has been given, and in practice it very often does. There's always a greater risk of the alibi not being believed, of course, and it could even lead to suggestions of a conspiracy . . .'

Still, if he were to wrap it up a little, Sir Makepeace had little doubt that it could be done.

'One more thing,' he said to me before Sam and I left, 'if I were you I'd get it all down on paper — now, while it's still fairly fresh in your memory — everything that's happened so far, starting with the day of the dinner itself. And when you've finished keep adding to it as you go along.'

'I'll do that,' I said.

And I started that same evening. I wanted to get it up to date before the first of the round of visits that I would now have to make took place.

v. Then

"Department for Inter-Service Co-ordination of Administration and Supply!" repeated Lieutenant Stephen Knightley witheringly.

His tone implied all the contempt of an active serving officer for those branches of the services that conduct their fighting from behind an office desk – particularly, I suspected in his case, for one that has its being in such an arch-pongo institution as the War Office.

Stephen's Captain Class Frigate was in at Portsmouth for refuelling and Molly and I had driven down from London that morning. When we had reached Portdown Hill, I had been surprised by the number of pennanted staff cars that were slowing down our progress and at the top we had pulled in to the side of the road to stretch our legs and look at what really was a sensational view. On the land-side Molly had pointed out two of the old Napoleonic forts while, in sharp modern contrast, the Solent itself was crammed with ships, some of the bigger ones having the bulbous grey shapes of barrage balloons moored directly above them. In the far distance was the hazy outline of the hills of the Isle of Wight.

I had left Molly sitting in the Rolls on the South Railway Jetty and I had been met at the top of the gang-plank by an alarming reception committee which consisted, as I discovered later, of the Quarter-Master, the Bosun's Mate and the Officer of the Day. The latter, a plumpish young man, had beamed at me but it was a moment or two before I had recognised him as Billy Bagot, whom I had known all my life. I had followed Billy to the Ops Room, one deck below the Bridge, which was clearly the brains of the ship.

In the harsh glare of artificial light lay bank upon bank of instrument panels profuse with knobs and lettering, white upon black. Lists, under perspex, covered every available inch of bulkhead, microphones and head-sets hung in festoons, there were telephones everywhere – their curled leads writhing out of

Then

sight. And it was here, on either side of what to me was just a glass-topped table in the middle of the room but which he referred to as 'the plot', that Stephen and I were now sitting.

"It's not quite as useless as it sounds," I said.

I embarked on the cover story that Brigadier Broadbent and his men had prepared for me. It had already become apparent that a number of acts had been committed by German officers that were far too serious to be dismissed as just the type of unfortunate incident that is likely to occur in the heat of the moment. The handling, and treatment pending trial, of what would be known as 'War Criminals' was going to be a matter of prime importance and my Department had been given the task of selecting the necessary personnel well in advance. Stephen Knightley's name had been put forward as one that might be suitable for consideration.

"I wouldn't want to leave my ship – now of all times," but Stephen was leaning forward, an expression of eager attention now on the trimly bearded face.

"That's all right," I said. "I don't suppose any of us will be needed until the war's nearly over, but I'm afraid I've got to ask you rather a lot of personal questions first."

"Then count me in. Er ..." any suggestion that it could be otherwise was clearly ludicrous, "... always provided I pass muster," he said.

Stephen Knightley had been born in 1918. His father had been a farmer, as had his grand-father before him, and there had never been any doubt in his mind but that he would follow the family tradition. All his school holidays had been spent working on the farm – his only other interest had been sailing – and when he had left Bradfield in 1936, which coincided with his father's sixtieth birthday, it had been made over to him. But he had joined the Royal Naval Volunteer Reserve in 1939 and since then he had not done at all badly. Second-in-Command of a Frigate, he told me with some pride, was for an R.N.V.R. officer unusually high.

"There's only one thing that worries me about you, as far as this particular job is concerned," I said. "You do seem to be more than usually bitter about the Germans."

"So would you be – if you'd had my experience," he said.

It had happened some two years previously. Stephen had been gunnery-control officer on board a destroyer when he had

Then

watched a German bomber attacking a hospital ship off the coast of North Africa. There could have been no mistake about it, it was the only ship in the area that had been fully lit up and there had been a huge illuminated cross between the masts which had been clear enough to him – and he had been nearly four miles away. The bomber had made a couple of low-level runs before dropping its bombs on the third and one of them had scored a direct hit. Stephen's captain had made for the area at full speed, within minutes they had been only a few hundred yards off and what they had then been able to see had been appalling. Wounded men in the water clinging to bits of ship, the few life-boats that they had been able to lower crammed with twice as many men as it was safe for them to hold, nurses, orderlies and lascars, all struggling in the sea. They had been near enough to make out the expressions of hope in the men's faces by the time that the bomber had returned. This was it, Stephen had thought, it was their turn now. He had stood there, directing the firing almost dispassionately, waiting for the bombs to fall on him. But no bombs came. Deliberately, the bomber had turned and machine-gunned the wreckage in the water with all the bodies clinging to it. And then, just as deliberately, it had flown away.

"I see," I said.

"Do you? Well, the next day it really was our turn. We were attacked by three German bombers of the same type and this time we managed to hit one. It came down in the sea with its engines on fire and several members of the crew climbed out onto the wing. I watched then, *in cold blood*, but I didn't give the order to cease firing until they were all dead." He was looking straight into my eyes. "What do you think of that?"

"I'll tell you what I think," I said. "I very much doubt if your blood *was* cold by that time."

I put the notes that I had been making away in a folder. I had been groping, as yet unsuccessfully, to establish some point of mutual interest that could form the basis of the social contact suggested by Brigadier Broadbent.

"I've never done any sailing," I said. "I've always wanted to."

"Really?" Stephen beamed. "I've been offered the loan of a boat and we're due in for boiler-cleaning in a week or two. Any chance of your being able to get a day off, if I give you a ring the night before?"

Then

"I'm sure I could. Do you mind if I bring Molly Stanton along with me?"

"Jolly good. I'll see if Monica – she's my girl-friend – can get off too. We'll make a four-some of it," he said.

* * *

"Well, how did you get on?" said Brigadier Broadbent.
I told him. "Of course, all that professed hatred of the Germans of his could be bluff," I said. "A sort of protective colouring."
The Brigadier nodded. "Possibly. Possibly. Hard to see what his initial motivation could have been, though. To say nothing of any opportunity for recruitment."
"He told me his best friend at school was a German. He went out to stay with him there after they'd both left Bradfield and the visit was returned a year later," I said.

* * *

"It's a *Dragon*," Stephen Knightley had told me on the telephone the night before – when at last the expedition *was* on.
"No! Really?" There had been something about the exaggerated nonchalance of the way in which he had said it that had warned me that I ought to be impressed.
"It's a *Dragon*," I told Molly now as we were leaving London in the Rolls on the journey south, using much the same tone as Stephen had done.
"Oh, that old thing," Molly said. "A cousin of mine and I used to knock about in one of those quite a bit, just before the war."
We had near as anything never managed it at all.
Stephen Knightley had rung me up early the previous afternoon – several weeks had gone by since our previous meeting and, in the intervening time, I had seen each of the other six at least once. His ship was back in at Portsmouth for the predicted boiler-cleaning; his girl-friend, Monica, had been able to get the day off too; the yacht was still available – its owner had been keeping it painted up and ready to go at any time – that was no problem. But there was a total ban on any form of sailing for pleasure, so there would be nothing for it but to call the whole thing off after all.

Then

"Why don't we all go out for the day in the Rolls somewhere, instead?" I had suggested. There had been a marked silence at the other end of the line. I had completely forgotten about Stephen's obsession over any mis-use of petrol. Then,

"As sailing's out, perhaps we'd better forget it."

"No hang on, I don't work in the War Office for nothing. I'll ring you back."

Brigadier Broadbent, however, had been far from optimistic. "You just don't know what you're asking, especially on that part of the coast," he had said.

But several hours later the telephone had rung again. He had achieved the virtually impossible. He had even arranged for the barbed wire to be cleared from the jetty and the *Dragon*, which was at the moment in a cradle on the slip-way, to be rigged and launched for us. There was only one proviso, we were to stay strictly within the confines of Chichester Harbour itself, where the yacht was kept.

"What happens if we do go out – by mistake?" I had asked.

"Happens? Happens? Blown up more than likely. The sea there's simply hotching with mines."

Molly and I left the Rolls at Petersfield Station and went on from there by rail. To spare Stephen's susceptibilities, I had thought that it would be more diplomatic if we were to arrive at Havant, where he and Monica were to meet us, as though by the London train. But when some twenty-five minutes later we alighted at our destination, the breeze that was gusting across the sun-lit platform bringing with it the yelps of wheeling sea-gulls and that astonishingly strong sea-salt smell, we could see no sign of Stephen at all. We almost walked straight past the only couple who were waiting at the barrier, a man with an unhealthily pallid face wearing a dark blue sweater and accompanied by a mousey-looking girl.

"Hello, Derry. Hello, Miss Stan . . . er, Molly. This is Monica."

We stopped and stared at him. Stephen gave us a rather sheepish grin and put up a hand to touch his now clean-shaven chin. "Monica didn't like it," he explained. "I say, guess what! We've just got engaged."

We shook hands and made the appropriate noises. She was a girl with no figure to speak of and a mouth disproportionately small for her face, but pretty enough in a dowdy sort of way. They

Then

had a fifteen-hundredweight truck, which Stephen had scrounged from the Royal Navy for the occasion, waiting outside. It did occur to me that it must use every bit as much petrol as my poor Rolls, but then perhaps his standards regarding the use of expensively acquired fuel were not actually intended to apply to Naval officers themselves. Molly and I scrambled into the back, leaving the front to them — it seemed the least we could do — and we drove some four or five jolting miles due east. Although Monica had held out her newly acquired three-stone diamond ring politely enough for our inspection, I had received the distinct impression that, in her view at least, our presence was surplus to requirements. It had hardly been an auspicious start for an enjoyable day.

But when we caught our first sight of the *Dragon*, for the moment at least all depression lifted. Lying well off from a rather amateur-looking, loosely piled stone jetty, an elegant little yacht made of varnished natural wood and about thirty feet long was rocking gently at her mooring. Even I could see how beautiful she was. Her white cotton sails were folded neatly on the deck and a slim mast, marginally taller than her length with a triangular burgee wafting at the top of it, pointed to the sky.

Monica clapped her hands together.

"Oh Stephen!" she said.

He put a hand awkwardly on her shoulder. "Like her, Old Girl? Not bad, is she?"

Even Molly was gazing with a smile of pure appreciation not untinged with awe.

There was a small dinghy made fast alongside the jetty, in which Stephen rowed the two girls out first. Then, when my turn had come and I had climbed precariously aboard, he put a bit of rope into my hand.

"Here's the halliard. Stand by to hoist the mains'l when I give you the word."

I obeyed his instructions but only after I had made him translate them into the King's English.

"Right then, hang on to the fore-sheet and don't aft it 'til I tell you. I'll go for'ard and let go."

It took some time before I really began to get the hang of it, but in the process I learned quite a lot. I discovered that a 'sheet' meant a rope and not, as one might have expected, a sail; I found

Then

out from painful experience that the 'boom' — the spar that was hinged in some way from the mast and to which the bottom of the mains'l was attached — had a mind of its own and distinct homicidal tendencies; it was also increasingly borne in upon me that Stephen was contriving to make me do the major share of the work.

The two girls sat crammed together in the small cockpit. Monica divided her attention between the new ring on her finger and Stephen, at whom she was casting the sort of adoring glances that would have been all right in a gun-dog but which in a girl I found faintly sick-making, while Molly, an expression of pure bliss on her face, trailed one hand in the water over the side. The sea was beginning to get pretty rough now.

"It's called the 'Solent Chop'," Stephen explained. "It's caused by the wind working against the tide." He pointed. "That's Hayling Island on the starboard bow. The entrance to the harbour's straight ahead."

"Well for goodness' sake don't go out of it," I said.

He looked at me pityingly. "Little chance of that. It's a narrow enough channel and with only a beginner to help we'd find outselves on a sand-bank for certain."

But from that moment on, as we tacked across and about the expanse of water, it seemed to me that he was deliberately doing his best to go as near to the mouth of the harbour as possible, each time we passed. It was on one such occasion that I really had to admit to myself that I was positively beginning to enjoy it. Stephen had not had to put me right for some time. Come to think of it, he had not said anything at all for some time.

I glanced round at him, secretly rather proud of myself, and after a moment or two he caught me eye.

"Don't look at me," he shouted. "Watch out what you yourself are doing."

He would have done far better to take heed of his own advice. The boom, which had obviously been lying in wait for just such an opportunity, chose that moment to swing round, clout him resoundingly on the back of the head and knock him senseless.

Monica let out a shrill squawk and sprang forward to minister to him.

Desperately I tried to call to mind just exactly what it was that Stephen had been doing each time as a complement to my own

Then

movements and to put that into action as well, but the *Dragon* failed to respond in much the same way that a horse will when it senses the inadequacy of its rider. I stood there swathed in ropes, trying vainly to restore some semblance of discipline to the damp flapping cotton. Molly, once she had seen that Stephen was all right, stretched herself out, comfortably alone now on the seat, roaring with laughter at my efforts as, stern towards the harbour entrance, we were being drawn by the ebb tide slowly but inexorably out towards the open sea.

"Don't just sit there, you dumb blonde," I yelled.

The mousey-haired Monica looked back reproachfully at me from where she was crouched over her stricken lover.

Molly leaned forward.

"Make fast the fore-sheet and keep her away from the wind a bit."

"Don't *you* start."

"Sorry. You see that bit of string on the bottom of the smaller sail? Tie it onto that hook thing on the side of the boat. Here, let me do it."

She came over and jiggled about with the various ropes; miraculously and with what seemed to be the minimum of effort the sails filled, we started to inch back within the confines of the harbour and, within forty minutes we were all standing safely on the jetty once more.

Stephen, fully conscious again, but his pallid face now having assumed an anaemic shade of green, grinned at us ruefully.

"Do you know the three most useless things in a small boat? A wheel-barrow, a step-ladder – and a Naval Officer!" he said.

When we drew up outside Havant Station, again, Stephen got out of the front of the fifteen-hundredweight carrying a suitcase.

"Monica's got to go back to London too," he said. "You'll be able to travel up together."

It was not quite the treat that he made it sound. As we went through the barrier, I took care to conceal the destination on the return halves of Molly's and my tickets from the others, but sooner or later we would have to pay on – Monica was bound to notice – and how on earth were we ever going to get the Rolls out of pawn?

I looked aghast at Molly. But she only gave a helpless though barely perceptible shrug.

Then

"I think I'll just go along to the book-stall for a magazine, if you don't mind," she said.

And she was skimming happily through the pages of her acquisition as the train slowed down for Petersfield Station.

Suddenly she looked up.

"Blast! I must have left my bag behind on the book-stall at Havant and it's got absolutely everything in it. Oh Derry, I *am* sorry. We'll just have to get off here and catch the next train back."

Monica offered rather half-heartedly to come back with us, but she did not need a lot of dissuading.

When we were safely installed back in the Rolls again and Molly was letting out the clutch, I looked across at her admiringly.

"What a girl you are! Not only do you save us all from a watery grave but now . . . hey, where are you going? London's that way." An awful thought struck me. "You didn't really leave your bag behind at Havant, did you?"

"Don't worry. The old girl behind the counter promised to look after it for me." Molly grinned. "Resourceful, that's me," she said.

6. *Now*

'I can't *think* what's happened to Stephen.'

Monica Knightley sat perched on the extreme forward edge of her armchair, sipping her tea desperately. She was a slight, mousey-looking woman and everything about her was in varying shades of nondescript brown. Her pale brown hair was set with a fluffy neatness that did nothing for her light beige face. The thin brown line of her lips turned down at the corners and I received the impression that, even if I hadn't done whatever it was that I was being accused of, there was something not quite nice about even getting one's self suspected. She was wearing a mid-brown coat and skirt and every now and then she would put her teacup down and pull the hem, over knees clenched primly together, even further down her thin fawn-stockinged legs.

'I do hope he won't be long,' she said.

Tisha and I had managed to find out a certain amount about each of the seven. As far as Stephen Knightley was concerned, he had left the Navy at the end of the war in order to stand as a candidate for his home constituency at the 1945 General Election. But his extreme right-wing brand of politics, together with the naval brusqueness with which he had sought to impose it on his electorate, hadn't gone down well at a time of immediately post-V.E. Day euphoria and he had lost what had up to then been regarded as a reasonably safe Tory seat. Since then he had settled down with his dull, worthy wife – and later his dull, worthy children – to the existence of a farmer coupled with local good works; she, among other things, being queen of the local Women's Institute and he, the dynamic moving force behind his British Legion branch. Earlier this year, he had allowed his name to go forward for selection as a candidate for the European Parliament elections, but memories among Hampshire Conservatives are long perhaps, because it was an offer that had been emphatically declined.

Now

Stephen had been friendly enough when I had rung him up the night before but he had sounded doubtful about my suggestion that Tisha and I should come down to see him. 'Hold on a minute.' There had been sounds of a muffled but protracted conference at the other end of the line. Then, 'All right, come about teatime,' he had said.

Tea as a formal meal being something that doesn't figure very much in my life, I never quite know what that means but Tisha and I had decided that four-thirty couldn't be far wrong. We had been shown into a cold bleak room reserved for rare social occasions and although we had done our best at first to make light conversation, Mrs. Knightley was obviously at a loss as to what one said to the criminal classes. After that we had just sat drinking tea at one another in silence and looking through streaming window panes out into the wet June day.

I had just been struck by the apalling thought that to a working farmer teatime might mean anything up to six o'clock and that there might therefore be fully another hour of this to endure, when there was the sound of an outside door slamming in the distance. This was followed by various thumpings in the hall, gumboots and outer garments being deposited no doubt, and the door opened and Stephen appeared, red face flushed even redder than usual, in an old navy blue sweater, corduroy trousers and stockinged feet.

'Slippers, Stephen.' The words were spoken quietly but there was an indefinable suggestion of menace in the tone. He paddled out again and reappeared a minute or two later, this time correctly attired for company.

'Sorry, m'dear. Hello, you two. Good-oh, tea!' he said.

He shook hands with Tisha and me and then leant over and planted a perfunctory kiss on his wife's gingerly proffered cheek, to be rewarded with a cup of tea and a slice of cake.

'Perhaps you'd better take Lord Thyrde along to your office.'

'Jolly good. We'll leave you two girls alone to chat together.'

With a momentary pang of sympathy for Tisha, I followed my host down the passage to a file-littered room, which nonetheless presented a welcome contrast to the forbidding atmosphere of the one that we had just left, and he and I settled ourselves in the two comfortably battered armchairs that it contained.

'Look, Stephen,' I said, 'I'm in one hell of a mess. If I didn't

Now

steal that central-heating device – and I didn't – then it must have been one of seven people. Well six, not counting you. As you can imagine, I've been thinking of very little else lately and I've come to the conclusion that you're the only one I can really trust.'

He leant forward. 'Good of you to say so, Derek. I appreciate that.'

'If I ever need any real help, you're the person I feel I can come to. But there is one thing I'd like to ask you now. You know all the others as well as I do. What's your assessment of each of them – my mind's going round in circles – who would you suspect?'

Stephen Knightley nodded wisely. 'I'll do my best,' he said.

Billy Candleford now, Stephen and he had been friends for years. But he'd rather lost touch with Billy, apart from the dinner of course. Never *had* tried to make anything of his life. May not be one of the world's brains, but he could at least try. And all those wives ... Dick Richards, he hadn't got any morals either but Stephen liked and admired everything else that he knew about him. Henry Matheson he couldn't say that he'd ever got on very well with, but he was as honest as the day was long – that's one thing he would go bail for. Roger Faulkner? Oh, I wanted Stephen to include him, did I? Quiet sort of chap but efficient with it. Even if he hadn't been head of the establishment that had been robbed, Roger would have been out of the question, in his view. Leonard Frost, he had to confess that he'd changed his mind about him over the years. Couldn't stand him at first but he'd mellowed and become totally different with age. Salt of the earth now. More than he could say about Peter Stobbs, though. Double standards, that was what just about summed up him. Stephen didn't object to socialists on principle. Didn't agree with them of course, but some of them were honest enough. Peter preached one thing and practised another and that was one thing he couldn't abide. Yes, if I asked him his opinion, for his money it would be Peter Stobbs all the way.

And that was all that I *did* manage to get out of him.

'How did *you* get on?' I asked, as I negotiated the Citroen out through the farm gates and onto the sodden surface of the road that led back to London.

Tisha shuddered.

'Ghastly. She never drew breath all the time you were out there. Said that what I needed was the advice of an older woman and she

Now

knew I wouldn't take it amiss because she was almost old enough to be my mother. *Almost!* Lectured me on the sanctity of marriage and said that I ought to persevere with it. Look at her own marriage, she said. *Look at it!* That it was intended to be a duty rather than a pleasure. *She can say that again!* That sex was unimportant. *Well, she's entitled to her view, I suppose.* And then she banged on quite a bit about the sins of the flesh and the evils of temptation. I rather think,' Tisha grinned at me, 'that *that* was *intended to mean you!*'

I looked her wistfully up and down.

'That I should be so lucky,' I said.

'I say, do you think we could go and visit Old Rollie and see how he's getting along?' said Tisha.

We were sitting in the library at Thyrde. Dutifully I got up, went to the telephone and dialled Mr. Barraclough's number. A minute or two later, I put down the receiver.

'We can go over this afternoon. But we're to prepare ourselves for a bit of a shock, the stage he's reached in the work-schedule at this moment,' I said.

Disconnect battery and put to store. Remove all body panels, doors, luggage trunk lid, wings and running boards. Remove engine unit, clutch and gearbox. (Send engine for specialist overhaul.) Steam clean chassis/body underside, wire brush as necessary preparatory to hand painting with protective bitumastic paint. Steam clean engine compartment ...

'Good God, that's not him, is it?'

I felt like somebody who goes to visit an old and valued friend in hospital only to find when he gets there that he's shown to the mortuary instead. We were looking at a shell, a dismembered corpse. It had four wheels still, but once you'd said that you'd said everything. Corrosion was showing where the various parts had been disconnected, there was a void where the engine had been and an assortment of frayed wires that ran along the bulkhead only served to make the sense of desolation more complete. Tisha looked up mournfully from where she had been trying unsuccessfully to rub one of the fresh greasemarks off the carpet. Mr. Barraclough passed her an old, once-yellow, duster.

Now

'Here, wipe your hands with this, me duck.' He turned to me. 'I did warn you, m'Lord. You may not believe it now, but it's all coming along very nicely.'

'I'm sure it is.' I tried to instil into the words a confidence that I was far from feeling. 'Thank you so much for letting us have a look.'

'My pleasure. Any time you're passing,' he said.

vi. Then

"Funny how all these Suffolk churches seem to look the same," I said. "We've already passed two that are the spitting image of that one."

Molly and I had been bidden to luncheon by Johnnie Bagot. We had started out from Thyrde in the Rolls that morning and we were well past Newmarket before I had found it necessary to look at the three-miles-to-an-inch road atlas. "Put that thing away," Molly had said scornfully. "We're on my home ground now." It was a perfect day for a drive, not a breath of wind and only enough tiny white clouds, miles up, to give emphasis to the brilliant blue of the sky.

"There's a reason for that, I'm afraid," said Molly. "Er ... you couldn't possibly get that map-book out again?"

It was only after the guidance of a friendly butcher's-boy, summoned across the road from his delivery-bicycle, that we were able to find West Candleford and draw up outside the low, white-painted shape of the Old Rectory. If it had not been for his tail-coat and striped trousers, the air of white-haired godliness that exuded from Coggins, the butler, who answered the door-bell would have mis-led the casual stranger into thinking that the house was still in ecclesiastical use.

"Take his Lordship in, please," Molly said. "I'll be quite happy walking in the garden. It's all my fault we're late."

And ten minutes later, as I sat explaining the new fictional enquiry dreamed up for me by The Department for Inter-Service Co-ordination of Administration and Supply, I could see her through the library window peering blissfully at the smudges of incipient colour on the rockery at the far end of the lawn.

"There's nothing I should like better," said Uncle Johnnie when I had finished, "and of course I'll answer your questions. But, if you don't mind me saying so, the re-establishing of Anglo-German friendship after the war seems a rum sort of thing for the

Then

War Office to be taking an interest in."

"Perhaps they've at last woken up to the fact that prevention is better than cure," I said.

Sir John Bagot, Bart., M.P., had been born, as I now had good reason to remember, on 29th March, 1894. Shortly after leaving Eton, he had joined the local battalion of the Territorial Army in Yorkshire, where he still owned over two thousand acres, and, as a captain newly commanding his company, he had been taken prisoner during the last advance of the Battle of the Somme, in November, 1916.

He had been sent to a prisoner-of-war camp at Gisfield, south of Erfurt. In January, 1918, the Germans had got wind of an escape that had been planned, the three who were to make the attempt had been warned in time and ironically enough it was he, who had narrowly missed being chosen to take part and had only happened to be passing, who had been the one to be caught. He had been wheeled in before the Camp Commandant and given a month's solitary confinement. It was only after it was over that the latter had somehow discovered his mistake. The Camp Commandant, who was a decent old boy, had had Uncle Johnnie in to apologise to him. His young daughter had been there – she was sixteen at the time – and the three of them had had a glass of wine together. He had caught a glimpse of her several times after that – and she had always waved.

In December, 1922, he had gone out to Germany again, this time as a member of a parliamentary delegation. Walking back to his Berlin hotel on the last evening but one, he had noticed a figure about which there had seemed to be something familiar, shuffling along the pavement in front of him in a shocking old overcoat. He had caught up with him and had barely been able to recognise Gundolf Insel, the Commandant of the prisoner-of-war camp. The old man had invited him back to the two rooms at the top of a crumbling tenement building that he now shared with his daughter, Fredeke. In the camp she had represented an ideal to him, the embodiment of freedom and hope, and that was how it was again, there in those appalling surroundings, she dressed in rags almost – to him ... *then.*

That night Uncle Johnnie had decided to prolong his visit indefinitely. He and Fredeke had been engaged in two weeks and married within six and the year that followed had been the

155

Then

happiest of his whole life. Until late November . . .

It was during the 1923 Election campaign that it had happened. It was going to be a close run thing and he had been out speaking late into the night. As for 'Freddie', that was what he had called her . . . Fredeke, his wife . . . it was only the eighth month so he had not been unduly worried. But it had been a question of saving her *or* the child and he was never consulted. They had not been able to reach him, so she had decided for herself . . . it was to be the child. It was a boy. They had both wanted a boy.

He sat there when he had finished, staring out of the window for a long time. There was something incongruous about the expression in the eyes of that tubby middle-aged figure clad in heather-mixture plus-fours. There was no sign of Molly now and for once I was glad of it. The sight of her just at that moment might have been too painful for him. Uncle Johnnie was back in 1923.

Suddenly he turned back to me and a slight smile crinkled the corners of his eyes. "So you can see what this suggestion of yours means to me."

I felt absolutely awful.

"It's all very tentative," I said miserably.

He leaned over and put a hand on my shoulder. "That's all right, old boy. Let's go and find that girl of yours. It's time for luncheon and I could eat a horse."

From that moment on, Uncle Johnnie was more cheerful than I had ever known him. Bringing it all out into the open must have been just what he needed, a sort of blood-letting. The roast duck was delicious.

"Coggins looks after these," he said, as we were finishing our first helpings. Over by the sideboard the butler smiled paternally. "Which of your charges is it? Not Gwendoline, I hope."

"I'm afraid it is, Sir John."

"Oh dear, and she was one of my favourites". He turned back to us. "She used to flap up onto that window-sill there and take a piece of crust right out of my hand. Ah well, have some more? I'm going to."

Molly shook her head weakly.

"Not for me, thanks," I said. I was feeling like a cannibal.

We watched, in horrified fascination, as Uncle Johnnie heaped his own plate.

Then

* * *

"So from the moment of his wife's death," said Brigadier Broadbent, "he resolved to devote the rest of his own life to fostering friendly relations between the two countries?"

"Until 1938. He's convinced now that he'd have seen through the Nazis far sooner if his father-in-law had lived. He became quite devoted to the old boy, but Gundolf Insel died in 1933 still regarding Hitler as something of a saviour."

The Brigadier nodded. "A lot of the Old Guard did."

"It was the annexation of Austria that finished Johnnie Bagot," I said. "I remember hearing my father talking about the sensation that his speech in the House of Commons, renouncing his former championship of Nazi Germany, made at the time."

* * *

"You're in here, my dear," said Uncle Johnnie, "and Derry that's you, next door but one. The bath-room's at the end of the passage there."

He had issued us with a standing invitation on our previous visit to come at any time. He had met us at the front door himself. The butler, it appeared, was immured in the kitchen, where he had just reached a critical stage in the preparation of dinner, and Johnnie Bagot had been anxious that he should not be disturbed. So he himself now had Molly's suit-case in his hand.

"Oh, by the way," he said as he put it down, "wouldn't do for you to be staying in the house alone with us two men. Coggins and his daughter live in a cottage in the village, but I've arranged for them to sleep in tonight and tomorrow. Young Vera's about your age and we've put her in the room between you and Derry." He looked up at her anxiously. "That makes it all right, doesn't it?"

Personally, I thought that he was being over-punctilious for these modern times and, in any case, the Victorian convention that one girl who is adequately chaperoned herself can in some mysterious way pass on that chaperonage to another has always struck me as being faintly illogical. But his thoughtfulness obviously pleased Molly, who gave him a flashing smile.

"Perfect", she said.

Coggins was standing reverentially by the side-board when we went in to dinner and with him a tallish girl, very pretty but on the plump side, whom Uncle Johnnie introduced to us as the daughter Vera. She smiled nervously as we shook hands with her, gave a slight bob to the room at large and departed in the direction of the back regions as we sat down.

Uncle Johnnie was a superb host, talking first to Molly – he knew her aunt slightly – then to me, but always taking care to see that the other was included in the conversation, pulling our legs gently at one moment and then telling a story against himself at another, keeping our glasses constantly filled – and his own – but never neglecting his own plate at the same time. The main course consisted of a boiling-fowl, half submerged in a thin clear gravy floating with carrots, onions and little fluffy dumplings and from which he carved us enormous helpings.

Only once did the round moustached face, above his braided maroon velvet smoking-jacket, lose something of its cheerfulness. Suddenly he turned to me.

"I had a letter from Billy, yesterday," he said. "He tells me he saw you not long ago."

"Er, yes," I said. "I promised to go down and see that friend of his, Stephen Knightley, about something and I ran into Billy at the same time."

Luckily, I had had the forethought to make Stephen promise not to tell any one what I was seeing him about, not even Billy – although *especially* Billy was what I had really meant.

Uncle Johnnie did not pursue the matter.

"He's a fine boy, Billy," he said. "Only wish he wasn't so bitter about the Germans, though. Still, he never knew his mother and I suppose it's no wonder, considering that experience of his."

And then he went on to tell us almost word for word exactly the same story that Stephen Knightley had told me about the German bomber sinking the hospital ship – only, as he told it, it was Billy himself and not Stephen who had been gunnery-control officer at the time!

He was silent for a moment or two after that, but the mood did not last. The excellence of the chicken dish amply repaid the undisturbed attention that Coggins had been able to give to it in the kitchen. Even so, my plate was still nearly half-full when Uncle Johnnie got up to carve second helpings.

"This really is delicious," I said. "One of yours?"

Then

I ought to have known better. Uncle Johnnie pivoted round enquiringly to the butler who was standing just behind him, the carving-knife in his right hand missing the latter's chin by approximately a quarter of an inch.

"Agnes?"

Coggins nodded mournfully as he retreated to a slightly safer distance. Resignedly, I laid aside my own knife and fork.

Molly looked up from the wish-bone from which she had been engaged in detaching the last fragment of meat.

"What was that?"

"We were just saying how good it was," I put in hastily.

Uncle Johnnie beamed. "More, Molly?"

"I'd love some," she said.

7. Now

'It *must* be that one,' said Tisha. We had reached the village of West Candleford from which Billy's father, old Johnnie, had taken his title.

Low and sprawling – the Old Rectory clearly dated from the days when parsons used to number their offspring in double figures – the outside had recently been repainted pink, not the conventional pastel shade but rather in a shriekingly vivid puce. A virginia creeper, mercifully still green, was climbing as fast as it could in a gallant effort to ameliorate the effect. It was only mid-July now, but I dreaded to think of the battle of colours that would ensue in the Autumn when its leaves had turned to red.

And a beaming Billy did indeed meet us at the door.

The interior of the house was a welcome contrast. Quiet wallpapers provided a perfect setting for framed water-colours, mainly of birds; the furniture was of exactly the right proportion, quantity and style for the room in which it stood; every bedroom seemed to possess its own bathroom (Billy showed us to a double one at first, but I hastily put him right about *that* – even before I had seen Tisha's face); the carpeting was hock-deep; all this, I reckoned, being a legacy from the most recent in the series of wives, while the outside paintwork resulted from a newly liberated Billy giving vent to his own more flamboyant taste.

Dinner was handed round by a joyous mountain of a woman, whom Billy had introduced to us as "Vera" and who stood by, beaming indulgently, each time our host replenished his plate.

'I try to force a little down at mealtimes – just to please her,' he said, with an enormous wink at us and a gesture towards Vera who was gathering up the at last empty dishes.

'Oh go on, do, Master Billy.' She giggled delightedly and left.

Contrary to public belief, I had been told, Billy Candleford had only managed to run through three wives so far. None of them had provided him with a son and heir and he was now engaged in

Now

the task of searching out, and enquiring into the qualifications of, likely candidates to be the fourth. It seemed to have become something of a full-time occupation with him over the years, which was perhaps just as well. Between leaving the Navy soon after the war and succeeding to his father's seat in the House of Lords, so far as my informant had been able to find out, he had had little else with which to occupy his time.

I found myself wondering whether Vera might not be cherishing secret ambitions to become wife number four.

It was not until the Madeira was on the table, Malmsey 1880 – vintage *not* solera, as Billy was at pains to point out, a dark brown treacly liquid which turned out to be pure nectar – that I had got down to the purpose of our visit. He was obviously enormously flattered to be told that he was the only one whom I could trust and, when I asked him if I could call on him for help if ever the time came, his whole manner assumed an air of conspiratorial importance.

'Count me in,' he said.

Billy's assessment of the other six members of the "1944 Club" was distinctly superficial. He never felt entirely at his ease, he said, with Peter Stobbs. 'Always will pick a fellow up so.' Stephen Knightley, one of the best, old Stephen, but he'd become a bit too stodgily worthy now for his liking. Henry Matheson was a pompous ass. Dick Richards, well Dick *was* at least prepared to talk to one without putting on airs of any sort, he was the one Billy really liked far the best. Leonard Frost was O.K. too, even though he was inclined to be a bit of an old bore . . . 'er, sorry m'dear.' And Roger Faulkner was out of the running of course . . .

He paused. An inspiration of pure genius had come to him.

'Tell you what, though. I bet he fixed the whole thing up to look like a theft and then took that central-heating thingummy off to sell it privately himself.' He thumped the table. 'Yes, that's it. Bound to be.'

Billy had solved the problem. He nodded his great tuber of a face proudly up and down.

'It'll turn out to have been the mad scientist all the time. You mark my words,' he said.

. . . Remove road wheels preparatory to specialist repair. Remove hood and send with hood cover as patterns for replacement.

Now

Remove all chromed and bright fittings, door handles, window winders, light bezels and body trim strips, auxiliary lights and instruments. Check instruments and send for specialist repair as necessary. Overhaul main and auxiliary wiring within conduits and refit ...

If anything it looked worse than before. Even the wheels had gone now and the poor old thing was supported on axle stands from the floor. There were bits of car everywhere, some of them unrecognisable, and cardboard boxes placed haphazardly along the work-bench obviously held more of the same. But ... the chassis frame now stood out, starkly black.

'Come and take a closer look, Derek,' Mr. Barraclough said.

Tisha and I walked apprehensively forward. The black of the frame was clean and shiny. In the interior, paper mats had been put down over the carpet where Tisha had tried to remove the grease-stain on our last visit. And the engine compartment was spotless too and had now begun to acquire an air of workmanlike efficiency with new wiring, neat and colourful, protruding from its little alloy channels, the still tabbed ends waiting to be connected.

Mr. Barraclough smiled paternally at our absorbed attention.

'Still coming along nicely,' he said.

vii. Then

"And what," said Mr. Frost — he paused to refresh his memory from the heading of the letter that I had written to him to arrange the appointment, ". . . can this 'Department for Inter-Service Co-ordination of Administration and Supply' have to do with me?"

We were sitting in what passed for arm-chairs in the sitting-room of his second-floor Westminster flat, which had been furnished with that peculiar form of modern austerity that contrives to combine the minimum of comfort with the maximum of expense.

I told him.

"It will be some form of military government at first, but your name has been suggested as some one who has been out to Germany and met some of the personalities involved."

"I see." His hands were at his hair again. It was a gesture that I was coming to the conclusion more often than not accompanied moments of particular indecision or stress. "Well, I'll do anything I can to help of course, but it'll have to be in a purely advisory capacity. My first priority must be at Westminster, particularly immediately after the war."

Leonard Frost had been born in 1912. His father had been the bank manager of a small-town branch in Sussex, who had resolutely turned down all offers of promotion, as this would have meant him moving to a bigger branch in a different town. A respected member of the Rotary Club, the Freemasons and the Bowls Club, as well as a number of other local recreational and charitable organisations, he had only one ambition — to see his son go to the neighbouring grammar school which, as the boy was soon regarded as a virtual certainty for a scholarship, seemed on the surface to be easy to achieve.

Young Frost had had other ideas, however. The last thing that he himself wanted was to be up-rooted from one set of school-boys whom he knew and liked and set down amongst quite another who had the reputation locally of being more than usually toffee-nosed. He had argued with his father endlessly and then, when arguments proved useless, he had taken the only other course of action open to him – he had sat for the examination and then deliberately failed it.

The old man had been mortified. Who did the examiners think that they were to turn down his son whom every one knew to be brilliant? He would pay the fees himself. The bank manager of the neighbouring town in which the grammar school itself was situated having just died, Frost senior applied for the vacancy and got it and the whole family had migrated there en bloc. It was a move that was to have disastrous consequences for them all. There had been a Rotary Club there too, as well as facilities for all the other interests – and more – that he had enjoyed, but his father would have none of them. He had become listless and tetchy and this had affected his mother too. As for young Leonard, he alone knew that it was he who had been entirely responsible – he could have won that scholarship without any doubt what-so-ever. The only way in which he had felt that he could make amends was by making a success of his career at his new school. He never revised his early opinion of the boys there – the only affinity that he felt with them was in games, particularly athletics for which he had a natural ability – so he had concentrated all his energies into his work. By the time that he won a scholarship to Balliol, his mother and father had both died.

"I don't know why I'm telling you all this. It can't be of the slightest interest to you or your department."

"No, do go on," I said.

Oxford in the early 'thirties was going through an exciting time politically. Young men of good families had started to question the values of previous generations as never before; some flirted with Communism, others with Fascism – he pronounced it '*fassism*' – but it was in the short-lived 'New Party' that Frost soon found his niche. Its adherents were predominantly from public schools but athleticism was one of their cardinal virtues and his prowess in running had ensured him an immediate welcome. It was his first political love and he had been far slower to become disillusioned than had more experienced politicians who had drifted into it and who were to drift just as quickly out again. He had stayed on therefore when the New Party had

Then

merged to form The *British Union of Fascists* in 1932. And it was as one of its members still that he had gone out to Germany to do a series of articles on *The Regime and its Personalities* in the Spring of 1935.

The actual incident that was to trigger off his disenchantment had been a relatively insignificant one. He had been in a small town, not unlike the one in which he had spent the earlier part of his childhood, when he had watched a middle-aged man being hustled into a car by two members of the Gestapo. Possibly there had been something about the man that had reminded him of his own father – who he was or what he had been doing, he had never discovered, he might have been a genuine criminal for all Frost knew – but, whatever it was, that had been the end of '*Fassism*' for him.

"I'm determined to find out more about politics myself," I said. "It's not good enough just following one's father blindly."

Mr. Frost looked at me sharply. Perhaps he suspected that I might be pulling his leg, but he seemed to be reasonably satisfied with what he saw. He got up, went over to a shelf, picked out one of the books and blew the dust off its top.

"If you're really interested, take this. You'll find it fascinating." I glanced at the title. It was *Theory and Practice of Socialism* by John Strachey. I could hardly wait for my next bed-time reading. "In the meantime, give me a ring and we'll fix up lunch together and talk about it," he said.

* * *

"He got into Parliament at a by-election in 1937. Lucky to do so really, but he did so well in the 1935 General Election, almost doubling the Labour vote against the national swing in what had always been regarded as the second or third safest Tory seat, that he was immediately taken on as candidate by this other constituency which was much more marginal."

"So ... either he underwent an instant conversion from extreme Right-wing to extreme Left," said Brigadier Broadbent, "or ..."

"Or not, as the case might be," I said.

* * *

Then

It was in one of those mean sinister looking streets that lead off Shaftsbury Avenue into Soho. *The George and Dragon* – dragons seemed to be figuring rather prominently in my life these days – was a narrow-fronted building on the left-hand side. The food was excellent, Mr. Frost had said on the telephone when he had suggested it, and you could only get in if they knew you. The restaurant was directly above the Saloon Bar.

Molly and I followed him up the stairs and into a room crammed with noisily occupied tables, where he put his arms round a fat little woman, black-dressed and white-aproned with shiny black hair, blacker than Frost's own, pulled back behind her head into a hair-pinned bun.

"This is Pilar," he said. "May I introduce . . . Miss Stanton . . . Lord Thyrde. Will you look after them when they come here in the future?"

Pilar flashed us a smile that was made up of equal proportions of white and gold. "The George and Dragon is always at your service, Milor' . . . Milady." ('Steady!' I thought.) Then she struck her bosom with a much-ringed hand. "Me, I'm the dragon," and she laughed until her whole body shook.

She installed us at the one still-empty table, by the window, and asked us what we wanted to drink.

"Have you got any whisky?" I suggested ambitiously, when it was my turn.

"For a friend of Senor Frost's, yes. For every one else – no!" and she roared and shook again.

At Frost's suggestion we agreed to leave the choice of food to Pilar and the Spanish proprietress, as he later confirmed her to be, nodded her still quivering head. "I bring you something good," she said.

The food which soon arrived was superb. Mr. Frost wiped his mouth with his napkin and turned to me.

"How did you get on with that book I lent you?"

"Er, well, . . ." I dragged my attention away from my gently steaming plateful and remembered guiltily that the volume in question still lay unopened on the hall table at Thyrde, "what with one thing and another . . ."

"Never mind, we'll make a start anyway."

And then he leaned forward and embarked on an exposé of his political philosophy, addressing everything he said to me, but at

Then

the end of each separate point turning back as though for confirmation to Molly. A lot of it, as I remember, had to do with something called *nationalisation* — a scheme whereby the Railways, the Coal Mines, the Banks and almost anything else that one could think of, would be bought up compulsorily from their private owners and run, like the Post Office is now, by the Government. Everything would immediately become immensely efficient, everyone would work incredibly hard and strikes would be a thing of the past — which, if true, seemed to me to be not a bad idea at all.

As we were finishing, Pilar came back to our table and she and Mr. Frost started talking to each other in very rapid Spanish, casting amused glances as they did so in the direction of Molly and me.

Frost turned back to us.

"Do you know what it is you've been eating?"

"No," said Molly, "but it's jolly good, whatever it is."

"Pilar tells me it's goat — or kid, to be strictly accurate."

I looked down at the polished whiteness of my plate from which I had shamelessly used my bread to mop up the last trace of gravy.

"Just so long as you don't tell us its first name," I said.

8. Now

'Yes, I suppose you could say I was a bit of a radical in those days,' said Lord Frost of Highgate. 'I held junior office in the Attlee administration immediately after the war and stayed on as an Opposition spokesman when the Tories came in, in 1951. But in 1954 my wife died — Tisha was only three at the time — and I reverted to the back benches. Since then . . . well, perhaps as one grows older one grows wiser, I like to think it's that.'

There was a slight pause before he went on — rather sadly, I thought.

'Or maybe it's just that one loses one's youthful ideals and enthusiasms,' he said.

We were sitting over two glasses of very good brandy at either end of the now cleared table in the ground floor dining-room of his house on Highgate Hill. Tisha had bought the food earlier in the day and we had arrived at 6 o'clock in good time for her to cook it. I had been looking forward to finding out how she rated in this particular form of feminine activity — I had never encountered Tisha's cooking before.

We had drawn the dining-room curtains to shut out the evening light of August and we had eaten with candles making flickering patterns on the green hessian-covered walls. Half avocado pears, at the peak of their smooth green creamy perfection, with sour cream mixed with caviar to fill the hole where the stone had been; *filet de boeuf en croûte* tender and red inside, its veneer of flaky pastry yielding to an ambrosial red wine sauce thick with chopped mushrooms, new potatoes of a flavour and tactile consistency that appealed to taste-buds and tongue alike, with a green salad, sweet and garlicky, on a separate half-moon plate at the side; fresh English outdoor peaches — the first of the season — and finally a *Brie*, each knifeful of which settled lovingly on its buttered hunk of crusty French bread the moment that it was applied.

Now

'Any more?' Tisha had said at last.

'Yes, I want to start the whole thing all over again from the beginning.'

She had got up grinning. 'I'll go and do the washing-up. No, honestly Derek, I know you want to talk to Daddy.'

Leonard had been given his life peerage in the dissolution honours of 1970 and, as I knew, he had been a regular though perhaps not over-assiduous attender at the House of Lords ever since. Then, with the sound of clattering dishes coming muted through the closed hatch from the kitchen, he listened in silence as I went through the same performance as I had done with Stephen and Billy. The real thief must be one of the other members of the "1944 Club". He, Leonard Frost, was the only one of the seven whom I felt that I could really trust. Could I rely on his help when and if the time came?

'Well, it's very kind of you to say so, my dear Derek, but if you'll take my advice you won't trust any one. Once you start doing it with one of us, however good the reason, you'll find yourself doing it with a second for quite another and it'll warp your judgment. But, having said that, I'll do anything I can to help, of course I will.'

'You probably know all the other members better than any of the rest of us?'

'Well, I'm certainly the only one who's hardly missed a dinner. Yes, I think that's probably true,' he said.

'Then who would you suspect?'

He stared at the guttering candle in front of him for fully two minutes and then he went through the list of names. Of Stephen Knightley, his assessment was very much the same as mine. Honest and, no doubt, hard working but not over-blessed with brains and perhaps inclined to be a little dull. Dick Richards, he'd always got on well with him, even though he was probably the one he knew least well. He'd followed his career in the newspapers of course, but Dick had attended fewer of the annual dinners than any of the others. Roger Faulkner, he was solid and reliable – not to mention a thoroughly nice chap. Yes, of course, he realised that the theft could have been faked, but he couldn't believe that any one with an international reputation such as his would stoop to such a thing. Peter Stobbs was still in the throws of those illusions of youth that Leonard had been talking about. But he'd grow out

Now

of them. They always do. Billy Candleford, well Billy was a fairly ineffectual sort of chap. But with his background, everything done for him, all the money he ever wanted – Leonard had said as much to old Johnnie, his father, on more than one occasion, but only got a flea in his ear for his pains – Billy had never really stood a chance. And finally Henry Matheson ...

At that moment the door of the hatch opened and Tisha stuck her head through.

'All finished now. I'm taking the coffee up to the drawingroom. No hurry, but come up for it when you're ready.'

The door slid shut again.

'No, the trouble is I like them all,' Leonard went on, 'each in a different way, of course, and I'd really rather not pick on any one of them.'

'You were going to say something about Henry.'

'Was I? Strange, rather aloof sort of character, Henry is, completely lacking in any form of sensitivity, I've often thought. I've made a point of keeping up with him since the break with Tisha. Felt it my duty to her.'

There suddenly came into my mind a possible solution to one of the problems that had been worrying me.

'I'm going to have to speak to each of the others,' I said. 'Not half as frankly as I have to you, of course, but as things are it might be a bit embarrassing for me to approach Henry. Do you think you could possibly fix something up for me?'

'Certainly.' Leonard Frost flipped open the half-hunter gold watch on the end of the chain in his waistcoat, studied it for a moment and returned it to its pocket. Then he smoothed his hair. 'Look, Derek old boy, I don't want to play the heavy Victorian father but ... have a care over Tisha, will you? Don't let her read into anything you say or do more than you really mean. She's been badly hurt over Henry, more than she ever lets on, and I'd hate to see it happen again.'

... Overhaul as necessary front and rear suspension and shock absorbers. Dismantle front and rear brake systems and handbrake. Overhaul brake rods and linkages, clean, lubricate and reassemble. Check, adjust or replace as necessary, steering rod ends, track rods and wheel bearings ...

Now

All the cardboard boxes had disappeared now – chrome parts gone to the platers, Mr. Barraclough explained – while, in their place on the workbench, laid out neatly alongside the newly-polished wood trim strips to the doors and windows, and each in its cellophane bag, were the various instruments from the dashboard, returned from the repairers. The two runningboards, their rubber strips replaced, were propped against a wall.

Mr. Barraclough leant over, put a hand on the steering-wheel and showed Tisha and me the easy swivel action of the steering.

'We'll have the engine back, next time you come. Fitted too, with any luck,' he said.

viii. Then

Colonel Matheson, in shirt-sleeves and army issue braces, had opened the door of his white-painted house in Camberley before I could ring the bell. With him was a dark-haired man, a year or two younger than myself, in civilian clothes. The skin on one side of his face was puckered up into a recently healed scar.

"This is my son, Henry – he was just going anyway – Lord Thyrde."

We shook hands and his father and I stood on the door-step while Henry Matheson walked off down the shrub-lined path.

"What does he do?" I asked.

"Joined the Fire Service, don'cha know. Should have liked to see him in the Regiment, though." He sighed. "Mustn't grumble, I suppose, recommended for some form of gallantry award last December – got himself badly burned in the process. But ... feller's a confounded conchie, if you please."

It was clear that it had shaken Colonel Matheson badly. But he brightened up again immediately.

"I say, isn't that Miss Stanton in the car there?" he said.

"Yes, my new job rates a driver but they hadn't got one to spare. Molly was looking for something to do, so they took her on."

He caught Molly's eye and waved. "Come along in, then, we'll talk in the gun-room. More comfortable there, don'cha know." I got the impression that he would have been far happier to see the roles reversed – Molly conducting the interview and I waiting in the car outside.

An enormous flat-topped desk filled the middle of what was an essentially masculine room at the back of the house. In one corner, justifying its name, stood a glass-fronted gun-cabinet while, over the fire-place, backed by a cork board, hung a Daily Telegraph war map of Central Italy on which a double line of pins, black-headed for Axis, red for Allies, marked the latest

Then

positions. That these were kept meticulously up to date was apparent from the folded copy of that morning's newspaper, on which a little clutch of spare pins of either colour lay.

"Now then, young feller, tell me what it's all about."

"Well, Sir, as I told you on the telephone, I've been temporarily posted to the War Office. This department of mine is carrying out a survey of ex-regular officers who are now employed in a subsidiary military capacity. The object is to find out whether any specialised knowledge or experience they might have is being wasted where they are."

I had been half-expecting at this stage to receive somewhat forthright views on the War Office in general and the *Department for Inter-Service Co-ordination of Administration and Supply* and this latest idiocy that they had dreamed up in particular. But Colonel Matheson seemed only too glad to answer my questions and, interspersed with a formidable supply of 'don'cha knows', I was given what amounted to the entire life history of the man.

Born in 1891, James Matheson had joined the Scots guards soon after leaving Wellington. He had finished the Great War as a Lieutenant-Colonel commanding his Battalion and left the army immediately after it in order to contest a seat at the forthcoming General Election, which he had won as a coalition candidate with a substantial majority. He had retained the seat as a Conservative in 1922, just held on to it in 1923, had an overwhelming victory in 1924 and lost it to Labour in 1929. In the same year his wife had died.

During his time at Westminster, he had become interested in, and acquired a considerable knowledge of, the comparative political systems of Europe. He had been invited over to Freiburg University in south-west Germany once or twice as a guest lecturer on the subject, by a professor there with whom he had corresponded. So when, in the Autumn of 1929, he had been offered a permanent job as *assistent* to his professor friend – this, he gave me to understand, being quite exceptional for some one who possessed no academic qualifications whatsoever – he had taken it on without hesitation.

The Albert Ludwig University of Freiburg was an old-fashioned establishment set in a Grimm's Fairy Tale town and Colonel Matheson had taken to the academic life immediately. It was a different world to any that he had been used to, or to be more exact three different worlds each distinct from the others – and he had had the run of all of them. First there were the Professors, they were god-like beings up in the clouds, but as a distinguished visitor of the past he had had the entrée there. Then there were the *Assistents* and Post-Graduates, that was his natural level. Finally there were the undergraduates, the fact that he himself had never taken a degree made him more acceptable among them than were his immediate peers. Added to this, he had enjoyed drinking the local wine, vintage *Ruländer* when he could afford it and *Mauerwein* from Baden-Baden when he could not; there was ski-ing not very far away in the winter and trout-fishing in Hollëntaal in the spring and summer.

"Sorry I went there now, though. Unsettling for the boy."

"You took him out with you then?"

"Had to. Wanted to make a clean break at the time."

The Mathesons had come home in 1935. Then, just as he had been wondering what to do next, he had had another stroke of luck. There was a vacancy for a National Government candidate in his old constituency, he had applied for it and got it, had regained the seat at the General Election of that year with almost as big a majority as he had had in 1924 and had been in the House of Commons ever since.

At the out-break of war, he had been given his present job as adjutant of the Camberley *Local Defence Volunteers* – now the Home Guard. The duties were not very onerous and fitted in well with his attendance at Westminster. He was particularly proud of the fact that, after twenty years, his old uniform fitted him without so much as an alteration, but he suffered from perpetual friction between himself and his immediate superior. I gathered that the two facts were not unrelated.

"Told me that he was my commanding officer and that I was only a captain and should dress as such. Wanted me to wear three 'pips' as he calls them. Stuck-up jack-in-office!" he said.

"Well, I think that's all," I said. "I say, is that a trout-rod in the gun-cabinet over there?"

"Yes, I've got a rod on a stretch of river not very far from here. Do you fish?"

"Only for salmon, I'm afraid." I told him about the Chanisgil. "But I've always understood that it's in trout-fishing that the real skill lies."

Then

"Skill? Nothing to it. Give me a ring when the season starts and we'll have an afternoon there together. Come on, let's get Miss Stanton in for a glass of sherry," he said.

* * *

"I see. I see."
Brigadier Broadbent was drumming on the table in front of him. "Well, I suppose the emotional state in which he went out to Germany would have been more than enough to make even a man like him pretty susceptible. Did he tell you what finally decided him to come home?"
"He didn't like the sort of friends his son seemed to be making," I said.

* * *

The water of the gravel stream, so clear that you could pick out the little stones at the bottom, flowed gently and evenly over its entire width of some forty or fifty feet between us and the trees on the opposite side. Colonel Matheson surveyed it thoroughly.
"Not a fish moving," he said at last. "It's a bit early in the year, yet – for any real hatch of fly, don'cha know – but this is a likely place. We'll go and practise somewhere else first and then, when you've both got the hang of it, we'll come back and have tea and try here afterwards."
We followed him some way down the river until he stopped and picked up a little piece of gravel and threw it into the river so that it fell with a *plop* up-stream from where we were now standing.
"We'll imagine that that's a trout rising. Remember what I told you, it's a wrist movement – not arm. Now watch. If I get it right, this time he'll come to me."
He held the rod in his right hand and his bare brown fore-arm did indeed hardly move as he went through the motions of casting, the fly never actually touching the water but each time his left hand letting out about two feet more line. With his final cast, he allowed the fly to settle onto the surface so that it landed two feet above, but floated down to cover the exact spot, where the little splash had been. Then he turned back to us.
"See? Nothing to it. Now you first, my dear."

Then

He showed Molly how to hold the rod and threw another little stone. Then he stood close behind her, his left hand on her shoulder and his right over hers, guiding the rod. The first of their joint efforts resulted in the fly embedding itself firmly in the branch of a neighbouring tree. With the second, the line struck the water in a splashy heap.

"I'm left-handed," said Molly after the sixth or seventh attempt. "Does that make a difference?"

Colonel Matheson was contrite. "Of course you must use your left hand. Stupid of me not to ask," he said.

She switched hands. The improvement was only marginal because although the new arrangement suited Molly far better it made things noticeably more awkward for him – but he persevered all the same.

When at last it was my turn, the Colonel threw the stones for me but that, so far as I was concerned, was to be the end of it. He stood further down the bank beside Molly and directed operations from there.

We had been about an hour, taking turn and turn about, before he was satisfied. We walked back up-stream again and sat down on the tartan rug and, while Molly poured out the tea, I undid the two white bakelite containers from the picnic-basket. There was a slab of nondescript yellow shop-cake in one and sandwiches which turned out to be of gooey red jam in the other.

"I wonder what they make the pips of?" I said when I had taken an experimental bite out of one of the latter.

"Sorry! I could only get raspberry this month," said Molly.

"And very good it is too." Colonel Matheson looked reprovingly in my direction. "You young fellers don't know you're born. You ought to try plum and apple. I had enough of *that* to do me for a life-time – in the trenches during the last . . ." He broke off and pointed towards the river.

"Look, there's a rise. Go on, Thyrde, see what you can do with that one."

I picked up the rod and crept on my knees towards the bank.

It was a pretty good cast too – the best that I had managed so far. The fly settled gently on the water just where I had intended it to, there was a little swirl on the surface well before it had reached the centre of the now widening rings. I felt the line tighten and then a sharp tug. I raised the point of the rod and the pull became

Then

stronger. Quickly I put my left hand on the cork grip so as to free my right for the reel ...

"Strike, man!" came the Colonel's voice from the tartan rug behind me.

I struck.

There was momentary resistance followed by a catapulting effect and line, cast and fly whistled wetly back towards me.

"Must strike," said Colonel Matheson happily, as he turned back to his conversation with Molly. I had been just those all-important seconds too late. I had missed the only chance that *I* was to have all day.

And some two hours later, throughout the twenty-odd-mile drive back to Camberley, I was regretting it still. But when we had dropped the Colonel off at his house and started out again through the magic of that spring evening on the long cross-country journey to Thyrde, it only needed one glance at Molly for the feeling of disappointment to vanish. Sitting in contented silence at the steering-wheel beside me, that hair, those eyes, the look of fulfilment on her face, she was the proud possessor of a three-quarter-pound trout which now reposed on its bed of a handful of grass in the boot – even though she had been given a good deal more help than I.

I put a hand on her bare arm.

"I'm so glad it was you who had the luck," I said and I really meant it.

Molly gave what in any one less beautiful I would have described as a snort.

"Luck nothing! It's just a matter of the skill of the person who holds the rod, that's all."

"Or of the person who's holding the person who holds the rod?" – I said.

9. Now

'Half a pint . . . or a pint?' said Henry Matheson, M.P. From the way in which the question was put, there was no mistaking the fact that the former was the expected answer.

I had met him at a prearranged point in the Central Lobby, to which I had come direct from the Tube Station so as to avoid the embarrassment both to them and to myself of encountering any friendly faces of policeman or doorkeeper from the House of Lords end of the Palace. He had suggested that we should talk over a drink and led me by an unfamiliar route of corridors and stairs until we hit the Strangers' Bar, which is situated at terrace level, some hundred yards of dungeon-like but gaudily decorated passage along from House of Commons Diningroom D, where all my troubles had begun. There was a noisily cheerful crowd inside – both Houses had just resumed after the Summer Recess.

To hell with it, I thought. 'A pint, please,' I said.

Henry's father, old Colonel James Matheson, had been drowned while bathing in the sea off Cornwall shortly after the 1945 General Election. There had been some talk of suicide at the time but this had been dismissed by most of his friends as unlikely. There had been no conceivable reason. Although a widower, he had always seemed to be a happy enough sort of chap and one who had been universally liked. But the same couldn't be said of his son, who had been elected unopposed at the subsequent by-election, at the age of twenty-one. Henry had never been offered, nor so far as any one knew sought, office – he had always spent more time on his numerous business interests outside the House. He had married Tisha as recently as 1974, but the break-up which was now common knowledge hadn't surprised anybody very much. He was nearly twice her age and it was rumoured that, for the past eight months or so, he had been keeping a mistress in a flat somewhere north of the park.

There were only two places vacant at one of the little tables that

Now

serve the green leather, bench-type seats and I made for them while Henry went straight to the bar for the *Federation* beer that I had asked for. I caught a glimpse of Peter Stobbs, three bottles of champagne held by the neck in one hand and a spray of glasses in the other, going out through the door on the far right, bound for the terrace. But he didn't see me and it wasn't long before Henry Matheson arrived with our glasses, my pint and his pointedly reproachful half.

'Perhaps you'd better tell me what it is that you want me to do for you,' he said.

I told him.

He seemed to accept as perfectly natural, and indeed no more than his right, that he should be the only one of the seven whom I felt that I could really trust. Well, he supposed so, but it would depend on the kind of help for which I asked, he said.

There was a cold uncompromising expression about that slightly twisted face of his as his eyes fixed on mine for a moment. 'You do realise, of course, that if anything should come to light that seems to me to point even remotely to your guilt, I should feel it my duty . . . indeed, I should have no option, but to pass it on to the appropriate authorities?'

I nodded.

'Well, so long as that's clearly understood from the start . . .'

I was left with the impression that the duty wouldn't be an unduly painful one. It might even be a positive pleasure instead.

He had the profoundest respect for Dr. Roger Faulkner. He, Henry, possessed a certain rudimentary knowledge in the field of electronics, purely through his business interests of course, but Roger was an acknowledged world expert. And General Dick Richards, Henry probably knew him better than the rest of us did. Fine military career. It certainly couldn't be either of them. Peter Stobbs was all right. Socialist, of course, and a left-wing one at that, he wouldn't put *anything* past him politically, but otherwise he reckoned he was honest enough. Leonard Frost, well surely I wouldn't expect Henry to discuss *him* with me. Billy Candleford, he frankly despised, but Billy was far too idle, not to mention stupid, to be able to carry out anything like that, even if he'd wanted to. Which only left Stephen Knightley. Henry's father had disliked Stephen from the start. Not that Henry would have let that prejudice him, of course, he was quite capable of making up

Now

his own mind. Stephen was devious. Henry had never been taken in by that stolid hard-working farmer image. Yes, *if* it were any of them, it would be Stephen Knightley. He lingered just a little bit longer on the word "if" than I thought was strictly necessary.

And that concluded the interview, which had turned out to be a mercifully short one. It was clear that the subject of Tisha was definitely not to be on the agenda for discussion between us. It suited me. I drank up thankfully and left.

... Clean off corroded sections of body inner skins, beat out and reshape damaged body main panels. Repair under part of both doors. Cut out rotten and damaged wood framing, make up and fit new ash framing in place ...

The overhauled engine was back – but lying there in its opened crate. Ranged on the crate-lid were the carburettor, the starter-motor, the water-pump and various other bits of equipment, all ready to be fitted. The clutch and gearbox, still in their wrappings, were on the concrete floor.

'The magneto's been giving them a bit of trouble apparently,' Mr. Barraclough said. 'We've been held up for that.'

The half-naked coachwork of Old Rollie himself was now a hotchpotch of various shades of grey and pinky-coloured primer paint. At the far end of the shed, stacked against their pile of new tyres, were the six re-spoked wheels. We went over to look at them. They were freshly re-enamelled – in black.

'Shouldn't they be in fawn too?' asked Tisha.

Mr. Barraclough nodded. 'They always come like that. We'll be painting 'em same as the body,' he said.

ix. Then

Roger Faulkner was silent for a moment or two.
"You're right, of course," he said at last. "Sc . . ience will be one of the most important factors, if Germany's ever to get s. . tarted on the right lines again after the war."

He and I were sitting perched uncomfortably on two hard-backed chairs in the office lent to us by Professor Tomkins at Farmwell for the purpose. The thick lenses of his spectacles, his prominent nose beneath, the way in which he tilted his head back to look at me, all combined to give him the appearance of a rather apprehensive bird − probably of the parakeet family. That must have been the actual safe from which the paper had originally been stolen, over against the wall there to his right.

Roger had been born in 1920. His grand-father, also called Roger, had been at Cambridge during the years that had seen the foundation of modern economic theory. He had been a friend and contemporary of both John Neville Keynes and his more famous son, Maynard − his own age had been approximately mid-way between the two − and like the latter he had studied under the great Arthur Marshall, after whom in due course his own son, Roger's father had been called.

In 1923, Roger's grand-father had been approached by one of his international connections, whom he had come to know as a rising young German banker before the war. Horace Greeley Hjalmar Schacht had recently been appointed as Reich Currency Commissioner at a time when the state of the German economy had been at its lowest. Could his old friend recommend an Englishman who would be capable of joining his team of assistants? Faulkner could and did. He had sent out his own son Arthur, accompanied by his daughter-in-law. He and his wife would take temporary charge of their grand-son, Roger, then aged three.

The choice had proved to be a wise one − whereas it had taken

Roger senior some twenty years to build up an international reputation as an economist, young Arthur had been regarded as a prodigy from the start – but it was to be short-lived. In December, Schacht had been appointed President of the Reichsbank; Arthur, who had been on a ski-ing holiday had been summoned back to Berlin at short notice and, his car skidding on the icy roads at night, he and his wife had been killed instantly. Old Faulkner, at the age of fifty-seven, had left for Germany immediately to carry on the work that Arthur had been doing so well, not as the intellectual equal to Schacht which he undoubtedly was, but in the same junior capacity. As a sort of memorial to him, he had insisted on literally taking his son's place.

As for young Roger, from that time on his grand-father's visits had been rare and the boy had been brought up in the rambling old house near Cambridge with only his grand-mother for company. He must have learned quickly to become self-sufficient and he barely remembered the death of his parents, but he now realised that its psychological effect on him must have been considerable. His stammer had originated from about that time.

In 1929, Schacht had left the Reichsbank over a quarrel to do with the reparations still to be paid by Germany, and consequently his grand-father had come home. The grey-bearded man who was almost a stranger had been willing to talk to him as an equal and an instant rapport had sprung up between the two Rogers, grand-father and grand-son. The old man had soon been able to pass on something of his own interests and enthusiasms to the boy. The success of Schacht and his team had indeed been phenomenal. By the device of linking the new Mark to the actual land, they had succeeded in stabilising the German currency to a degree that would never have been believed possible. As school holidays had succeeded school holidays, Roger senior had instructed his grand-son in the principles of first elementary and then increasingly advanced economics until, without any conscious decision having been taken, it had become generally accepted that this was what he too would do with his life.

In 1933 – young Roger was in his first half at Eton – the Nationalists had come to power in Germany, the Nazis were on the verge of taking over, and Schacht had been invited to return to the presidency of the Reichsbank. Almost his first act had been to ask Faulkner to rejoin him.

Then

Once again, Schacht's success had been spectacular. In a way that was applauded as financial wizardry by some and frowned on by others as amounting almost to sharp practice, he had arranged a series of bi-lateral trade agreements with poorer countries who could not afford to turn down such a relationship with Germany, and financed thereby a programme of re-armament and public works. All this Faulkner had described in regular bulletins to Roger and it was agreed that as soon as he left Eton, he himself should come out to Germany and spend a year with his grand-father before going on to Cambridge. This was a trip that was planned and looked forward to by both of them with equal enthusiasm, but in 1936 old Faulkner had died.

This sudden and totally unexpected event had left an appalling gap in the boy's life, but it had also resolved something of a conflict of loyalties in which he had been finding himself. Before leaving for Germany the second time, Faulkner had written to an old Cambridge friend, none other than Professor Tomkins who had at that time been a science beak at Eton and asked him to befriend his grand-son.

"You've met him, of course, Derry?"

I nodded. "He was billeted on us until just the other day."

"Well then you know what a m. .arvellous person he is."

Just as his grand-father had aroused in him an interest in economics, so had Professor Tomkins done with his own subject, physics, and no less with his closely allied spare-time obsession, operational research in wireless. Roger had been feeling drawn more and more towards the latter and the time had come when he would have to choose the subjects in which he would specialise during his last two years at school. It had been an apalling conflict of loyalties as yet unresolved, but with Faulkner's death he had felt that he could make the change. He was to have taken mathematics and economics, but he now chose mathematics and physics instead. Professor Tomkins had become his tutor and for the remainder of his time at Eton he was so absorbed in this new passion that he had scarcely noticed what was happening in the world outside.

Then in June 1938 he had received a letter from Dr. Hjalmar Schacht. His old friend, he wrote, had often talked about the planned visit of his grand-son and he would now like to honour this commitment himself. Would Roger come out as his personal guest? Roger had accepted gratefully, but for a shorter period than the previously envisaged year.

He had gone out to Germany at the end of July. On his arrival he had been received with great courtesy by Schacht himself, but he had actually been escorted around the country and shown everything by a man little older than himself. At first he had had nothing but admiration for what he saw. Nor did the trouble over Czechoslovakia, which was just then coming to a head, worry him unduly. The German aspirations to the Sudetenland, as explained to him by his hosts, seemed to him to be eminently reasonable. He had not gone out of his way to obtain the English newspapers, so the rising indignation felt by his own countrymen about it had largely passed him by. Surely this was no more than a mild disagreement between two friendly nations which would soon be settled – and settled it duly was.

But by the time that this had happened, the initial excitement and enthusiasm of his visit had worn off and Roger had been able to look about him more objectively. He became aware for the first time of the erosion of freedom that had been taking place in Germany. Disillusionment had turned into anger and he had been home in a matter of days. Was it for this that his own mother and father had gone out all those years ago and in doing so had met their, admittedly accidental, deaths? Was it for this that his beloved grand-father had worked so hard for the closing years of his life?

Even so, Roger now found something attractive about The Department for Inter-Service Co-ordination of Administration and Supply's proposal that he should go out to Germany at the end of *this* war to make use of his own different expertise, but in much the same way as his father had done before him, in 1923.

"Come over and have dinner at Thyrde one night?" I said. "I'll see if I can get that American, Dick Richards, to come too."

"I'd l. .ove to. By the way, Derry, whatever happened in the end about that p. .aper you showed me?"

I told him.

At first I thought that I was about to witness some form of controlled scientific eruption – but apparently he thought better of it.

"I don't su. .ppose it really matters," he said.

Out in the car-park, I found Molly sitting in the Rolls staring intently through the window in front of her. She did not look round as I opened the passenger door.

"Look at that car," she said. "The one straight ahead."

I looked. It was a Morris Ten, a dark blue one this time. At first sight it seemed to be immaculate – not a blemish to be seen.

"What of it?"

"Look at the off-hind mud-guard and the bumper just below it. You can see that they've been damaged and straightened out at some time. The whole thing's been re-painted recently – re-chromed too."

"Well yes," I said, "but that doesn't mean very much. There must be hundreds that have had a knock like that."

"Walk forward . . . casually now . . . and look through the rear-window."

I did so. Through the lozenge-shaped glass, I could see a mascot lying wedged against the left-hand end of the rolled-up blind, its short length of cord dangling loosely over the back of the seat.

It was a Mickey Mouse. It only had one hand.

* * *

"And it was only *after* Munich that he decided to cut his visit short?" said Brigadier Broadbent. "At a time when some of her bitterest opponents in this country were reluctantly coming to the conclusion that it might be possible to live with Nazi Germany after all?"

"Apparently the young chap who'd been told off to show him round made no attempt to conceal his delight at the duping of Mr. Chamberlain."

"And, at the same time, your friend Professor Tomkins had been asked to start up the hush-hush establishment at Farmwell and needed his young protegé with him? Handy! Handy! Bit of luck you two spotting that Morris, though." He looked at the bit of paper on which I had jotted down the registration number. "You'd better leave that end of it to us now, but I'll do what I can to see that you're in at the kill."

"What do Molly and I do in the mean-time?" I asked.

He told me.

And that was exactly the question that Molly herself asked,

Then
when I rejoined her out in the Rolls afterwards.

I told her.

" 'Do? Do? Why, just carry on as you have been doing, my dear boy,' " I said.

10. Now

'I assume,' said Dr. Roger Faulkner, 'that you've tried all the traditional approaches to the problem – motive, opportunity and so on?'

He had sounded distinctly cool over the telephone and at first I had thought that he was going to refuse to see me. I suppose that in the circumstances I could hardly have blamed him, but then apparently he had relented. 'I'd like to believe it wasn't you, Derek. As you know, I was at school with your father.' Even so, he wouldn't come to lunch. If it were all the same to me, he could be at Thyrde by about ten minutes to two. So Tisha and I had had ours early and then, taking advantage of weather surprisingly mild for late November, walked in our oily green *Barbour* coats down by the water-garden, waiting for his arrival. At 1.50 on the dot, we had seen his old black Ford car coming up the drive.

I nodded.

'They're all fairly well off and, as for opportunity, any one of them could have done it,' I said.

'I see. Yes, it's the financial gain aspect of the thing that's been worrying me too. Selling that device – even to an eager buyer – there really would have been comparatively little in it, you know.'

'Even less than you think,' I said.

In spite of Sir Makepeace's instructions to the contrary, I told him about my interview with Lord Stanstead at Enerco and about the exact sum which had been paid into my own bank account. Roger broadly agreed with Lord Stanstead's calculations, his only reservation being that he thought that the latter had, if anything, erred on the high side.

'Hmm, interesting.' And then he asked the same question as Sir Makepeace had asked. 'Have any of the other six got any sort of grudge against you?'

I gave the same answer. 'Not that I've been able to think of,' I said.

Now

'Well, there could be another explanation. Have you ever been to the "Black Museum" at Scotland Yard?'

'No.'

'One of the exhibits that they've got there is a postal order which was bought as a three-and-sixpenny one back in the days of the first world war. But somebody had then gone to infinite time and trouble to alter the sum to *eight* shillings and sixpence everywhere it occurs, three times in figures and no less than thirty-two times in *words*, and they did it with such extraordinary skill that the forgery is virtually undetectable. All that work, to say nothing of the risk of incurring a prison sentence of anything up to fourteen years' hard, for the gain of a mere five bob – even if that would be . . .' he did a rapid mental calculation, 'about three pounds twenty-five in present day terms. There's a certain type of mentality to whom breaking the law and getting away with it can have its attractions for its own sake. There might be an element of that in this.'

'It's certainly worth a thought,' I said.

'I think that the most constructive thing we can do is to examine the characters of each of them, bearing that possibility – and it's only a possibility – in mind.'

And this he proceeded to do, going anti-clockwise round the imaginary dinner-table and starting with Peter Stobbs on his right.

Peter's was a complex character in that it reflected the result of a basically easy-going man being tugged in opposite directions by a variety of conflicting influences. First there was the crusading zeal of a pushful and near-fanatical wife versus the complacence born of possessing a safe Labour seat coupled with comfortably adequate financial backing from his Trade Union; then there were his own genuine left-wing ideals which fought a constantly losing battle with his pronounced weakness for those luxuries of life which are more often associated with a capitalist society; and superimposed over the whole was the "small man's complex" which, in Peter's case as so often happens, expressed itself in unnecessary flamboyance. Though how any of this fitted in with the *postal order syndrome* was hard to see.

'Henry Matheson.' Roger paused for a moment. 'I'm sorry, Tisha, but I think it's only fair to Derek if I . . .' Tisha nodded emphatically. 'Forget I'm here,' she said. Henry too was a man of tremendous enthusiasms but the difference between him and Peter was that he persevered with all of them. His trouble was that he diversified too much. He gave the impression of wanting to be an expert in everything he touched and perhaps he resented his inability to do this, not realising that he never left himself the time fully to master one thing.

'One of the others was saying that he was completely lacking in sensitivity,' I said with a slightly nervous glance at Tisha.

'I know what he means but I think that that's overstating it. His overriding interest is in work of various kinds, that's all. It is with some of us, you know,' Roger gave an apologetic laugh and turned to Tisha too. 'I don't suppose that Henry allows himself a lot of time for any sort of leisure activity?'

'Ski-ing and golf! Only trouble is, he treats both of those as though they were businesses too,' she said.

'Leonard Frost'. Again Roger looked enquiringly at Tisha. Again she nodded. Leonard had been possessed of a driving single-minded political ambition when he had first known him. Looking back at it now, it seemed strange that he had never achieved a greater impact with his life. But the drive had become noticeably blunted when he had married Tisha's mother. That was understandable, he supposed. 'Do you remember her?' 'Barely,' Tisha said. 'And then, when she died it seemed to disappear altogether.' He'd still had plenty of energy, of course, but for little, relatively unimportant, things. Such as this? Such as being the organising spirit behind the "1944 Club", certainly. Roger doubted whether it would have lasted quite so long as it had done – if it hadn't been for him.

Stephen Knightley's character was the result of a totally protected environment. Luckily the whole pattern of his life had been provided for him ready-made from the start because he had limited intelligence and precious little imagination, but he made up to a certain extent for these inadequacies by dogged hard work. Roger reckoned that he had probably made an adequate, run of the mill, Naval Officer, no more and no less, and that thereafter he had run his farm efficiently enough.

'In the parable, he would have been the fellow who buried his one talent safely in the ground,' he said.

Billy Candleford was the complete opposite of Stephen in almost every particular. He had somehow acquired an image of being the amiable buffoon and this he seemed to go out of his way to play up to, although it was far from being an accurate one. He, Billy, possessed both intelligence and imagination to a marked degree and if he ever got the right motivation Billy would be a hard man to stop.

I told Roger about the ridiculous pettiness that Billy had shown over the matter of his father's will and the bequest to me.

Dick Richards's was far and away the most powerful character of the lot – he was the only one of the six to have achieved anything like world recognition in household name terms. He always knew exactly what it was that he wanted – he had a strong sense of idealism coupled with a certain ruthlessness. Nobody ever seemed to be able to say "no" when Dick asked them to do anything for him and he was of the type to go at anything he did single-mindedly to the exclusion of all else, not to let any one or anything stand in his way.

He tilted his head back until his gaze, which up to that time had been focused through the thick-lensed spectacles onto the notebook in front of him, was brought up to rest on me without having incurred the inconvenience of actually having to shift the position of his eyes.

'Which brings me round full circle,' he said, 'back to myself. Would I be right in thinking that you've said much the same thing to each of the others as you have to me? About being the only one you felt you could really trust?'

'Er . . .' I said.

He smiled. 'Don't worry. I'd probably have done much the same myself.'

Roger had gone up to Cambridge in 1945, he told me, to take his degree in electrical engineering and subsequently his doctorate. His leaving there had coincided with the inauguration of the Foundation for Technological Research and he had thus been able to return to the place where, as an embryo boffin, he had spent the war years. Since then, Farmwell had become his life. Of course he realised that he himself *could* have planned the theft and faked the evidence but it would be like robbing his own family.

He smiled. 'Not that I wouldn't have found it a stimulating mental exercise,' he said.

So there I had it. No, he would rather not speculate further but he hoped that what he *had* been able to say would be of some help

Now

— if only to clarify my own mind.
It was only after he had left that a rather odd thing struck me. During the whole time that he had been with us, *Dr. Roger Faulkner hadn't stammered once.*

... *Reassemble ancillary equipment and fit to engine unit, refit clutch and fit to vehicle. Refit gearbox and connect transmission line. Replace all instruments and radiator. Connect repaired cooling system and replace hoses as necessary. Static run engine and adjust* ...

'That's not the same engine, is it?' said Tisha. 'It looks enormous.'

Mr. Barraclough nodded happily. 'They don't make 'em like that no more, not even Rolls-Royce don't,' he said.

The general appearance of the car hadn't changed very much, except that the wheels and the radiator were back on. Most of the body panels had yet to be replaced and the primer paint was still multi-coloured and rough to the touch, but the engine in its shiny compartment did indeed seem bigger and infinitely more powerful than I remembered it. With the oil and fuel pipes in their now pristine state, it might have been a product of the very latest technology.

'Can we take him out for a drive?'

Mr. Barraclough pursed his lips.

' 'Fraid not, m'Lord, not without doors and brake-lights and such-like. Tell you what though, I'll take her over and put her on the "rolling road" for you, in the shed across the yard.'

A few minutes later I was sitting at the controls, Tisha beside me on the clean dust-sheet that had been provided to cover the seat, marvelling at the gentle purr of the engine and watching the needles creep across the dials on the instrument panel, each telling its story.

'Don't switch off for the moment,' Mr. Barraclough said. 'Come round and have a look at this.'

He took a 50p piece out of his trouser pocket and balanced it on the radiator-top. Then he removed his hand and, miraculously, with the engine still running the coin stayed there – poised on one of the seven facets of its edge.

191

x. Then

"This outfit of yours must be pretty high-powered," said lieutenant Dick Richards. "You'd be surprised if I told you the name of the man who signed the authority for me to talk to you."

We were sitting in an austerely functional room at Chelveston Aerodrome, he on one side of a bare white-wood table, I on the other. The only picture was a framed photograph of Franklin D. Roosevelt, seated as always, on the wall behind him. There was a furled *Stars and Stripes* propped against the corner to my right.

"No door is closed to the Department for Inter-Service Co-ordination of Administration and Supply," I said.

Alan Richards had been born in 1920. His father had been the middle brother of three, all of whom had worked for a light engineering firm outside Stuttgart which had made parts for Mercedes but which had gone out of business a few years before the Great War. Their name had been 'Reichardt' then. The eldest, Franz, had been taken on by Mercedes themselves but the two younger brothers had emigrated to Charlottesville in the United States to set up making cars on their own account there. They had changed their own name, as well as that of their company, to 'Richards' as soon as America had come into the war.

The Richards 'Trix' – they had only made the one model, boat-shaped with two seats in front and one behind – had always had a reputation for reliability but the development that had given it such a tremendous vogue in the early nineteen-twenties had come about by accident. They had been experimenting with a means of improving the cooling-system, by running pipes from the radiator back round the inside of the body of the car, when they had found that it had a side effect of making the leather of the back seat noticeably warm. They had been about to scrap the whole idea when they had realised its potential. The single passenger behind, who had lacked the protection afforded by the wind-screen, now had a distinct advantage of his own and they had advertised it as

Then

such. It had caught on immediately. The car had acquired the popular nick-name of 'the hot-seat buggy'. Even today there are people who believe – mistakenly – that it was that, the invidious position of the spare man or woman who was left on his own in the back while the driver and his girl-friend sat companionably together in the front, that was the origin of the expression 'being on the hot seat' – and not the electric chair. The Richards brothers had sold out to one of the major companies in 1928.

This realisation of the family capital had enabled Dick – the name 'Alan' had not survived the first few years of his life – to be brought up in an atmosphere of modest affluence. His parents had bought a house in the country a few miles from Charlottesville; he had been given his first pony – the local pack of fox-hounds, *The Farmington*, had been formed at about this time; and there had been holiday visits paid by the whole family to his Uncle Franz in Germany, who had still kept the name 'Reichardt'. From High School he had gone to Princeton, where among other things he had taken a flying course on the side, and from there into the United States Army Air Corps. As a co-pilot, he had been shot down near Frankfurt in 1943.

The rest of his crew had been captured. He himself, as the only German speaker among them, had gone ahead to reconnoitre a near-by village and on his return he had almost run straight into the rest of them being marched off by the local Gestapo. He had made for Stuttgart and within three days he had been working as a mechanic for his Uncle Franz. As soon as an opportunity arose, he had been sent with a consignment of spare parts to Occupied France, where he had managed to contact the local resistance movement who had taken over. And when he had reached England again he had been promoted to being first pilot of a B 17.

"About this job," I said. "If the Russians should turn nasty when it's all over, it might mean working – even fighting – *with* the Germans against *them*. It won't be for me to decide, of course, but if you were to be selected would that put you off?"

"Not a bit. I'm one myself, remember." He grinned. "I speak English pretty well for a German, wouldn't you say?"

He had indeed got hardly a trace of any kind of accent.

"You don't speak it all that badly for an American either," I said.

Then

* * *

"What if the uncle had turned him in? Taking a bit of a gamble on that, wasn't he?"

"He didn't think so," I said. "His only worry had been whether it would be fair on the old boy himself, to expect him to take the risk if he didn't."

"And he was in Germany for how long?"

"The best part of six months, I understand."

"H'm," Brigadier Broadbent said.

* * *

"Roger's been to Stuttgart," said Dick. "He knows my Uncle Franz."

Roger peered along the table in my direction. "I only m. .et him once, very briefly at a party," he said. "It was that time I was telling you about, Derry, just a year before the war."

We were sitting next door to the main dining-room, in the little room that we sometimes use nowadays whenever we have a dinner-party of our own. I was at one end of the oval table with Molly on my right and, at the other, Dick in his olive-green Air Force uniform and Roger in a well-worn blue suit sat on either side of my mother. Her frail form – she hardly ever ate anything, it seemed to me – was covered in a dress made up from inch-wide-checked gingham stuff, which I happened to know had started its existence as the pantry curtains. It went rather well with her hair.

"Why is your mother's hair that peculiar shade of green," Molly had asked me soon after her first arrival at Thyrde.

"Oh that," I had said. I hardly noticed it myself now. "It's the village war effort."

"Sort of woad effect? Scare the enemy into surrender?"

"That too, of course." My mama's hair, I had explained, had been white for years but Thyrde, in common with neighbouring villages, had been allotted the voluntary job of making camouflage nets for the army. A large wooden vertical frame, known as a 'horse', had been set up in what used to be the billiard-room; over this, folded in two at the top and tied down at the base on either side, a completed net formed the pattern from which to work; and over this again each new net was arranged. My mother,

Then

together with women volunteers from the village, would thread strips cut from rolls of a canvassy material known as 'scrim', in black and two different shades each of brown and green, into the mesh of the new net so as to match exactly the pattern beneath.

The dye that had been used for the lighter of the two greens always came off in a fine powder which covered everything.

"The billiard-room not only has green walls now but a green floor to match. It rather suits it."

Molly had thought for a bit. Then,

"I think it suits your mother too," she said.

Although they had sat next to each other at the birthday party, I had been surprised at how well Dick and Roger had got on together from the start. They had talked to my mother to begin with, of course, but her answers although outwardly displaying polite interest had been monosyllabic and she had kept casting anxious little glances over her shoulder to the double doors beyond which the billetees were having their own dinner. After a bit, they gave it up and talked across her to one another. We were almost finishing when I realised that, without any prompting from me, they had got onto the subject of Germany and, at my signal, Molly stopped what she had been saying in mid-sentence and we both listened.

"Dick, there's something that p. .uzzled me about your uncle," said Roger. "I've only just remembered it, but . . ." At that moment the butler came in and put the port decanter on the table. It was the first of the 'twenty-seven and old Andrews had been worried that it might still be too young, but it tasted all right to me and the others seemed to enjoy it.

"Go on," I said. "You were going to say something about Dick's uncle."

"W. .as I?"

It had totally gone out of his mind again – or so he said.

My mother caught Molly's eye soon afterwards and they both got up and left. They went out by the side door that leads directly into the hall, but after a few moments I could hear filtering through the double doors that connect with the main dining-room the sound of clucking mother-hen enquiries followed immediately by a chorus of reassuring male-voice replies.

My two companions meanwhile had found yet another interest in common. Dick had elicited from Roger the fact that a

Then

significant proportion of the research work which was being carried out at Farmwell had to do with the latest modern developments of aeroplanes and Roger started off on a long exposition about something called a *jet engine*. It was all highly technical and I was letting it flow over my head until suddenly I noticed Dick putting a warning finger to his lips with a glance in my direction. From that moment on until the decanter was finished their talk consisted of nothing but trivialities, into which they both took care that I was equally drawn. And, hard though I tried, neither then nor later when we had joined the ladies in the drawing-room was I able to persuade either of them to revert to the subjects of Germany or Farmwell again.

Any one would have thought that it was I who was the German spy!

11. *Now*

'I've never danced with a lord before.'
She was a model, she had told me, but *not* one of the modern near-skeletal variety. Christmas, which Tisha and I had spent platonically together at Thyrde, had come and gone and Dick Richards had invited us to dine with him at this restaurant hidden away in the recesses of Soho. Virginia, who was Dick's own contribution to the evening, had withdrawn her head for a moment so that those grey-green eyes, which were set in a deliciously pneumatic pink-and-white face framed in hair of rich auburn profusion, could gaze deep into mine.
'Really? What's it like?' I said.
'Dreamy. I must try it again, some time.'
Dancing with her to the soft rhythm of the solo pianist was indeed like a dream visit to a tropical island bathed in an atmosphere of lascivious innocence. Every part of her body had been suggesting, at its point of contact, adventuresome possibilities to the equivalent part of mine.
And then reflectively, 'Of course I've been to bed with two or three of them,' she said.
The music stopped and, with a good deal of reluctance on my part, we followed in the wake of Dick and Tisha back to our table. And back to reality again.
Dick Richards had finished the war with the rank of Captain and since then his rise had been dramatic. Major by 1948 and Lieutenant-Colonel by 1951, he had been sent out to Korea where his being shot down at the very point of success in a near-suicidal mission and his subsequent escape, alone and on foot from a good hundred miles behind enemy lines, had made world headlines and earned him the Congressional Medal of Honor. His promotion to full Colonel had followed shortly afterwards. The Korean war over, he had been given a staff assignment in the Pentagon as a Brigadier-General and this had been followed by appointments to

Now

Air Staff College, to Europe as a Wing Commander, to War College, to being Commandant of cadets at the Air Academy and to Vietnam as the Major-General commanding an Air Force unit. After Vietnam, to being head of the U.S. Tactical Air Force as a Lieutenant-General, to a NATO assignment on the Military Standing Committee, to being Commanding General U.S. Air Force Europe (as a four-star General) and finally to being Deputy Assistant Chief of Staff, U.S. Air Force at Washington D.C.

There had recently been moves to try and persuade him to go into politics, possibly even as the next Republican candidate for the Presidency, so Leonard's joke at the dinner about him coming over on a State Visit had not been all that way off the mark.

'Well now, let's get down to business,' he said.

Dick doubted whether, over the years, he'd seen any one of the six more than a dozen times at the most. But, if that were so, he clearly had a talent for drawing people out which amounted almost to genius because he was able to produce interesting side-lights on the lives of each of them which I for one had never heard about. Billy Candleford, for instance – Dick had never even met *him* before the night of the last dinner, although he had sat next to him then of course. Billy had surprised him by displaying a remarkably erudite knowledge of military history. Not that he made any practical use of it – he seemed to have acquired it purely for his own amusement.

'I've always had a bit of an interest that way myself, but Billy told me any amount of facts and figures that were entirely new to me. Quoted sources for most of them too.'

Roger Faulkner, it seemed, used what little spare time he had to indulge a private passion for orchids, to the propagation of which he had been able to bring what was, for an amateur, an unusually scientific approach. He had developed new culture media for the growing of seeds, which were not dissimilar to those used for the cultivation of bacteria; by means of X-rays and chemical agents he had managed to produce chromosome variations and his crossing of the different genera had resulted in hybrids of superb size and colour, but unfortunately most of them had turned out to be sterile.

'He suggested that I should come down rather earlier that day than the rest of you, so that he could show it all to me. He's quite open about it of course, but I got the impression that he's rather

Now

ashamed about using the resources of Farmwell for what is after all an entirely personal interest.'

Leonard Frost had become quite an expert on *Ufology* – the science of Flying Saucers. He'd started it more as a joke than anything else but then he'd really become bitten with it. Apparently he had been grilling poor Dick quite mercilessly about United States Air Force sightings, refusing to believe that the latter didn't know a great deal more than he was prepared to let on.

'But I expect that you've heard more about it than I have.'

Tisha shook her head.

'He never mentions the subject. Knows I think it's all a lot of nonsense,' she said.

Stephen Knightley had gradually developed an uncharacteristic interest in racing. He hardly ever managed to sneak off to an actual race-meeting because, even without him doing so, his wife had been vociferous in her disapproval. But he studied the breeding avidly and had all the up-to-date form papers delivered to him regularly.

'And apparently he's got a clandestine television set stashed away somewhere on that farm of his, which Monica hasn't been able to discover yet.'

Peter Stobbs's secret vice was playing the stock-markets. Dick didn't know how successful he was nor even what sort of sums were involved, but he reckoned that he took it seriously enough. I remembered what Roger Faulkner had said about Peter's character being the result of a number of conflicting influences. This was obviously just one more example.

'Perhaps he's just set on regaining the family fortunes,' I said.

Henry Matheson – 'And I doubt if even you know about this, Tisha.' Over the past weeks, Henry had become closely involved with some sort of Community Centre which was doing a tremendous job in one of the poorer parts of the East End of London.

'It's not just sitting on committees or fund-raising either. He goes down there at least twice a week and actually takes his coat off and gets his hands dirty. Apparently the girl who runs it is a friend of his. And that, I'm afraid, is just about as much as I *can* tell you about any of them,' he said.

I asked Dick the same question that I had put to each of the others.

Now

'If you were in my position, which of them would you suspect?'
He shook his head. 'If I have any thoughts on the subject, I'll let you know, but I have got one suggestion to make which may or may not appeal to you. How would it be if I got them all together round the table and then you could ask each of us any questions you liked in the presence of the others?'

'That would be marvellous, but ... would they come?'

'They'll come,' said General Dick Richards, U.S.A.F.

Later, when the girls were away doing whatever it is that is euphemistically referred to as "getting their coats," 'How did you get on with Virginia?' Dick said.

'Words fail me.'

He grinned. 'I thought that I ought to bring you two together. She was my alibi for that night.' Then the grin faded. 'Oh, by the way, about that question you asked me. I couldn't very well say so in front of that young lady of yours but, if I had to pick on one of them, I'd settle for Leonard Frost. Don't ask me why, it's just a feeling I've got,' he said.

... Refit all body panels, fit new draught excluder and weather strips, rehang doors and adjust catch plates. Remove all interior upholstery and carpets for cleaning and repair. Mask up body, fill, prime flat as necessary and undercoat, preparatory to final paint ...

'That looks more like it!' I said. The bright work and chrome parts had yet to be fitted and were laid out on the work-bench, separately packaged and labelled. Every inch of glass was covered up and a vast expanse of heavy brown masking-paper completely covered the top of the body in lieu of the still missing hood, but all the panels were back in place now. Even if Old Rollie wasn't quite a Rolls-Royce again, he did at least look like a motor-vehicle of some sort — probably something more along the lines of a rather up-market pick-up van.

We walked over and I put a hand on the paintwork. It felt smooth and even, now.

'Is that the final colour?' I asked. It was the one thing about which I was feeling slightly disappointed.

But Mr. Barraclough shook his head. 'It's only the undercoat, so far, even though there are four coats of it.' He gave an

Now

encouraging slap to the fawn rump. 'This'll give you the rough idea but she's still not a patch on how she'll look when she's finished.'

Tisha beside me was gazing with the wide-eyed wonder of a child witnessing the transformation scene at its first pantomime.

'He's going to be effing brill!' she said.

xi. Then

"No, not in there," said Lord Greyfield hastily. "Frightful muddle. Use the drawing-room."

I had been quite unable to think up any adequate reason as to why an obscure War Office department, represented by a Captain in the Grenadier Guards of all people, should have been entrusted with the handling of the post-war German economy, but Greyfield himself did not appear to find anything unusual about it. It was Nanny's day off, he had told me, and Lady Greyfield had taken their young son out shopping so we would have the house in Grosvenor Square to ourselves. The door to my front at the top of the stairs had been open, disclosing a small cluttered room in which most of the actual living was obviously done and I had started towards it, but he had opened the door on the right.

All the furniture was swathed in dust-sheets, but Lord Greyfield pulled one of these off a sofa, silk-covered with its frame carved walnut. Its upholstery was sagging underneath and there was a label tied onto one of the legs on which I could make out the name of a well-known antique shop. The panes of both windows were criss-crossed with strips of gummed brown paper against bomb-blast. A chandelier hung from the ceiling, a cascade of shimmering Georgian glass droplets, and that had a label on it as well. I had had his cheque for two pounds fourteen and threepence returned to me, marked 'Refer to drawer', that morning and I had been wondering whether to mention the fact to him. Perhaps not, I thought now.

"On the point of moving. Smaller house. Can't get the staff, these days," he said.

Peter Stobbs, second Earl of Greyfield, had been born in 1907. His grandfather had been a fish-monger in the Greyfield district of the East End of London, who had died in 1877 leaving a shop, *Stobbs' Fish – Bloaters a speciality*, and unpaid debts amounting to five times the cash available to settle them. This inauspicious

Then

beginning had been the making of George Stobbs, the eldest son. He had dabbled in a number of enterprises, each more profitable than the last, and formed them into a limited liability company which, with rather endearing sentimentality, he had called after his father's principal sales line, but this had only been a prelude to the fortune that he was later able to make for himself, out of shipbuilding and steel, during the 1914–18 War. He had given enormous sums to the political party that he had supported and in 1919 he had been awarded his earldom – not for this, you understand, so much as for the contribution that his business interests had made to the progress of the war.

After the 1921 crash, the shares of the *Bloater Corporation* had come under some suspicion on the Stock Exchange – they fell to an all-time low of seven and six-pence in 1922 – but the newly ennobled Lord Greyfield had already sold out three-quarters of his four million shares at four pounds per share. In 1923, at the peak of the hyper-inflation there, he had used half his capital to acquire a controlling interest in *Schlesische Steinkohlen Gruben A.G.* and another in *Mitteldeutsche Stahlwerke*. By 1928, with the German holdings alone worth ten million pounds, his shares in the Bloater Corporation which he had been steadily re-buying, a country house and three thousand acres in England and a vast estate in Scotland, he had become a rich man even as he understood the term. But things had then started to go badly wrong. Owing to the world recession, the *Bloater Corporation* had begun to make heavy losses and this time Lord Greyfield had been determined to save it. He had sold out his English and Scottish land at rock-bottom prices in 1931 in order to raise the necessary capital – but all to no avail. It had been put into liquidation in 1932 and the old man had promptly died.

"So you were left with nothing," I said. "But I thought . . ."

"No. Still had the German holdings. Worth a million. Even then."

If the second Earl of Greyfield had been prepared to cut his losses, all might have been well. But his father had resolutely refused to let him have anything to do with the various businesses while at the same time allowing him all the money that he wanted. He had seldom been out of the gossip columns, the expression '*bloatered* plutocrat' occurring and re-occurring with sickening regularity, and his only serious interest had been in racing. If he could make a profit out of owning race-horses, he had then argued to himself, why not in business too – and the former had indeed been an unqualified success. Why not indeed? He had gone out to Germany, become enthusiastic about what he saw there and accordingly decided to owe the Inland Revenue three hundred thousand pounds' worth of death duties for the time being. By 1936, both the coal and steel companies had started to pay dividends again and the value of their shares had appreciated considerably. There was only one drawback – German Foreign Exchange regulations made it impossible to transfer money back to this country and the Inland Revenue were pressing for the death duties on his father's estate.

It was then that young Greyfield had made his second major mistake. He had borrowed half a million pounds – this to be repaid over a period of three years – on the security of the German shares. On the fourth of September, 1939 – the third, on which war had been declared, having been a Sunday – he had heard from a representative of the Swiss Bank who had chanced to be in London on a visit, demanding immediate repayment of the money. In a panic, he had hurried round to see him. The banker had been quite charming about it, they had no alternative but to foreclose, of course – the Germans would seize all his assets including the accumulated dividends if they did not – but Lord Greyfield had no need to worry. The shares would be returned to him, less of course any money that might still be owing to them, after the war was over. It had been small comfort. The bank would be hard put to it to recover even the major part of their loan and there would certainly be nothing left over for him, once Germany had lost yet another war.

"Look here, Thyrde. Put my cards on the table. That job of yours. Need the money," he said.

As with Johnnie Bagot, I started to have a severe attack of conscience about the false hopes that I had been arousing.

"You'd have to speak German pretty well," I said, searching frantically for a loop-hole.

He smiled. "Ich bin auf allen Gebieten der deutschen Sprache äusserst bewandert, besonders in der Sprache der Geschaftswelt und der Akademikerkreise." Then he translated, "I am fully versed in all aspects of the German language, particularly those appertaining to the business and professional worlds."

Then

There was no answer to that one.

"Come and have lunch or dinner with me one day so that we can talk about your horses. Bring your wife," I said.

* * *

"So he'd be infinitely better off if the Germans did win the war?" said Brigadier Broadbent.

"Yes, but he's never thought for a moment that they would do, not even in the worst days after Dunkirk, he says."

* * *

I asked them to dinner at the International Sportsmen's Club. I had thought of taking them to Pilar's, but I had decided that on the whole it would be safer not and it only needed one glance at Lady Greyfield, a long thin querulous streak of a woman, to convince me now that my caution had been well-advised.

"We've brought Peterkin with us. It's Nanny's evening off and we knew you wouldn't mind. *Everybody* loves Peterkin," and I noticed for the first time that, standing behind them in tweed knickerbockers, was a more than usually repulsive-looking small boy.

"Yes of course that's all right," I said and I held out my hand.

The boy ignored it. He fixed me through a pair of black-rimmed spectacles with an unwaveringly hostile stare.

"I'm going to Harrow," he informed me, in a tone that implied that this sorted him and me out into our relative places once and for all. I was struck with a momentary and uncharacteristic pang of sympathy for Harrow. It was hard to see what even *that* establishment could have done to deserve such an affliction, but I did not say so.

"Shall we go in?" I said.

The waitress, who was rather a friend of mine, brought us the menus in the low, green, women-dominated dining-room. Lady Greyfield studied hers for a long time, then she turned it over as though she had suddenly realised that it was all a practical joke and that the real selection would be disclosed on the back. But the back was bare. She let it slip through her fingers onto the table.

"Oh, I don't know," she said. "Anything will do for me."

Then

"I'll have chicken soup followed by turbot," said Molly without hesitation.

"How about that for you too, Lady Greyfield?"

She closed her eyes. "*Anything!*"

"Peter?" He had told me to call him 'Peter'. "Yes, we'll all have that please," I said to the waitress hurriedly.

I was not going to give Peterkin the chance.

It was hardly the most enjoyable of meals. The food when it arrived was not bad at all and I was feeling ravenous, but Lady Greyfield picked at hers and left most of it behind on her plate. Poor Molly was left to cope with her. Lady Greyfield's conversation, what little of it filtered through to me, seemed to consist of one long series of complaints; food and rationing; clothes and rationing; transport and the misery of having no petrol ration at all; the difficulty of getting any decent servants, these days; their inefficiency and intransigence when at last one had managed to do so. Her nanny, if in fact that elusive functionary ever existed, did indeed seem to enjoy an inordinate amount of time off.

Peter Greyfield, on the other hand, ate everything that was put in front of him, chattering away to me non-stop about his racehorses, in disjointed but enthusiastic sentences. The financial embarrassment that had been so apparent at our last meeting seemed to have been totally forgotten.

"Start 'em all up again. Do even better. After the war," he said.

Peterkin never uttered once – until the pudding arrived.

"I can't eat *this*," he said, looking down with indignant horror at the pat of greyish material that lay before him. I must admit that it did look pretty nauseating, going slightly hard round the edges.

"It's what you ordered – semolina pudding," I said.

"I can't eat semolina pudding without jam!"

"Peterkin *always* has jam with his semolina pudding," put in Lady Greyfield fondly.

I beckoned over the friendly waitress and whispered in her ear.

"Well I don't know about that, dear, there *is* a war on, you know."

But she bustled off just the same, to return a few minutes later shielding in her hands from the gaze of less privileged diners, something which was disclosed to be a tea-spoon holding jam of a

Then

sickly green colour. She deposited it triumphantly in the middle of Peterkin's semolina pudding, giving the whole thing the appearance of an extremely suspect fried egg.

The conversations resumed their desultory course.

It was only when we were all finishing that what sounded like a half choked-off giggle made me aware of the smirk of self-satisfaction that was being directed to me through the smeared lenses of Peterkin's spectacles. Although what he could have to be self-satisfied about was beyond me. I glanced downwards.

And then I knew.

Every grain, every vestige of semolina pudding had disappeared, even the spoon and fork had been licked scrupulously clean, but there in the middle of the plate, surrounded like an island by a wide sea of gleaming white china and totally untouched, lay that tea-spoonful of sticky green jam.

* * *

"Ugh," said Molly, "that woman. I've had enough of her to last a life-time and as for Peterkin ..."

"But I thought you liked her. You seemed to be getting on so well together." I reached over a hand to touch hers. "Look, we never did have our evening at *The Four Hundred*. Shall we go there now?"

The smile that Molly gave me was devastating.

"Oh Derry, do let's," she said.

* * *

"They don't seem to be enjoying it very much, do they?"

Molly stood for a moment looking at the picture that hangs in the entrance hall – a couple in evening dress at one of the tables, frozen at one moment of time in the mid to late nineteen-twenties but now condemned for ever to sit and gaze at arriving and departing members, she with a cigarette and he with a glass in his hand.

"Oh, I don't know. A bit blasé perhaps, but remember they're here every night. Come on, let's take our coats off and see if we can do any better."

"No, hold on, they're playing *Called to Arms*. Can we just

Then

listen to that first? It's my favourite tune of the moment and they may not do it again."

We walked forward. Straight ahead of us lay the dimness of the dance-floor crowded with gently moving figures; beyond them the band, marginally better lit, with the single beam of a spot-light from the ceiling picking out the flower arrangement on top of the grand piano; the red glow of the tables was on our right. As we stood there, listening to the music, she still in her beige fox-fur coat, I in my British Warm, the words from the record by Ambrose and his Orchestra, in the tones of his male voice singer, ran through my mind.

> *Say, do you remember that day in September,*
> *The day that we waltzed through the night,*
> *When I was the guy in black tails and white tie,*
> *And you were the girl all in white?*
> *'Though I'd only just met you I'll never forget you*
> *The way that your eyes first met mine.*
> *Oh the dances we danced then, the glances we glanced then,*
> *The music, the moon-light, the wine.*
> *And the clouds we saw rise on the distant horizon*
> *Quite failed to arouse any qualms*
> *Until— I was called to the Colours*
> *And you were called to Arms.*

We were given a table by the wall. The red flocked paper behind us looked like pleated velvet but, when I reached up to touch it, it had the consistency of sand-paper. Molly put her hands down in front of her — she had lovely hands, slim with long tapering fingers. But there seemed to be something different about them.

"Where's your ring?" I asked suddenly. Always before she had worn an eternity ring, rubies in a white-gold setting.

"Oh, a stone came out and I dropped it in at the jeweller's this morning. It was my mother's. I feel odd without it," she wriggled her fingers, "almost indecent, somehow."

"Here, borrow mine." I took the signet ring off my own little finger and leaned over and put it on the third finger of her right hand. It fitted perfectly.

Molly held it up to the red-shaded table lamp to look at the effect.

"What a dear little owl. May I really? Yes, that feels much

Then

better," she said.

Several dances later Molly looked at me speculatively. We were back at our table again.

"Will you do something for me?" Her eyes glinted. "Will you take me on to the *Bag o' Nails*?"

"Certainly *not*!"

"Lots of my girl-friends have been and I've always wanted to."

I shook my head. "We'd be bound to run into men you know and think of the embarrassment to them." Actually I was far more worried about one specific, and even more embarrassing, encounter that we might have had.

I moved the table out and got up. "Come and dance again – but *here*," I said.

Molly floated in my arms as we did one long slow delicious circuit of the dance floor in silence. Then,

"What was she like? The girl at *The Bag*, I mean." I had told her about Irene.

"I don't know. I never got that far."

Her whole face suffused into a delightfully uniform mid-pink colour.

"You know perfectly well what I meant."

"Oh, wonderful figure, very pretty, danced like a dream and her hair was a lovely rich deep chestnut colour." I put up a hand to touch Molly's. "None of that insipid pale stuff that one sees so much of about, nowad... OUCH!"

"Serves you right for dancing with a mere amateur," Molly said.

And it was considerably later when the message was brought to our table. Molly's hand had somehow just found its way into mine.

"It's the Department for Inter-Service Co-ordination of Administration and Supply at the War Office, on the line for you, M'Lord."

I went to the telephone. As always I had kept them informed where I could be found that night.

"That you, Thyrde? You remember I promised you that you should be in at the kill? Well, I can't say more on an open line, but it looks as though it may be tomorrow. Got Miss Stanton with you? Good. Good. Haven't interrupted anything, have I?"

"Er ... no, Sir."

Then

I heard the Brigadier's chuckle at the other end of the line. "I'll see you both here, in . . . let's say half an hour," he said. I went back to the table – and Molly. "It's tomorrow," I said. "Come on, there's just time for one more dance before we go."

The floor was far less crowded now and the band-leader at his piano caught my eye as we danced slowly past, and inclined his head.

"Is there anything special you'd like me to play for you, m'Lord?"

"Thanks, Tim. Molly?"

"Can you play *Called to Arms*, please?" she said.

He signalled to the rest of the band who stopped in mid-note and broke immediately into the strains of the considerably slowed down but still recognisable waltz.

After a bit Molly, her cheek against mine, began to sing softly in my ear.

> *From love that enthralled us our Country has called us*
> *We've each got a job to do.*
> *Now you're in a suit that is khaki but cute*
> *And I am a girl dressed in blue.*
> *Our chances of meeting are precious but fleeting*
> *And soon we'll be summoned away.*
> *But while we're together what ever the weather*
> *Today is a wonderful day.*
> *For these moments at least all our troubles have ceased*
> *And we're safe from war's alarms,*
> *Although – you've been called to the Colours*
>   *And I've been called to Arms.*

The music changed again, to a slow fox-trot this time. I lowered my left hand which was holding her right, until they hung loosely twined together at our sides. Then I let her hand go and put mine behind her waist, my palm feeling the warmth of her through the flimsy stuff of her dress, and at the same time sliding my other hand down her back to join it so that the finger-tips met. Gently but with increasing pressure, I drew the dawning responsiveness of her body close against me. Tentatively at first, I sensed her cool arms creeping round my neck but soon her fingers were ruffling the hair at the back of my head. We were barely moving now and imperceptibly almost I slid my cheek over hers until, for the first time, I felt the wonder of her soft warm lips on mine.

12. Now

Some four feet away from me, Tisha was gyrating wildly. Annabel's was crowded that night, even for it. Then, in one of her more extravagant variations, she inadvertently cannoned into a nondescript, middle-aged sort of man who was entwined so inextricably with an over-blown blonde that one couldn't help wondering whether they hadn't been born with that affliction. Oops! She watched, an expression of horrified remorse on her face, as they shot apart like a dog and bitch who have just received the benefit of a bucketful of icy water on an already cold day. But she didn't let up. She was still convulsing.

'Sorry, Martin,' I said. 'My fault. Took me eyes off the road for a moment and the bird spun out of control.'

The male half of the recent combination nodded in an absent-minded but friendly sort of way and patiently set about the laborious process of re-establishing the status quo.

Tisha came up close to me until we were separated by a bare eighteen inches. 'Who was that?' I couldn't hear a word but the contortions of her lips made the question instantly understandable. I told her. 'Don't worry, he's only one of the minor dukes,' I said.

We went back to our table where we had left the Stobbs's on guard. I had met Peter quite by chance in Piccadilly that morning. He had suggested that I should dine with his wife, who possessed the unlikely name of "Euthalia", and himself after he had voted in the ten o'clock division at the House of Commons that night; I had already promised Tisha that I would take her to Annabel's; and, in the end, we had agreed that the two plans could be satisfactorily combined.

Peter, rather to my surprise, had turned up in a faultless dinner-jacket, his only aberration being the inevitable floppy bow tie, white spots on red – perhaps the horn-rimmed spectacles would have felt lonely without it – while his might-have-been countess,

Now

an earnestly hygienic mid-blonde, was in a long wispy brownish-grey evening dress, which plunged with calculated audacity where there was precious little to reveal. We had confined ourselves to trivialities over dinner and Peter had monopolised Tisha, who was wearing a three-quarter length dress in what I can only describe as "shocking-green". The two of them had chattered and laughed away non-stop together — which had left his wife free to concentrate on me.

Euthalia Stobbs's brand of party conversation had consisted of one long catalogue of the unfortunates of the world, the championship of whose cause was clearly her self-appointed task and who ranged from the genuinely destitute of Africa and Asia to women everywhere, who were being deprived through sheer malice it seemed of delights and services, mainly obstetrical, which I doubt if they knew existed and which they probably wouldn't have wanted if they had. Roger Faulkner, I remembered, had suggested that it was she who was the driving force behind Peter Stobbs's extreme left-wing views. Her brown eyes had been fixed earnestly and unwaveringly on mine as she invited me to share her abhorrence at each fresh revelation and her valedictory comment on every item before going on to the next was "*Dis graceful*", an epithet which she managed to make into two separate and distinct words without even the token link of a hypen in between.

As we rejoined them now, Euthalia was regarding the fresh orange juice that she was holding with the guilt-ridden expression of one who knows that every sip that she takes will be depriving the starving millions of the *Third World*. Peter was showing no such inhibitions over his sixth or seventh glass of champagne.

'Nice to see how you gilded parasites on the body politic live, once in a while,' he said. 'I'd have been a multi-millionaire myself if my old man hadn't somehow managed to piss the whole lot up the wall. You'd be finding me here — or somewhere like it — every night, if I had.'

'*Dis graceful*!' muttered Euthalia, although whether this was prompted by her husband's professed ambition, by his having been deprived of the means of gratifying it or merely by his choice of words, was not quite clear.

'How did it happen?' I asked.

'Never did find out for sure. All I know is, the very week before

Now

I was due to go to Harrow — clothes bought, bags packed, everything — I had to be taken off the list and was sent to the local council school instead. Narrow squeak, I can tell you. If it hadn't been for that I might be right in there defending the bastions of privilege just like the rest of you, instead of showing them up for what they are.'

He glared at me in silence for a moment or two and Euthalia reached forward and patted his hand proudly. I had often heard it said that Peter Stobbs had a monumental chip on his shoulder and it might well have dated from then.

I ordered another bottle. It was now past midnight. Leap Year day!

'It must be pretty obvious what I want to ask your advice about, Peter. I don't feel that I can talk like this to any of the others somehow but, if you were in my position, who would you suspect?'

'If I were in your position? Why, *you*, my dear Derek!' The whinny that followed was mercifully drowned by the music.

'No, seriously.'

'All right, let's see now.' The eyes from behind the spectacles stared into space for a moment or two. 'Roger Faulkner, he'd hardly be likely to rob himself. Stephen Knightley, I don't think it's likely to be him. Doubt if he's got the intelligence to steal a pat of butter from one of his own cows. Billy Candleford, he's even more idle than you are, never done an honest day's work in his whole life. But he's no fool, it could be him. Dick Richards, I don't know a lot about. But, if he's anything like some of the Americans I've come across, he'd rob his own mother — think it was just good sound business practice and sleep like a child afterwards. Then there's Leonard Frost and Henry . . .' He stopped short and looked at Tisha. Then he turned back to me and grinned. 'Perhaps I'd better leave it there. No, I think if I had to make a guess I'd plump for Dick with possibly Billy as a long shot.'

'But Billy's got all the money there is.'

Peter snorted. 'That sort never think they've got enough.'

'Look, Peter, if the time ever comes that I need some help, can I count on . . .'

'Would somebody mind telling me what all this is about?' Euthalia said.

'Oh, didn't I tell you?' Tisha and I sat in silence while Peter

Now

gave his wife a brief run-down on the events leading up to and including the visit of the "1944 Club" to Farmwell and the subsequent robbery. She had been looking from one to the other of us for the past few minutes but it had never occurred to me for a moment that she wouldn't have heard all about it. When he had finished, she cast an accusing glance in my direction.

'*Dis graceful*!'

'Hey, but it wasn't me. I didn't ...' and then I saw the expression in her eyes and realised my mistake. Whether or not I had done it was immaterial. I was now the underdog, the persecuted minority, and as such amply qualified to be taken to Euthalia Stobbs's bosom, a twin organ that bore some affinity to Dr. Who's space ship *The Tardis* in that, skimpy – negligible even – when viewed by the casual passer-by from without, it had any amount of room inside.

She got up, held out her right hand peremptorily for my left and led me, still without another word, towards the dance floor where, once we were installed as an integral part of the maelstrom, she placed a pair of protective arms about me and clamped her bony cheek tepidly to mine.

Tisha sat silent beside me as I drove the Citroen off through the London streets. Nor did she comment when, reaching the point where the routes to her flat and mine diverged, I selected the latter. The two standard lamps in the sitting-room were controlled by a switch at the door and I dimmed them to little more than a glow with the rheostat below it which was my latest toy. I walked over to the corner cupboard, poured out two glasses of *Christopher's Curious Old Virgin Brandy* and took them over to give hers to Tisha, who had curled herself up at one end of the sofa, legs beneath her, into a mouth-watering bundle. But there was still one more thing to do. I went across to the hi-fi system, selected an old Francoise Hardy L.P., put it on and turned the volume low.

'Don't you think,' said Tisha, 'that I'm rather too big a girl to fall for quite this sort of thing?'

The spell was shattered. I cut Miss Hardy off in her prime.

'Just you wait,' I said, 'I think I've got something else here that really is your scene.'

On top of a bookcase across the room there stood what must have been the great-grandfather of all modern gramophones. It consisted of a little square box of stained wood, turntable on top, with projecting out from its nickel pick-up head a long straight trumpet-shaped brass horn. I walked over and wound it up, picked from the attendant pile of single-sided records one at random, which I secured to the green-baize covered platen by means of the little gadget which screwed into the spindle, released the brake and lowered the needle onto the start of the groove.

The strident words of a long-forgotten music-hall song blared scratchily out until they filled the room. Tisha was standing beside me now, a look of near-ecstasy on her face. Eventually, after all too long a time it seemed, the instrument staggered to a merciful silence.

'Derek! Where *did* you get that?'

'Oh, it's been in my family for yonks. My mother ...'

'I know, gave it to you on condition you never sold it. Like Old Rollie. Right?'

'Wrong,' I said. 'She never could stand it. I only just rescued it from being sent off to the village jumble sale and even then she made me pay up the full 50p.'

Tisha turned to face me and, at the same time, I felt her soft hand take hold of mine.

'I will if you really want to, Derek, but ... if you wouldn't mind too dreadfully, I'd far rather wait until we're both absolutely certain. And ... somehow I've got a feeling that it'll be quite soon now.'

There wasn't very much that I *could* say in answer to that one.

I drove her home.

'Ah, you so got my message,' said Mr. Barraclough. 'Good of you to look in, Derek, and you, Mrs. Matheson. No, nothing new to see on the Rolls yet, I'm afraid. The men from Connolly's, the specialist leather people, are working on the upholstery now. But they found this ...' He rummaged in a drawer and pulled out a wristwatch, '... right inside the seat. Must have been there a year or two, I reckon, but even so I thought as how you might be glad to have it.'

He passed it over. It was remarkably undistinguished-looking, one of its worn brown crocodile straps was broken off short at the point where it had met the buckle and the round case was of stainless steel, but through the badly scuffed glass it was still just

Now

possible to make out the name "*Patek Philippe & Co., Genève,*" on the face beneath.

'Thanks,' I said. I put it in the right-hand pocket of my coat.

'Well, it's been a long old job restoring that old lady, but it's been a labour of love, I do assure you. And there's not a lot left to do now. Let's see.' Mr. Barraclough picked up the dog-eared work schedule from where it lay on the top of his desk.

'*. . . Spray final colouring paint and lacquer coats. Refit interior upholstery, trim and carpets. Fit new hood and cover. Refit lights etc. and bright parts. Fit coachwork furniture and chromed trims. Road test and make necessary adjustments. Complete cleaning interior and wax polish exterior to finish.*'

He scratched his head. 'Can't say offhand how long that little lot'll take. I'd best give you a ring, p'raps, when she's ready to collect.'

Sir Makepeace Brotherton had not been unreservedly enthusiastic when I had first told him about Dick Richards's offer to get all seven together round a table for me.

'It's worth a try, of course,' he said now. 'You'd be able to question them all about their alibis, for one thing. When you went round seeing each one individually, the "*You're the only one that I can really trust*" gambit precluded that. And we're going to need all the help that we can get. I hear the case is coming up on old Pierceworthy's list.'

'Is that bad?'

'It's not good. He's been known virtually to take over himself when he feels that the prosecuting counsel's not doing the job properly. No, I think that the time has come when we must take some positive action of our own. Here's what I suggest.'

I listened carefully while he outlined his plan. If Dick Richards's solution didn't work there was just a chance, I thought, that Sir Makepeace's might. One of the two had better, because time was rapidly running out now.

And, late that night, I was still turning the various possibilities over in my mind until I fell asleep.

xii. Then

"Wake up," I said to Molly, "I think that's the street ahead."

The sky was getting quite light now and from where I had pulled the Rolls in, some twenty-five yards short of a T-junction, I thought that I could just make out the numerals '10' on the door of a house across the road to our front. It was a street of terraced houses which looked as though they might have been built in the mid to late nineteen-thirties, but nearly five years of war-time stringency had left their outside paint-work in sad need of repair.

I had reached for the handle of the door and was just about to open it when I heard a warning hiss from Molly and at the same time felt her restraining hand on my left elbow. I froze. A bent figure had just appeared on the pavement that ran round the wall of the corner house to our half-right and was shambling towards us, its eyes intent on the gutter. The man stopped and bent down to pick up a cigarette-end, examined it distastefully, lit it in cupped hands, threw spent match and empty box away and came on. At the same moment, he seemed to notice us. Surreptitiously, he allowed the fragment of cigarette to fall from his lips, trod it out with his next step and slouched over to where I had the window half-way down.

"Got a fag, Mister?" he whined. He was wearing a filthy old mackintosh, fastened tightly round the throat with one of its only two remaining buttons. He held out a grimy blue-mittened hand.

"Sorry," I said. "I only smoke a pipe."

"I think I've got one," said Molly and she rummaged in her bag as the tramp shuffled round the long bonnet of the Rolls to reach her side.

He put the proffered cigarette between his lips and, as Molly flicked on her lighter, he leaned towards her — but not quite far enough to reach the flame. The air of dejection left his eyes for a moment as he glanced past her to me and gave me a barely perceptible wink.

Then

"Lord Thyrde? You won't see number seventeen from here, it's round the corner to your right on the other side of the street. There's no number on it, but it's the only house with a blue door. He's in there, all right, and the Morris is in the garage. Good luck, Sir."

Then he allowed the cigarette to meet the flame and straightened up.

"Gawd bless you, Lady," he said. He gave a notional pull to his fore-lock and slouched on past us down the road along which we had come.

I watched him in the driving-mirror through the slit of a rear window until he turned off down a side street. I gave him a minute or two and then I got out, walked diagonally across the road to the corner and peered round. The house was unmistakable, blue front door with a bow window beside it and two smaller windows above painted in a similar colour. It was at the end of that section of the terrace and a rickety wooden garage, doors held shut by a large padlock, filled the space between it and the first house of the next.

I turned and came back, taking the pipe and tobacco-pouch out of the pocket of my British Warm as I did so, and crossed the road behind the Rolls. I was badly in need of a stroll to stretch my legs and I hoped that that was how it would appear to any one who might be watching. I walked on, filling the pipe as I went. I glanced down the side-street as I passed it, but there was no sign of the tramp now and there did not seem to be any one else about. When I had covered about a hundred yards, I came to where the M.G. was pulled in with young Tom Barraclough at the wheel and there I stopped to light my pipe. I leaned down, ostensibly to do so out of the wind but taking care not to look in his direction, and between puffs I described the house to him and told him what I wanted him to do. Then I strolled on for another ten paces or so, before turning and retracing my steps back to the Rolls. Molly had shifted over to the driver's side and I got into the passenger seat beside her. After a minute or two, Tom drove slowly past us in the M.G., pulled in to the side of the road in front and inched forward until he had the house in view. Then he swivelled his head round and nodded to us.

"Your turn to get some sleep," said Molly. "I'll keep watch."

I wedged the pipe into a safe position on the ledge in front of me, leaned my head back gratefully against the leather upright

Then and closed my eyes.

   * * *

It had actually taken nearer three-quarters of an hour between the time of my hanging up the telephone receiver at *The Four Hundred* and the moment when Molly and I had pushed open the door of Brigadier Broadbent's room on the top floor of the War Office, in the very early hours of that morning. But I thought that in the circumstances the additional minutes that we had stolen were forgivable and, even if he had noticed, the Brigadier had not mentioned the fact.

Commander Jackson had had no difficulty in tracing the owner of the Morris Ten. He was a Belgian called Pierre Janssen, aged 43, height 5 ft. 6, weight 8 st. 4, who with three others had managed to escape across the Channel in an open boat in 1941. Like all refugees from Occupied Europe, he had been taken to the interrogation centre known disarmingly as the Royal Victoria Patriotic School in Clapham, where he and his few personal belongings had been subjected to, and had passed, the most rigorous of tests – not quite rigorous enough as it now seemed. He was an analytical chemist of a type which had been very much in demand at that stage in the war, and for the past two years he had been working at Farmwell. But he was employed in a section that was not engaged in work of particular secrecy and in a relatively minor capacity, little more than that of laboratory assistant, so to avoid arousing any suspicions Commander Jackson had felt that he had no option but to leave him where he was. The most that it had been thought safe to do had been to monitor all telephone calls and correspondence that Janssen received, both at work and at home, as was already being done so far as was possible with each of the other seven.

The Brigadier put a photograph into my hand. Did I perhaps recognise it as some one whom I might have seen that evening on the underground train when I had had my pocket picked? It was of a man with dark hair, a small round face and a moustache – hardly the sort who would stand out in a crowd. I shook my head.

Late the previous evening, Janssen – whether or not that was his real name was uncertain, it is apparently the Belgian equivalent of our 'Smith' – had indeed received a call, probably

Then

from a public box because there had been no matching one reported from the homes of any of the others, telling him to meet the caller and pick him up at a pre-arranged, and therefore undisclosed, time and place on the following day.

Commander Jackson's men were to cover each of the seven suspects – but this would tax his resources to the uttermost and he would only be able to spare a man to watch the accomplice until we could get there to take over. The task of following Pierre Janssen was to be left to Molly and me.

"But surely," I said, "we've known for some time that the spy himself is one of seven people, now that you know the actual identity of the accomplice, why don't you just pull in all eight?"

"Good question," said the Brigadier. "Good question. I was wondering whether you'd ask that."

We knew for certain that a second man was involved and, if two, why not a third? The third man, to whose identity we had no clue whatsoever, might either have actual possession of the paper himself or at least know of its whereabouts, might already have been given his own instructions and could therefore make his own arrangements to get it out of the country: if not on this occasion on another soon after, now with the certain knowledge of the extreme importance that we placed on it. It was a risk that we dared not take.

Our instructions were simple but categorical. We were to wait within view of Pierre Janssen's house until he came out and then we were to follow him, taking the greatest of care not to be seen ourselves, until he picked up the spy. As soon as that happened, the senior of the men who were tailing whichever of the seven suspects it turned out to be would make himself known to us and we were to take our further orders from him.

"What happens if he doesn't make contact with us?" I asked.

"He will. He will. He'll find that Rolls of yours easy enough to spot."

"So," I said, "will the spy."

There was a long pause. The Commander must have realised the danger of such a thing happening and for some reason discounted it, but Brigadier Broadbent had clearly not been briefed on the answer to that one.

"Or he might have managed to shake off Commander Jackson's men by that time."

Then

"See what you mean. See what you mean. Well, in that unlikely event," said the Brigadier cheerfully, "you're on your own."

But, even then we were just to follow and make no positive move of our own – yet. They might be intending to pick up the third man later, if such a one existed, and it might indeed be he who had the paper with him. Or it might already be hidden away at some place near to its eventual point of departure, forwarded to some fictional name 'care of' a post office for example, to be collected for security reasons at the very last moment. It was only when they seemed to be reaching whatever destination it was for which they were ultimately making that we were to take any action at all. Then, and only then, we were to use our own judgment and do whatever seemed to us to be necessary. *At all costs*, the Brigadier emphasised this, the '$2\frac{1}{2}$ C.A.' paper must be prevented from leaving the country.

Finally, he made Molly and me independently repeat all the instructions until he was satisfied that we both had them right.

As I drove Molly back to her digs in Jermyn Street, we had talked over my doubts about what seemed to me to be a very risky operation indeed and we had formulated at least some sort of a plan. While she was changing back into her tweed coat and skirt, I had rung up my agent, James Ford and, with abject apologies for the ungodliness of the hour, I had asked him to knock up Tom Barraclough with a message. Then I had driven the seventy odd miles back to Thyrde – we had agreed that Molly, who had once been sent to the police school at Hendon for a week-end course on tailing cars, should take over once we really got started – with she getting what sleep she could at my side.

I had found young Tom waiting for us at the village garage with the M.G. filled up and ready and, I holding the nozzle while he cranked the handle, I had given him his instructions as we did the same for the Rolls. I was amused to see that he had put on his Home Guard battle-dress in honour of the occasion, but the look of sheer horror on his face as he surveyed his former charge increased my feeling of guilt at the condition into which, without really noticing it, I had allowed her to deteriorate over the past weeks. Gone was the immaculate depth of sheen, hidden under a thin coating of oil and dust; there was at least one dent to be seen now, not to mention innumerable scratches; and I had thought that I detected distinct signs of corrosion through the paint-work

Then

of one of the rear mud-guards only the day before.

We had driven in convoy to the south-west outskirts of the town of Northampton, where I had had no difficulty in following Brigadier Broadbent's directions to the street in which Pierre Janssen lived. Tom had kept well behind me and he had stopped and pulled in to the side of the road as soon as I had. The last thing that I wanted was for *him* to be noticed by one of the Commander's men.

* * *

I felt Molly's hand shaking my arm – I could have sworn that I had only been asleep for ten minutes at the most.

"We're on our way," she said.

The Rolls was already turning the corner into bright sun-light. I glanced down at my wrist-watch and found that it was already gone ten o'clock. There were people about on the pavement now. One woman was buying a loaf of bread from the back of a horse-drawn van. Another was on her knees, scrubbing her front door-step. As we passed the house with the blue paint-work, I saw that the garage doors were open. There was nothing inside but a large patch of oil on the floor. The M.G. was disappearing off to the right at the far end of the street. The Morris Ten was no longer in sight.

"Don't lose him, whatever you do."

"Me?" said Molly. "I'm an expert, remember. I did nothing else but this – over a whole week-end!"

We turned to the right ourselves, then left, then right again. I sat there tensely, willing myself not to back-seat-drive. She seemed to be leaving an awful lot of distance between us and the M.G. in front. Tom Barraclough, oddly enough, I felt no worries about. I knew that he drove most days, doing taxi jobs for that garage of his, and he would not be likely to risk making a mess of the one chance that he was ever likely to get of doing anything active during the whole of the rest of the war. But there was not a lot of point in him keeping up with the Morris if we, in our turn, lost touch with him. He would hardly be in a position to do anything by himself, even if he had known exactly what it was all about, when the moment came. But, as we turned corner after corner, there he always was in front of us and once or twice I caught a

Then

glimpse of the Morris ahead. It was not long before I began to feel more confident and once we were well out of Northampton on the Bedford road, the same general direction towards which Thyrde lay, I knew that I really could relax. Tom knew every by-road for miles around – and so, for that matter, did I.

"Well done!" I said to Molly. "But we ought to be taking the lead now. Give Tom the signal."

She reached forward for a little silver-coloured knob on the dash-board and switched the spot-light beam on and off several times in quick succession. Unlike the main head-lights, it had never been equipped with a black-out visor – I had only replaced the bulb, which had been carefully stored away in a cardboard box in the boot, early that morning.

The M.G. shot forward. Molly increased our own speed proportionately, but still keeping a respectable distance behind it, until it pulled out onto the crown of the road to overtake a car, which we could now see was the Morris Ten, accelerated again, and soon disappeared out of sight round a bend ahead.

Immediately Molly slowed down to match the speed of the Morris.

I swivelled round in my seat and watched out of the rear window. After a mile or two, I saw the M.G. nose out of a side road behind us and follow in our wake. Then I turned my head again and relaxed back into my seat.

"That's all right. He's with us again," I said.

The plan which we had worked out after leaving the Brigadier's room at the War Office was this. The main danger points, it had seemed to us, were at the beginning and at the end of the operation. The Rolls was a quite unmistakable car and Janssen could easily catch a glimpse of it when he came out of his house, or while he was threading his way through the back streets of Northampton, and recognise it as the car that had given chase to him after he had left Covent Garden underground station several weeks before. If he did, he would certainly try and shake us off before he made for the rendez-vous.

He might even give up his journey altogether, leaving the spy and/or the third man to carry on alone. For all we knew, they could have planned for just such an emergency.

For this reason, we had decided that Tom, in the far less conspicuous M.G., should lead to begin with. But, once we were

Then

out onto a main road in the open country-side, Molly's experience in following cars would tell, and we would take over. Any large towns with adverse traffic-lights through which we might have to go would present a risk, of course, but with any luck there would be other vehicles behind which we could take a certain amount of cover.

There would be even greater danger when Janssen stopped to pick up the spy, because at that point there would be two of them who might spot us rather than one. We had therefore arranged that if the Morris turned off onto a minor road, either in a town or in the countryside, or showed any other indications of stopping, Tom would take the lead again. If it turned out to be a false alarm and the Belgian had stopped for any other reason, we would carry on as before. But, once the pick-up had taken place and Commander Jackson's man had made himself known to us, we would give Tom another signal by means of the spot-light and he would make for home. I was sorry to have had to insist on this, because it had obviously been a great disappointment to him when he had heard that he was not to be in at the finish. But I wanted to keep his involvement from the Commander if I possibly could, and, in any case, we would have all the help that we needed by then. There was always the possibility that, for one reason or another, Commander Jackson's man might fail to make contact with us and we had to make provision for that too. If that should happen, then we *would* keep Tom and the M.G. with us, we taking the lead again just as soon as the Morris was well on its way.

Of course, it might not work out like that at all, but that had been the best that, at such short notice, we had been able to devise. And, so far, things were going according to plan.

We passed through Bedford, with its ring of looming elephant-grey barrage balloons, and along the flat plain in the direction of the Great North Road. There, we turned left.

"He'll probably turn off right again in a mile or two," I said. "Assuming that he's making for the East Coast, that is, but if he'd been going any further north I doubt if he'd have come this way."

He did indeed turn right, over a long narrow bridge and into the little town of St. Neots, steadily through it and out into the open country beyond. As we passed the cross-roads at Caxton Gibbet, I looked down the road to the right at the gaunt black wooden post, with its single gruesome arm, which gave the place its name.

Then

Whether it was a true survival from earlier days or merely a modern reconstruction, designed to act as a sign for the public house that now stood there, I had always been meaning to find out – and somehow never had. Probably the latter, I thought. But I could not help wondering whether Janssen too had noticed it and, if he had, just exactly what forebodings it might have aroused in him.

We left Cambridge by the Newmarket Road.

There was rather more traffic about than usual, most of it military of one kind or another – but luckily no convoys, or rather none going in the same direction as ourselves! We passed lines of poplars, their leaves reddy-brown in the spring sun-shine; cowslips full-open by the road-side; and, once, a beech wood, with blue-bells dusting the entire surface between its tree trunks into a continuous powder-blue splash. I sat back in my seat and watched the road with its bordering hedgerows rolling back towards us. Sometimes I glanced backwards to check that the M.G. was still following, sometimes towards Molly who was driving in relaxed confidence beside me.

And always ahead was the Morris Ten, often out of sight but never quite out of touch, pottering along with what seemed to be a total lack of concern in front of us, covering mile after mile and doing a steady forty most of the way.

* * *

"Where are we?" I said. "I must have dropped off for a moment."

The Rolls had come to a stop with the engine still running. Molly had her arm out through her open window and was beckoning Tom Barraclough on.

"Not far short of Bury St. Edmunds. Don't worry, he's just turned off down that little road ahead."

She pointed with her hand as the M.G. drew level and I saw Tom nod in reply. Molly let out the clutch as he disappeared down a turning to the left and we followed him round. It was a narrow winding road, little more than a lane, with high banks lined with trees on either side. Their branches met at the top and the sun was shining through the newly opened leaves, stippling the gritty road surface into a intricate pattern of light and shade.

Molly kept about fifty yards between us and the M.G.

Then

"Look out!" I said.

We had slowed down considerably in order to negotiate a sharp bend when I had suddenly seen the other car close in front and realised that it was reversing towards us. But Molly had seen it as soon as I had and reacted immediately and she pulled in behind it when the M.G. came to a stop. Tom got out and walked back.

"Coo, that were a close one, nearly over-ran him, I done. Pulled into a pub just round the corner. Don't think he saw me though, and he'll be there for a bit. Locked his car before he went in."

"What's it like?" I said. "Did you see anywhere we can put the cars so that we can watch without being seen?"

Tom grinned. "Thought you'd ask that. Yes, the pub's on the left and there's a bit of a green lane on the right just short of it. Reckon it'll be out of sight of the windows too."

"Right-ho," I said. "We'll go in first and see if we can reverse into it. Give us a minute or two and then you back in after us."

Molly just managed to manoeuvre the Rolls past the M.G. and drove on at walking pace until almost immediately we saw the green lane on our right. The grass had been deeply rutted by cart-wheels but the surface looked firm enough and there, sure enough, was the free-standing sign of a public house – it had no picture and the faded lettering was impossible to read at that distance – with the Morris parked by it, on the other side of the road some thirty yards ahead. Molly inched the Rolls forward until we could just see the brick wall at the far end of the actual building and then she put the gear into reverse. We could still see the sign and the Morris beside it, as we backed off the road and into the rutted grass lane, until both were hidden by the high hedge on our right. After a minute or two we watched as Tom repeated the process in the M.G. He reversed well back towards us and then moved slowly forward again – and stopped. His hand came out to give us a thumb-up sign.

I looked down at my watch. It was ten-past one.

"Perhaps this isn't the actual meeting-place," I said. "He may only have stopped for lunch."

Suddenly I realised how hungry I was. Molly and I had had nothing to eat since dinner on the previous day and here we were stuck in a hot dusty car while, all the time, that wretched little traitor of a Belgian was stuffing his beastly tummy with all sorts of unimaginable delicacies.

Then

"Hard-boiled *eggs*," I said out loud. "Ham rolls and a pint of bitter beer in pewter tankard; possibly even a piece of crusty pork pie with freshly-made mustard!"

Molly leaned her fair head back against the leather, closed her eyes and moaned gently.

"Stop it, I can't bear it," she said.

Visions of the Berkeley Buttery began to float through my mind, although why it should have been that particular restaurant I am not quite sure. In my imagination, I sat at a table and went through the menu, selecting what I would choose just at that moment. I eventually settled for *Pigeons à la Buttery* – was that what they called them? – dark yielding flesh in a thick rich gravy. There was an unkind rumour that they were apt to arrive with 'Trafalgar Square' stamped on their breasts, but what could I not have done with one of those just now?

"Beg pardon, Mr. Derry." Tom was at my window holding up a patched leather shopping bag. "Mother hoped you wouldn't think it was a liberty, but she was putting up my dinner and she sent this for you and Miss Molly."

"That's marvellous. Just what we were needing," I said, trying not to let too much greed creep into my gratitude. I took it through the window and passed it to Molly. "Oh, by the way, could you keep an eye open and see how many people get back into the Morris? If he has a passenger hold up two fingers, if he's by himself, just one."

"Very good, Mr. Derry."

Molly had immediately started delving into the contents of the bag. There was a lever-topped fizzy lemonade bottle full of what looked like cold tea with a couple of enamel mugs – and two packets wrapped in grease-proof paper besides.

"Tom, it looks *delicious*," she said.

A slow grin of gratification came over his face. He stood there for a moment and then turned and ran back to the M.G.

"Just look at *this*," said Molly and she put an enormous sandwich into my hand. Made of rounds cut from the widest part of a cottage loaf, their spongy whiteness buttered with no skimpy war-time scrape, there must have been the best part of a week's ration of cheese, together with a dark-brown jammy substance which was obviously home-made pickle, inside. I took a first expectant bite.

Then

Any remaining thoughts of the Berkeley Buttery instantly disintegrated. *Nothing* that the kitchens or cellars of that admirable establishment provided could have tasted one quarter so delicious as those cheddar cheese and home-made pickle sandwiches and that cold sweet milky tea.

We were just finishing up the last lingering crumbs, when Tom put his hand out with one finger held up. Seconds later the Morris flashed past. We followed the M.G. back along the way we had come, through the leafy tree-tunnel until, approaching the main road again, we saw its left-hand indicator arm shoot out.

"Better give Tom the signal again," I said, as soon as we ourselves had turned the corner. Molly did so and, this time, the M.G. slowed down and kept over to the left-hand side of the road so that we could over-take. We had decided that it would be unwise to use the *over-taking and waiting in a side-road* trick more than once and that after that we would revert to the more conventional method. And we soon had the Morris Ten in sight again, proceeding on its apparently still-unsuspecting way.

* * *

"This *must* be it," said Molly. "That's the railway station ahead."

We had passed through Bury St. Edmunds, Stowmarket and Needham Market without incident. When we had reached the outskirts of Ipswich, the Morris had turned off down a little street to the left and Molly had waved Tom on past us, so that the M.G. could again take the lead. We had followed in the Rolls, taking care to keep a good distance between us and them, as the two cars in front had turned right and left and right again. Then turning left once more at a '*HALT. Major Road Ahead*' sign we had found ourselves back on the same road and Molly and I had come to the conclusion that the sole purpose of this complicated manoeuvre must have been to avoid a road-block connected with the ten-mile-wide strip of 'Protected Areas', which had come into force at the beginning of April and which ran round the entire coast-line from The Wash to Land's End. We had decided that it would hardly be worth-while to change the order again until we were clear of the town and, sure enough, the M.G. had come to a stop at the far end of a long bridge. I could just see the right-hand side of the drab yellow-brick Victorian station building with its upper

Then

windows framed in two courses of red, across the road at the T-junction to our front.

The door of the M.G. opened and Tom got out, crouching and peering forward. Then he straightened up and walked back towards us.

"It's all right. He's gone in."

"Good," I said. "Better get back though, we don't want to lose him now."

Tom nodded and ran back to the M.G., where he adopted the same crouching and peering attitude, and it seemed that he was only just in time. He held up two fingers in our direction, jumped into the car and drove off. He turned left and as we followed, driving on past the station and weaving our way through the streets and over another bridge, all the time I was gazing round me searching for some sort of a sign from Commander Jackson's men. It was not until we had left the town and seemed to be heading eastwards down a little country road that I finally had to admit to myself that none would be forthcoming.

"That's torn it," I said. "Who-ever he is, he must have managed to shake them off. It's the worst possible thing that could have happened."

"I doubt if Tom'll agree with that," Molly said.

She gave the M.G. the signal which meant that it was to stay on with us and, as he pulled well into the side to give us room to overtake again, I saw through my open window that there was indeed a grin of pure happiness on Tom Barraclough's freckled face.

We went along a series of lanes, narrow but surprisingly straight in places. There were little banks, unkempt hedges along the top of them spaced irregularly with trees – oak and elm predominantly, on either side.

We nearly ran straight into them, when it happened. It was certainly no fault of Molly's, but this time they did see us – of that there could be no doubt at all. We had just rounded a sharp bend and there was the Morris Ten, stationary at a cross-roads in front of us, and Janssen – he was easily recognisable from his photograph – was standing beside it in a dark blue suit, consulting a map. He looked up, startled, as the Rolls juddered to a halt, shot back into the car and was off in it along the road on the left. I was just able to make out the indistinct blur of a face from the

Then

passenger seat, staring back at us through the rear window, as the Morris disappeared out of sight.

Molly stared at me aghast. "What do we do now, Derry? Catch 'em up and stop 'em?"

"We can't," I said. "Not yet."

There was a sudden screeching of brakes behind us. Young Tom had arrived.

I had a flash of inspiration. "Look," I said, "I'll change places with Tom. You and he catch up with the Morris in the Rolls, follow them for a bit but, as soon as you're certain that they've seen you again, pretend to let them lose you. Then let me past in the M.G. and I'll take over from there."

Molly wasted no time in arguing. "All right. But why don't you swap jackets with Tom too? Now that his moustache has grown and he's trimmed it a bit, he's not at all unlike you at a distance."

I was out on the road by this time and I immediately started to do as she said. "Quick, give me your blouse," I said to the bemused Tom who had left the M.G. to come up and join us. "Thanks. Put this on and jump in the Rolls. She'll explain as you go." I thrust my service dress jacket with the unbuckled Sam Browne belt still on it into his hands, snatched up the loaded Smith and Wesson .45 revolver from the floor in front of the passenger seat, threw my forage cap in after Tom and then ran back to the M.G., struggling into his battle-dress blouse, which was far too small for me, as I went. Tom had left the engine running and I put the car into gear, let out the clutch and started after the Rolls, as it too was disappearing down the road to the left.

Molly drove like a demon. Time and again, I saw her wheels mount up on the grass verge on one side or the other, throwing up sprays of dirt and weeds as they did so. God knows what would have happened if she had met something coming towards her, although I realised afterwards that it would almost certainly have hit the Morris first.

For a plan thought up on the spur of the moment it was not at all a bad one, although I do say it myself. Even now, I cannot see how it could have been bettered. And it would have worked too — if it had not been for that confounded level-crossing.

Almost in slow motion it seemed I watched the action, as it unfolded with an awful sense of inevitability in front of me. The Morris Ten was already through. A little old man, in railway cap

Then

and uniform, had the gate on our side part-shut. Molly blared on her horn and he paused and beckoned her on with a series of quick impatient waves. Then as she scraped through with a couple of inches clearance on either side, he drew himself up and gave her a very smart but quivering military salute. Some forty yards back I was just accelerating to follow her through, but he held up one hand, palm towards me, in an imperious gesture. A Rolls Royce with a pretty girl at the wheel might be one thing but a battered old M.G. driven ostensibly by a Home Guard private was clearly quite another and one from which he was prepared to put up with no nonsense whatsoever. With a jerky little run, he continued to push the heavy gate towards me and I managed to pull up with a foot to spare as he slammed it shut in my face.

"For God's sake let me through," I shouted. "This is a matter of life and death."

"Can't, mate. Train's coming," and he jerked his thumb towards where, over the top of the hedge, I could indeed see a puffing line of smoke approaching from down the line on the right.

I sat there subconsciously counting the wagons, 1, 2, 3, 4 ... *Molly must have seen my predicament through her rear-mirror* ... 10, 11, 12 ... *She would realise that she and Tom were on their own now* ... 18, 19, 20 ... *What, in the changed circumstances, would she feel that they must do when they did catch up with the Morris?* ... 29, 30, 31 ... *The possible consequences were too dreadful to contemplate* ... 36, 37, 38 ... *To Molly!* ... 40, 41, as a seemingly endless goods train trundled by.

Of course he *would* have to go and open the far gate first.

When, eventually, he did get around to my side, I remember hoping at the time that the fright which I gave him, as I shot through before there was really room for the M.G. to do so, would last him for the remainder of his life. I roared down that road, thumb permanently down on the horn button, praying that there would be no turning off before I could catch up with them. But I knew in my heart that it was a forlorn hope. They had far too good a start on me for that.

I over-shot the cross-roads before I had realised that it was there. I trod on the brakes, slammed the gear into reverse and raced backwards. Then I got out and gazed about me helplessly. A choice of three ways. I had no means of knowing whether, in

Then

their hurry to escape us, they had taken the road that they had intended when we had surprised them at the previous cross-roads. Which way, therefore, would they have selected now?

But for once luck was on my side.

I spotted the blue and gilt of my forage cap first. Dust-bespattered by the loose gravel from which it had obviously been kicked, it lay upside-down on its flat top, half-hidden in the grass on the left-hand side of the road. And, almost at the same moment, I saw the dishevelled figure of Tom Barraclough, service-dress jacket flapping loosely about it, stagger to its feet from the bank against which it had been slouched, put its hands to its head and sit down heavily again.

"They went that way, Mr. Derry, Sir." He pointed to the right. "Don't worry about me. They've . . . they've got Miss Molly – and the Rolls," he said.

"I'll be back," I called over my shoulder as I ran back and into the M.G. and I shot off again in the direction that he had indicated, scattering poor Tom with gravel as I went.

The metalled road on which I now found myself was in tolerably good condition and I trod the accelerator pedal down into the floor-boards. The car was going better than I had ever known it to do – Tom had fulfilled his charge well – and I was certain that it had the legs of the Morris Ten, not to mention the Rolls. The Rolls meant *Molly* now and I was straining my eyes ahead as I drove, desperate to catch a glimpse of that familiar fawn shape.

I reached for the Smith and Wesson, took it one-handed from its holster and laid it ready on the seat beside me. Any qualms that I might have had about using it in earnest had disappeared now.

A more than usually slovenly private soldier was standing by the road-side, a rifle slung over his shoulder. He removed the cigarette from his mouth as I approached him, made a token effort to hide it behind his back, and started to wave me down with the other hand. I paid scant attention but I discovered the reason just as soon as I had rounded the next bend. A temporary road-block had been set up. The Morris it seemed had already been checked and was stationary some sixty or seventy yards beyond; but there, blessed sight, still on the near-side of the barrier and an all too uncomfortably short distance ahead, was my Rolls-Royce, JB 5555.

Then

Once again, Janssen was standing out in the road, gesticulating as he talked to two more soldiers, another private and an equally scruffy sergeant.

"Stop that man," I yelled, as I skidded to a halt.

Three heads turned. Three faces gaped at me, their bodies transfixed, as I jumped out of the car and ran towards them, the revolver now in my right hand. The Belgian had a look of almost comical incredulity on his face but he was the first to move. Suddenly he ducked under the red and white counter-weighted pole and scuttled off along the road towards the waiting Morris. Without a moment's hesitation, I raised the revolver and fired – aiming for his legs.

At first, I thought that I had missed him. The little man continued on for a couple of paces but before I could fire again he just seemed to crumple, fell and lay by the road-side in a dark blue pin-striped heap.

Molly! I rushed back to the Rolls, flung open the door, pulled forward the upright of the seat and there she was in the space behind. I reached in both arms and eased her gently out. Bound and gagged, the blindfold having slipped just enough to reveal two blue eyes softening in recognition, her near-white hair tousled, she had a bruise over one of the eyes and two large smuts over the other but never had she looked more adorable.

"Thank God you're safe," I said and I started to carry her to the side of the road, preparatory to untying her.

" 'Mm—'mmm!" the eyes were blazing at me furiously and she jerked her head in order to divert my attention from her to what was happening further down the road. I glanced quickly round. The driver of the Morris already had his car moving, leaving his unfortunate accomplice to whatever fate might be in store for him. "Look after her," I thrust Molly into the arms of the astonished sergeant. "And him," I added, pointing with the revolver to the still inert Belgian. I jumped into the Rolls.

"And get that b****y barrier up," I said.

The private soldier moved with quite astonishing agility but, even so, I was too quick for him. As the long fawn bonnet glided forwards, the rising metal pole struck the flying lady mascot a glancing blow on her head.

The road had narrowed considerably now; the banks pressing in on either side were smothered with masses of tall yellow wild

Then

flowers of a type which was not familiar to me; stalks and leaves of a succulent apple-green, the whole impression being that of a particularly venomous-looking variation on the general idea of cow-parsley, they surrounded the two pill-boxes that I passed set in the hedge-row and softened and mellowed the stark white concrete outlines in the late afternoon sun; there was a distinct whiff of the sea.

Whatever combination of pressures, threats to his family, the hopelessness that comes with total defeat, weakness of character or just plain financial greed, had prevailed upon Janssen, that pitiful bundle which I had barely managed to avoid where it lay unmoving yet by the road-side, to work against his own country and ours, alive or dead he would get, or had already got, his just deserts now. But the man in the Morris Ten ahead... whichever of the seven it was, and I would know that soon enough, there could be no excuse for him.

This man – spy, traitor, call him what you will – had of his own free will taken the deliberate and cynical decision to sell out to the enemy, to betray his King and Country and to live a life of pretence and deceit among his friends. Only I was in a position to stop him now, to expose him for what he was and, above all, to prevent the ultimate catastrophe of the '$2\frac{1}{2}$ C.A.' paper leaving the country. And he had dared to lay his filthy hands on Molly... the Rolls became a weapon of war in my hands, an avenging chariot, as I rammed it down that peaceful Suffolk lane.

I must have been on the point of catching up with him, even if he had not stopped. But there at last, drawn up alongside a gate on the left-hand side of the road ahead of me, smoke-like exhaust fumes emerging from beneath its squat rear end, driver's door still swinging slowly shut as I came upon it and obviously only just left empty, I saw the newly painted dark blue of the Morris Ten. And at the same moment, help arrived too. Even as I scrambled from the Rolls, a motor-bicycle appeared coming flat out towards me from round the bend in the road beyond, braked sharply as its rider, a red-capped Military Policeman, saw me and drew up with a roar and a spray of gravel.

"Follow me," I shouted, beckoning with the revolver as I ran, and I made for the gate.

I already had one foot on the second rung and there was just enough time, in much the same manner as the split second of exposure allowed by the camera-shutter onto the surface of a roll of film, for the details of the scene which was now in front of me to imprint themselves on my mind. A slope gently descending to a wide expanse of water, the strong west wind swaying and rippling the coarse grass into an ever-changing pattern of varying tones of green, the figure of a running man who had still covered less than half the distance to where a flying boat was bobbing amongst the white-topped waves of the estuary below. I had five shots left and I could, would, *must* stop him now, when ...

"Hey, you!"

The words came from close behind me and, at the same moment, my arms were grabbed, the Smith and Wesson slipped from my fingers, I felt myself being jerked backwards from the gate to fall and hit the ground with a jolting, breath-expelling thump and the next thing I knew was that there was a heavy hand pinning down each of my shoulders and I was lying on my back gazing stupidly upwards, past a pair of double chevronned khaki-clad arms, to the red cap and the equally red face below it that were looming over me.

"And where do you think you might be going?"

For a full minute I just lay there. I was incapable of speech.

Then, "That will be enough, Corporal," I said wearily.

Half-winded as I still was, there must have been enough of authority left in my voice, because he let go immediately and helped me to my feet. It was then that the muted throbbing sound, that had progressively been trying to insinuate itself into my consciousness, made itself apparent over the sound of the wind. Together we turned back to the gate.

The flying-boat, which must have taxied several hundred yards down-river before turning inland again in order to begin its run into the wind, had already passed the point where it was directly opposite to us and it was now skimming along the water at considerable speed. As we watched, it seemed to use the waves as a launching-ramp, rose on its hull and became air-borne. It gathered height steadily until, when it had almost reached the limit of our view, it made a wide turn in the air and started coming back towards us again. As it approached, the sound increasing with every second, the details of its ungainly shape came more and more into focus. The floats on either wing-tip; the double set of wings, upper and lower, the single engine perched incongruously

Then

in the centre of the space between, as though the designer had somehow forgotten all about it and then stuck it in there as an after-thought; the red-white-and-blue roundels, which it still bore on wing and side, belying its present ownership because it was clearly in enemy hands now; even the pink blob that was the pilot's face. At a height of about two hundred feet, it passed directly over our heads, the white of its now massive body becoming dark for a moment in contrast to the light above, and, as the roar of the engine which had risen to an almost unbearable volume began gradually to diminish again, so the flying-boat itself became smaller and smaller until it was no more than a speck, soon to disappear altogether into the sea-mists of the eastern sky.

Instinctively we both looked back to the estuary, to the place where it had been – and beyond it. A little motor-boat, already three-quarters of the way across, was making its escape towards the other side.

The Military Police Corporal turned to face me and, at the same moment, he seemed for the first time to take in the stuff of which my shirt and tie were made, my service-dress trousers, my dark brown shoes under the scuffed dustiness of which traces of their former high polish were still to be seen. His mouth had been gaping already, but his jaw dropped still further into an expression of exaggerated, almost stage bewilderment. In other circumstances I could have felt sorry for him. I realised later that, capless as I was, ill-fitting battle-dress blouse unbuttoned at front and cuffs, hair blown all over the place and unshaven since the previous morning, the best part of thirty-six hours before, his mistake was at least understandable – how I had been able to bluster my way past the soldiers at the road-block, I still do not know. But after all those weeks of uncertainty, of painstaking effort and frustration, after the events of the day itself culminating in the past half-hour or so of desperate, gut-binding anxiety, to have had the prize snatched from me, at the very moment when success had seemed to be certain, by the blundering officiousness of this oaf beside me, sympathy was just about the last emotion which I was capable of feeling now. I looked into his great bovine face.

"If it's of any interest to you," I said, "you've probably just lost us the war."

13. Now

'What on earth is this?' said Tisha.
I glanced round. We were standing in the hall at Thyrde, I by the window out of which I had been looking, she by the fireplace. She had in her hands a model of a rather grotesque-looking biplane.

'Oh, that. It's a Supermarine Walrus. But for goodness' *sake* be careful, it belongs to my mama and it's one of her most treasured possessions.' Tisha put it down on the mantelpiece again as though it were a *T'ang* dynasty porcelain horse. 'She always swears it's one of those that might have made the whole difference as to whether we won or lost the war.'

I looked back through the window down the long straight drive, flanked on either side by the leafless tracery of the young lime trees, at whose base the daffodils were just beginning to show. There was a car turning in through the gates at the far end. Then another.

'Look out, they're coming,' I said.

We had agreed that she was to go and spend the day with my mother and Bridget, the collie, who was beginning to accord to Tisha the same, only marginally secondary, degree of devotion that had previously been reserved for my twin sister and myself. Tisha's presence, combined with that of her husband, her father and myself, would have made what was in any case going to be an embarrassing occasion almost intolerable.

She nodded and slipped out through the green baize door.

When they had all arrived, I took them into the dining-room where there were eight chairs round the table. It was only after we had sat down that I realised that, without any prior consultation, we had instinctively made for the places that we traditionally occupied at the annual dinner, I in the middle on one side, Leonard on my left, Henry at the foot of the table, Peter, Roger

Now

and Dick opposite, Billy at the head and Stephen on his left and my right. It was the American who spoke first.

'This is a unique occasion in the relatively short history of the "1944 Club", Gentlemen, and I'd like to begin by expressing my personal thanks to each of you for being here.' It did indeed say quite a lot for his powers of persuasion that everybody had agreed to come. 'But one of our number is in trouble and I considered that the circumstances warranted it. You all know what happened at Farmwell on the night of our visit. One of us eight, and I don't exclude you, Derek, nor you Roger,' he smiled, 'nor even myself, *must* be the thief. Now the rules of the game are these. I'm going to invite Derek, here, to put any questions at all that he may consider necessary to any of us and, as it's going to be difficult enough to establish the truth, I think that we should all consider ourselves under oath to answer fully and frankly and not to hold anything back.'

There were stirrings of unease round the table.

'That's all very well,' said Billy Candleford, 'but if Derek's been wrongly accused, the same thing could happen to any of us. Why should we stick our necks ...'

'Just a minute, Billy. None of you was compelled to come here and you are all perfectly free to go, either now or at any time that you wish. But I think that I should warn you of the possible conclusions which the rest of us might draw from such an action.'

He looked round the table. Nobody moved.

'Very well. Derek, the floor is yours.'

'I still don't like it,' Billy said.

It gave me as good an opening as any. 'I must say, I'm very much inclined to agree with Billy,' I said. 'What you're all doing is beyond the call of friendship and I really am most awfully grateful – especially to you, Dick. Now what I'd like you to do first is to fill in one of these.'

I passed round seven bank paying-in slips, on the top of each of which I had had the appropriate name typed, with the figure 1 against it. I told them the date, "12.4.79", the name and address of my bank, that they should be credited to "The Viscount Thyrde" with my own account number, and the four sums that I wanted them to fill in against the £20, £10, £5 and £1 slots respectively, with the total at the bottom. I had contrived these latter in such a way that, taken in conjunction with the date and

Now

account number, each digit including nought appeared at least twice. Finally I asked them to put the name of the payer-in as "P. JANNSEN" in block capitals.

I watched them while they did it.

'Thank you very much. No don't give them back yet.' I passed round seven more slips, each with the figure 2 against the typed name. 'Now, will you all do exactly the same again, please, but this time using your left hand – that'll be the right as far as you're concerned, Leonard.'

'If I'd known we were going to be asked to play round games, I wouldn't have come,' Henry said.

The second operation took considerably longer and when it was finished I collected all fourteen slips.

'Thank you'. I picked up a sheet of typescript from the table in front of me. 'Now you were all kind enough to give Dick Richards an account of your movements on the night of the Farmwell visit. I have his notes here and I'm afraid I must ask you to go into them in rather more detail.'

There was a tangible silence round the table. Then, very much to my surprise, it was broken by Henry Matheson who nodded approvingly.

'That's much more like it,' he said. 'I came prepared for that.'

Henry had arrived at the hotel where he usually stayed in Birmingham but where, on this occasion, his booking had gone astray, at about 7.0 p.m. He had had dinner there before beginning his search and he had not reached the motel where he had eventually been able to find a room until 10.30 or 11.0. He had left it again at 8.30 in the morning and been at his board-meeting punctually at 9.0.

'I was in Birmingham last week and, quite by chance, I found it again.' He put a hand into his inside breast pocket and produced a wodge of papers. 'Here,' he unfolded one of them and held it out to me down the table, 'is a Xerox copy of the relevant page of the register. I've marked the entry in yellow.' I glanced at it. "3.4.79. Henry Matheson, M.P., 217 Lumford Mansions, Westminster. British", it read.

'And this,' he passed me the other, 'is the carbon copy of the receipt they gave me.' Headed Lucky Cat Motel, the exact sum charged for bed and breakfast was indecipherable – it looked like "£17.53" – but the date was clear enough, "3rd April, 1979".

239

Now

I turned to my left. 'Leonard?' I said.

After Tisha and I had left him, Lord Frost of Highgate had eaten his supper in front of the television set, watching a programme on B.B.C. 2. Could he remember what it was? Well, oddly enough he could. The police had asked him exactly the same question when they had come round to see him and it had stuck in his mind. It was one of David Attenborough's *Life on Earth* series, this particular programme being "Life in the Trees", all about mountain gorillas in Rwanda and monkeys in Japan. This had been followed by a quiz programme of some sort which had bored him, but he had kept it on because he had wanted to watch *Man Alive* afterwards, before going to bed.

Peter Stobbs had driven on up to his constituency in the North-West, stopping for dinner at a motorway service station on the way. He had arrived at his little one-up, one-down house in Blaresley at about 11.30, rung up Euthalia briefly so as to reassure her as to his safe arrival and gone straight to bed. He had met his agent, as planned, at 10 o'clock on the following morning. Not a lot of help, he realised, but that was the best that *he* could do, he was afraid.

Stephen Knightley had dumped his suitcase in his room at the Farmers' Club, off Whitehall, at about 7 o'clock. He'd gone straight out again, by himself, to a Chinese restaurant in Soho. No, he didn't remember its name, but he was sure that he could find it again if it was important. Then he had walked to the Curzon Cinema to see Chabrol's *Violette Noziere*. Hadn't I seen it? (I got the impression that I suddenly went down in Stephen's estimation.) Well, there was this adolescent French girl who was trying to find an identity of her own in sexual liberation and who finally finished up by murdering her father. And then he had taken a taxi back to the Farmers' Club. Oh, eleven, eleven fifteen, he supposed. Could any one vouch for the time that he had got in – or the fact that he hadn't gone out again later? Not really. He had taken his key out with him and the porter served the whole building, of which the club was only a part, and would hardly be likely to remember such an irregular member as him.

Dr. Roger Faulkner had little to add to what I knew already and I had heard most of that twice – once from the police at the time of my day-long questioning and again from Dick. Working on late in his office until 11.0 p.m. precisely, back to his own

Now

house in a different part of the Farmwell Foundation and into bed by approximately 11.30 (all of their timings seemed to be following a remarkably regular pattern) taking care not to waken his wife.

Billy Candleford had reached his house in the village from which his title had been taken at approximately 7.30, he thought. It could have been nearer 8.0. He'd cooked himself an omelette (of gargantuan proportions, no doubt), and eaten both it and a pudding that had been left in the refrigerator for him, before sitting down in front of the television. He couldn't say what he'd watched and, in any case, he must have dropped off at some time or another, because he distinctly remembered waking up in his armchair to find that the screen had gone blank. He had gone up to bed without bothering to look at the time and the next thing he had known had been the devoted Vera knocking on his door with his breakfast tray at 9.30 a.m.

I glanced down at my watch and then half-right across the table. 'I'm sorry, Dick. You too, I'm afraid ...' After all the trouble that he had been to on my behalf, I had been reluctant to subject the American to even the possibility of embarrassment but, with perfect timing, the telephone extension on the sideboard chose that actual moment to ring.

'Hold on,' I said, 'somebody's bound to answer it.'

But nobody did.

'Oh hell!' I got up from the table, went over and picked up the receiver. 'Hello?'

'*Can I speak to Viscount Thyrde, please?*' It was a slightly nasal voice with a distinct north country accent.

'I'm Lord Thyrde. Who's that?'

'*You don't know me, but I may be able to help you.*'

'Help me? How?' I said.

'*I was at Farmwell that night. Nobody knew I was there, but I saw what happened.*'

'But ... why haven't you said anything about it before, then?'

There was a slight pause.

'*I got the sack, didn't I? That's why I was there late, clearing up my things. I wasn't going to tell them anything, but I'll tell you — at a price!*'

'How much?'

'*A thousand pounds. Cash down — in advance.*'

241

Now

I gave myself just long enough to think before replying. It was a lot of money. But I could afford it – now! And it would be worth that, and more, to get a line onto the identity of the real thief.

'How do I know that what you're going to tell me is any good?'

'*You don't. You'll have to take a chance on that.*'

'Five hundred now, then, and the other five when I know what it is?'

There was another pause. Then, '*Six now, four later.*'

'Right,' and I jotted down his instructions as he gave them to me.

'That,' I said as I went back to the table, 'looks like being just the break I've been waiting for,' and I gave them the gist of the other end of the telephone conversation – omitting of course the details as to the actual meeting place.

Dick Richards rose to his feet and put a hand on my shoulder.

'Many congratulations, Derek. You'll let us know in due course how you got on, I hope?'

'I'll do better than that. Look, I'm seeing this chap somewhere in London at ten-thirty tomorrow morning. Why don't you all come to my flat at eleven?'

They all got out their diaries. There were two or three objections but these were very soon overcome by Dick.

'Thank you all very much,' I said. 'I won't have to bother you any more now, so let's go into the library for a drink and that'll give them a chance to lay the table for lunch. And I think I've got something rather special in the way of port to offer you.'

It was a bottle of Croft '45, which had been given to me by Sir John Elton, Julia's father. I had been saving it up for some slightly more pleasant form of occasion, but – I really felt that I owed them at least that.

In my London flat that same evening, I sat down by the telephone with a piece of paper on which I had written down their numbers. I dialled the first on the list.

'Hello. Derek Thyrde, here. You remember my once asking you if I could call on you for help? Well the time has come. That meeting in my flat tomorrow. Don't tell any of the others, but I'm not actually seeing the chap who rang until 11 o'clock, so I won't be back there until at least half past myself. I've arranged with the porter to let you all in. Do you think you could possibly make a

Now

point of being there in good time and keep the others happy until I come? Let me know afterwards which of them, if any, arrives particularly late. Oh and keep an eye open to see if any of them seem to be behaving at all out of character. You know, jittery or ill at ease.'

'*Well yes, a promise is a promise*,' said Henry Matheson, M.P. But he didn't sound any too enthusiastic about it.

'*I'm game*,' said Billy Candleford, excitedly. He seemed to have forgotten all about his misgivings of that morning.

'*Certainly, my dear Derek*,' said Leonard Frost.

'*Hold on, I'll take it upstairs*,' whispered Stephen Knightley and the more than usually intense classical music which had been flooding the background was cut off with a click. When the extension receiver was lifted, he made me repeat it. '*I'll be there*,' he said. But he was still whispering.

'*Of course I will, I'll be glad to*,' said General Dick Richards.

There was a pause while Roger Faulkner consulted his diary. '*Well, I've got a l. .uncheon engagement at one, but it's in London so I think I can manage that and still be able to keep it.*'

'*Flat by 11.0 a.m. sharp; keep happy 'til approx. 11.30; note of late arrivals; jittery or ill at ease. Right!*' said Peter Stobbs, M.P.

I could see the white-painted front of the café across the road, clearly reflected in the plate-glass window of the shop outside which I was standing. For the fourth or fifth time I put my hand in my inside breast pocket and felt for the envelope — I had been surprised how relatively thin it was with the sixty new ten-pound notes, drawn from the bank the previous afternoon, in it — it was still there.

I glanced idly over the contents of the window — it was a secondhand gramophone record shop — and the blue label of one of the old seventy-eights caught my eye. *Called to Arms* by Ambrose and his Orchestra. That had always been my mama's favourite record, bar none. I can still visualise the awful scene

Now

when, as a child of six or seven, I had broken her original copy. She had come into the room smiling and then when she saw me standing there, holding the pieces, she just slumped down onto the floor and dissolved into great heaving sobs. Come to think of it, it's the only time that I ever remember seeing my mother cry.

I turned round. There was a convenient gap in the traffic and I walked across the street to the café, opened the door and went in. It was 10.55. I was dead on time.

The establishment consisted of nine or ten red-formica-topped tables with a counter running the length of the far end. I sat down in the chair that was nearest to the door. There was only one other customer, sitting facing me at the table in the opposite corner. He was a little man in a dark blue overcoat. There was a battered carrier-bag on the table in front of him and he was staring dismally into the cup round which he was warming both his hands. Behind the counter, in cheerful contrast, a middle-aged woman was humming to herself as she polished a glass with a cloth. She looked up, noticed me for the first time and came over.

'Coffee, please,' I said. 'White, without sugar and cold milk if you've got it.' She went back to her station behind the counter, manipulated various levers thereby causing a hissing emission of steam and returned with the full cup and saucer which she put carefully down.

'That'll be thirty p, dear.' I thanked her, gave her thirty-five and took a couple of sips while she went back to put the money in the till. It was surprisingly good. I took the white foolscap-size envelope out of my pocket and put it on the table, taking care that it should overlap the edge by at least three inches. Then I picked up the cup and started drinking again. It was cool enough, so it didn't take long.

The man in the opposite corner had just finished his. He stood up, wiped the back of his hand across his mouth, picked up his carrier-bag and started for the door. As he passed my table, the edge of his overcoat brushed against the envelope, knocking it down onto the floor.

'Sorry, mate.' He bent down, picked it up and put it back on the table in much the same position but this time away from the edge. Then, with a demeanour that seemed to suggest that this had been just the crowning disaster in a day that had already been crammed with appalling incidents, he went out of the door.

Now

The whole thing had been accomplished with extraordinary dexterity. I could have sworn that it was the same envelope but, as I put it back in my inside pocket, I could feel that it was noticeably thinner now. I got up, called out my renewed thanks to the waitress and left myself. It was exactly 11.0 a.m.

On the pavement outside I stood for a moment and looked around me. Immediately the Snaffles print of the Irish jockey riding in the Grand National, "*Oh Murther! The dhrink died out of me and the wrong side of Bechers*" came into my mind. There was rather too much sensation in the pit of my stomach – and far too little in my knees.

Adrenalin! I had once asked a doctor friend why it was that adrenalin, which, we are always told, is intended to key one up to cope with a difficult or dangerous situation, almost invariably prevents one from coping with it instead. He had explained it like this. "Imagine that you are a caveman suddenly confronted with a woolly rhinoceros. Your brain flashes a message through the sympathetic nervous system to your body and your body immediately produces just enough of this mysterious substance to enable you to take whichever instantaneous action occurs to you first, either to stand and hit it over the head with your club or alternatively to shin up the nearest tree. Modern man, however, is cursed with the power of rational thought. He pauses to decide whether to opt for fight or flight and, however short this pause may be, the adrenalin keeps on flowing. Too much of it has precisely the opposite effect and the woolly rhinoceros, who acts first and thinks afterwards, wins the day."

I stopped pausing and walked quickly on my way. As I walked I kept my left hand on the opposite lapel of my overcoat. Were the second envelope to contain anything like the sort of information which I had been led to expect on the telephone the day before, it would be worth to at least one other besides myself infinitely more than the six hundred pounds that had been in the first. I approached the first of the turnings that I would have to take, cautiously. I peered through the window-glass on the front of the shop at the corner and, as far as I could see on through the pane at the side which was set at rightangles to it, the pavement beyond that again seemed to be clear. There was a slight drizzle now, which gave me the excuse to turn my coat collar up and do up the button at my neck, thereby leaving both hands free. I thought with

Now

regret of my *priest*, now reposing no doubt in a drawer at some obscure police station, with an exhibit label attached to it. What wouldn't I have given for the comforting weight of it in my pocket now?

The street along which I was now walking consisted of shops which dealt exclusively in a single form of commodity. The name of one of them caught my eye, "*Porn*broker", and the sign that accompanied it was authentic in every detail but one – it omitted the third brass ball. There were a number of men looking in through the various windows, some of them even wearing raincoats that could actually be described as "dirty". But none of them paid the slightest attention to me.

I turned the second corner, this time into Cambridge Circus, on under the canopy of the Palace Theatre where two or three people were looking at the posters and stills of *Jesus Christ, Superstar*, and I stopped a yard back from the corner of the pavement at Shaftesbury Avenue, waiting for the light to change.

Instinctively I sensed somebody coming up beside me and I swivelled round sharply. It was only a small boy wearing a vivid orange T-shirt with the cryptic slogan "I B4 U" stencilled on it in royal blue. It was clear from the poised determination of his attitude that he meant it and I let him go first for his pains.

I could see one of the underground entrances ahead of me now, across the road and well on beyond the row of secondhand bookshops, where I had often spent an idle and self-indulgently expensive hour. I walked on still without incident, past the first entrance on my side – that one looked a little too deserted for my liking – and turned into the second, which seemed to be the main one, set under *The Talk of the Town*. I had mentally divided the journey home into three phases – from the cafe to Leicester Square tube station, the underground itself and the walk from Knightsbridge back to my flat at the other end. Phase one over ... and not a woolly rhinoceros to be seen.

The booking-hall was milling with people. I went quickly across to the forty-pence ticket-machine and, one by one, fed into it all the 10p coins that I had in my pocket. One by one, it spat them contemptuously out again. I gave it up and made for the nearest ticket office, instead.

Back again to the barrier, through and onto the top of the escalator that led to the Piccadilly line. I stood on the right rather

Now

than walking down, and for once I refrained from leching at the advertisements as I was carried past them. The steps rolled out empty below me, so I kept my head turned upwards in order to keep an eye open for anybody who might be getting on at the top. I was halfway down before the first person did so, a woman grappling with an overweight Scotch terrier, and she too remained standing. But there were one or two others from behind who walked on past her and I started walking myself so as to maintain the distance between us. Off at the bottom, straight ahead for the Piccadilly line, then a right turn, followed by a left. Down a short flight of steps and the westbound platform was to the left again. It was empty – a train had obviously only just gone out. I walked halfway along to a point in front of the wooden bench below the station sign, with its blue bar set on a large red circle, and I stood there waiting, well back from the platform edge.

The platform started filling up again, but I couldn't see any one that I recognised. Suddenly I heard a sharp rattling sound close beside me and again I whipped round. This time it was a woman wrestling with her *Daily Telegraph* in a vain effort to subdue it. And then from the tunnel away to the left, and unmistakably bound for our direction, came the distant vibration of an approaching train.

I was exactly midway between two sets of the doors which opened in front of me and I chose the one on the left. I went straight across to the opposite doorway, turned and stood holding the upright metal bar. The doors shut. The train started moving. We were on our way.

Often in the past, but never with so good a reason as now, I had whiled away such a journey by speculating on my fellow passengers, where had they come from, where were they going and for what purpose and, brought together in such close proximity for this one short interlude, would the lives of any of us ever touch again?

The woman with the *Daily Telegraph* was there – she had got in just ahead of me – as was the woman with the Scottie. They were to my right front, sitting next to each other but looking in opposite directions. The Scottie had begun to sniff at the other woman's shoe. Opposite them, sat a man in a well-worn clerical grey suit. Every few moments he would tilt his old-fashioned black Homburg hat up from the front with one hand to scratch the

Now

side of his head with the other. *Solicitor's office? Bank?* Something like that – I judged him to hold a relatively important position in a relatively unimportant grade. To my left was a man in a blue regimental blazer, with a black beard trimmed into a style such as I had never seen before but which must have been what I have always heard described as "spade-shaped". He was sitting nearest of all to me but he was far too sinister-looking to be a likely suspect. Across the gangway from him but further along, a girl with hair dyed to an unlikely silvery-blonde – *shop-assistant?* – was engaged in painting her nails a fluorescent purple colour. She was blowing on each one to dry it, as soon as she had completed it to her satisfaction. Further along again, three men in overalls sat together. The one on the right had a brown canvas bag of tools at his feet and the one on the left was holding several planks of wood, while the one in the middle had nothing. From the fact that he was marginally older and seemed to be talking more than the other two, he was probably the boss of the three. And standing at the far end, a little knot of five schoolgirls, who were darting quick little glances at each of the rest of us in turn, giggling and pointing, completed the team.

At Piccadilly the schoolgirls left, giggling still, and quite a number of people got in. I decided to concentrate on the eight who remained out of the original thirteen.

At Green Park, the woman with the *Daily Telegraph* and the woman with the Scottie left, now chattering away happily to each other. It only lacked the dog to be carrying the newspaper for the rapport to be complete.

At Hyde Park corner, the man with the itchy head left by one set of doors, the three men in overalls by another – the man from the middle leading the way.

At Knightsbridge, I myself left, preceded by a couple of the more recent arrivals. Nobody had jostled apologetically into me. Nobody had come within arms' reach of me. Nobody ... The man with the spade-shaped beard and the girl with the fluorescent nails sat on and, as the doors slid shut behind me and the train moved off again, were carried on their way.

Along the platform to the "Way Out" sign, through it, left up the stairs, left again by the railing type barrier put there to prevent ascending and descending passengers from fraternising with one another, onto the escalator and up to the top. I gave up my ticket

Now

to the inspector, turned right across the hall, more steps – a flight of thirteen first followed by one of ten – round and out into Sloane Street. And that completed the second phase.

I was beginning to feel like a man who has survived the first two rounds of a three-round game of Russian Roulette, in the certain knowledge that, the longer he has gone on playing with impunity, the more dangerous it gets. I was going to be late now, later even than the thirty minutes that each of the seven was already individually expecting, and I quickened my pace accordingly. I dodged in and out of the people on my side of the road but as far as they were concerned, laughing, talking, window-shopping or just walking, it seemed that I wasn't even worth a glance. Then I turned off right ... and left ... and right again ... and the feeling of impending inevitability inside me grew more and more intense. And ... there, at last, lay the entrance to my own street ahead.

I walked steadily up it, counting the paces out deliberately as I had often, but subconsciously, counted them out to myself in the past. Sometimes there had been as few as 175 of them, sometimes as many as 178.

1, 2, 3, 4 ... *That row of four rendered Georgian cottages just ahead. Three of them had had their fronts repainted during the previous month, but the fourth had only just had its scaffolding put up in readiness. Could there be somebody lurking there? ... 40, 41, 42 ... What about the single plane tree which we're all so proud of – the sole survivor of the avenue that had once lined both sides of the road? Its trunk was broad enough, surely ... 72, 73, 74 ... I didn't like the look of that porch, though. It was far too solid and came down right out onto the pavement ... 89, 90 ... That post office van, there, could be dangerous ... 108, 109 ... Or the cars parked beyond it, there could be somebody crouched behind one of those ... 117, 118, 119 ... HEY, OR ANY OF THE ONES WHICH I'D ALREADY PASSED, FOR THAT MATTER! Surely I hadn't had my pocket picked already without my noticing it? ... 133 ... No, still there ... 137, 138, 139 ... Steady on, I must take a grip of myself ... 148, 149, 150 ... Even so, it must be soon ... 166, 167 ... Nearly there now ... 173, 174,* 175, one hundred and seventy-six and I was on the steps of my own block. Suddenly I was struck with a flattening, blood-draining sense of anti-climax. I had reached home base – nobody in his right mind would dream of waylaying me now.

Now

I turned and looked back along the street down which I had come. It was no longer empty. There was a small figure approaching and I stood and waited for it to come up to me. It was the man from the café, swinging his carrier-bag as he walked, noticeably more sprightly now.

'It didn't work, did it?'

'No,' I said. The disappointment was almost more than I could bear.

'Aye, I did a spell of intelligence work in the army after the war and I'd be prepared to swear you weren't followed. Hard lines, lad! Well, I'd best be giving you this back then.'

He took the original envelope out of his pocket and handed it to me. I put it back to join its mate in my own.

He laughed. 'The things I do for that Establishment brother of mine! Who'd have thought to see me of all people going out of my way to help a bloody lord?'

'It really has been most awfully kind of you. Thank you very much indeed, Mr. Brotherton.'

'Call me "Thack",' he said.

I had been expecting them to be in the sitting-room where, by scrounging a couple from the bedroom, I had made sure that there were enough relatively comfortable chairs. But I found them in the little dining-room, sitting round the table, instead.

They turned and looked up at me, all but Billy Candleford who refused to meet my eye in the sulky manner of a spoilt child who has suddenly been deprived of a promised toy. Stephen Knightley was tapping the table in front of him impatiently with a pencil; Leonard Frost shook his head at me in reproachful slow motion; Henry Matheson's face was more than usually twisted by a scowl and Peter Stobbs was pursing his lips; Roger Faulkner had an expression of benign interest, as though my behaviour presented a species of scientific conundrum which, given time, he would be bound to solve. I sat down in the empty place and the "1944 Club" was in plenary session yet again. Again it was Dick Richards, every bit the General this time, who spoke first.

'It seems,' he said, 'that you've been playing some sort of trick on us all. Nobody, as I remember, betrayed a confidence. It just came out. Well, for your information, we all of us arrived here by four minutes to eleven at the latest and not one of us appeared to

Now

be . . .' he paused and the next words were in palpable inverted commas . . . "jittery or ill at ease". So perhaps you would now be good enough to inform us just exactly what, if anything, you've achieved by this charade.'

I took the thinner of the two envelopes out of my pocket, opened it and withdrew the single sheet of A4 paper, which I unfolded and showed to them. Then I turned it over. It was blank on both sides.

'I . . .' I began miserably, but Dick held up his hands.

'I think I understand what you were setting out to prove,' he continued rather more gently. 'You were hoping to panic one of us seven into following you and making some sort of move to take this mythical information off you before you could get back here and tell it to the others – or at least arranging for some one to do it for him, thereby giving you a lead to him. Nobody would have been more delighted than I if it had come off, but you must see, Derek, that by seeking to establish your innocence in this way – and failing – you have achieved precisely the opposite effect. I for one am now not at all sure what to believe.'

From the murmuring round the table, the feeling appeared to be unanimous.

I was even beginning to have doubts about it myself.

The whiteness of the adjacent buildings had gleamed in the light of the morning sun as my taxi swung round the corner.

'This is the Old Bailey, Sir. This is where it all happens,' said the driver as I paid him off. He clearly took me for a disinterested spectator with time on his hands, out for a vicarious thrill.

The gold figure of Justice with her sword and scales – was it my imagination, or were they tilted slightly? – loomed directly above me as I approached the imposing doorway with its sliding iron gates. I tried them but they wouldn't budge. It struck me as ironic that, just at this moment, locks and bars should be employed as a means of keeping me *out*.

'Not this one, Sir,' said a friendly bearded policeman. 'They use the lower entrance, nowadays.' I thanked him and walked down to it.

But not in. Not yet!

There were still some twenty-five minutes to go and I decided that I would spend at least ten of them in the freedom of the sunlight outside.

xiii. Then

I was ten minutes early. The chill falling from the walls of the basement passage in Norfolk House did nothing to alleviate the even more icy feeling in the pit of my stomach. Several weeks had gone by since the débâcle over the flying-boat in that Suffolk estuary. I was waiting outside Commander Jackson's door.

The Military Police Corporal had done his best, he had escorted me on his motor-bicycle to the nearest place where I could use a telephone and Brigadier Broadbent had received the news with remarkable equanimity.

Molly and I were to motor back to Thyrde and await further instructions there. He would arrange for everything to be taken care of locally, including the Belgian and the Morris Ten. The former had already been carted off in an ambulance by the time that I arrived back at the road-block, where I found Molly sitting disconsolately in the back of a fifteen-hundredweight, a blanket draped round her shoulders, sipping a mug of hot sweet army tea.

"They were lying in wait for us," she said, when I had told her my end of the story. "Tom and I could do nothing, it all happened so quickly. And, oh Derry, he took your ring."

"Never mind about that, you're safe and that's the only thing that matters. But . . . which of them was it?"

Amazingly she still did not know. Tom had only reached the M.G. again outside Ipswich Station just in time to see both front doors of the Morris pulled shut. And Molly herself had never actually seen the other man.

"But how on earth?" I said. "It must have taken the two of them to tie you up like that and bundle you into the back of the Rolls."

"Well, it happened like this . . ."

They had driven round a bend to find the Morris slewed across the road in front of them and Molly had had to stop dead. The Belgian must have been lurking somewhere by the road-side

Then

because, before Tom who had already started to get out could do so, he had used some form of heavy instrument to knock him out. Then he had run round to Molly's side of the Rolls, just as she herself was getting out to come to Tom's assistance, twisted her left arm behind her back and used the other hand to hold her head-scarf over her eyes as a blindfold. It had only been then apparently that the spy had left the Morris and come and stood in front of her. He had gripped Molly's right wrist with one hand and then taken her left from Janssen with his other thereby leaving the latter both his hands free to tie the head-scarf properly behind her head.

Molly had struggled like anything and had in fact managed to get her left hand free, finding herself grasping something from the spy's wrist – a watch probably, or it could have been some form of identification bracelet – which must have come off in the process. In a moment of defiance, she had flung it in the direction where she imagined the open window of the Rolls to be. Anyway, it must have caused the spy to lose his temper because she had received a punch on the forehead and then he had immediately taken my ring off her finger, no doubt in retaliation. And the respite had been only temporary, because the spy had had no difficulty in catching hold of her free hand again – half-dazed as she was by the blow – and had passed both of them to the Belgian, who had by then completed the blind-fold and used her own handkerchief to gag her as well. The Belgian had held her hands securely behind her back, while the spy had first knelt to bind her ankles together and then gone round behind her to do the same for her wrists.

All this happened extremely quickly and not a word had been spoken between them during the whole process. Together they had lifted her into the back of the Rolls, and, pausing no doubt to drag the unconscious Tom – whom for all we knew they still thought to be me – onto the side of the road, they had driven off again almost immediately, only to stop when they had reached the road-block where I had managed to catch up with them.

The two gormless soldiers had not been a lot of help either. They had taken hardly any notice of the driver of the Morris – they were pretty sure that he had been able to produce a regular resident's pass, but they had been far too preoccupied with the following, and more spectacular, Rolls at the time.

We had spent several fruitless minutes searching the Rolls for

Then

whatever it was that Molly had thrown into it; she and I had driven the two cars, I the M.G., back to the cross-roads where we had found Tom waiting patiently where I had left him – his mind now a complete blank for the half hour that had led up to the incident; he had joined us in searching the road itself and the grass at the side – again to no avail; and at last we had driven in convoy back to Thyrde where we had given him over into his mother's capable hands.

At 9.30 the following morning, the Brigadier had rung up as promised. Janssen had been found to be dead on arrival at the hospital and had never regained consciousness in between. Nobody at Ipswich Station had been able to identify any of the seven photographs which they had been shown as someone who had got off a train there that afternoon. And discreet enquiries later in the day had shown that all of the suspects were still in the country and going about their lawful occasions, including Lieutenants Stephen Knightley and Dick Richards, who by sheer chance were each spending the night in London having been given a twenty-four hour pass. "So it's up to you two. Up to you two," the Brigadier had said cheerfully. Once again, Molly and I were to carry on as before.

And, once again, we had.

Of the seven, only Stephen Knightley had proved to be totally unobtainable. His ship had been almost constantly at sea. But Molly and I had eaten our way through a seemingly inexhaustible supply of Uncle Johnnie Bagot's household pets. We had had several more days' trout-fishing with James Matheson – on one excruciating occasion the son, Henry, had come with us. He had not fished himself but had spent his whole time issuing instructions to the rest of us which, rather to my surprise, his own father had meekly obeyed. Dick Richards had continued to have difficulty in deciding whether it was Molly or the Rolls that he coveted most – sometimes he seemed to favour one, sometimes the other. Roger Faulkner had proved to be a lot more human on further acquaintance, but Leonard Frost's political tuition had grown more and more abstruse. Peter Greyfield had become more and more ineffectual and his wife more and more querulous. Peterkin had not got any worse – that would hardly have been possible. He had merely dreamed up new and ever more ingenious ways in which to allow his awfulness to show.

Then

And then, eventually, the telephone had rung and this time it had not been Brigadier Broadbent – whom I had been expecting – but Commander Jackson himself. Molly and I were to report to him in Norfolk House at some unearthly hour the following morning. That had been last night.

We had left Thyrde in the Rolls just as the dawn was beginning to redden the clouds above the tree-tops, and the sky had been simply full of aeroplanes all the way to London. On our arrival, Molly had been told to wait on the ground floor. Commander Jackson would see me – alone! And small wonder. I had not even been able to save at least something out of the wreck by establishing the identity of the spy. To be sent back to my battalion in disgrace was the very best that I could expect.

I looked at my watch. It was 0815 hours precisely, on Tuesday, the sixth of June, 1944. I knocked on the door and went in.

Commander Jackson's eyes were every bit as piercing as I had remembered them, his uniform just as worn and faded, but it hung perhaps a little more baggily on him now, as he got up and came round his desk towards me, because he had left off the cardigan underneath.

"I'm terribly sorry, Sir," I said when I had saluted, "I'm afraid I've failed – all along the line."

"On the contrary, my dear chap, you've succeeded – almost beyond my wildest dreams," he said.

I gaped at him and then at something that he picked up from the desk, unfolded and put into my hands. It was a piece of cartridge paper, of approximately foolscap size, and the design on it was made up of lines and blobs and dots and numbers. There, was the little tear from one of the drawing-pin holes to the edge of the paper; there, the ink-blot; and there, in the corner, was the brown circle with its curious inscription, '$2\frac{1}{2}$ C.A.', written in thick blue crayon.

"You've ... you've got it back. Thank God for that, but how ..." and then I stopped.

The Commander was shaking his head.

"We never lost it – not the second time, that is. Perhaps you'd better sit down. This may take a little time to explain."

* * *

Then

The invasion had actually started. In the early hours of the morning, Allied forces had been landed on the coast of Normandy. The first official announcement had not been due to be made until nine-thirty but the B.B.C., it seemed, had been monitoring German broadcasts and had jumped the gun already. It was on the news at eight.

Active planning for the invasion had been going on for well over a year now, he told me. The first thing had been to examine all the possible target areas and to select the most suitable. Of the many that had been considered, the choice had eventually been narrowed down to two – the area of the Pas de Calais and the stretch of coast around Caen in Normandy. The German High Command must have been going through exactly the same mental processes, with very much the same criteria to guide them, and thus far it was fairly certain that they would have reached the same conclusions. So when Normandy had finally been decided on it had been realised that, if the invasion was to achieve any element of surprise at all, it was vital that the Germans should believe that it was in fact the Pas de Calais that had been chosen and innumerable subterfuges had been adopted to achieve this end.

Another important consideration had been to find some means of keeping the Allied Expeditionary Force supplied until such time as ports of large enough size could be captured and any damage that the retreating Germans might have done, in order to deny their use to us, repaired. The planners had hit on an entirely new concept, an artificial harbour which could be made in floating sections in this country and towed across to be assembled on the other side. Once the general location for the invasion had been fixed, specific sites for two such harbours had also been selected, one for the use of the American forces and one for our own. Work on the component parts had been completed just in time and the first batch were on their way over even now.

The research establishment at Farmwell had been working on a refinement to the British harbour, a catapulting device that would enable fighter aeroplanes to be launched from its top, so as to defend it from attack by the air. This particular development had subsequently been shelved as impracticable and all the relevant papers – there had been a number of them – locked away in the safe of Professor Tomkins the establishment's head. Only one had contained any information that would be of real value to the enemy — the over-all site plan — and this was the paper that had been stolen, the one that I now held in my hand.

"Your pal, Knightley, got it right. Those two irregular lines, the continuous one at the top and the dotted one below it, are the high and low water-levels at a place called Arromanches and the figures show the depth in fathoms from the shore right out into the deep water. That chart is as good as a finger-print, it would have given the Germans pretty well the precise location of where the invasion was planned."

Once the paper itself had been so providentially recovered, Commander Jackson's immediate inclination had been to leave it at that. But then he had had second thoughts. Why should he not turn what might have been a disaster of overwhelming proportions into a positive advantage? He had had a replica made — even down to the ink-blot that Professor Tomkins had allowed to get on it after I had handed it over to him. Well, almost a replica . . .

"For the high and low water-levels — you remember I drew those particularly to your attention — and the depths in fathoms, I had substituted a set belonging to an equivalent stretch of coast-line near the Pas de Calais. If they fooled you, there was at least a sporting chance that they might also fool the spy."

"Then you . . . you meant it to be stolen . . . all the time. That's all very well, Sir," I was up on my feet again now, "it doesn't matter about me, but Molly . . . anything might have happened to her — damned near did — how could you have exposed *her* to a thing like that?"

Commander Jackson looked at me for what seemed to be a very long time indeed. Then he nodded slowly.

"Ah, so that's how the land lies. Well, let me tell you this, if I were twenty years younger, ten even . . ." He paused. "Anyway, I don't suppose that my feelings about Molly Stanton are very different from yours. But there really was comparatively little danger, my men were following you the whole time. And as for Molly, how do you think she would have felt if I'd sent some one else in her place?"

I sat down again. I already knew the answer to that.

Then an awful thought struck me.

"Did Molly know the truth about what we were actually

doing?"

"No more than you."

"But why didn't you tell us? It would certainly have saved years off my life if I'd known all along that that paper was a fake?"

"I'll answer that question with another. Just how good an actor do you think you are? As I arranged things, the only deception you had to carry out was to pretend not to know how important the paper was when you showed it round the first day. After that you didn't have to act. Could you have kept it up, day after day, week after week?"

The chief stock-in-trade of the illusionist through the ages, he told me, has been to keep one jump ahead of the people whom he is seeking to delude. Palming off the fake paper had only been the start of it. After that, it had been necessary to convince the spy, not only that the information that it contained was genuine, but also that it was too late in the day for plans to be changed and that it would therefore continue to be valid – hence our desperate though unavailing efforts to get it back. To do this, the pressure had to be seen to be kept up on him right up to the day of the invasion itself and everything that Molly and I had been instructed to do had been geared towards this end. Our use of the Rolls-Royce, for instance, rather than some less easily identifiable car.

"It really was an incredible piece of luck that you, who found the paper, should have shown it first to one of the handful of people who was able to recognise it immediately for what it was. Nobody could possibly have foreseen that."

As far as the spy was concerned, my suspicions would only have been aroused when the false telephone message had been used to separate Molly and myself and my pocket had subsequently been picked on the underground train.

What would have happened then? I would have gone to some one in authority and the description that I had been able to give of the paper might well have been connected with its theft from Farmwell, which by that time could have been discovered. It was then, that Molly and I would have been seconded to Intelligence and given the job of going round to each of the suspects in turn and questioning them again and again by means of some cover story, with the object of tracing the stolen paper and recovering it

Then

before it could leave the country or, failing that, at least discovering the identity of the spy.

Thus we had been given our 'one jump ahead'.

"Then he wouldn't have been taken in by all that *Department for Inter-service Co-ordination* ... business?"

"Not for a moment. The man's a professional, remember. I'd have been disappointed in him if he had."

The chance recognition by Molly of the re-painted Morris Ten had been an unlooked-for bonus. This had given us two the opportunity of being in hot pursuit at the very moment when the false paper was being taken out of the country. Commander Jackson had not been able to predict either the flying-boat as a means of conveyance or the actual point of departure, although neither of them had been very much of a surprise to him after the event.

"It was a Walrus – they're Amphibians, actually. Ugly-looking brutes, aren't they? *Shag-bats*, we call 'em, probably one of the ones that we had to leave behind at the end of the Norwegian campaign. And the choice of that particular estuary makes a lot of sense too. It's on the direct approach to R.A.F., Woodbridge, which is often used as a convenient base for our own aeroplanes, limping home damaged. The coastal defence around there are always seeing unidentified ones on their R.D.F. screens."

Even our endless slogging round the suspects since then had been an essential part of the plan. To add to the illusion, Commander Jackson had even arranged for two of the concrete caissons of which the artificial harbours were made up to be towed off in the direction of the Pas de Calais, although these would be diverted again in time to be fitted into their allotted places. And it had paid off. From early reports as to the volume of resistance that our troops had been encountering, the Germans seemed to have swallowed the bait completely. All this was still Top Secret, I was to understand, and I must not breathe a word of it outside this room – even to Molly. He would have her in afterwards and tell her as much as he thought she ought to know.

I sat there in silence after Commander Jackson had finished speaking.

"You don't look too happy about it. You really mustn't underestimate the part that you two played in it."

"Well, it still makes me feel no end of a mug," I said.

Then

"If it's any consolation to you, you were too darned good. I had one hell of a job selling you the story in the first place, if you remember. And, not once but *twice*, you all but succeeded in the task that you believed you'd been given. That Military Police Corporal at the estuary was one of mine of course and, if my chaps hadn't managed to arrange that convenient blow-out for you on the very first evening near Whipsnade, the whole thing would never have got off the ground. Still, that's what they were there for."

"I thought you said they were there to protect Molly and me."

"Er . . . that too, of course."

"But you still haven't told me – which one *was* the spy?"

The Commander slowly shook his head.

"But surely . . . you had each of the seven followed?"

"No, that story was for your benefit alone, I'm afraid. You just don't know how many men it takes to lay on an operation like that – it took all the experienced ones I had available simply having you properly followed. They saw through that second car you used almost immediately, of course, but your changing clothes with that Home Guard chap was little short of brilliant. That's what I meant about you being too darned good – at first they thought it was *you* left out cold by the road-side – threw 'em completely. After that they had all their work cut out stopping you from catching the fellow and I've got no more idea who he is than you have – probably never will know now."

"*What!*" I stared at him. "But you can't let him get away with it."

"Have to. Too many other things on hand. Tell you what I have done, though. I've arranged for the whole story, of how he lost the paper in the first place and then allowed himself to be duped by you, to be passed on to the Germans – we've channels open to us to do that sort of thing. That'll clip his wings, they'll never use *him* again. No, let him live with the knowledge that he had in his possession the means of possibly pulling the whole war out of the bag – and then let it slip literally through his fingers."

"*I* didn't do much duping," I said bitterly. "Rather the reverse, if anything."

"Cheer up, he's not to know that. Now then, you've certainly earned a spot more leave. Ten days suit you? Your lot aren't due over for a week or two yet and you'll still be back with your

Then

Battalion in time."

"Thank you very much indeed, Sir." I hesitated, but it was only for a moment. "Can Molly have leave too?"

This time the pause was barely noticeable before he replied. "Very well. Yes, I think I owe you at least that."

I stood up, came to attention and saluted.

"Er . . . there is one other question I'd like to ask. What is that brown circle that looks like a stain left by a tea-cup?"

"That," he said, "is a stain left by a tea-cup."

"And '$2\frac{1}{2}$ C.A.'?"

"Oh that? Well, it seems that your mother rang up Professor Tomkins at Farmwell one afternoon and asked him to be sure and buy her two-and-a-half pounds of cooking-apples on his way home. This paper was the only thing he had by him at the time to make a note on . . . and the cream of the joke is that he went and forgot 'em after all."

He picked the paper up, held it out at arm's length and gazed at it. Then, for the first time in our brief acquaintance, Commander Jackson laughed out loud.

"I'd give my right arm," he said, "to know what the Boche has been making of that."

* * *

Out in St. James's Square again, Molly and I paused for a moment before getting into the Rolls. We stood there, looking across at the dripping green of the plane trees in the middle. And then we looked at each other. As we did so, we began to hear, low at first and then rising to one long, clear, all-pervading triumphant note – symbolic somehow – an air-raid siren, sounding the 'All Clear'.

* * *

"Blast!" said Molly. "I'd forgotten the ruddy radiogram's bust."

I had dumped her luggage upstairs and come down into the Fords' sitting-room to find her looking disconsolately into the modern mahogany monstrosity, its lid open to emit that distinctive woody smell. She was holding a gramophone-record, still in its brown-paper sleeve, in one hand.

Then

"What have you got there?"

"*Called to Arms* by Ambrose and his Orchestra. I slipped out and bought it while you were closeted with old Jacky this morning, but I might just as well have saved myself the trouble."

"I've got a gramophone over at the house," I said. "It's a bit old but it still works. I'll go and get it."

And ten minutes later, I was back depositing an unwieldy chest, covered in dust and dark green oil-cloth, on the sitting-room floor.

"What on *earth* is that?" said Molly. She watched, with growing horror, as I took out the component parts one by one – the wooden arm, some eighteen inches in length with the playing-head at one end and the wire support for the widest part of the horn to rest on at the other, the brass horn itself, long, straight and flared, the square wooden box, nine inches by nine by four with the protruding metal bar, from the end of which the needle-arm could pivot, and the green-baize-covered turn-table on top – and started to assemble them.

"There you are," I said when I had finished, "one gramophone, as per order."

"Haven't you got anything better than *that*?"

"There isn't anything better. If you look at the label on that record of yours, you'll see that it's meant to be played on a machine like this."

Molly glanced down at the label showing through the circular hole in the paper sleeve. Then she put her little pink tongue out at me. "It's *Decca*, not *His Master's Voice*," she said. "Anyway, it won't work without the dog." But she gave it to me, just the same.

I put it on, screwed on the cap to hold it in place, released the brake, applied the needle and stood up. I held out my arms and Molly came into them. We danced on the carpet. As we glided slowly round, my mouth found hers almost immediately. And time stood still.

Her lips parted slightly and I could feel the intoxicating dampness between them, as Ambrose's male singer started on the last verse.

Do you mind if I speak of the blush in your cheek,
Which you stole from a way-side rose?
And I'd mention as well that your lips are just swell –
Was it rubies you robbed for those?

Then

Oh your eyes are like two little pools that are blue,
Your hair is as golden as straw,
And I don't think I've missed very much from this list,
Which explains why it's you I adore.
So, if I am so bold as to reach out and hold
You, just blame it on your charms.
'Cos if – I've been called to your colours
    Then you've been called to my arms.

The music stopped but we went on dancing. I slid my lips round over Molly's cheek until I could whisper something in her ear.

She stopped dead and took a step backwards. "What was that?"

"Will you marry me?" I repeated.

"Yes please. When?"

"Oh, I don't know. After the war's over, of course."

Molly shook her head. "Now. Just as soon as we can get a special licence."

"No, there's any amount of things to be considered first and ..."

"We've got a whole ten days' leave ahead of us."

"Yes, but ..."

She stuck her little chin forward. "*Now!*"

"Look," I said, "what I really mean is, I might easily be ... anything might happen to me and it simply wouldn't be fair on you. I won't allow it and that's final!"

"We'll see about *that*," Molly said.

Slowly but deliberately, she took her coat off and dropped it onto the floor. "Hey, what are you doing?" One by one, she was undoing the buttons of her blouse.

"I'm going to seduce you that's what. And then you'll *have* to make an honest woman of me."

"Do that blouse up." Her eyes glinted. "*Immediately!*"

"*Bloose*," she corrected. "My aunt Emily would be shocked to the core if she ever heard you call it that."

"What would she say if she could see what you're doing now?" I watched in fascination, helpless. However it was pronounced, it was undone completely. She was pulling it off over one shoulder and she only had on the flimsiest piece of silky stuff underneath. Her slim figure was looking far from boyish now.

Then

"You win," I said quickly. "I want you more than anything else in the whole world, but . . . I don't want it to be like this."

And, with not very steady fingers, I began to do up the buttons of her . . . oh, all right! . . . *bloose.*

14. Now

'Come to bed,' I said, 'come directly to bed; do not pass "GO"; do not collect two hundred pounds.'

'Why not?' said Tisha. 'I could do with two hundred pounds just now and the labourer is worthy of her hire.'

She was.

But she didn't get it.

Later, I glanced at her where she lay on the bed beside me. The half-inch figures of the digital clock on the bedside table emitted just enough of a green fluorescent glow and the contours of her body were picked out like the hillocks and valleys and wooded areas of some strange planet in the light of a science fiction moon. She was breathing regularly and her eyes were shut, but I knew that she was still awake. There was a smile, as of a contented child, on her face.

It had been a ghastly day – the whole trial so far couldn't have gone much worse for that matter. In spite of Sir Makepeace Brotherton's prediction, the judge had hardly interfered once. He hadn't had to. The prosecuting counsel – The Attorney-General, no less – had been doing his job only too well. Sir Makepeace had subjected each of the other members of the "1944 Club" to the most rigorous questioning about their alibis for the night of the third of April, but not one of them had shown the slightest deviation from the stories that they had already told us. A handwriting expert had testified that the paying-in slips couldn't have been filled in by me, but he had been equally emphatic about all of the other seven. There still remained, as damning as ever against me, the evidence about the *priest* and the signet-ring. And Tisha herself had been absent from the courtroom for the greater part of the day.

When I had seen her outside afterwards, she had been remarkably cagey about what she had actually been doing. But I had taken her out to dinner at the restaurant we'd been to on the

Now

night when we'd first met – neither of us had been back there since – we had both ordered exactly the same meal as we had had before and, from that moment on, the evening had been an unqualified success. In the taxi home, I had looked at Tisha with a certain amount of apprehension when I had given the driver my address rather than hers, but she had tilted her head back and grinned back at me in unspoken reply. And it was better, far better, than that first time. There was none of that feeling of guilt lurking in the background. Whatever might happen in the short term, life had suddenly begun to open up in front of the pair of us in a seemingly endless vista ...

'Hey, don't go to sleep. I haven't finished with you yet.'

I opened my eyes again. She was leaning on one elbow now, her whole body positively, tantalisingly alert.

'I must,' I said. 'It looks like being a crucial day tomorrow. Neither Sam Thornton nor Sir Makepeace has said anything yet, but I've got a feeling that they think things are going badly wrong.'

'Don't worry. Things are going to get better from now on, I know they are.'

A bare arm tentacled over and I felt her fingers exploring the sensitive areas of my chest.

I was woken by the sound of the coffee-percolator erupting. The bedclothes on the other side were flung back, the door was open and there was a smell of frying filtering through from the direction of the kitchen. I sprang up, washed, shaved and dressed as quickly as I could, and went towards it. Tisha, standing by the stove and looking ravishing in a little apron which she must have dug up from somewhere, turned when she heard me come in and held out a loaded plate. There were two fried eggs, their yolks showing pink under a thin veneer of the white, a mound of bacon, of just the right crisply succulent consistency and kidneys, dark brown, oozing slightly red.

It was a moment or two before I understood – there had been none of those things in the refrigerator – and then she winked at me. She must have bought them the day before and brought them with her, been planning the whole thing, in fact. I grinned back.

She sat and talked to me, drinking coffee while I ate.

'I've got a surprise for you,' she said when I'd finished.

Now

'I know, I've had it. More than one, to be strictly accurate, and I liked all of 'em.'

'No, this is something else. Give me about ten minutes and then come on down.'

I did as instructed. And when, ten minutes later, I came out of the front door onto the sunlit street, I saw at once what it was she had been away doing the day before. She had the hood down. Old Rollie had now been transformed into an open two-seater to dream about. The three near-side wheels, front, rear and the spare which was positioned against the side of the bonnet, together made up an off-centre triangular pattern achieving a perfect balance against the sweeping fawn body-lines that ran long and straight above, from *The Spirit of Ecstasy* on the radiator-top, through the base of the gently tilted windscreen and the chocolate canvas of the hood-cover to the boot-lid, and long and curved below.

I walked round the car to her side. 'Let me drive. Please,' I said, 'it'll bring me luck.' She moved over and I slipped in to sit beside her, in the place where she had been. Then, the gear-lever moving like a warm spoon through golden syrup, I let out the clutch and we were on our way.

A long expanse of gleaming fawn bonnet-top away to the front of me, the wings of the mascot seemed to be soaring now until the tyres skimmed the surface of the tarmac. I settled back in my seat, the tang of leather upholstery pleasant in my nostrils, the steering-wheel solid and reassuring – a symbol of power and security – in my hands, an awareness of the lovely girl beside me ever present in the forefront of my consciousness, while the engine sang softly along the road like an automated Paul McCartney.

At the Old Bailey, I stopped and got out. Tisha shifted over into the driving-seat again and smiled up at me.

'I'll be back first thing this afternoon, promise.' She had an appointment with her husband's solicitors, which I knew was going to last the better part of the morning. She put up her lips to be kissed.

'Goodbye, darling,' she whispered.

It was the first time that she had called me that.

It was at the luncheon adjournment that it happened. He had taken off his wig, but he still had his gown on. He came to the point straight away.

Now

'I'm sorry, Lord Thyrde, but I think that we're going to have to produce your alibi witness now.'

I had been expecting it, of course. Not quite so soon perhaps and the state of euphoria that I had been in, born of my new-found relationship with Tisha, didn't make things any easier either. But the sudden shock of it, coming on that of all days, rendered me for the moment quite incapable of saying anything in reply. Even now I hadn't got the slightest idea how she would react.

My silence only seemed to irritate Sir Makepeace.

'I don't think you quite appreciate the seriousness of your position, young man. This may be your only hope now.'

'Yes, I know,' I said miserably, 'but . . .'

His whole manner suddenly became gentle again. 'Tell me about it.'

I told him. I told him everything, right from the beginning.

'Where is this young lady of yours? I'm quite certain that you're worrying unnecessarily.'

'She'll be here this afternoon. She had an appointment this morning but she promised to be back by two.'

He reached up and put a hand on my shoulder.

'Look, why don't you let me have a word with her?'

'Would you?'

'Leave it to me,' he said.

She was a forlorn figure, pitifully young and defenceless-looking standing there in the witness-box, and she wouldn't look at me. It was late in the afternoon. Sir Makepeace had held off for as long as he had dared, in a final effort to spare her the ordeal altogether, but it had been hopeless. The judge had been pretty scathing about our application to produce an alibi witness, at the very last moment and without having given the proper notice at the proper time – but he had agreed in the end. She took the book in her right hand and repeated the words on the card.

Her name was Beatrice Anne Matheson . . . She lived at 217, Lumford Mansions, Westminster . . . She was the wife of Henry Matheson, M.P. . . . She had first met the defendant on Tuesday, the . . . Sir Makepeace's manner couldn't have been more kind and reassuring as he took her through the preliminary questioning – he was holding both sides of his gown and with every question he inched them upwards so that, each time, the neck hung infinitesimally lower down his back – but it was clear to everybody that she was going through sheer hell. I sat there watching her, gripping with both hands the wooden front of the dock, worn smooth by countless similar reactions of the past. I thought that I could see a tear starting to run down her cheek as he approached what would be the crucial part of her evidence. *The priest? Yes, she remembered seeing the priest. She had asked me what it was earlier on.*

'And it was left behind in the car, when you got out at the door of your block of flats?'

'I think so ... yes, I'm sure it was.'

'What time was that?'

'I ... I don't really know.'

'This is important. Try to remember, Mrs. Matheson.'

'About eleven o'clock, I suppose. It could have been earlier.'

'But not later?'

'No.'

'And you went up together to your flat?'

'Yes.'

'What happened then?'

'I gave him a drink. A glass of brandy and I poured one out for myself. Then we talked for a bit.'

'And then perhaps you had another drink?'

There was a slight hesitation. 'Yes.'

'And after that?'

'He ... I mean, I ... We ...'

'Let me put it another way. What time did Lord Thyrde leave?'

This time there was a long pause. Then she did look at me, but it was only for a moment. 'It must have been at about a quarter-to-six in the morning.'

'So he stayed the night. I'm sorry, Mrs. Matheson, but I must ask you this, did he sleep in the same room as you?' Then, far more quietly, '*In the same bed?*'

'Yes.' It was almost inaudible.

'And you are able to vouch for the fact that between the hours of, say, 11.0 p.m. on the night of Tuesday, the third of April, last year, and 5.45 on the following morning – and I must remind you that you are under oath, Mrs. Matheson – the defendant never once left your sight?'

'Yes,' there was another pause and, the very next moment, my

Now

whole world fell apart as she corrected herself, '... *no!*' she said.
    I was only dimly conscious of the explosion of sensation which instantly devastated the courtroom. All my attention was on Tisha who, tears streaming down her face, was looking full at me now. 'You only stayed for that one quick drink — you know you did — and then you left. I'm sorry, Derek, I know I promised but ... I can't. I thought I could but *I can't*. I'm under oath, you see, and I didn't know what it would be like.' She looked back up to the Bench and there was a plea in her voice, 'I can't, my Lord.'
    The Judge leaned forward consolingly. 'Of course you can't, my dear.' He straightened up again and, for fully a minute it seemed at the time, he glared at me. Then he turned to my Counsel who was just standing there, his mouth open, his hands loose at his side, his gown all anyhow on his back. 'Perhaps Sir Makepeace has yet another surprise witness whom he wishes to call? No? Very well then, I think that we might adjourn for the day.'
    I was fully expecting my bail to be rescinded on the spot and myself to be taken into custody. But it didn't happen. Somehow I found myself out among the chattering throng in the hall outside.
    I nearly ran slap into Tisha. Her husband was with her, one arm around her shoulders. I looked straight at her, into her slightly swollen face and reddened eyes, and felt ... nothing. In much the same way as, when you've just come back from a visit to the dentist, the whole of one side of your face is sometimes numb — only this time it was my mind. I was brought back to reality by Henry.
    'You *bastard!*' he said.
    Tisha turned to him. 'You go ahead and fetch the car, I'll join you there in a minute or two. I want to talk to Derek — alone.'
    He didn't move. He just tightened his protective grip slightly.
    'The car, Henry. Please.'
    And at that he did go, but not before he had cast one more look of utter contempt in my direction.
    'Derek ...' she was looking up at me beseechingly, 'let me at least try and explain. This morning, at the solicitors ... I'd thought it was going to be something about the divorce, but it wasn't that at all. They told me Henry wants me back. Oh, I was so confused at first ... I didn't know what to think. And then I realised that I still loved him ... that I have done all along. And

Now

later, standing there in the witness-box – I was going to do this one last thing for you, Derek, I swear I was – but then it suddenly came to me that if he ever found out I'd been unfaithful while we were still ... before he'd actually left me, it'd be the end of everything. He's so proud, you see. And I know I'm being selfish, I know that I can't expect you to forgive me ... ever, but do please try and understand.'

I didn't say anything. I couldn't have done so, even if I'd wanted to. Even if there'd been anything to say.

And she too went.

Gradually, I became aware that some one else was standing in the place where she had been. It was my Uncle Charles, grey-haired, grey-moustached and looking immensely serious.

'Was that your cast-iron alibi?'

'It *was*,' I said.

'Look, Derek, go straight back to your flat now and don't move a yard from there until I come and join you. I shall have something for you. I've no idea what it is, or even if it'll be the slightest help, but I was to see that you were given it "only if you were ever in such severe trouble that there seemed to be literally no way out". Those were the exact words.' He smiled. 'That's not a wholly inaccurate description of the position that you're in now, wouldn't you say?'

It was several hours later. Uncle Charles had come and gone, leaving behind him a bulky package wrapped in faded buff-coloured paper. 'Your father left this for you with the conditions I've already told you about. No, I won't stop now, but give me a ring if you'd like me to come back – however late it is.'

I broke the seals and folded back the outer covering. On top was a square, once-white envelope, which I found to contain a gramophone-record of the metal home-made variety and this I put carefully to one side. The rest consisted of a thick bundle of lined foolscap paper, held together through the matching holes at the top left-hand corners by one of those little lengths of green cord with a tag on either end. I glanced at the top sheet –

It all started with that confounded birthday party. Not that I did not enjoy it at the time. In fact it was a jolly good evening ...

and I recognised the writing at once, from the captions in his photograph albums which I still have at Thyrde, as being in my

Now

father's neat hand. I took it over to the armchair by the fireplace and began to read.

Abstractedly at first but then with growing interest I learnt of the origin of the "1944 Club" and its aftermath until, as I turned the pages, I became wholly absorbed in the doings of its founder members, during those spring and early summer weeks so many years ago. Johnnie Bagot, very much as I myself first remembered him; the endearingly amorous Colonel Matheson, Henry's father; Leonard Frost, the uncompromising radical; Dick Richards as a brash young American pilot; Stephen Knightley, with the aggressive efficiency of a serving naval officer and the even then intolerable Monica; Roger Faulkner in his embryo scientist days; the ineffectual Peter Greyfield with his nagging, whining wife.

Then the three sons – Billy Candleford, although his had been the merest walking-on part; Henry himself, as a pompous *young* man; the odious child who was to grow up into Peter Stobbs, M.P. – I knew that I wouldn't be able to think of him as anything but "Peterkin", ever again.

And my own father ... the shadowy figure, that had hovered never very far above my head throughout the early years of my childhood at Thyrde, took on flesh and blood and bones as he and his Molly hunted their spy over the countryside of leafy wartime England and in and around the landmarks of long dead London; the legendary *Four Hundred* and its more earthy counterpart, *The Bag o' Nails*; the trams that used to sway and rattle down the embankment, left at the end and into their own exclusive tunnel; *Gamages'* department store and *The International Sportsmen's Club*; all gone. *Harrods* remains, of course, and so does *White's*.

But then they always will.

Only when I reached the scene in the sitting-room of the Fords' house, on the afternoon of D-Day, did I pause for a moment. Just how far would my mama have gone, I wondered, if my father had called her bluff? Ever since I could remember, there had been the odd male admirer about the place but I had always looked on *those* as being strictly platonic. Come to think of it, there wasn't a great deal about the comfortable triviality of my mother's existence now that I *could* recognise in the spirited twenty-year-old Wren of my father's story. I suppose that everybody has much the same difficulty in believing that their parents really were young once. Either way, I was glad that things had turned out as

Now

they had — for his sake. He'd earned his happiness, poor old boy, short-lived though it was to be. And then I was brought up short again. Poor *old* boy? At the time when he had been killed, my father had been a good ten years younger than I was now.

Suddenly I realised how hungry I was and I got up and went into the kitchen. There was no fresh bread but there was a sliced loaf in the deep-freeze and I put a couple of pieces into the toaster and made myself a mammoth sandwich. Then I poured out a whisky and soda to accompany it and, armed with these, I went back to the chair by the fire and began my father's final chapter.

xiv. Then

We were married, your mother and I, three days later. We could have got the special licence in two, but I had thought the extra day well lost in order to give Molly at least the semblance of a proper wedding. As it was, the few front pews of St. Margaret's, Westminster, which we had managed to sprinkle rather than to fill, achieved much the same impression that a couple of cabin-boys might have done, had they somehow contrived to get themselves left behind on the *Marie Celeste*.

My brother Charles being still in mid-Atlantic – en route home from his training as an Observer in Canada – I had asked Brigadier Broadbent, immaculate as ever and eye-glass gleaming, to be my best man. Molly's friend Pat, who shared digs with her in Jermyn Street, was her only bride's-maid and Commander Jackson gave the bride away.

I cannot remember a lot about the reception – which was held in the *Patience Room* at The Savoy – it all passed in a mist of happiness. A table, put there by the door for that purpose, had acquired a respectable mound of wedding presents in spite of the shortness of the notice. Molly and I had ordained that there should be no speeches, but Uncle Johnnie Bagot proposed our joint healths formally. Roger Faulkner seemed to be dashing around all over the place in a highly unscientific manner. Leonard Frost never mentioned politics once. Stephen Knightley's shaven face, now suitably weathered, carried an almost perpetual smile. Even Lady Greyfield gave every impression of enjoying herself, while her husband, Peter, positively sparkled. Colonel Matheson, to my certain knowledge, kissed the bride five times. And, outside in the hotel fore-court afterwards, Dick Richards produced a hunting-horn from somewhere and, as Molly and I got into the Rolls and drove off, blew a more than passable 'Gone Away'.

* * *

Then

We spent the honey-moon at Thyrde. I showed Molly the warren in the meadow where rabbits could be stalked with a four-ten on a sunny summer evening or, if none were showing, could be lured out with a noise made by sucking the heel of one's thumb, as old Barraclough the keeper had taught us how; the five-barred gate that my pony had bolted, and jumped with me one day, to the port-glass-frozen horror of an entire lawn meet; the trees that my brother Charles and I used to climb, by far the most difficult being the old beech that stands by itself at the far end of the lawn, its vast trunk bare and slippery for fully twenty feet up. I was basking in the glow of Molly's flattering incredulity ... and then she had to go and spoil it all by kicking off her shoes, swarming up it there and then and laughing down at me from astride the lowest branch.

But it was the garden that fascinated her most. We spent hours wandering round it, she planning out loud the use that she would make of the free hand that I had promised her.

"Haven't you got a lake?" she asked me at one point, almost accusingly.

"Sorry, no lake."

"My grand-father used to say that a garden without water was as bad as a room without a looking-glass."

I was guiltily counting up in my mind the number of the rooms at Thyrde that lacked this apparently indispensable amenity, when luckily something caught her eye and she ran off, beckoning me after her. It seemed that, if we were to dam the small stream at its narrowest point, the lie of the ground was such that we might be able to achieve something really quite respectable in the way of a water-garden. It would hardly be a lake, but it would be the next best thing.

We had left the opening of the wedding presents until the third day.

* * *

"Derry, *darling!* Just look at this," said Molly.

We were in the library, she kneeling on the floor in a sea of wrapping-paper, with an ever diminishing stack of parcels on one side of her and an ever growing hoard of loot on the other. Some instinct had prompted me to abstract before-hand a square white envelope that I remembered noticing among the presents on the table at the reception as having no label on it. It felt as though it contained something very like a gramophone record and it was now reposing safely in the drawer of the desk at which I was sitting making a list of the items as she called them out with the name of the donor written against each.

I went over and had a closer look at what she was holding. It was a model aeroplane, painted, accurate down to the minutest detail and I recognised it immediately. I could hardly have failed to. That single, almost obscenely naked engine, the floats at either wing-tip, a "shag-bat" Commander Jackson had called it, it was irrevocably graven on my mind.

"Very nice," I said dutifully, but Molly was purring over it as though none of the other presents counted for anything in comparison.

"It's from Jacky, he makes them himself in his spare time. He's done one of almost every type there is. Spends weeks and weeks over them and he's simply never been *known* to give one away."

It was early in the evening before I first got a chance to examine the envelope. It did indeed contain a record and I smuggled it up to my old bed-room where I had taken the much maligned gramophone.

It was made of aluminium, less than six inches in diameter, and there was a red label in the middle carrying the inscription '*Voice Records Ltd.*' together with a picture of the world. There was an advertisement for '*De Reske Minor*' cigarettes on the reverse side. I put it on the turn-table, wound up the motor and set it to play.

"Hello, Derry, and you too, Miss Stanton, if you're listening. Or should I say Lady Thyrde now? No, you still don't know who I am and there will be no point in your trying to recognise me by my voice. This is not a wedding present, although it masquerades as such. Look on it rather as an aural form of greetings-card, a message of congratulation from a loser to a winner, for I must concede that you have at least merited my respect. You have shown an ability and an intelligence of which I did not believe you to be capable – and about that I have no complaint. You too must have your ideals and it is right that you should fight for them, just as I know that I have been right to fight for mine. But you have done it in such a way as has been calculated to bring the

Then

maximum of discredit down upon me amongst those whom I have been proud to serve – and that I cannot forgive. It is something that, however long it may take, I will now make it my business to repay. Have no fears for your wife, I do not make war on women. But do not take comfort, either, from the thought that, if you yourself do not survive the war, it will end there. I have always envied our Latin friends their custom of Vendetta. The sins of the fathers can always be avenged on the sons instead – and now you may well soon have one. Oh, I almost forgot, I have your ring. It will be returned to you when the debt is paid."

I played it through several times. It took exactly one minute twenty-eight seconds and he had been right about one thing. Spoken quickly with very little inflection, in a voice that was clearly disguised by coming from the back of the throat, it was totally impossible to make the vaguest guess as to his identity. The quality of the recording was such that it would almost certainly have been impossible to do so in any case and even this began to deteriorate noticeably at the fourth or fifth playing. So I played it through just once more, a sentence or two at a time, while I wrote down the exact words of the text.

Was it no more than a malicious practical joke – the whole thing had an air of theatrical unreality about it, particularly the reference at the end to a symbolic returning of the ring – or did the message present a genuine threat? And if the latter, what steps should I take?

I could hardly go to the police, as this could not be done without my having to divulge privileged information which really would get me into trouble. As for Commander Jackson, his attitude as expressed to me on D-Day gave me little confidence that he would take the thing seriously. All that I would be likely to get from him would be a specific embargo, should I ever feel it necessary to do so, against my taking any further action myself. The spy had undertaken not to do any harm to Molly and this part, at least, did to my mind have the ring of truth about it. He would be hard put to it to get his own back at me personally, where I would shortly be going, and as to my having a son, and the chances of that happening before I was back from the war to take care of him myself must be remote, I could worry about that when the time came.

Then

I was rapidly coming to the conclusion that the worry imposed on me by receiving the threat in the first place was intended to be revenge enough and that, if it were not, there was precious little that I could do about it in any case, when Molly arrived to rout me out. When I heard her at the door, there was just enough time for me to hide the thing by putting a normal gramophone record down on the turn-table on top of it. She gave one genuinely withering look in the direction of the unfortunate instrument before dragging me, with simulated severity, away.

The four remaining days of our leave passed at that pace peculiar to periods of extreme happiness, in that while they were actually happening, they seemed to flash by in as many hours whereas, looking back afterwards at everything that Molly and I had managed to cram into them, it was hard to imagine that they could have taken less than a similar number of weeks.

I took the train from Bedford to St. Pancras, crossed by taxi to Victoria and so down to Brighton. The officers' mess was in the Dudley Hotel. Most of the preparations had been completed by the time that I got there and I even managed to spend one more night with Molly in London. We embarked on Friday, the thirtieth of June.

* * *

And after that I had other things on my mind.

First there was another period of waiting, relieved only by the occasional journey forward in a jeep to watch a real live battle taking place. Then, after about a fortnight, the abortive attempt to break out of the bridge-head beyond *Caen*. A second unsuccessful attempt a few days later, in which the Guards Armoured Division did not take part. The fighting which followed in the *Bocage*, that part of Normandy particularly unsuited to tanks, consisting as it did of a crazy patch-work of woods and cider-orchards, interlaced with narrow winding lanes between banks of anything up to ten feet high. The eventual break-out – *that* was achieved by the Americans – a quick lift on tank-transporters as far as the *Seine*, then on, on our own tracks, to the *Somme* and far beyond. The liberation of *Brussels*, a set-piece repetition, but on an infinitely larger scale, of the joyful welcome that we had already encountered all the way along. The slower,

Then

harder-fought, progress thereafter which took us over, first the *Albert*, and then the *Escaut* canals.

All this time, Molly had been writing to me every alternate day, cheerful chatty letters, and these I had received irregularly, sometimes two or three, sometimes a whole batch at a time.

I can vividly remember the occasion of the particular letter arriving — it was around the middle of September, shortly before the abortive advance to *Arnhem*, which alas was only to reach *Nijmegen*, began — the leaky barn that had been taken over as the officers' mess of the moment, the rain pouring down outside, the constant stream of drips inside finding their way through from above in certain places, the heaps of musty hay strategically placed so as to avoid them, the Tilly-lamps, the food on enamelled tin plates. She had wanted to be absolutely certain, she said, before she wrote and told me. After that somebody had produced half a dozen bottles of champagne from somewhere and it had been an evening of celebration. It only occurred to me later that this now put a completely new complexion on the gramophone record and the threat contained in it. He did not make war on women, he had said, and I had believed him. And, although this had obviously been meant to refer to Molly herself, it must apply to a daughter too. But what if the child should turn out to be a boy?

Over the preceding months there had been a slow but regular disappearance of well-known faces from the Battalion, some killed, some wounded. Oddly enough, it had simply never occurred to me to begin with that I myself might be killed. But I had been having more than my fair share of near misses lately — our Shermans seem to be particularly vulnerable to the German anti-tank 88's and the even nastier short range bazookas — and it had been progressively borne in upon me that such luck could not last. I was reinforced in this view when, some days later in Nijmegen itself, a sniper's bullet from an unexpected angle near the post office in the middle of the town severed the strap of my steel helmet clean through, leaving me with nothing worse than a headache and a slight burn mark on the under part of my chin.

I came to the conclusion that there was one thing that I *could* do and that was to put down in writing a record of everything that had happened to me since my first fortuitous recovery of that stolen paper. There was always a chance that there might be some

Then

detail, the importance of which I myself had not yet been able to recognise, which just might provide a vital clue in the unlikely event of the spy at some unspecified time in the future actually trying to carry out his threat. And this, whenever I had a spare moment from the events of the weeks that followed – the failure to break through and relieve the First Air-borne Division at *Arnhem*, the drawing back to re-open the narrow corridor from *Eindhoven* and the move south and east to *Gangelt* – I proceeded to do.

Three days ago, shortly after we had been relieved from this, our first brief spell within the borders of Germany itself, the second piece of news came. For no apparent reason your grandmother had died peacefully in her sleep.

Home leave is not due to start until after the New Year but, by a lucky chance, the Grenadier Group had been asked to send an officer back to the War Office in London for consultations, leaving that same evening. And the chap who had originally been chosen very sportingly insisted that I should go in his place.

Not only has this enabled me to be here for the funeral, which is to be this afternoon, but it has also presented me with an ideal opportunity to make provision for the safe keeping of this manuscript of mine – and this I am going to do now. I have been finishing the last few pages this morning. The rest of today and tonight I spend at Thyrde with Molly. Tomorrow I go back.

And I, Derek John Altramont Mallicent, second Viscount Thyrde, being of sound mind and in the clear knowledge that I may, at any time in the near future, be called upon to meet my Maker, do swear by Almighty God that, to the best of my knowledge and recollection, the fore-going is a true account of the events which have happened to me personally since the twenty-ninth day of March, Nineteen forty-four.

Signed: Thyrde
Witnessed by: James Ford
Land Agent

Thyrde House,
Northamptonshire.

18th December 1944.

Then

On a separate sheet of paper there was attached a post-script, which was clearly intended to be for my eyes alone.

If you should be reading this, three things will have happened. You will have been born a boy; I myself will be dead, probably long dead; and you will now be in trouble – trouble of the severest kind. I hope and believe that this trouble will not have been of your own making. If I am right in this confidence, one of the seven men who figure in the attached account may conceivably be responsible. I have had my own suspicions as to which of them it might be of course but, as these have varied from time to time and as I do not want to distract your mind by adding to fact what can only be conjecture, I have thought it right to keep them to myself.

God bless you, my dear son – for so I may now presume you to be – and may you be able to find whatever relief might be necessary, having regard to the position in which you now find yourself. It is little enough that I have been able to tell you. It could be any one of the seven – and I still do not know which.

15. Now

But I knew!

I knew it just as surely as if my father had written the name down in capital letters for me and then underlined it as well.

Not immediately, of course.

My first reaction had merely been one of amazement that any one should have gone to so much trouble to avenge an imagined wrong after so many years – and then only on the son of the man whom he believed to be responsible. For that the two crimes were connected – the one being the direct result of the thwarting of the other – was certain beyond any doubt whatsoever. The threat contained in the gramophone record, the use of the Belgian accomplice's name, *Janssen*, on the paying-in slips and, above all, the planting of the signet-ring, proved that.

And then I thought – was it really so very surprising?

The palming off of the fake *Mulberry Harbour* paper had been only one of many deceptions that the Allies had employed at that time in order to convince the Germans that it was the Pas de Calais and not the coast of Normandy that was to be the target area for *Operation Overlord* – but it could have been the conclusive one. If the real paper had got through, by depriving us of the element of surprise it might well have given the enemy time to bring their secret weapons into more devastating effect; the submarines that could stay submerged for long periods of time and travel under water at high speeds, which only made their appearance in the Spring of 1945; von Rundstedt's crack Sixth Panzer Army, the very existence of which nobody on our side even suspected until it was brought into action in the late Autumn of 1944; the V 1 and V 2. Taken in conjunction with these, would it have made a difference to the final outcome of the war?

Perhaps not – but the spy may have thought that it would, and that was what mattered. This man, who might reasonably have been expecting to hold a high position in a German–occupied

Now

Britain, honoured and rewarded for the part that he himself had played in achieving it, must have been forced instead to stand by and watch the approach and eventual achievement of our own victory and the general rejoicing that followed it, knowing all the time that he was being despised for his gross carelessness and subsequent gullibility – which, by the same reasoning, had been directly responsible for it – by his late German masters whose respect he craved.

Perhaps the mere worry caused by the promise of revenge contained in the gramophone record had indeed been intended to be reprisal enough in itself – *at the time*. And then, as the years had gone by and he had brooded more and more on all that he had lost and the disgrace that he had incurred in losing it – as he believed, at my father's direct instigation – the bitterness had eaten away inside him until it became an obsession. Until what had been conceived as an empty threat had grown into a reality. A debt of honour that – in spite of the risks involved, because he could never have known for sure how much my father and mother had found out, and she passed on to me – for his own peace of mind must be repaid.

But which of them had it been? Three out of the original seven were already dead and that at least narrowed down the field to four.

Or did it?

The man on the gramophone record had talked of a vendetta – but didn't that work both ways? Revenge could be taken not only *on* a son but by a son as well. It didn't seem to be very likely, but was I entirely safe in thinking that I could discount the other three?

I picked up the gramophone record itself. My recently acquired hi-fi system was for some reason incapable of playing at seventy-eight revolutions per minute, but I still had the old fashioned gramophone over on the bookcase. It was an eerie sensation listening to those same words, issuing out of that same brass trumpet, just as my father had done all those years before.

It left me no further forward than it had him.

I read through my father's manuscript again, more quickly this time but keeping an eye open for any points that I might have missed before. Then I got out the notes that I myself had made and went through those. Finally, I put the two together and read

Now

them as nearly as possible in conjunction – his story *then* and my story *now*.

And it was then that I got it.

Late as it was, I went over to the telephone, leafed through the little red-leather-bound book which I kept beside it and dialled the number that I found.

'Yes, I really do believe you're right,' he said at last.

He had arrived some forty minutes earlier, looking every bit as spruce as he had when I had last seen him and giving the impression that being called out of bed at three o'clock in the morning was not only nothing unusual in his life but also something that he positively enjoyed. I had explained my processes of reasoning to him and read out the relevant passages, those from the account that my father had had the forethought to leave for me and those from my own. Then I had unlocked the drawer of my desk and shown him the wristwatch that Mr. Barraclough's upholstery men had found. I had had the strap replaced in brown crocodile of an almost identical shade.

'But we'll never be able to prove it,' I said.

'Maybe not. But I think I just might be able to get him to admit it,' said Sir Makepeace Brotherton.

And he told me how.

Court Number One at The Old Bailey. The Dock. 10.30 a.m.

To the front of me was the Bench with its five chairs. The one in the middle was empty and would remain so. Traditionally it is reserved for The Lord Mayor of London who in days gone by was chief judge of The Central Criminal Court but who never sits now. The Judge himself, in short plain horsehair wig and scarlet robes, was occupying the one just off-centre to the left.

Below sat the Clerk of the Court. Between him and me ran a long table, a highly bemused-looking Sam Thornton sitting on one side of it and the two officers in charge of the case – Detective-Chief-Inspector Harding glancing benignly about him and beside him his gaunt companion, the sinister Sergeant Pollock – on the other; the latter was studying his own fingernails as though he suspected even them of having committed some nameless crime. To the right of that, and parallel to it, were the benches reserved for Counsel, their respective Juniors behind them; Sir

Now

Makepeace's was scribbling away busily, although what he could have to scribble about at this early stage in the day's proceedings only God and he knew; the great man himself was shuffling papers about, as though he were practising some highly involved legal three-card trick which he was preparing with a view to confusing the opposition into submission; while at the far end the Attorney-General was sitting with arms folded and a gentle smile on his face; as far as he was concerned, I was there for the plucking – no such manoeuvres were necessary for him.

Behind me to the left, sat the seven members of the "1944 Club". Each of them in turn caught my eye and then looked away again; Leonard as though his faith in human nature had received an irretrievable blow; Henry angrily; Billy petulantly; Stephen self-righteously; Dick with detached dignity; Roger displaying mild interest; only Peterkin's expression being inscrutable behind the thick horn-rimmed spectacles and above the floppy red-and-white spotted bow tie.

To my half-left were the members of the Press, pencils poised at the ready, each glancing about him as though seeking to establish the most favourable route that would bring him first to the nearest telephone when the time came.

Immediately behind them were the twelve members of the Jury, seven men and five women. None of them would look at me, neither would Tisha – she was on one of the benches reserved for distinguished onlookers on the far right. That was hardly surprising considering the performance of the afternoon before, but then nor would any of her neighbours on that side or the members of the more general public in the gallery above. As had been the case with the seven, any who did chance to meet my gaze looked quickly away.

There was a difference in the atmosphere today, something that hadn't been there before – not even during the worst moments of yesterday. A sense of anticipation, an animal excitement – predatory, almost – of which, while that thronged courtroom was secure in the self-justifying knowledge that collectively it couldn't help itself, I was left with the impression that each individual unit of it was still just a little bit ashamed. It reminded me of – what? Spectators in a motor-racing stand? No, that wasn't quite it. And then I did manage to place it – the crowd that gathers on the pavement below when, several storeys up a high building, a man

Now

has clambered precariously out onto a narrow ledge. They were waiting to be in at the death.

My death.

And then . . . I became aware that there was *one* person there who didn't quite fit in. Sitting six or seven places along from Tisha, that hair which couldn't quite make up its mind whether it came into the category of "blonde" or not, those high cheek-bones, the very slightly crooked nose which in being not quite perfect somehow achieved something more than perfection. Julia. She was looking full into my eyes but tentatively, anxiously, questioningly . . . I grinned back at her and instantly her features relaxed and broke into a breath-stopping smile, as she raised a small gloved hand.

Sir Makepeace rose to his feet.

'May it please your Lordship, new evidence has come into my possession which I believe that the Court should hear. May I respectfully request an adjournment?'

The Judge jerked his head back and blinked twice with an expression of mock incredulity. Then he leant forward again and peered querulously over his half-moon spectacles.

'What is the precise nature of this . . . ah . . . evidence that you seek to adduce – and for how long, may I ask?'

'I would ask your Lordship not to press me at this stage. I cannot properly be ready to present the evidence before the Jury until after the luncheon adjournment.'

The Judge turned to the Attorney-General. 'Have you any objection, Sir Thomas?'

'No, my Lord.'

'Very well, the Court is adjourned until five minutes past two.'

He stood up. 'Be upstanding in Court,' called the Usher and, with a distinct flounce of his robes, the Judge stalked out of the courtroom to the right.

It was mid-afternoon.

The man stood under the canopy of the cosy little wooden witness-box, as though it had been designed and put there for his own especial comfort. He had walked there with confident unhurried steps. Only six of the "1944 Club" members were now left sitting behind me – otherwise the entire cast and audience, in their various locations about the courtroom, were very much the same.

The Judge had been pretty scathing about the submission as new evidence of a document of that length at such short notice and at first I had thought that he was going to refuse to allow it. But then, surprisingly, the Attorney-General himself had intervened. His learned friend had been kind enough to show the manuscript to him privately during the adjournment and he considered it to be in the interests of justice, he had said.

Calmly and succinctly, Sir Makepeace had summarised the events that had happened to my father, his chance recovery of the stolen paper, his showing a suitably prepared substitute round his seven friends, the taking of that too, the enquiries that followed and how it had finally left the country. Then, just as dispassionately, but in rather more detail, he had explained the facts that conclusively connected the wartime traitor with the recent Farmwell theft. He had included, almost as if they were totally extraneous and even unconnected incidents, my mother's grabbing something off the spy's wrist at the time of her struggle with him and his Belgian accomplice and the finding, earlier this year, of the wrist-watch in the upholstery of the Rolls-Royce.

James Ford, our former agent summoned to London that morning from his retirement home in Cheltenham, had not only testified to the authenticity of the signature that he had witnessed, but he had also volunteered the information that, before signing, my father had read out loud the declaration at the end of the manuscript, putting his hand as he did so on a copy of The Bible that had lain on his desk.

Sir Makepeace Brotherton had then turned to the Judge. 'Not quite a death-bed statement perhaps, but not so very far short of one either. I can if you wish, my Lord, call his brother, Mr. Charles Mallicent, who will testify that, on the day that that declaration was written and signed, the late Lord Thyrde was under the strongest of premonitions that he would shortly be killed in action.'

'I don't think that will be necessary, Sir Makepeace.'

My Counsel had given a slight bow and then called the man who was to be the last witness in the whole trial instead.

There was silence now as the man in the witness-box stood with an expression of polite enquiry, waiting for the examination to begin. Sir Makepeace fumbled under his gown, produced the

Now

wrist-watch out of his trouser pocket and held it up high for a moment or two, swinging it gently by the buckle of its strap. Every one stared at it, as though they were expecting the little man suddenly to make it disappear or perform some other trick.

'I'd like you to take a look at this, please.' His voice was as mild as before.

The Usher walked over with it and the man in the witness-box took it from him and examined it with the air of indulgent puzzlement of one who is prepared to humour a rather unpredictable child. Then he turned it over in his hand and looked at the other side.

'Is that watch yours?'

'No.'

'Have you ever seen it before?'

'Not to my knowledge.'

With each of the two questions there had been that infinitesimal upward movement of the gown with Sir Makepeace's hands.

'Will you put it on, please.'

The man in the witness-box looked at him. The child was verging on the naughty now – indulgence could be carried too far. But he did so just the same.

'Do you always wear your watch on your right wrist?'

'*When* I wear one ... yes.'

'You are left-handed, then?'

'I am. What of it?'

Quoting from either manuscript the same points that I myself had done to him in the early hours of that morning, but mustered in a far more logical sequence, with total economy of words and what one would have thought would have been devastatingly incisive reasoning, Sir Makepeace told him *what*.

There was no reaction. None at all. Not even the revelation that every *Patek Philippe* watch bears a serial number engraved on its working parts – I myself had elicited this piece of information by ringing up *Garrards Ltd.* of Regent Street during the adjournment – from which the identity of the original owner could almost certainly be established, seemed to shake the man in the witness-box in any way whatsoever.

Suddenly I was assailed by the cold cramp of incipient panic. I had started out that morning secure in the confidence that my acquittal would be little more than a formality, but it was all going

Now

terribly wrong. Today was turning out to be a repetition of the fiasco of yesterday – worse, far worse, the second time round. If this too failed, I reckoned that I could well be in prison for the rest of my natural life.

I glanced frantically back to Sir Makepeace, his gown all awry now but from the way in which he was standing, eyes fixed on the man in the witness-box, he was giving every impression of being as unconcerned as he.

'You have heard me speak of a man,' the voice became progressively harsher now, each word distinct and honed to razor-sharpness, 'who had sunk so low from the accepted standards of decent human behaviour that he saw fit, in wartime, to ally himself with perhaps the most depraved and corrupt regime that history has yet known and, in seeking to promote its ends, to betray his own country. His actions were such – the full consequences of which only the prompt intervention of the late Lord Thyrde, the defendant's father, was able to avert – that I doubt if there is more than one man present in this court-room today who would hesitate utterly to condemn. (*The man in the witness-box shrugged his shoulders and looked away. It was a gesture that could have meant anything or nothing— total indifference or merely taken-for-granted acceptance of a generally held view.*) I would ask you now to consider a man who has done what some would consider even worse – he has betrayed a friend. A man who has born a grudge against another and fostered that grudge until, in the words of the gramophone record, it has become a family vendetta. A man who, by weaving a whole web of lies and deceit and false trails, has deliberately and calculatingly caused this friend to be wrongfully accused of a crime for which he himself is responsible, a crime moreover which he committed with that one purpose in mind. And all for nothing. Because, not only did this friend's sole fault lie in the fact that he was the late Lord Thyrde's son, but also that man's whole warped hatred of the late Lord Thyrde and every one connected with him was based on ... a misconception.' (*Sir Makepeace paused and the man in the witness-box looked up. Was it my imagination, or had his expression wavered just the very slightest bit?*) 'Yes, a misconception,' Sir Makepeace picked up the manuscript and struck it with his other hand, 'because this account, written by him and solemnly declared by him to be true at a time when he

believed his own death to be imminent, makes it clear that, contrary to what the man whom I have been describing to you believed, the late Lord Thyrde had never been told about the substitution of the papers . . .' (*The man in the witness-box looked at me. His mouth opened and for a moment I thought that he was going to say something directly to me. But no words came.*) '. . . that the part which he himself played in the deception therefore was a wholly unwitting one and that all his actions then were directed towards the sole purpose of preventing information that he still believed to be valid from falling into enemy hands. The question that I have to ask you now is . . .
"*Were you that man?*" '

With the accomplice holding her headscarf over her eyes behind her as a blindfold, the spy had stood in front of Molly gripping one of her hands in each of his. It was her left hand which she had managed to wriggle free and, in the position in which they were standing relative to each other, it must have been held in his right. The thing from his wrist that she had found herself grasping might have been some form of identification bracelet – and in a way it was – but it was in fact a wrist-watch. Only left-handed people usually wear their watches on their right wrists – therefore the spy was left-handed. Molly herself was left-handed so that would also explain – her stronger held in his weaker – why she had found that particular hand easier to free.

The man in the witness-box said nothing. There was total utter silence with every eye in the courtroom focused upon him – I myself had been forgotten, I was merely one of the spectators now – but it was a silence that somehow achieved the decibels of a rock group. The near certainty of exposure hadn't worried him, nor had the imminent possibility of a long prison sentence. In a strange perverse way, he might even have welcomed it as a means of purging his guilt, not at having betrayed his country but rather at having failed those for whom he had been glad to betray it, and, by coming out into the open at last, of reaffirming the faith which his concealment over the years had by implication denied. But it was the revelation that my father had been duped, even as the then unknown spy had been duped – and the consequent realisation that the whole of his own life since then had been geared to the

Now

sole purpose of achieving a revenge that would have been empty, because it was misdirected which, just as Sir Makepeace had known it would, was beginning to break the man in the witness-box now.

'WERE YOU THAT MAN?'

None of the three who had been at the birthday party but who had since died, had been left-handed – Johnnie Bagot, spinning round to ask the butler a question and narrowly missing him with the carving-knife held in his right hand; James Matheson, finding it more difficult to guide Molly's casting when she switched to her left hand, because it had meant him using his own left rather than his right; and Peter Greyfield, propping his cheque-book awkwardly against the wall of the House of Lords dining-room with his left hand, must have used his right with which to fill it in.

The man in the witness-box still did not reply. It was a duel, fought first with words and then with sheer naked personality projected in the concentrated power of a laser-beam, between him and Sir Makepeace and, as the one began to dwindle in ascendancy, so the other grew until, even from that distance, he gave the impression of towering menacingly over him. Now it was as though there was one of those transformation scenes from the cinema taking place – Dorian Grey's own face, when that of his hideously distorted portrait has been smashed, changing slowly but inexorably to match it, Dr. Jekyll becoming Mr. Hyde. I looked across to where Tisha was sitting – Tisha the willing ally, who had only failed me right at the last moment; Tisha the kind and gentle, who could become such a tigress in bed; Tisha the strangely modest, who had always been so reluctant to allow that side of her nature to show; Tisha the superb actress, who could play each of these parts to perfection and who, in addition, possessed the rare attribute of being able to summon up tears at will. I caught her eye and one glance at her expression now was enough to confirm what I had been ninety-five per cent certain of already – she had been in it all along, right up to her adorable slim white *treacherous little neck!*

'WERE YOU THAT MAN?'

Now

Of the seven existing members of the "1944 Club" who had filled in the first set of paying-in slips during that meeting in the dining-room at Thyrde, only one had done so using his left hand.

I was told afterwards that the judge ought to have put a stop to the whole thing long before this. It was wholly improper that the witness-box should have been turned into a dock, the witness into the accused, his examination into an indictment... even a verdict. But Mr. Justice Pierceworthy was sitting up there on the Bench gazing open-mouthed at the man in the witness-box, stupefied just like the rest of us — incapable of movement, incapable of speech. As for myself, nothing that this man had done or had tried to do, to my father, to his Country, to myself, could justify this torment that was going on in front of us and I found myself willing it, longing for it, praying for it to end — this destruction, this total disintegration before our eyes, of what had been a man.

And then... just when it was finally becoming unbearable, just when it seemed that the utmost level of tolerance was being reached and even passed, Sir Makepeace Brotherton put up both his hands and, gripping the sides of his gown at some point behind and below his shoulders, jerked it over and downwards to fall perfectly back into place in one sharp continuous movement, with the sound of a *whiplash*... which didn't break the tension — if anything it served to heighten it — but instantly diverted the mass absorption of the courtroom from the man in the witness-box back to himself.

Even as it did so, he himself seemed to shrivel in stature until all that there was left for us to look at was a rather ordinary little man, dressed neatly but perhaps a trifle incongruously in the archaic trappings of his profession.

And his voice when he spoke next was very quiet, the tone gentle and conciliatory — apologetic, even.

'Thank you, Lord Frost. No further questions,' he said.